record
of
a
spaceborn
few

Also by Becky Chambers

The Long Way to a Small, Angry Planet
A Closed and Common Orbit

record
of
a
spaceborn
few
becky
chambers

HARPER Voyager
An Imprint of HarperCollinsPublishers

RECORD OF A SPACEBORN FEW. Copyright © 2018 by Becky Chambers. All rights reserved. Printed in the United States of America. No part of this book may be used or reproduced in any manner whatsoever without written permission except in the case of brief quotations embodied in critical articles and reviews. For information, address HarperCollins Publishers, 195 Broadway, New York, NY 10007.

HarperCollins books may be purchased for educational, business, or sales promotional use. For information, please email the Special Markets Department at SPsales@harpercollins.com.

Originally published in Great Britain in 2018 by Hodder & Stoughton, a Hachette UK company.

Harper Voyager and design are trademarks of HarperCollins Publishers LLC.

FIRST US EDITION

Library of Congress Cataloging-in-Publication Data has been applied for.

ISBN 978-0-06-269922-0
ISBN 978-0-06-285115-4 (hardcover library edition)

23 24 25 26 27 LBC 15 14 13 12 11

For Anne, who showed me I could.

With the exception of the prologue, the timeline in this book begins during the final events of *The Long Way to a Small, Angry Planet.*

FOUR STANDARDS EARLIER

TESSA

'Mom, can I go see the stars?'

Tessa looked up from her small workbench and down to her even smaller daughter. 'I can't take you now, baby,' she said. She nodded toward the cleanerbot she was trying to coax back to life. 'I want to finish this before your Uncle Ashby calls.'

Aya stood in place and bounced on her heels. She'd never in her life been still, not while sleeping, not while sick, not while she'd grown in Tessa's belly. 'I don't need you to go,' Aya said. 'I can go myself.'

The declaration was made boldly, laden with enough self-assurance that Tessa set down her screwdriver. The words *I don't need you* made a part of her shrivel in on itself, but then, wasn't that the point of being a parent? To help them need you less and less? She turned to Aya, and considered. She thought of how deep the elevator shaft to the family cupola was, how easy it would be for a bouncing almost-five-year-old to slip off the bench and fall a full deck down. She tried to remember how old she herself had been the first time she'd gone down alone, but found she couldn't. Aya was clumsy, as all people learning their bodies were, but she was careful, too, when she put her mind to it. She knew to buckle her safety harness on the ferry, to find an adult if she heard air hissing or metal groaning, to check for a green pressure light on any door before opening it. Aya was a kid, but a spacer kid, and spacer kids had to learn to trust themselves, and trust their ships.

'How would you sit on the bench?' Tessa asked.

3

'In the middle,' Aya said.

'Not on the edge?'

'Not on the edge.'

'And when do you get off of it?'

'When it gets to the bottom.'

'When it *stops*,' Tessa said. It wasn't hard to picture her daughter jumping off while still in motion. 'You have to wait for the bench to stop *all the way* before getting off of it.'

'Okay.'

'What do you say if you fall?'

'I say, "falling!"'

Tessa nodded. 'You shout it real loud, right? And what does that do?'

'It makes . . . it makes the . . . it makes it turn off.'

'It makes what turn off?'

Aya bounced and thought. 'Gravity.'

'Good girl.' Tessa tousled her kid's thick hair with approval. 'Well, all right, then. Go have fun.'

Her daughter took off. It was only a few steps from Tessa's table at the side of the living room to the hole in the centre of the floor, but running was the only speed Aya knew. For a split second, Tessa wondered if she'd just created a future trip to the med clinic. Her fears gave way to fondness as she watched Aya carefully, carefully unlatch the little gate in the kid-height railing around the elevator shaft. Aya sat on the floor and scooted forward to the bench – a flat, legless plank big enough for two adults sitting hip-to-hip. The plank was connected to a motorised pulley, which, in turn, was attached to the ceiling with heavy bolts.

Aya sat in quiet assessment – a rare occurrence. She leaned forward a bit, and though Tessa couldn't see her face, she could picture the little crumpled frown she knew had appeared. Aya didn't look sure about this. A steep, dark ride was one thing when held firmly on your mother's lap. It was another entirely when the only person taking the ride was you, and nobody would catch you, nobody would yell for help on your behalf. You had to be able to catch yourself. You had to be able to raise your voice.

Aya picked up the control box wired to the pulley, and pressed the down button. The bench descended.

I don't need you, Aya had said. The words didn't sting anymore. They made Tessa smile. She turned back to the cleanerbot and resumed her repairs. She'd get the bot working, she'd let her daughter watch ships or count stars or whatever it was she wanted to do, she'd talk to her brother from half a galaxy away, she'd eat dinner, she'd call her partner from half a system away, she'd sing their daughter to sleep, and she'd fall sleep herself whenever her brain stopped thinking about work. A simple day. A normal day. A good day.

She'd just about put the bot back together when Aya started to scream.

ISABEL

Isabel didn't want to look. She didn't want to see it, didn't want whatever nightmare lay out there to etch itself permanently into memory. But that was exactly why she *had* to go. Nobody would want to look at it now, but they would one day, and it was important that nobody forgot. Somebody had to look. Somebody had to make a record.

'Do you have the cams?' she asked, hurrying toward the exit.

Deshi, one of the junior archivists, fell alongside her, matching her stride. 'Yeah,' he said, shouldering a satchel. 'I took both packs, so we'll have plenty to— holy shit.'

They'd stepped out of the Archives and into a panic, a heaving chaos of bodies and noise. The plaza was as full as it was on any festival day, but this was no celebration. This was terror in real time.

Deshi's mouth hung open. Isabel reached out and squeezed his young hand with her wrinkled fingers. She had to lead the way, even as her knees went to jelly and her chest went tight. 'Get the cams out,' she said. 'Start recording.'

Her colleague gestured at his scrib and opened his satchel, and the camera spheres flew out, glowing blue as they absorbed sight and sound. Isabel reached up and tapped the frame of the hud that rested over her eyes. She tapped again, two short, one long. The hud registered the command, and a little blinking light at the corner of her left eye let her know her device was recording as well.

She cleared her throat. 'This is senior archivist Isabel Itoh, head of the *Asteria* Archives,' she said, hoping the hud could pick up her voice over the din. 'I am with junior archivist Deshi Arocha, and the date is GC standard 129/303. We have just received word of— of—' Her attention was dragged away by a man crumbling soundlessly to his knees. She shook her head and brought herself centre. '—of a catastrophic accident aboard the *Oxomoco*. Some kind of breach and decompression. It is believed a shuttle crash was involved, but we do not have many details yet. We are now headed to the public cupola, to document what we can.' She was not a reporter. She did not have to embellish a moment with extraneous words. She simply had to preserve the one unfolding.

She and Deshi made their way through the crowd, surrounded by their cloud of cams. The congregation was dense, but people saw the spheres, and they saw the archivists' robes, and they made way. Isabel said nothing further. There was more than enough for the cams to capture.

'My sister,' a woman sobbed to a helpless-looking patroller. 'Please, I think she was visiting a friend—'

'Shh, it's okay, we're okay,' a man said to the child he held tight against his chest. 'We're gonna be home soon, just hold on to me.' The child did nothing but bury xyr face as far as it would go into xyr father's shirt.

'*Star by star, we go together*,' sang a group of all ages, standing in a circle, holding hands. Their voices were shaky, but the old melody rose clear. '*In ev'ry ship, a family strong . . .*'

Isabel could not make out much else. Most were crying, or keening, or chewing their lips in silence.

They reached the edge of the cupola, and as the scene outside came into view, Isabel suddenly understood that the clamour they'd passed through was appropriate, fitting, the only reaction that made any sense in the face of this. She walked down the crowded steps, down as close as she could to the viewing glass, close as she could to the thing she didn't want to see.

The rest of the Exodus Fleet was out there, thirty homestead ships besides her own, orbiting together in a loose, measured cluster. All was as it should be . . . except one, tangled in a violent shroud of debris. She could see where the pieces belonged – a jagged breach, a hollow where walls and homes had been. She could see sheet metal, crossbeams, odd specks scattered between. She could tell, even from this distance, that many of those specks were not made of metal or plex. They were too curved, too irregular, and they changed shape as they tumbled. They were Human. They were bodies.

Deshi let out a wordless moan, joining the chorus around them.

'Keep recording,' Isabel said. She forced the words from her clenched throat. They felt as though they were bleeding. 'It's all we can do for them now.'

EYAS

'Do they know how many yet?' someone asked. Nobody had said much of anything since they'd left the *Asteria*, and the abrupt end of quiet startled Eyas out of wherever she'd been.

'Forty-three thousand, six hundred,' Costel said. He cleared his throat. 'That's our best estimate at this point, based on counting the evacuees who scanned in. We'll get a more accurate number once we— once we collect the rest.'

Eyas had never seen her supervisor this rattled, but his halting words and uneasy hands mirrored her own, mirrored them all. Nothing about this was normal. Nothing about this was okay. If someone had told her the standard before – when she'd finally shed her apprentice stripes – where accepting this profession would lead her, would she have agreed to it? Would she have continued forward, knowing how this day would unfold?

Probably. Yes. But some warning would've been nice.

She sat now with the other caretakers from her segment, twenty of them in total, scattered around the floor of a volunteered cargo ship, headed to the *Oxomoco*. More cargo ships and caretakers were on their way as well, a fleet within the Fleet. This ship normally carried foodstuffs, she could tell. The smells of spice and oil hung heavy around them, ghosts of good meals long gone. Not the smells she was accustomed to at work. Scented soap, she was used to. Metal. Blood, sometimes. Methylbutyl esters. Cloth. Dirt. Rot, ritual, renewal.

She shifted in her heavy exosuit. This, too, was wrong, as far a cry as there was from her usual light funerary garments. But it wasn't the suit that was making her uncomfortable, nor the spices tickling her nose. *Forty-three thousand, six hundred.* 'How,' she said, working some moisture into her mouth, 'how are we supposed to lay in that many?' The thought had been clawing at her ever since she'd looked out the window thirteen hours prior.

Costel said nothing for too long a time. 'The guild doesn't . . . we don't know yet.' A ruckus broke out, twenty questions overlapping. He put up his palms. 'The problem is obvious. We can't accommodate that many at once.'

'There's room,' one of Eyas' colleagues said. 'We're set up for twice our current death rate. If every Centre in the Fleet takes some, there's no problem.'

'We can't do that, not all at once,' said another. 'You'd fuck up the carbon–nitrogen ratio. You'd throw the whole system out of whack.'

'So, don't do it all at once. A little at a time, and we . . . we . . .'

'See,' their supervisor said. 'There's the issue.' He looked around the group, waiting for someone to step in with the answer.

'Storage,' Eyas said, shutting her eyes. She'd done some quick math while the others spoke, much as she hated to reduce something this important to numbers. One hundred and eighty Centres in the Fleet, each capable of composting a thousand corpses over a standard – but not at the same time. A Human body took just under four tendays to break down fully – bones and all – and there wasn't space to lay in more than a hundred or so at once. Even if you could set aside the carbon–nitrogen ratio, you couldn't change time. You'd have to store tens of thousands of bodies in the interim, which the morgues could not handle. More importantly, you'd have to tell tens of thousands of families that they'd have to wait to grieve, wait to hold a funeral, wait their turn to properly say goodbye. How would you choose who went first? Roll dice? Pick a number? No, the trauma was great enough without adding anything smacking of preferential treatment to the mix. But then . . . what would they do? And how would those same families respond when told that the people ripped away from them would not be joining their ancestors' cycle – would not transform into nourishment for the gardens, would not fill the airways and stomachs of those who remained – like they'd always been promised?

She put her face in her hands. Once more, silence returned to the group, and this time, no one broke it.

After a while, the ship slowed and stopped. Eyas stood, the pain inside stepping back to make room for the task at hand. She listened to Costel give instructions. She put on her helmet. She walked to the airlock. One door closed behind her; another opened ahead.

What lay outside was an obscenity, an ugliness she would wrestle another time. She blocked out the ruined districts and broken windows, focusing only on the bodies floating between. Bodies she could handle. Bodies she understood.

The caretakers scattered into the vacuum, thrusters firing on their backs. They flew alone, each of them, the same way that they worked. Eyas darted forward. The sun was muted behind her tinted visor, and the stars had lost their lustre. She hit her stabilisers, coming to a halt in front of the first she would collect. A man with salt-and-pepper hair and round cheeks. A farmer, by the clothes he wore. His leg dangled oddly – possibly the result of some impact during the explosive decompression – and a necklace, still tied around his neck, swayed near his peaceful face. He *was* peaceful, even with his eyes half-open and a final gasp at his lips. She pulled him toward her, wrapping her arms around his torso from behind. His hair pressed against her visor, and she could see the flecks of ice woven through it, the crunchy spires the cold had sculpted. *Oh, stars, they're going to thaw*, she thought. She hadn't considered that. Spacing deaths were rare, and she'd never overseen a funeral for one. She knew what normal procedure was: vacuum-exposed bodies got put in pressure capsules, where they could return to normal environmental conditions without things getting unseemly. But there weren't enough pressure capsules for the *Oxomoco*, not in the whole Fleet. No, they'd be piling frozen bodies in the relative warmth of a cargo hold. A crude half-measure improvised in haste, just like everything else they were doing that day.

Eyas took a tight breath of canned air. How were they supposed to deal with this? How would they give these people dignity? How would they ever, ever make this right?

She closed her eyes and took another breath, a good one this time. 'From the stars, came the ground,' she said to the body. 'From the ground, we stood. To the ground, we return.' They were words for a funeral, not retrieval, and speaking to corpses was not an action she'd ever practised (and likely never would again). She didn't see the point of filling ears that couldn't hear. But this – *this* was the way they would heal. She didn't know where this body or the others would go. She didn't know how her guild would proceed. But she knew they were Exodan. They were Exodan, and no matter what threatened to tear them apart, tradition held them together. She flew back toward the ship, ferrying her temporary charge, reciting the words the First Generation had written. 'Here, at the Centre of our lives, we carry our beloved dead. We honour their breath, which fills our lungs. We honour their blood, which fills our hearts. We honour their bodies, which fuel our own . . .'

KIP

Not in a million years would Kip have wanted to be held up –
that was for *kids*, not eleven-year-olds – but he couldn't help but
feel kind of envious of the little droolers sitting comfy around
their parents' heads. He was too big to be held, but too short to
see over the forest of grown-ups that filled the shuttledock. He
stretched up on tiptoe, swaying this way and that, trying to see
something other than shoulders and shirt sleeves. But no, whenever he found a gap to look through, all there was beyond was
more of the same. Tons of people packed in tight, with kids up
top, making the view all the more impossible. He dropped his
heels down and huffed.

His dad noticed, and bent down to speak directly in Kip's ear.
'Come on,' he said. 'I've got an idea.'

It wasn't easy for them to push their way back out of the
middle, but they managed – his dad leading the way, Kip following
the grey-striped print of his father's shirt. It was a nice shirt, the
kind of shirt you wore to naming days or weddings, or if someone
important came to the hex for dinner. Kip was wearing a nice
shirt, too – yellow with white dots. He'd struggled with the
buttons, and his mom had had to help him get it closed. He
could feel the fabric tugging tight over his chest every time he
took a breath, just like he could feel his toes pressing against the
ends of his shoes. His mom had shaken her head, and said she'd
go over and see if his cousin Wymer had any bigger hand-me-
downs lying around. Kip wished he could get brand new clothes,
like the ones the import merchants hung outside their stalls, all

crisp and straight and without stitches where somebody else's elbows had poked through. But he could see stitches on his dad's shirt, too, and on most of the shirts they pushed past. They were still nice shirts, though, as nice as people could manage. Everybody wanted to look good for the Aeluons.

No matter whether the shirts were new or stitched, there was one thing everybody had on: a white band tied around their upper right arm. That was what people wore in the tendays after funerals, so other people knew to cut you some slack and give you some kindness. Everybody had them on now – everybody on the *Asteria*, everybody in the whole Fleet. Kip didn't know anybody who'd died on the *Oxomoco*, but that wasn't the point, Mom had said while tying cloth around his arm. *We all lost family*, she'd said, *whether we knew them or not.*

Kip looked back once they'd cleared the crowd. 'Where are we going?' he asked with a frown. He hadn't been able to see anything where they were, but the empty dock was far away now, and the ship would be arriving any minute. They weren't going to *miss it*, were they? They couldn't.

'Trust me,' Dad said. He waved his son along, and Kip could see where they were headed: one of the cargo cranes perched nearby. Some other people had already got the same idea, and were sitting in the empty gaps of the crane's metal neck. His dad put his hand on Kip's shoulder. 'Now, you should *never, ever* do what we're about to do any other time. But this is a special occasion, yeah? Do you think you can climb up there with me?'

Kip nodded. 'Yeah,' he said, his heart pounding. Dad didn't break the rules often. Ever, really. No way would Mom have gone for this. Kip was secretly glad she hadn't come.

They climbed up the crane's service ladder, then clambered along the fat metal supports. The crane was way taller than it had looked from the floor, and Kip was a little scared – not like *scared scared,* he wasn't a baby – but the climb wasn't hard. It was kind of like the obstacle course at the playground, only way bigger. Besides, he was with his dad. If Dad said it was okay, it was okay.

The other people already on the crane smiled at them. 'Pull up a seat,' one lady shouted.

Dad laughed. 'Don't mind if we do.' He swung himself into an empty spot. 'Come on, Kip.'

Kip pulled himself alongside, letting his arms hang over one support beam and his feet swing free below another. The metal below his thighs was cold, and definitely not designed for sitting. He could already tell his butt was going to go numb.

But the view . . . the view was awesome. Being far away didn't matter so much when you were up top. Everything looked small – the people in the crowd, the patrollers at the edges, the in-charge group waiting right at the dock. 'Is that the Admiral?' Kip said, pointing at a grey-haired woman in a distinctive green council uniform.

'That's her,' Dad said.

'Have you ever met her?'

'No.'

'I did, last standard,' said the friendly, shouting lady. She sipped something hot from a canteen. 'She was on my sanitation team.'

'No kidding,' Dad said. 'What'd you think?'

The lady made a *yeah, not bad* kind of face. 'I'd vote for her again.'

Kip felt a knot start to unravel itself, a mass that had been tangled in him ever since the crash. Here was his dad, climbing up a crane with him and chatting easily with strangers. There was the crowd, assembled in the smartest clothes they had, nobody crying or screaming anymore. There was the Admiral, looking cool and official and powerful. Soon, the Aeluons would be there, too, and they'd help. They'd make things right again.

The dock lights turned yellow, indicating an incoming vessel. Even up high, Kip could hear the crowd hush. All at once, there it was. It flew into the dock silently – a smooth, gleaming Aeluon skiff with rounded corners and pearly hull. It almost didn't look like a ship. Ships were angular. Mechanical. Something you bolted and welded together, piece by piece, chunk by chunk. This ship, on the other hand, looked like it had been made from something melted, something poured into a mould and polished for days. The entire crowd held their breath together.

'Stars, that's something,' Dad said quietly.

'Get 'em all the time over at cargo,' the lady said. 'Never get tired of it.'

Kip didn't say anything. He was too busy looking at the most beautiful thing he'd ever seen. He almost asked his dad what this kind of ship was called, but his dad obviously hadn't seen one before, and Kip didn't know the lady, so he didn't want to ask her. He'd look up Aeluon ships on the Linkings when he got home. He knew all the types of Human ships, and he also liked to know stuff about alien bodies, but he hadn't ever thought to learn about *their* ships. It was easy, in the Fleet, to think that Human ships were all there was.

A hatch yawned open. How, Kip couldn't say, because there weren't any edges on the outer hull to suggest doors or seams. The crowd broke into a cheer as three Aeluons stepped out. Kip had really wanted to see them up close, but even at a distance, they made his heart race. Bare silver heads he knew were covered in tiny scales. Patches on their cheeks that swirled with colour. Weird grey and white and black clothes that, he guessed, had never been anybody's hand-me-downs.

'Why are they wearing masks?' Kip asked. 'Can't they breathe oxygen?'

'They can, and do,' Dad said. 'But sapients who don't live around Humans tend to find us, ah . . . pungent.'

'What's pungent mean?'

'We stink, kid.' The lady laughed into her canteen.

'Oh,' Kip said. He wasn't sure how he felt about that. And the longer he sat there, the less he was sure how he felt about anything. His insides began to tangle themselves again as he watched the Admiral greet their otherworldly neighbours. Her uniform no longer looked cool, the crowd no longer looked smartly dressed, and the dock no longer looked normal, not with a big flying gemstone resting in the middle of it. The Aeluons were here to clean up a mess the Fleet couldn't, a mess that wouldn't have happened without busted ships and worn-out tech. They shook hands Human-style with the stinky, stitched-up council, and beneath Kip's excitement, beneath his wonder, a sadness spread.

He watched the Aeluons, and he felt ashamed.

SAWYER

The trick to living on Mushtullo was knowing which sunrise to wait for. Ressoden came up first, but only spacer merchants and little kids made the mistake of going out that early. Ressoden was dinky, capable of providing usable light but not enough warmth to burn off the cold. The pre-dawn fog carried the kind of insidious wetness that wormed its way to your bones, and you couldn't be blamed for deciding to wait for the third sun – big, fat Pelus – to banish the clouds entirely. But that, too, was a rookie mistake. You had about a half an hour after Pelus' appearance until the surrounding swamps started to evaporate, and the roasting midday air became thick enough to chew. The second sunrise – Makarev – was where it was at. Makarev held court for an hour and sixteen minutes, just long enough for you to get up and catch a tram to wherever it was you needed to go. Not too damp, not too muggy, not too hot, not too cold. You didn't need to layer, and you wouldn't show up to work with a sweaty shirt that wouldn't dry out. Ideal.

Sawyer pressed his palm against the inner wall of his capsule bunk, and he could tell that Makarev was just about there. His capsule was supposedly temperature controlled – and okay, sure, he hadn't frozen to death or anything – but the insulation was as cheap as his rent. He lay under his blankets, waiting for the wall to hit that level of warmth that meant . . . *now*. He sat up on his mattress and hit one of the buttons on the wall. The sink shelf slid out, a thick rectangle with a basin and a pop-up mirror and the almost-empty box of dentbot packs he needed to restock.

He rinsed his face, drank some water, cleaned his mouth, combed his hair into place. He pushed a different wall button. The sink retracted, and a larger shelf extended, holding a quick-cooker and a storage box full of just-add-water meals. He knew he had a long day at work ahead, so he opted for two packs of Magic Morning Power Porridge, which were still heating up when he checked his scrib and discovered he had no job to get to.

He didn't bother to finish reading the soulless form letter his (former) employer had sent. He knew what it said. Unforeseen funding shortage, blah blah, sincerely regret the abrupt notice, blah blah, wish you the very best of luck in future, blah blah blah. Sawyer fell back onto his pillow and shut his eyes. He was nineteen, he'd been working since twelve, and he'd had ten jobs by now. The math there was not in his favour.

'Great,' he sighed, and for a while, he considered staying in bed all day, blowing the extra creds needed to cool his capsule while Pelus was out. But now his creds were even more precious than before, and if he'd been laid off, that meant everybody else at the factory had, too. They'd all be descending on the commerce square, ingratiating themselves to business owners until one of them offered a job. That was how things worked with Harmagians, anyway. No résumés or interviews or anything. Just walk up and hope they like you. With other species, finding a job was a less tiring to-do, but Harmagian jobs were where the creds were at. There were jobs in his neighbourhood, probably, but Human-owned work didn't get you very far. Much smarter to head out to the square and try his luck. He could do it. He'd done it before.

With a weary will, he sat back up, ate his porridge, and put on clean clothes (these, too, were stored in the wall). He scooted off the end of his mattress and out the capsule hatch, planting his feet on the ladder outside in a practised way. He gripped his doorframe as he started to lower himself down, and immediately withdrew his hand with disgust. 'Oh, come on,' he sighed, grimacing at the grey gunk smeared across his fingers. Creep mould. The grey, greasy stuff loved the night-time fog, and it grew so fast you could clean it up before bed and find a fresh new mat in the morning, just like the one inching over Sawyer's tiny home now. He wiped his palm on an old shirt and resumed his exit, taking care to not get any of the gunk on his clothes. He had new bosses to impress, and this already wasn't his day.

It would be, though, he decided, hoisting his mood as he climbed down. He'd go out there, and he'd find a job. He'd find something even better than the job he'd had yesterday.

He headed out into Mushtullo's second morning, weaving his way through the neighbourhood. The narrow paved streets were as packed as the tall buildings that lined them, and the general flow of foot traffic was headed for the tram stations, like always. He saw a few other better-dressed-than-usual people in the crowd, and he quickened his step. Had to get to the square before the good stuff got snapped up.

Out of the corner of his eye, he spotted something out of the ordinary: a small crowd – old people, mostly – gathered by that little weather-worn statue of an Exodan homesteader over by the grocery. They were decorating the statue, laying wreaths of flowers and ribbons over it, lighting candles around its base, scrubbing creep mould off of it. Sawyer dimly remembered talk at work a few days before, something about a homesteader exploding, or decompressing, or something. Some horrible shit. He figured that was the reason for the crowd, and would've kept going on his way were it not for one face he recognised: Shani Brenner, one of the supervisors from the factory. She wasn't headed for the trams, she was helping some old – no, *ancient* – lady light a candle. Did she not know about the layoffs? Had she not checked her scrib?

Sawyer hesitated. He didn't want to waste time, but Shani was all right. She'd shared her lunch with Sawyer once, when he'd been short on creds. This day hadn't had a lot going for it yet. Maybe, Sawyer thought, helping somebody out would get the universe back on his side.

He changed course and hurried toward the statue. 'Hey, Shani!' he called with a wave.

Shani looked up, first with confusion, then with recognition. She patted the old woman (who was sitting on the ground, now), then met Sawyer halfway. 'Shitty morning, huh?' she said, rubbing the back of her neck.

'You heard,' Sawyer said.

'Yeah. Got a letter, same as I bet you did. No idea it was coming. Stingy bastards. I gave Tolged a thanks-for-being-my-boss gift three days ago and everything.'

Sawyer jerked a thumb toward the street. 'Aren't you going to the square?'

Shani shook her head. 'Not today.' She nodded to the statue. 'That's my grandma over there. You hear about the *Oxomoco*?'

'That homesteader that . . . ?'

'Yeah. She was born there. Came here when she was seven, but still. Roots, y'know?' Shani eyed Sawyer. 'You Exodan?'

'I mean . . .' Wasn't everybody, at one point or another? 'Like way, way back. I— I don't know what ship, or anything. I've never been.'

Shani shrugged. 'Still counts. Wanna come sit with us?'

Sawyer blinked. 'Thanks, but I—'

'There'll be jobs tomorrow,' Shani said. 'I'm not worrying about it, and neither should you. We'll both land on our feet, yeah? Things work out.'

Over Shani's shoulder, Sawyer could see other people joining Grandma Brenner on the ground. Some were weeping. Some held hands, or passed a flask around. Some were speaking in unison, almost like a chant, but he could only catch a few words. His Ensk was scattershot at best.

Shani smiled at Sawyer. 'Up to you,' she said as she walked away. She, too, sat on the ground, and held her grandmother close.

Sawyer did not join them, but neither did he turn back. There was no reason for him to stay, and yet . . . and yet. He imagined the jam-packed frenzy that awaited him at the commerce square, the lines of eager people desperate to impress. It was the antithesis of the scene in front of him, this quiet mourning, this shared respect. The idea of joining them felt awkward. He didn't want to intrude. He wasn't one of them, didn't belong there. But as he watched them share tears and songs and company, he wished that he did. He didn't have anything he was a part of like that. Even in grief, it looked like a nice thing to have. Maybe *especially* in grief.

He thought, as he rode the tram to the square, of the recited words he'd managed to make out. They circled his mind, over and over as he watched crowded neighbourhoods blur through mouldy windows.

From the ground.

Part 1

· · · · · · · · · · · · · · · · · · ·

FROM THE BEGINNING

Feed source: Reskit Institute of Interstellar Migration (Public News Feed)
Item name: The Modern Exodus – Entry #1
Author: Ghuh'loloan Mok Chutp
Encryption: 0
Translation path: [Hanto:Kliptorigan]
Transcription: 0
Node identifier: 2310-483-38, Isabel Itoh

[System message: The feed you have selected has been translated from written Hanto. As you may be aware, written Hanto includes gestural notations that do not have analogous symbols in any other GC language. Therefore, your scrib's on-board translation software has not translated the following material directly. The content here is a modified translation, intended to be accessible to the average Kliptorigan reader.]

———

Greetings, dear guest, and welcome! I am Ghuh'loloan Mok Chutp, and these words are mine. I hope my communicative efforts will be sufficient to make any time you spend on this feed here worthwhile. I shall exercise my skills to the best of my ability, with the aim of educating and entertaining you. If I fail in these endeavours, please accept my sincere apologies and know that such failings are mine alone and are not reflective of my place of employment, my schooling, or my lineage.

If you are unfamiliar with my work, allow me to provide a brief introduction. I am an ethnographic researcher based at the Reskit Institute of Interstellar Migration. I have worked in this field for twenty-two standards, and my focus is on transitory and orbital communities in the modern era. I am proud of my work thus far, with a few exceptions. I am confident that I am qualified for the task I will describe momentarily. I hope you will agree.

What do you think of, dear guest, when I mention the Exodus

Fleet? You could define the term literally: the collection of ships that carried the remnants of the Human species away from their failed planet. Perhaps the Fleet sparks some deeper association in you – a symbol of desperation, a symbol of poverty, a symbol of resilience. Do you live in a community where Humans are present? Do you know individuals born within one of these aged vessels? Or are you from a more homogeneous society, and therefore surprised to learn that the Fleet is still inhabited? Perhaps the entire concept of the Fleet baffles you. Perhaps it is mysterious, or exciting. Perhaps you yourself are Human, dear guest, and think of the Fleet as home – or, conversely, a place as alien to you as to the rest of us.

Whatever your background, the Fleet is a source of curiosity for all who do not have some personal connection to it. Unless you have a close Human friend or are a long-haul merchant, it is unlikely you have travelled there. While Humans living in GC territories and planetary colonies outnumber Exodans in aggregate, the Fleet is still where you will find the largest concentration of their kind outside the Sol system. Though many Humans have never set foot in the great homestead ships, the journey of the Fleet is a history they all consciously carry. That lineage has inextricably shaped every modern Human community, regardless of foundational philosophy. In one way or another, it affects how they think of themselves, and how the rest of us see them.

So what is the Fleet today? How do these people live? How do they view the GC? Why have they continued this way of life? These are the questions I will attempt to unravel in the time ahead. I, Ghuh'loloan, will likewise be a guest. As I write this, I am on my way to the Exodus Fleet, where I will be staying for eight tendays. I will be living aboard an Exodan homestead ship, interviewing Exodan citizens, and learning Exodan ways. Much was written about the state of the Exodan Fleet following first contact and leading up to GC membership, but little mainstream record has been made of them since. The assumption, I fear, is that their presence in multispecies communities means they have integrated into our varied societies and left their old ways behind. Nothing could be further from the truth. I cross the galaxy now in search of a more honest story.

It is my hope, dear guest, that you will join me.

TESSA

Received message
Encryption: 0
Translation: 0
From: Ashby Santoso (path: 7182-312-95)
To: Tessa Santoso (path: 6222-198-00)

Hey Tess,

I don't know if you've seen the feeds, but if you have, I'm okay. If you haven't, some bad stuff went down at Hedra Ka, but again: I'm okay. The ship's suffered a lot of damage, but we're stable and out of immediate danger. I've got my hands full with repairs and my crew, so I'll get on the sib when I can. I'll send a note to Dad, too.

More soon, promise. Hug the kids for me.

Ashby

————

In the grand tradition of siblings everywhere, Tessa wanted to kill her brother.

Not *permanently* kill him. Just a casual spacing to get her point across, followed by a quick resurrection and a hot cup of tea. *That*, she'd say, as he sat shivering on the floor, clutching his mug like he used to when he was little. *That's what you put us through every time you go off the map. We all stop breathing until you get back.*

Tessa tossed her scrib across her desk and rubbed her eyes with her fingertips. 'Shit,' she breathed, furious and relieved. She'd seen the feeds. Of course, they hadn't said *which* civilian ship the Toremi had fired on, but Tessa had known where Ashby had been headed for the past standard, what he'd been hired to do. 'You stupid . . .' She exhaled, her eyes stinging. 'He's okay.' She inhaled, her voice steadying. 'He's okay.'

She'd gone to the cargo bay immediately after the news feed had wrapped up, despite her shift not starting for another two hours, despite her father telling her to stay home until they knew whether to relax or plan a funeral. Tessa had no stomach for how Pop had decided to deal with it: holding vigil in front of the pixel projector, watching every feed over and over until something new uploaded, smoking and muttering and tossing out anxious theories. She saw no point in sitting around waiting for news, especially when you had no idea when it would arrive. She'd addressed the fist squeezing her heart in her own way. She'd dragged Aya out of bed, given Ky a cake bite to keep him from fussing at the change in schedule, given Aya a cake bite so she wouldn't cry unfairness, and told Pop to get on the vox if anything changed.

You'd know if you stayed home, he'd grumbled, shoving fat pinches of redreed into his pipe. But she hadn't budged, and he hadn't pushed, for once. She'd patted his shoulder, and sent the kids across the way to the Parks' – who, as Tessa had figured, had been asleep, but that's what hexmates were for.

Aya had pestered her for an explanation every step toward the door. *Why are we up so early? Why can't I stay here? Do I have to go to school? Why was Grandpa mad at you? Is Dad okay?*

Your dad's fine, Tessa had said. That was the only question she'd answered directly. Every other query got a *because I said so* or an *I'll tell you later*. There was no way to say *your Uncle Ashby's ship may have been blown up by aliens and this is my way of coping* to a nine-year-old, and no way a nine-year-old would respond to that sentiment in a way that wouldn't freak out the two-year-old as well. Let the kids have a quiet morning. The grown-ups could worry enough for everyone.

Tessa stretched back against her desk chair, cracking the tight points between ribs and spine. She turned her head toward the wall vox. '224-246,' she said. The vox chirped in acknowledgement of a home address. 'Pop, is your scrib on?'

'No,' her father shouted back. He'd never grasped the concept that even though the vox was on the other side of the room, he didn't have to yell like he did with the old models. 'Why?'

Tessa rolled her eyes. *Why*, asked the man who'd been looping feeds all morning. 'Ashby wrote to us. He's okay.'

The vox relayed a long sigh, followed by a softly spoken 'shit.' He started shouting again. 'How's his ship?'

'He said stable. He didn't have time to write much, just that he's okay.'

'Is he still on board? *Stable* can change fast.'

'I'm sure Ashby knows whether or not his ship's safe.'

'These Toremi weapons they're talking about on the feeds, those things can really—'

'Pop, stop watching the feeds. Okay? They don't know what's going on either, they're just filling time.'

'I'm just saying—'

'Pop.' Tessa pinched the bridge of her nose. 'I have to get back to work. Go to the gardens or something, yeah? Go to Jojo's, get some lunch.'

'When are you coming home?'

'I don't know. Depends on how the day goes.'

'Okay.' He paused. 'I love you.'

Pop wasn't withholding or anything, but he didn't throw those three words around lightly. Tessa softened. 'I love you, too.'

The vox switched off, and she took another opportunity to clear her lungs. She stared out the workroom window, out into the cargo bay. Rows of towering shelves stretched on and on, full to the brim with wires and junk, attended by the herd of heavy-duty liftbots following assignments Tessa had punched into her terminal. There were stacks of metal, too, the pieces too big for the shelves, the pieces nobody'd had time to cut down. This was her domain, her project. It was her job to track comings and goings, to make sure everything got logged and weighed and described, to keep track of stuff the merchants and foundries weren't ready for yet, to wrangle the unintelligent machines who shuffled goods from where they had been to where they were needed. A complicated job, but not a taxing one, and one where you could count on most days going exactly the way you'd thought they'd go when you woke up. Compared to the constant familial chaos of home, she valued that.

When she'd first started working in cargo, way back in her twenties, Bay Eight had been a tidy place. She remembered the neatly packed bins of raw materials, the imported crates with exciting labels printed in multiple alien alphabets. Twenty years down the road, and you couldn't find a one of those in her bay anymore. Imports and processed stock were elsewhere. Bay Eight was one of three on the *Asteria* dedicated to the remains of the *Oxomoco*. Every homestead ship was made the same: a massive central cylinder full of vital systems, a flat ring of thousands of homes anchored around it, a cluster of chunky engines at the back. The *Oxomoco* didn't look like that anymore. Half of it was a ragged husk, dragged far from the Fleet's orbit but still out there, still scaring the boots off anyone who saw it grimacing through a shuttle window. The other half was in pieces, gathered and shoved away in cargo bays like hers. So now, instead of alien crates, she dealt with a never-ending backlog of support trusses, floor panels, empty oxygen tanks. Things that had been vital. Things that had been viewed as permanent. All it had taken was one malfunctioning shuttle, one unlucky trajectory, one stretch of fatigued bulkhead. Just one combination of small things that led to the deaths of tens of thousands, and to cargo bays packed with what was left of the place that had carried them.

Pop's words stuck in her head. *Stable can change fast.*

'M Santoso, you okay?'

Tessa looked over. Kip was peeking around the doorway, his pockmarked face scrunched in concern. She sighed and gave her head a light shake. 'Yeah,' she said. 'Yeah, I'm fine.' The scrunch persisted. Explanations that worked for a nine-year-old had no chance against a sixteen-year-old. Tessa gave an acknowledging smirk and waved him in. 'Just family stuff. Would you pour me some mek?' She paused. 'You can have one, too, if you want.'

The boy raised his eyebrows. 'My shift's not over.'

Tessa gave him a wry smile. 'You've got two days left with me, and we both know you're not going to apprentice here.'

Kip smiled sheepishly as he poured two mugs of mek from the brewer in the corner. 'Come on, M, I'm not *that* bad.'

'You're not,' Tessa said. 'You *could* be decent at managing inventory if you put in the practice. You've got the kind of logicky brain you need for sorting stuff. But we both know this isn't for you.' She accepted the mug with a nod, trying to brush away the lingering mental image of kicking Ashby in the shins. 'But that's the point of job trials, yeah? You've gotta find a good fit, and you won't know what you like and what you don't until you give everything a try. You worked hard for me, and you didn't slack off.' *Much*, she thought.

Kip sat down, a lanky assemblage of too-long limbs and patchy stubble. The kid would be handsome in a year or two, but puberty wasn't going to let him get there without a fight. 'What was your first trial?' he asked.

'Fish farms with my dad,' Tessa said. 'I lasted three whole days.'

'Did you not like killing them, or what?'

'No, that part was fine. It was more that Pop and I were gonna kill each other.' She took a sip of mek and *did not think about Ashby*. 'Have you thought about trying the food farms?'

'I did bugs,' Kip said.

'And?'

'I didn't like killing them.'

This surprised her not a bit. 'But you eat 'em, yeah?'

'Yeah,' he said, with the same goofy smile. 'I'm just good letting somebody else . . . y'know. Do that.'

'Fair enough,' Tessa said. Inwardly, she found that mindset silly. If you were okay with eating something, you had to be okay with it being dead. But Kip was a nice kid, and she wasn't about to make him feel bad for having a soft heart. 'Any idea what you want to try next?'

'I dunno. Not really.'

'You've got plenty of time. And besides, there's tons more for you to try. Always something to do in the Fleet, yeah?'

Kip's mouth smiled, but his eyes didn't. 'Yeah,' he said. 'I guess.'

Tessa took in the kid's face. She knew that look – that restless, empty-handed look. She'd seen it on her baby brother's face, just a standard or so before he packed his bags and tearfully promised them all he wouldn't disappear. He'd made good on that. They got letters and sib calls regularly. He visited when he could. He sent them more credits than any of them knew how to thank him for. But there was a room in the Santoso home that was used for storage now. There were a lot of rooms like it in the Fleet. Empty rooms had been a luxury once, Pop often said. Nowadays . . . nowadays folks could spread out more, take longer showers, hear their voices echo a little louder in the public walkways. She looked at Kip, drinking his mek, probably bored out of his mind. She wondered if his room would end up empty, too.

ISABEL

Isabel had worked in the *Asteria*'s Archives for forty-four years, but she never tired of days like this. These days were some of the best, and she'd prepared in kind. The assembly hall was most often used for lectures and workshops and so on, but today, it had been transformed. She and the other archivists had hauled out the decorations they'd long ago made for such occasions: hanging sunbursts made of scrap metal, bright streamers of recycled cloth. A long table stood waiting to the side, ready to receive home-cooked food and drink. Another table held new seedlings brought in from one of the nurseries, available for those present to bring home to their neighbourhood gardens. Floating globulbs hovered around the room's upper edges, radiating yellows, greens, and blues. Life colours. Growth colours. At the front of the room, by the big screen that projected the view of the starry black beyond the bulkhead, there was a podium. It was covered with streamers and fully-grown plants and, at the top, held Isabel's scrib. This was the most important piece of all.

The person being honoured there would not remember any of it, but the others present would, and they would relay the story one day. That, in a nutshell, was what Isabel's profession was for. Making sure everybody was a link in a chain. Making sure they remembered.

Guests began to arrive, festively dressed, carrying containers dewy with steam and fragrant with spice, syrup, toasted dough. Isabel would not need dinner after this. One of the finer perks of her job.

A boy pleaded with a man to let him have *just one* of whatever they'd brought to the shared table. The man told the boy to be patient. The lack of patience in his own voice indicated that this was not the first time this conversation had been had that day. Isabel smiled. She'd been in both their shoes.

Two musicians set up near the podium. Isabel knew them both, and greeted them warmly. She remembered when they'd been kids begging at the table, too. The same was true for many of the people entering the room, except for the ones she'd shared a childhood with so long ago. There weren't many faces here she didn't know.

The room filled, and at last, two people entered, carrying a tiny third. This was Isabel's cue. She walked to the podium, stepping with practised care in her formal robes. The hum of voices started to fade. She met eyes with one of the musicians and nodded. The musicians nodded to her, then to each other. *One and two and* . . . she saw them mouth. A sheet drum and a long flute leapt into merry action. The final voices disappeared, and the gathered bodies parted to allow the trio to make their way to Isabel.

The young couple stood before her, smiling, proud, perhaps a little shy. Their infant daughter wriggled in the woman's arms, more interested in the glint of her mother's necklace than anything else.

Isabel raised her head to the room as the song reached its end. Faces looked back at her, smiling, waiting. Everyone there knew exactly what would come next. She'd said the words hundreds of times. Thousands, maybe. Every archivist knew how to say them, and every Exodan knew their sound by heart. But still, they needed to be said.

Isabel's body was old – a fact it constantly reminded her of – but her voice remained strong and clear. 'We destroyed our world,' she said, 'and left it for the skies. Our numbers were few. Our species had scattered. We were the last to leave. We left the ground behind. We left the oceans. We left the air. We watched these things grow small. We watched them shrink into a point of light. As we watched, we understood. We understood what we were. We understood what we had lost. We understood what we would need to do to survive. We abandoned more than our ancestors' world. We abandoned our short sight. We abandoned our bloody ways. We made ourselves anew.' She spread her hands, encompassing the gathered. Mouths in the crowd silently mirrored her words. 'We are the Exodus Fleet. We are those that wandered, that wander still. We are the homesteaders that shelter our families. We are the miners and foragers in the open. We are the ships that ferry between. We are the explorers who carry our names. We are the parents who lead the way. We are the children who continue on.' She picked up her scrib and addressed the couple. 'What is her name?'

'Robin,' the man said.

'And what name does your home carry?'

'Garcia,' said the woman.

'Robin Garcia,' Isabel spoke to the scrib. The scrib chirped in response, and retrieved the citizen registry file she had created that morning. A blue square appeared on screen. Isabel gestured for the mother to step forward. The baby frowned as they manoeuvred one of her bare feet onto the square, pressing tiny toes and heel against it. The scrib chirped again, indicating that a new file had been added to the mighty towers of data nodes that stood vigil a deck below. Isabel read the record to the room. 'Robin Garcia,' she said. 'Born aboard the *Asteria*. Forty Solar days of age as of GC standard day 158/307. She is now, and always, a member of our Fleet. By our laws, she is assured shelter and passage here. If we have food, she will eat. If we have air, she will breathe. If we have fuel, she will fly. She is daughter to all grown, sister to all still growing. We will care for her, protect her, guide her. We welcome you, Robin, to the decks of the *Asteria*, and to the journey we take together.' She cupped the baby's head with her palm, weathered skin cradling new. She spoke the final words now, and the room spoke with her. 'From the ground, we stand. From our ships, we live. By the stars, we hope.'

SAWYER

He stood at the railing outside the dockside bioscans, luggage in hand, breathing in the recycled air. It was different than the air he knew, for sure. It wasn't what he'd call *good* air, not like what you'd get around a forest or a field. There was a slight metallic edge to it, and though the walkways were lined with healthy planters exhaling oxygen back his way, something about each breath just *felt* artificial. There was no wind here, no rain. The air moved because Humans told it to, and maybe in that, it had lost something along the way.

But Sawyer smiled. *Different* was what he was after, and everything he'd encountered in the twenty minutes since coming aboard was as different as could be. What struck him was the practicality of the architecture, the intense economy. On Mushtullo, people embellished. There were mouldings on the tops of walls. Roofs twisted and fences spiralled. Even the ships were filigreed. Not here. Nothing in the foundation of this vessel had been wasted on sentiment.

But while the ship's skeleton was simple, the people within had spent centuries fleshing it out. The metal walls were disguised with inviting paint: warm tan, soft orange, living green. On his way to the railing, he'd come upon an enormous mural that had stopped him in his tracks. He'd stood for a minute there, as other travellers split their busy stream around him. The mural was vibrant, almost gaudy, a spree of colour and curves depicting dancing Exodans with a benignly burning sun beneath their feet and a starry sky above. Myriad professions were on display – a farmer, a doctor, a tech, a musician, a pilot, a teacher leading children. It was an ordinary sort of theme, and yet there was something about it – the lack of actual ground, perhaps, or something in the sweeping style – that was undeniably foreign. You'd never see a mural like that on Mushtullo.

Sawyer let his reality sink in: he was in the Fleet. The Fleet! He was finally, actually *there*, not just reading reference files or pestering elderly folks for any scraps they could remember about what *their* parents had told them about the ships they'd left behind. He'd made it. He'd made it, and now, everything was right there for him to explore.

There were no other species in the crowd, and it left him both giddy and jarred. The only times he'd seen anything close to this many Humans in one place was on holidays or at parties, and even then, you'd be sure to see other sapients in the mix. There'd been merchants from elsewhere on the transport with him, but as soon as they reached a branching sign that read *Cargo Bays* on the right and *Central Plaza* on the left, all the scales and claws went right. Everyone around him now had two hands, two feet, soft skin, hairy heads. He'd never blended into a public group like this, and yet, he felt like he stuck out more than he ever had.

Sawyer had thought perhaps some part of him would recognise this place, that he'd feel himself reversing the steps his great-great-grandparents had taken. He'd read accounts of other grounders visiting the Fleet. They'd written about how connected they felt to their ancestors, how they felt immediate kinship with the people there. Sawyer hadn't felt that yet, and part of him was a touch disappointed. But no matter. He'd been there for all of twenty minutes, and the only person he'd talked to was the patch scan attendant. So far, he'd dipped a toe in the water. It was time to dive in.

He took an elevator down to the market floor, an expansive grid of shop fronts and service centres. It wasn't like other market-places he'd been to, where everything sprawled and piled as if it were alive. The Fleet, as he'd read and as had already proven true, was a place of orderly geometry. Every corner had been considered, measured, and considered again. Space efficiency was the top order of business, so the original architects had provided future generations of shopkeepers with defined lots that could be assigned and repurposed as needed. The end result was, on the surface, the tidiest trading hub Sawyer had ever seen. But once he got past the neat exteriors, the underlying business was bewildering. Dozens of signs, dozens of displays, hundreds of customers, and he had no idea where anything was.

He eyed the places that served food – all open-air (if that was the right term to use inside a ship), with shared eating tables corralled behind the waist-high metal walls that defined each lot's edges. Sawyer found himself drawn toward a cheery, clean cafe called *My Favourite*. The menu posted outside was in both Klip and Ensk, and the fare was things he recognised – beansteak skewers, hoppers, jam cakes. It looked like a respectable spot for a non-threatening meal. Sawyer pointed his feet elsewhere. That was a place meant for merchants and visitors. Tourists. He wasn't here to be a tourist. He was after something *real*.

He spied another eatery of the same size and shape. *Jojo's*, the sign read. Or it would have, if the pixels on the second *j* hadn't been twitching themselves nearly illegible. There was no posted menu. The only other signage displayed the hours of business, which were in Ensk numerals and Ensk numerals only. (Standard time, though. They only used Solar for age, or so he'd been told.) Behind the corral, some folks in algae-stained coveralls wolfed down whatever was for lunch. A group of five or six elderly folks were arguing over a game taking place on an old pixel board. Nobody had any luggage.

Perfect.

No one greeted Sawyer as he walked in. Few looked up. There were two people behind the counter: a wiry young man chopping something, and an imposing middle-aged woman peeling shells off steamed red coaster bugs. The woman was absorbed in a loud vid on a nearby projector – a Martian period drama, it looked like. She cracked each shell segment with speedy precision, without so much as a glance down at her work. Sawyer had no real way of knowing, but he got the unshakable sense that this was her place.

The woman gave a short, mocking laugh. 'This Solan shit,' she said in Ensk, shaking her head at the projector. The vid music hit a melodramatic crescendo as a character in a clunky exosuit succumbed to a sandstorm. 'Why does anybody watch this?'

'You watch it,' an old woman piped up from the board game table.

'It's like a shipwreck,' the shell-cracker replied. 'Once it starts, I can't look away.'

The scene changed. A tearful group of terraformers sat huddled in their dome. 'This damned planet,' one actor cried. He wasn't about to win any awards for this, but stars, he was trying. 'This damned planet!'

'*This damned planet!*' the woman repeated, laughing again. Her eyes snapped over as she noticed Sawyer at last. 'Hey,' she said, glancing at his bag. 'What can I get ya?'

Sawyer walked up to the counter. He was more or less fluent in Ensk, having crammed Linking language lessons hard over the past few years, but the only person he'd been able to practise speaking with had been the lady at the shoe shop back home, and her slang was about twenty years out of date. He screwed up his courage, and asked: 'Do you have a menu?'

Every person in Jojo's looked up. It took Sawyer a moment to realise – *accent*. His accent. He didn't have the distinctive snap of an Exodan, the silky smoothness of a Martian, the muddle of someone who did a lot of bouncing around. His face said *Human*. His vowels said *Harmagian*.

The woman blinked. 'No menu,' she said. She jerked a thumb back toward the wiry man, still chopping away. 'It's ninth day. That means we've got twice-round pickle on a quickbun and red coaster stew. Only, we're out of red coaster stew.' Exoskeleton crunched between her hands. 'I gotta make more, and that's gonna be at least an hour.'

'Okay,' Sawyer said. 'I'll have the other one.'

'The pickle?'

'Yeah.'

'You ever had twice-round pickle?'

Sawyer grinned. 'Nope.'

The woman grinned back, but it wasn't a good grin, not the kind of grin that shook hands with his own. This was a different look, a look that knew something he didn't. Sawyer felt his mood slip a bit. He was pretty sure the board game crew was still watching him.

'Okay,' the woman said. 'One pickle bun. Comes with tea.'

It took him a second to realise she was asking him a question. 'Tea would be great.' She searched for a mug by way of reply. Sawyer took a chance, trying to coax more conversation. 'Are you Jojo?'

'No,' the woman said flatly. 'Jojo was my mom.'

'And she was a lot nicer than this one,' an old man with a pipe added from the back.

'*Ch,*' the woman said, rolling her eyes. 'You only say that 'cause she slept with you once.'

'I would've thought she was nice even if we hadn't.'

'Yeah, well. She always was a sucker for ugly things.'

The board game crew cracked up – the old man in particular – and the woman grinned, a real grin this time. She filled a mug from a large decanter and set it on the counter as the wiry man silently assembled Sawyer's lunch. Sawyer tried to see what was going into what he'd just ordered, but the man's body blocked his view. Something was chopped, something was ladled, a few bottles were shaken. Twice-round pickle looked . . . involved.

The woman stared at Sawyer. 'Oh,' he said, understanding. He hadn't paid. He pushed back his wristwrap. 'Where should I, ah . . .' He looked around for a scanner.

The woman pursed her lips. 'Don't take creds,' she said.

Sawyer was elated. He'd heard about this – Exodan merchants who operated on barter and barter only. But there was a problem: that was as far as his knowledge of the practice went, and he didn't know what the protocol was. He waited for her to suggest an acceptable trade. Nothing came. 'What would be good?' he asked.

Another short laugh, like the one the sandstorm victim received. 'I dunno. I dunno what you've got.'

Sawyer thought. He'd only brought one bag of essentials and didn't have much he was willing to part with, not for the sake of a sandwich. He scolded himself for not planning for this with a bag of circuit chips or something. 'Do you need some help in the kitchen? I could wash dishes.'

Now *everyone* laughed. Sawyer had no idea what the joke was, but he was starting to wonder if the tourist cafe would've been the better option.

The woman leaned against the counter. 'Where are you from?'

'Mushtullo.'

'What now?'

'Mushtullo.' No response. 'Central space.'

She raised her eyebrows. 'Huh. You got family here?'

'No,' Sawyer said. 'But my family came *from* here.'

'*Oh*,' the woman said, as if she understood everything now. 'I see. Okay. You got a place to stay?'

'I figured I'd sort that out once I got here.'

'Oh boy,' the woman said under her breath. The wiry man handed her a plate, which she pushed across the counter. 'Here. On the house. The food of your ancestors.'

'Wow, you sure?' Sawyer said.

'Well, now I'm not.'

'Sorry, um . . . thank you.' He took both plate and mug. 'That's really kind.'

The woman resumed her shell cracking without another word. Sawyer looked around, hoping one of the groups might wave him over. None did. The algaeists were stacking up their thoroughly cleaned dishes, and the old folks had resumed their board game.

Sawyer dropped his bag in an empty chair and sat in another alongside it. He studied his food – a large mound of wet, shredded vegetables, piled on top of two halves of a nondescript bun, dressed with whatever Jojo's daughter's assistant had dashed on top of it. He lifted one of the halves. It leaked, sending purple liquid running down his forearm. He paused before opening his mouth. There was a smell, fetid and sharp, maybe a bit fishy. He thought of the other customers, chowing down with satisfaction. He took a bite. His throat tightened, his sinuses shot open, and his bravery died. The stuff tasted exactly as it smelled, only now it was inescapable, mingling with a bitter, tangy undercurrent he wasn't sure he wanted to identify. He couldn't taste the bread, but despite the sour liquid now dripping all over his hands, the texture was distractingly dry. The pickle didn't crunch, as he'd expected. It just softly surrendered.

It was, without a doubt, the worst thing he'd ever eaten.

Okay, he thought. *This is okay. It's an adventure.* Not the start he'd been hoping for, but it was a start, and that was something. He forced another bite of pickle, washing it down with a huge swig of tea (the tea, at least, was good). There was no way he wasn't going to finish his meal. This was a test. The locals were watching, his ancestors were watching, everybody back home who thought this plan of his was bonkers was watching. He would clean his plate, and find a place to stay, and everything would be great.

Sawyer heard the woman laugh again. He thought for a moment it was directed at him, but no. Another Martian terra-former had died.

KIP

Lunch breaks were the best part of Kip's day. No teachers, no job trials, no parents. Nothing that needed doing or that he might screw up. Kip savoured every second. This was *his* time, and he always did the same thing with it: get a choko and a hopper at Grub Grub, park himself on the bench facing the oxygen garden, and try to stretch out his brief bit of freedom as long as possible. Chane in biology class said Sianat Pairs could slow time with their brains, and Kip didn't think that was true, but if it was, he'd seriously trade an arm or something if it meant he could do that. Both arms, maybe. Maybe even his eyes. Okay, not his eyes. But limbs, definitely.

Somebody jumped him from behind, pulling his shirt up over the back of his head. '*Tek tem*, fucko!'

Kip had his shirt back down and a hand swinging before he could get a look at where it would land. Not a mean fist or anything – he'd never punched anybody for reals. Just a soft slap that wouldn't even hurt, much less bruise.

His hand landed in Ras' ribs. Ras shoved the slap away with one hand and grabbed for Kip's choko with the other. 'Gimme.'

'*Dosh*,' said Kip, stretching his drink out of reach. 'Fuck off.' In one fast move, he reached out and mussed Ras' hair.

Ras withdrew at that, as he always did. 'Aw, come on,' he said, combing away the minimal damage with his fingers. 'Uncalled for.'

Kip chuckled into his drink, scrunching his eyes tight. He wiped his hand on his pants, trying to get rid of the hair glue remnants he'd picked up. Ras always put too much shit in his hair.

The scuffle ended as fast as it had started. He and his friend sat in an easy slump, watching the crowd for the unlikely chance of something interesting happening. Kip passed the choko bottle to Ras. Ras took a long pull of the sweet fizz and passed it back. It was a rhythm they fell into without any thought. There'd been a lot of shared snacks over the years. That was what had eventually led to them getting assigned work day and school day schedules that didn't overlap – too many passed-between packs of cake bites in class. *A persistent disruption to other students*, M Rebane had called him and Ras. Whatever. At least they still had lunch at the same time.

'You know Amira, at the tech shop?' Ras said.

'Yeah.'

'I think she likes me.'

Kip almost got choko up his nose. 'Okay.'

'Seriously,' Ras said. 'I saw her looking at me.'

Kip kept laughing. 'Okay.'

'What? I did!'

'Amira. From the tech shop.'

'That's what I said.'

'She's, like, twenty-five or something.'

'So?'

'So she probably just thought your hair looks stupid and couldn't stop staring.'

'*Remmet telli toh.*' Ras cuffed him, but grinned. '*Your* hair looks stupid.'

'Yeah,' Kip agreed. No argument there. Had he combed it this morning? He couldn't remember.

The crowd went back and forth, back and forth. Same faces, same patterns as every other day. 'What do you wanna do after work?' Ras asked.

'Don't you have history this afternoon?'

Ras shook his head with an expression that said he *did* have that class lined up, but there was no chance of him being there for it. 'Wanna go to the hub?'

'Nah,' Kip said. There weren't any new sims out, and they'd played all the ones worth playing. Ras was always down for *Battle Wizards,* but Kip was kind of sick of it.

'Wanna go look at the new transport pods?'

'We did that yesterday.'

'So? They're cool.'

Kip shrugged. New pods were the kind of thing that were cool only when you'd never seen them before.

'Okay,' Ras said. 'What do *you* want to do?'

Kip shrugged again. 'I dunno.'

Ras took ownership of the choko. 'You have a bad day or something?'

'It was fine. M Santoso kind of just let me hang out. Let me have mek during my shift.'

'That's cool.'

'Yeah,' Kip said, taking the choko back. 'She's all right.'

'I dunno why you're doing job trials anyway. Exams are coming up.'

This was Ras' grand plan, unchanged since they were twelve: take the qualification exams and get into university (the fastest ticket out of the Fleet – all there was at home were trade classes and apprenticeships). After that, get a cool job, get on a big ship, and make lots of creds. That was as good of a plan as any for Kip – and more than he'd ever been able to come up with on his own – but he wasn't as sure as Ras that he'd be able to come along.

'When I don't pass, I'm gonna need a job,' Kip said.

'You'll pass,' Ras said.

'I suck at tests.'

'Everyone sucks at tests.'

'You don't suck at tests.'

Ras didn't say anything, because he *didn't* suck at tests, just like he wasn't doing job trials because he knew he wouldn't need them. When Ras said he was gonna do a thing, the thing *happened*. Sometimes Kip was jealous of that. He wished he could be more like Ras. Ras always knew what to say, what to do, what was happening. Kip was real glad they were friends, but sometimes he didn't know what Ras got out of the arrangement.

'Hey, M Aksoy,' Ras called out. The grocery seller was walking past them, followed by an autocart carrying . . . ? 'What is that?'

M Aksoy turned his head, gestured at the cart to stop, and waved them toward him. 'Come on and see.'

Kip and Ras ambled over. Among the recognisable boxes – mek powder, root sugar, bottles of kick – there were three plex tanks full of water, like jellyfish tanks. But whatever was inside wasn't jellyfish, no way. They were long and wispy, covered in soft spines. They shivered their way through the water.

'Special order from the Archives,' M Aksoy said.

'Are they pets or something?' Ras asked. 'Some kind of science thing?'

'Nope,' M Aksoy said. 'They're called—'

'*Pokpok*,' Kip said, saying the word before he realised he knew it.

Ras turned his head. 'The hell'd you know that?'

Kip had no idea. Something from when he was little? Like something in a learning sim, or a Linking book, or . . . he couldn't say. He'd been a dork about that kind of stuff as a kid, and it had been a long time since that was his thing. But wherever *pokpok* had come from, the dusty old memory remained active. He could feel Ras looking at him, though, so he just shrugged and didn't say anything about the bit where he was pretty sure the swimming things were Harmagian food. Ras was real smart, and Kip didn't want to look stupid by saying something wrong.

'You're right, *pokpok*,' M Aksoy said. 'M Itoh has a Harmagian guest arriving today. These, apparently, are one of their favourite things to eat.'

Kip watched the *pokpok* wriggle around the tank, looking like spiky snot brought to life. He felt his nose pull into itself.

Ras mirrored his expression. 'Do they fry them or—'

The grocer's eyes crinkled at the edges. 'You know, I don't know if they cook them at all.'

Kip groaned with disgust. Ras looked at him. 'Give you twenty creds if you eat one.'

'You don't have twenty creds.'

The grocer laughed. 'One of these'd cost you well more than twenty creds, and they're not for you anyway. But here.' He reached into one of the crates on the cart, and pulled out two snack bags. 'Free sample, all the way from the independent colonies.'

Kip accepted the bag and looked at the label. *The One and Only Fire Shrimp*, it read in Klip. There was another line that ended in the word *hot*, but the word before it he didn't know. He pointed it out to Ras. They both used Klip all the time, but Ras was super good at it – *real* Klip, classroom Klip, not just a few words stuck into Ensk like everybody did (everybody who wasn't old, anyway). Ras was definitely going to university.

'*Soolat*,' Ras read. 'That's like, uh . . . horribly.'

'*Devastatingly*,' M Aksoy said. 'That's a better translation. *Devastatingly hot.* I don't know if they're any good, but if you like them, you know where to trade for more.'

'Thanks, M,' Ras said.

'Yeah, thanks, M,' said Kip.

The grocer gave them a nod and started back on his way. 'Hey, M,' Ras called after him. 'You said the Harmagian's gonna be at the Archives?'

'Far as I know,' M Aksoy called back as he disappeared into the crowd.

Ras looked at Kip. 'Ever seen a Harmagian before?'

Kip shook his head. 'Just in sims.'

'When you gotta be back at work?'

Kip shrugged. M Santoso hadn't given him a specific time

that he needed to be back, and given their conversation that morning, he didn't think she'd care too much if he was gone a while.

'Well, then, let's go.' Ras headed for the elevator to the transport deck.

Kip followed. Going all the way to the Archives just to look at an alien seemed like a stupid thing to do, but then, *everything* seemed like a stupid thing to do, and at least this stupid thing was a stupid thing that didn't happen every stupid day. He sighed.

Ras noticed. 'Yeah, I know, man.' He shook his head as they weaved through the crowd. 'The Fleet sucks.'

EYAS

A bot could have carried Eyas' load easily, but some things needed to be moved by hand. Not that it made any difference to the things being carried. Bots could've got them to the same place, and probably faster, too. That wasn't the point. The point was that some weights needed to be felt, and that hands convey a respect bots never could.

She pulled her wagon along, the canisters inside rattling slightly. The people she walked past recognised the sound, no question. Her cargo was unmistakable. Eyas sometimes wondered what it was like for merchants to carry boxes that passersby didn't know the contents of. Perhaps it felt a bit like a birthday, like having a good secret wrapped away. Eyas' canisters were no secret, but they were good all the same. They were undeniably good, even though some of the glances they received took a moment to sort themselves out.

'Thank you, M,' a woman said as she passed her. The woman was grey-haired, at least twice her age, and yet, still, 'M.' She had long grown used to that.

Eyas was tired, and not in the best of moods. She'd awoken with a headache and had skipped breakfast, which she'd regretted after a mere hour at work. She smiled and nodded at the woman anyway. That was part of her job, too. To smile. To be the opposite of fear.

She continued down the thruway, heading into the buzz of a neighbourhood market. The smells of crispy fish, warm starches, and fresh-cut veggies greeted her. Her stomach growled.

The environment shifted slightly as she moved through it, as it always did. She passed through the familiar blanket of long glances, murmured thanks, the occasional exhale. Someone appeared in her periphery – an older man, coming right toward her. 'M Parata,' the man said. He opened his arms wide.

Eyas didn't remember the man when she went in for the hug, but an image surfaced as she was squeezed tight. A face at a ceremony two – no, three – tendays prior. 'M Tucker,' she said. 'Please, call me Eyas.' She pulled back, leaving a friendly hand on the man's arm. 'How are you?' It was a difficult question, she knew, but simply saying *I care* was awkward.

'Oh, well,' M Tucker said. His face struggled. 'You know.'

'I do,' Eyas said. She did.

M Tucker looked at the cart. He swallowed hard. 'Is that Ari?'

Eyas raced through some math. 'No,' she said. 'Not for at least four tendays yet. If you'd like to come by then, I can prepare a canister for you myself.'

The man's eyes watered. He squeezed Eyas' upper arm. 'Do you like bean cakes?' he asked, gesturing back at his stall. 'I've got both sweet and savoury, fresh out of the oven.'

Eyas wasn't huge on bean cakes, but she had never, ever turned down a gift under these circumstances, and her stomach was willing to accept anything at this point. 'I'd love a sweet one.'

M Tucker smiled and scurried back to his workspace. He lifted a fat bean cake off a teetering stack and wrapped one end of it in a thin piece of throw-cloth. 'You have a good day now, M Eyas,' he said, handing over the bundle.

Eyas thanked him and continued on. She received more hand-outs before she reached her destination – a pack of vegetable seeds, which she had no use for but would keep for trade, and a mug of strong tea, which she desperately needed. She paused in her walk, sat on a bench, and consumed her gifted meal. The bean cake was fine, as far as bean cakes went, and the tea soothed a tightness she hadn't known was there. She found a nearby recycling station and put the mug and the throw-cloth in their respective bins, from which they would be collected, washed, and reused. She resumed her walk, dragging her own recycling along behind her.

Her destination was the oxygen garden, the central hub of any neighbourhood, a curved green assemblage of places to play and places to sit and plenty of room to think. She parked her wagon in its usual spot, put on her apron and gloves, and selected a canister. She stepped over a plex barrier into one of the planters, treading carefully around all that grew there. The grasses couldn't be easily avoided, but she did her best to not trample the flowering shrubs and broad leaves. She crouched down near a bush and unlocked the canister lid. The heady smell of compost greeted her, a smell she spent so much time alongside it was a wonder she noticed it anymore. She spread the stuff around the roots with her gloved hands, laying down handful after handful of rich black nutrients. She wouldn't have minded getting compost on her bare skin but, much like pulling the wagon, it was a matter of respect. Compost was too precious to be wasted by washing it from her hands. She was meticulous about brushing off her gloves before folding them back up, about doing the same with her apron, about shaking every last crumb out of the canister. Each bit had to make its way to where it had been promised it would go.

Eyas emptied every canister in turn, tending the recipient plants carefully. She made sure not to walk where she'd worked, and took care not to touch her face. She stuck a small green flag in each planter as she finished, letting others know the area had recently been fertilised. There was nothing about the compost that could harm a person, but it wasn't the sort of thing most would be comfortable accidentally sticking their hand in. It didn't matter that compost was just compost – nitrogen, carbon, various minerals. People got so hung up on what a thing *had been,* rather than what it was *now.* That was why publicly distributed compost was reserved for oxygen gardens and fibre farms, the only public places in the Fleet that used soil. You could use compost tea in aeroponics, sure, but the food farms got different fertiliser blends, ones that came from plant scraps, bug husks, fish meal. Some families did indeed use their personal compost canisters on food gardens at home; others recoiled from that practice. Eyas understood both sides. Clear divisions between right and wrong were rare in her work.

As she neared the end of her batch, she felt the shapeless tingle of someone's gaze. Eyas turned to see a little boy – maybe five or so – watching her with intense focus. A young man was with him – a father or uncle, who could say – crouched down to the child's height, explaining something quietly. Eyas didn't have to guess what the topic was.

'Hello,' Eyas said with a friendly wave.

The man waved back. 'Hi,' he said. He turned to the boy. 'Can you say hi?'

The boy presumably could, but did not.

Eyas smiled. 'Would you like to come see?' The boy shifted his weight from foot to foot, then nodded. Eyas waved him over. She spread some compost on her gloved palm. 'Did M here tell you what this is?'

The boy rubbed his lips together before speaking. 'People.'

'Mmm, not anymore. It's called *compost*. It used to be people, yes, but it's changed into something else. See, what I'm doing here is putting this onto the plants, so they grow strong and healthy.' She demonstrated. 'The people that turned into compost now get to be part of these plants. The plants give us clean air to breathe and beautiful things to look at, which keeps *us* healthy. Eventually, these plants will die, and they'll get composted, too. Then *that* compost gets used to grow food, and the food becomes part of us again. So, even when we lose people we love, they don't leave us.' She pressed her palm flat against her chest. 'We're made out of our ancestors. They're what keep us alive.'

'That's pretty neat, huh?' the man said, crouching down beside the boy.

The boy looked undecided. 'Can I see in the tube?' he asked.

Eyas made sure there wasn't any compost on the outside of the cylinder before handing it over. 'Careful not to spill,' she said.

The boy took the cylinder with two hands and a studious frown. 'It looks like dirt,' he said.

'It basically *is* dirt,' Eyas said. 'It's dirt with superpowers.'

The boy rotated the cylinder, watching the compost tumble inside. 'How many people are in this?' he asked.

The man raised an eyebrow. Eyas threw him a reassuring glance. It was not the weirdest thing she'd ever been asked, by far. 'That's a good question, but I don't know,' Eyas said. 'Once the compost reaches this stage, the . . . the stuff that makes it gets jumbled together.'

The boy absorbed that. He handed the canister back.

Eyas reached into her hip pouch and pulled out a flag. 'Would you like to put this in the dirt? It lets people know I've been working here.'

The boy took the flag, still not smiling. Eyas understood. It was a lot to think about. 'Where can I put it?'

'Anywhere you like,' Eyas said, gesturing to the dirt around them.

The boy considered, and chose a spot near a bush. He stuck the flag down. 'Does it hurt?' he asked.

'Does what hurt?'

The boy tugged at the edge of his shirt. 'When you get turned into dirt.'

'Oh, no, buddy,' the man said. He put a reassuring hand on the boy's back and kissed the top of his head. 'No, it doesn't hurt at all.'

ISABEL

Aliens did not make Isabel uncomfortable. In her youth – a period of her life she was sure her grandkids didn't truly believe had taken place – she'd spent three standards hopping tunnels, crashing in spaceport hostels, gobbling up every strange sky and unknown city until homesickness finally won the day. She'd bunked with a Laru for one leg of a trip, become the drinking buddy of a quartet of Aandrisks on another. That was a long time ago, to be sure, but she'd had contact with aliens since – merchants, mostly, when she ordered something special for import. But in recent years, she'd found herself in the odd, delightful position of being a person of interest to certain individuals from the Reskit Institute of Interstellar Migration. The Exodus Fleet had drifted back into academic fashion, and, as the head archivist of the *Asteria*, Isabel did not have to ask why they'd sought her out. Every homesteader had its Archives and archivists, but Isabel was the current oldest of her profession, and even among aliens, that counted for something.

She was biased, of course, having worked in the Archives for most of her adult life, but the files she kept watch over were nothing short of magic. The first Exodans had crammed old-timey server racks full to bursting with records of Earth and personal stories, and every generation since had added to their work. *What is it you're looking for?* she asked anyone who made the trip to the spiralling chamber of data nodes (the server racks had been retired well before her time). Art? Literature? Family history? Earthen history? Earthen life? Whatever topic you needed, if Humans deemed it worth remembering, the Archives kept it safe.

Her life spent in service to the past was why she now found herself doing a rather-out-of-the-ordinary task, something other than helping students or doing node maintenance or conducting record ceremonies. Today, she was meeting with an alien, and as transgalactic as her correspondence was, it had been a long time since she'd shared a room with one.

Ghuh'loloan had come straight from the shuttledocks to the Archives, and given what Isabel knew of her, she doubted she'd checked into her guest quarters yet. The Harmagian was the most enthusiastic of Isabel's Reskit Institute pen pals, and they'd been friendly colleagues for years. But this was their first time meeting in person, and, as was to be expected, Isabel found herself reconciling the person she knew from letters with the person now sitting before her. The dog-sized, speckled-yellow, wet-skinned person, lying legless on a motorised cart, with no feet and no bones and no real shape at all until you got to the wreath of grasping tentacles and smaller tendrils centred around a toothless maw, crowned with a pair of retracting eyestalks that made Isabel stare despite her best efforts.

Stars, it really had been a long time.

'I'm sorry I couldn't meet you at the dock,' Isabel said. 'Today's ceremony took a long time to clear out.' They were in her office now, at her meeting table, away from the towering technology and busy staff. Well, ostensibly busy. Isabel had seen more than a few of her peers undertaking tasks of dubious value that steered them conveniently past her office windows. Everyone wanted a glimpse of the visitor.

Ghuh'loloan flexed her facial dactyli. Isabel knew Harmagian facial gestures were important communicative cues, but they were lost on her. She could follow only her colleague's words, which dripped with a deliciously-burred accent. 'Nonsense,' Ghuh'loloan said. 'You have work, and I am the one disrupting it! I feel nothing but joy in sharing your company, for however much time you can spare.'

Harmagians, Isabel knew, had a tendency to lay it on thick. 'I'm looking forward to working together as well. Was your journey all right?'

'Yes, yes, entirely adequate. I've had better, but then, I've had plenty worse.' Ghuh'loloan laughed with a wavering coo. Her eyestalks studied something. 'Do you have trouble understanding me?'

'No, not at all.'

'But then—' Ghuh'loloan pointed a tentacle toward Isabel's face.

It took Isabel a moment to understand. 'Oh,' she chuckled, removing her hud. A faint border disappeared from her field of vision, an edge she barely noticed until it was gone. 'Sorry, I'm so used to having it on I often forget to take it off. I've even worn it to sleep, once or twice.'

'Ah,' Ghuh'loloan said. 'For filing, then, not translating?'

'For everything, really,' Isabel said, looking at the clear lens set in a well-worn frame. 'It's much faster than my scrib, and it keeps my hands free.'

'I wouldn't know,' Ghuh'loloan said in a good-humoured tone. She pointed at her delicate, swaying eyes, incapable of wearing Isabel's favoured gadget. 'But it sounds very useful.'

Isabel smiled. 'Well, I envy *that* a bit,' she said, nodding at Ghuh'loloan's cart. 'My knees aren't what they used to be.'

'I wouldn't know about knees, either.'

They both laughed. 'Would you like something to drink?' Isabel asked.

'Mek, if you have it.'

Isabel knew that she did, as the other archivists hadn't rioted. 'You take it cold, I assume?' She'd learned to do a Harmagian-style flash cold brew in the tenday before her colleague arrived.

But Isabel's new skill was to be untested. 'I do,' Ghuh'loloan said, 'but if I wanted cold mek, I would've stayed home. Please, make it for me as you'd make it for yourself.' She paused. 'Although, perhaps not *too* hot.'

Isabel nodded with understanding as she opened the tin of mek powder. Introducing scalding hot liquid to mollusk-like skin would not end well. She glanced over and laughed, seeing that Ghuh'loloan had opened a storage compartment on her cart and removed both scrib and stylus. 'Are we getting started?'

Ghuh'loloan curled the tentacles around her mouth. 'I had questions before I arrived, but after seeing these wonderful ships of yours with my own eyes – oh, I hardly know where to start! Everything. I want to know everything. Let's begin with the ships. I saw so many things on my way here that I wish to understand better.'

'You'll have to tell me what you already know about them, so I don't walk the same corridors twice.'

'No. My understanding may be flawed, and if I assume that I already know something, you won't know to correct my mistakes. Besides, it is such a rare opportunity to get information that is not filtered through a screen. Tell me of the ships as if I know nothing of them. Tell me as if I were a child.'

'All right then.' Isabel gathered her thoughts as the mek brewer rumbled. 'The original architects based everything around three basic principles: longevity, stability, and well-being. They knew that for the Fleet to have any chance of survival, the ships had to be something that could withstand both distance and time, something that the spacers within could always rely on, and something that would foster both physical and mental health. Survival alone wasn't enough. *Couldn't* be enough. If there were disputes over food, resources, living space—'

'That'd be the end of it.'

'That'd be the end of it. These had to be places Humans would *want* to live in. In that long stretch between leaving Earth and GC contact, we were utterly alone. Those who lived and died during that time only knew planets from stories. This' – she gestured at the walls – 'was everything. It had to feel like a home, rather than a prison. Otherwise, we were doomed.'

'Longevity, stability, well-being,' Ghuh'loloan repeated, writing on her scrib in her strange boxy alphabet. 'Please, go on.'

Isabel put her own scrib on the table between them and launched a sketch programme. Floating pixels followed her stylus as she drew in the air. 'Architecturally, every homesteader is the same. At the centre, you have the main cylinder, which is essentially life support storage. It houses the water tanks, the air tanks, and the batteries.'

'Now, the batteries,' Ghuh'loloan said, still taking notes. 'Those store kinetically harvested energy, yes?'

'Originally, yes, mostly. Well . . . right, let me back up. When the Exodans first left Earth, they burned chemical fuels to get going, just to tide them over until enough kinetic energy had been generated through the floors. They also had hydro-generators.'

'Water-powered?'

'Yes, using waste water.' The brewer dinged, and Isabel filled two mugs. 'As it flows back to the processing facilities, it runs through a series of generators. That system's still in use. It's not our primary power source, but it's a good supplement.' She placed the mugs between them, and considered bringing out the tin of cookies stashed away in her desk. She decided against it. Harmagians had famously finicky stomachs, and she didn't want to hospitalise her colleague over ginger bites.

Ghuh'loloan reached for the mug closest to her, eying the tiny wisps of steam. She gave the surface of the drink a few tentative raps with the tip of her tentacle – one, two, three. Apparently finding the temperature suitable, she wrapped a portion of her limb around the handle and brought the mug aloft. 'See, this is why I wanted to start with the basics. How fascinating. Might we be able to visit the water generators?'

'Absolutely,' Isabel said. Not a place she would've been excited to visit on her own, but Ghuh'loloan's enthusiasm was catching.

'Wonderful. But I'm getting you off-track. Do I correctly glean that kinetic energy is no longer your primary power source?'

'That's right. Once the GC gave us this sun, we started collecting solar power.'

'Yes, I saw the satellites as I flew in. Those were provided by . . . ?'

'The Aeluons.' Isabel's tone was matter-of-fact, but she felt a slump in pride. Her colleague had assumed correctly that the Exodans couldn't have built such tech on their own.

Lacking lips, Ghuh'loloan held the Human-style mug up, flattened her face back into her body so that it lay almost horizontally, and poured a little waterfall into her wide mouth. Her whole body shivered. 'Ho! Oh *ho!*'

'Too hot?' Isabel asked with dread.

'No— no, I'm just unaccustomed. What a feeling!' She executed a longer pour. 'Ho! That's . . . stars, that's *thrilling.* I may never take mek cold again.' She shivered once more, then cradled her mug between two tentacles. 'Oh dear, where was I?'

'Satellites.'

'Yes, and Aeluons. They provided you with artigrav, too, yes?'

'That's right.'

'A generous people,' Ghuh'loloan said. 'I wish I could say the same of mine.' She laughed. 'I suppose it is in your best interest that we did not win their war against us, eh?'

Isabel chuckled, but took that as a sign to steer the conversation back to the topic at hand. The war invoked was very old, very ugly history. Clearly, Ghuh'loloan didn't mind a bit of self-deprecation, but Isabel didn't want to cross the line from cultural ribbing into insult. 'Indeed. So, the main cylinder.'

'The main cylinder.'

'Unlike the habitat ring – which I'll get to – the cylinder interior was never designed for gravity, so you won't find artigrav nets there. Everything is arranged in a circle, around a central core.'

Ghuh'loloan set down her cup. 'Do you mean that when you go in there—'

'We have to work in zero-g, yes.'

'Incredible! I had no idea there were still species doing that. Not within the hull, at least!'

'Tamsin worked there, until some years back,' Isabel said, knowing her colleague knew her wife's name even though they hadn't properly met yet. 'I'm sure she'd be happy to talk to you about it.'

'Oh! Yes. Yes, that would be marvellous.' Ghuh'loloan scribbled furiously. 'Please, please, go on.'

'At the aft end of the cylinder – as much as anything can be aft in space – we have the engines. They're . . . they're engines.' She shrugged and laughed. 'Not my area of expertise.'

'And they don't get much use anymore.'

'We use them to correct orbital issues, but no, nothing like they did back in our wandering days. Now, the ring – that I can talk on for days.' She directed the pixels into shapes she walked through every day. 'Six hexagons, each joined to another around the main cylinder.'

'And this used to spin, before artigrav.'

'Right. It was a big centrifuge.'

'Was that not unpleasant?'

Isabel shrugged. 'I don't know. I've only ever lived in artigrav. I'm sure there's an account of how centrifugal gravity felt.' She made a mental note to go searching for that.

Ghuh'loloan made a note as well, on her scrib. 'So, six hexagons comprise the ring.'

'Six hexagons. And within those, you find more hexagons. Let's start small and work our way up.' She thought for a moment. 'Ah, I have just the thing.' She accessed an animated image file intended for young kids. A lone hexagon appeared. 'Okay, so we start with a single room. A bedroom, let's say.' She gestured. The hexagon shrank, and was joined by six others, creating a mathematical flower. 'Six rooms, surrounding a seventh room. This is a home.' The geometry expanded again. 'Now you have six homes, surrounding a common area. We call this, predictably, a hex. You'll hear this term a lot. Somebody's hex is their primary address.' Another expansion. 'Six hexes surround a hub. This forms a neighbourhood.'

'And in a hub, you will find . . . ?'

'Everyday services. Grocery stands, a medical clinic, tech swaps, cafes, playgrounds, that kind of thing.' She gestured again. 'All right, here's where it starts to get big. Six neighbourhoods to a district. The space in the centre is the plaza. The amenities here vary from district to district, but in general, this is where you find your big stuff: schools, recycling centres, entertainment, long-term medical facilities, council offices, marketplaces, big gardens.'

'We are in a plaza now, yes?'

'Yes. And from there . . .' The image blossomed into one final shape – six triangles comprised of six districts each, arranged around a final colossal hexagon. 'So, all of this' – she circled it with her hands – 'is a deck.' The middle area is the nucleus. That's where you get farms and manufacturing. At the centre of everything is, well, the Centre.'

'Where you dispose of your dead.'

'I . . .' Isabel chose her words carefully, knowing her colleague hadn't meant any offence. 'I'm not sure we'd use the word "dispose", but yes.'

'And then above and below the residential deck, you have . . . ?'

'Directly above, the transport deck, where you can hop from district to district in a pod. Below, waste processing. And below *that*, observation.'

'Yes, I'm very excited to see your viewing cupolas. I don't know of any other ship architecture quite like that. Most have windows on walls, not the floor.'

'That goes right back to the need to prevent fighting over living space. If some people have rooms with a view and others don't, you're going to have problems. And if centrifugal gravity is pulling our feet toward the stars, then you *can't* have windows on most walls. The only people who could would be the ones with homes on the edges of each deck, and that . . . well, that would invite trouble.'

'Ahhhhh. Yes, I see. I see.' Ghuh'loloan's eyestalks traced over her notes. 'Six homes to a hex, six hexes to a neighbourhood, six neighbourhoods to a district, thirty-six districts to a deck, four decks to a . . . ?'

'Segment.'

'A *segment*. And six segments to a homesteader.'

'You've got it.'

The Harmagian studied the children's images again. 'It's rather beautiful, in a way. Nothing wasted, nothing frivolous. Simple exponents.'

Isabel smiled. 'It's like a . . . oh dear, I only know the word in Ensk.' She shifted linguistic gears. '*Honeycomb*.'

Ghuh'loloan flicked her mouth tendrils. 'I don't know that word. My Ensk is poor enough that I'd call it non-existent.'

Isabel gestured at her scrib and accessed another image file. '*Honeycomb*. It's a structure made of interlocking hexagons. Incredibly strong and space-efficient.'

'Ahhhh. I've seen configurations like this, but I don't know that there is an easy word for them in Klip. Or Hanto, for that matter. *Honeycomb*.' She stretched her face forward toward the image. 'Wait, is this . . . organic? What is this?'

'A relic from Earth. A communal insect species built nests with walls of this shape out of . . . spit, I think. I don't know off-hand.'

'How strange. Well, I am looking forward to seeing your own *honeycomb* nest.' Her tendrils changed, taking on a slight slackness. 'Will my presence be intrusive for the families there? I am not overly familiar with Human social custom when it comes to the home.'

'They know you're coming, so it won't be any trouble. In fact, I was hoping you'd join me for a meal at my home tonight. I had originally thought of taking you to a restaurant, but—'

'Bah, restaurants! At some point, yes, I would enjoy that, but on my first day here, I would much rather be *your* guest than someone else's.'

Isabel took serious note of that term – *guest*. She'd done research on that front before Ghuh'loloan's arrival, spurred by a slight shift in her colleague's letters. Once arrangements for the visit to the Fleet had been made, Isabel found herself no longer being addressed as *dear associate* but *dear host*, and Ghuh'loloan's phrasing had become deferential. This was an important thing, Isabel had learned, as was the entire concept of *hosts* and *guests* in Harmagian culture. By anybody's definition, hosts were expected to be accommodating and guests to be gracious, but Harmagians put considerable stock into everyone performing those roles well. A bad host would be shunned – or, as the rules extended to merchants as well, bankrupt – and a bad guest was on par with a petty thief (which made an odd sense, Isabel decided: guests did eat your food and take your time). There were entire books written on host/guest etiquette, the most seminal of which – *Rules for Guests of Good Lineage* – had been the go-to for over a hundred standards. Isabel had skimmed a few opening paragraphs and left the rest of the tedious tome unread. Using her own alienness as a social buffer, she figured her Good Host status was assured by providing a non-poisonous meal on clean plates in friendly company.

She hoped so, anyway.

TESSA

Tessa approached the playground, a box of piping hot cricket crunch in hand. 'Aya!' she called. No heads turned on the swings, nobody paused on the obstacle course. She looked over to the scrap heap, where a pack of youngsters were hauling other-wise-unusable sheets of fatigued metal – edges sanded smooth, of course – in an attempt to assemble . . . something. A shelter, maybe? In any case, her daughter wasn't there, either. 'Hey, Rafee,' she said to a kid running toward the construction project with a bucket of pixel paint.

The boy stopped. 'Hey, M Santoso,' he said, glancing at his comrades. This crew was on a tight schedule.

'You seen Aya around?'

He turned and pointed. 'I saw her in the tank,' he said before running off, hauling his cargo two-handed in front of his chest.

Tessa made her way to the small plex dome. Inside, about a dozen or so kids of varying ages enjoyed the freedom of disabled artigrav nets. The tank was, in concept, intended as a place where kids could learn how to do tasks in zero-g. There was a panel on the wall covered with buttons, knobs, and blocks that needed to be placed in similarly shaped holes. A tiny girl was attentively working on the block problem. A slightly older boy was running at break-neck speed over the tank's inner walls with a pair of cling boots, looping upside down and sideways and backwards, over and over and over. The rest of the kids were engaged in a classic – the only thing you really used the tank for – seeing who could kick off the wall and do the most flips in a row. Tessa's personal best had been four.

She watched as a familiar head of choppy black hair launched forward, curled inward, and flipped, flipped, flipped. Tessa counted. *One. Two. Three. Four.* She grinned. *Five.*

That's my kid.

Tessa stepped forward and knocked on the plex. Aya displayed the surprise all kids did when they saw an adult outside their expected context. Teachers lived in schools, doctors lived in clinics, parents could be found at work or home. *Why are you here?* Aya's expression said. It wasn't an accusation, just genuine enquiry.

Tessa held up the box of cricket crunch and gave it a tempting shake. She couldn't hear the kids behind the plex, but Aya's mouth formed the words: 'What? Yes!'

With a quickness Tessa could barely remember having, Aya made her way to the tank exit, grabbing soft support poles to pull herself along. She worked her way down to the floor, then stepped out the airlock, tripping over herself as gravity took hold again. Tessa had never gotten the hang of that, either.

Aya fetched her shoes from a nearby cubby, slipped her socked feet inside, and began to tie them with dogged concentration. As she did, Tessa watched unsurprised as the cling boot kid paused in his circuit and casually threw up. The other kids' faces contorted in laughter, disgust, and unheard shouts. A cleanerbot undocked itself from an upper corner, its gentle boosters propelling it through the air toward the floating mess. Tessa rapped on the plex again. 'You okay?' she called to the kid, mouthing the words as clearly as possible.

The kid gave a weak nod, holding the sides of his head.

Tessa flashed him a thumbs-up. They'd all been there.

Aya ran over as soon as the shoe-tying was complete. She put out both hands with a broad smile, her twin rows of teeth checkered with empty spaces. 'Yes, please.'

Tessa gave her the box. 'Careful, it's hot.'

Aya tucked into the sugar-fried bugs without hesitation. Tessa caught a wince as her daughter burned her tongue. Neither commented on it.

'Come on, it's our family's night to cook,' Tessa said. They began to walk together.

'I know,' Aya said. She frowned. 'I'm not late, right?'

'No, you're not late.'

'Then how come you came to get me?' She looked at the snack box in her hands, the realisation dawning that she'd been given a sweet treat *before* dinner. 'How come I get cricket crunch?'

'Just 'cause,' Tessa said. 'I guess I'm feeling sentimental.'

Aya tucked a mouthful into her cheek. 'What's sentimental?'

'It's . . . caught up in your feelings. The way you feel when you're thinking a lot about the people or things you care about.'

Tessa had stopped looking at her daughter, but she could feel her staring back. 'You've been weird today,' Aya said.

Tessa didn't want to have the conversation, and she knew there were parts she'd have to tread extra carefully around for Aya's sake. But Pop would bring it up the second they were home, so: 'You're right, I have been. I'm sorry. Something happened you should know about. Everything's okay. That's the first thing you should know.'

Aya listened intently, still chewing.

'You know how Uncle Ashby went to build a new tunnel?'

'Yeah.'

'Well, there were some sapients there who weren't very nice' – she wasn't sure Aya was ready for *Ashby was on the business end of the first shot in what looks like a territory war* – 'and they damaged his ship.'

Aya's face went rigid. 'Are the bulkheads okay?'

Tessa put her hand on Aya's shoulder. She knew why the question was being asked. Despite counselling, despite patience, despite everybody's best efforts and five more years of growing up, Aya still crumbled at the idea of any breach between *in here* and *out there*. She remained uncomfortable around airlocks, she avoided cupolas as if they were on fire, and *bulkheads* were a matter she fixated on to a concerning degree. 'His ship's stable,' Tessa said. 'He wrote to me this morning, and he's okay. There are a lot of repairs to do, but everyone is safe.'

Aya processed that. 'Is he coming here?'

'Why would he come here?'

'For repairs.'

'There are plenty of spaceports he can do that in. But you should know, before we get home, your grandpa's pretty shook up.'

'How come?'

'Because Ashby's his kid, and parents can't help but worry about their kids.' She tousled Aya's hair. 'So be extra nice to Grandpa tonight, okay?'

'Did they use a gun on Ashby's ship?'

Guns were another subject of fixation – an exotic, abstract danger Aya knew of from sims and news feeds and whatever kids talked about among themselves. 'Yes,' Tessa said.

'What kind?'

'I don't know.'

Aya crunched and crunched. 'Was it Aeluons?'

Tessa blinked. 'Was what Aeluons?'

'The aliens who broke his ship.'

'No. Why would it be Aeluons?'

Crunch crunch crunch. 'They have the biggest guns and go to war all the time.'

'That's—' Tessa struggled to unpack that technically accurate statement. 'The Aeluons have a big military, that's true. But they're our friends. They've done a lot of good things for us in the Fleet, and they wouldn't hurt Ashby.'

'Have you ever met one?'

'An Aeluon? Yes. I've done work with a few Aeluon merchants, a long time ago. They were all very nice. Well, except one. You gotta remember, baby, other sapients are people just like us. There are good people and bad people and everything in between.'

Crunch crunch. 'Then who shot at Uncle Ashby?'

'A species called the Toremi.'

'What do they look like?'

'I don't actually know. I don't know much about them. We can look it up on the Linkings when we get home.'

'Have you met one?'

'No. How could I have met one if I don't know what they look like?'

'Why were they mad at Uncle Ashby?'

'I don't know. I don't think it was about *him*, just the GC in general.'

'Why—'

'I don't know, honey. Sometimes . . . sometimes bad things just happen.'

The crunching had stopped. 'Will they come here?'

'No,' Tessa said with a firm voice and a reassuring smile. 'They're very far away. The Fleet's a safe place. It's one of the safest places you can be.'

Aya said nothing. Her mother was sure she was thinking of bulkheads and damaged hulls.

SAWYER

Everybody had a home, and nobody went hungry.

That was one of the foundational ideas that had first drawn Sawyer in when he'd started reading about the Fleet. Everybody had a home, and nobody went hungry. There was a practical necessity in that, he knew. A ship full of people fighting over food and space wouldn't last long. But there was compassion, too, a commitment to basic decency. Too many people back on Earth *had* been hungry and cold. It was one of the copious problems the first Exodans had vowed not to take with them.

Sawyer stood in a home now – one of the empties left behind by a family that had gone planetside, now opened to travellers like himself. The grass was always greener, he supposed, but he couldn't understand why anyone would travel in the opposite direction he had. Colonies had hungry people. They had people without homes. He'd seen both plenty of times back in Central space – sapients picking through trash or carrying everything they owned. The GC tried, they really did, but planets were big and settlements were vast and taking care of everyone was hard. Things were better in sovereign territories, but in neutral colonies like Mushtullo, where trade was the primary drive and nobody could agree on whose rules they should follow . . . well, it was easy for people to fall through the cracks. Sawyer had been mugged twice in the past standard, once by some messed-up woman with a badly installed headjack, then again by someone he never even saw. Just a pistol in his back and a hand he couldn't identify twisting his arm around to scan his patch and drain his credits. The bank got the creds back, but that wasn't the point. Someone had been willing to kill for the sake of . . . what? Some new clothes? A few tendays of groceries? That had been the last straw for Sawyer. That had been the moment he decided he was leaving.

He set his bag on the floor and looked around. An entry-and-storage room, a common room, a bathing room, and four more bedrooms, all the same size and shape as the others, all window-less, all spread out around the circular hatch that led down to the family cupola. The home was tidy and filled with basic furniture, all signs of previous ownership erased by cleanerbots. There were tables and chairs, a couple of couches. Cupboards for food and belongings. Empty planters waiting for seedlings and a guiding hand. It looked like a package home, like something that popped out of a box. There was no sign that anyone else had ever lived there – except one. Sawyer walked with reverence toward the wall in the common room, the one the cleanerbots had known to leave alone. It was covered with handprints, pressed in paint of every colour. Big handprints, little handprints, smudged infant feet. *Belkin*, someone had painted above it – the name of the first family that had lived here, and the name that every other family who lived there after had taken, regardless of genetics. This was one of the many Exodan customs he admired. When born, you took your parents' name. When you grew up and started a family of your own, you took the name of the home you settled in. In a lot of cases, your name didn't change at all, not if you kept living with your parents and grandparents and so on. If you settled in the home of your partner, you took your partner's family name. If you both decided to live in a separate home entirely, apart from both of your families, you'd both get the name of whoever'd taken care of that home before you. Sawyer liked that.

He looked up at the bold, painted letters above his head. He wasn't a Belkin. It wasn't his custom yet, and this placement was temporary. He ran his hand along where others had been. 'Wow,' he whispered. He didn't need to count the prints to know that there were at least nine generations represented here, all the way back to the first. He crouched down, looking toward where the wall joined the floor. The prints there were faded, and covered with others, but their shapes were clear as day: six adults, three children, one baby. He tried to imagine what they must have felt, watching their planet fade away through a window in the floor, pressing painted hands to an empty wall with the hope that one day the wall would be full.

Sawyer put his hand over the tiny footprint. That kid had grown up never having known the ground. That kid had grown old and died in this ship, and all xyr kids besides. The enormity of it almost made him dizzy.

He straightened back up and looked around the room. The wall was full, but the home was empty. So empty. It was a space meant to house three generations at least, where kids could run around and adults could relax and everyone would be together. But right then, it held only him. Just him in a big room full of ghosts. There were families outside, in the homes the Belkins had shared a hex with. Sawyer knew the kitchen was for his use as well, and the digestive punishment of Jojo's ninth day special had faded enough for him to be hungry again. But he wasn't sure about going out there. When he'd gone to the housing office, he'd hoped to be put in a home with another family – a spare room, like he'd read about. When he'd gone to the hex number he'd been given, he'd hoped for a big welcome, with shaken hands and big smiles, introductions all around. Granted, he'd gotten his hand shook and a few names and nods, but the smiles had been hit or miss and mostly confused, and everybody seemed too busy for him. There were kids to chase, vegetables to chop. They all looked at him, though, with questioning eyes and words whispered out of earshot. He got it. He was a stranger, the new neighbour, the guy who'd just moved in. They had their own days to get about, and ice-breaking would come soon enough. And truth be told, Sawyer was tired. It had been a long haul, and a long day. One adventure at a time.

He stuck his head in each of the bedrooms, trying to determine a favourite. Each was the same as the last. He settled on the middle-left, and sat on the edge of the bed. The air filter whirred quietly. He could hear a faint rushing in the pipes below the floor, the odd click in the walls. But other than that, nothing. No drunk idiots out on the street, no skiffs zipping past at every hour, no delivery vehicles rumbling along. It was nice. It was odd. It would take getting used to.

His stomach growled. He reached into his bag and pulled out the bean cake he'd bought on his way. He was used to wrappers that crunched and rustled, but even the throw-cloth was silent. He took a bite. It was just a cheap sweet, but his taste buds bloomed with gratitude for something sugary. Take that, pickle bun.

Sawyer sat alone and ate his snack. Okay, so it wasn't the first day he'd imagined, but hey, the sentiment held true. Everybody had a home, and nobody went hungry.

KIP

There was a delicate balance to getting the dishes done fast. Do it too quick, and a parent or a hexmate would make him do it over. Too slow, though, and . . . well, then you were still cleaning dishes. Nobody wanted to be in those shoes.

He picked up a plate from the eternal stack and scraped the food remnants into the compost bucket. Crumbs, flecks, whatever oil and sauce hadn't been soaked up by quickbread. Kinda gross, but he supposed it could be worse. He remembered one time watching this crime-solving vid set on Titan – *Murder on the Silver Sea* – where some characters were at a fancy restaurant having this crazy smart conversation where the investigator and the informant both think the other one's the killer and they were saying it but they're not really *saying* it – and also they kind of wanted to bang each other? That scene had *layers*, seriously – and when the conversation was done, they just . . . left their food. Like, let the server come get it while they walked out of the place. The scene would've made sense if one of them wasn't hungry or had a stomach ache or something, but if that were the case, then the other one would've reached over and eaten the leftovers. But no. *Both of them left.* They left half-plates of food on the table. It was the weirdest shit. He couldn't imagine what cleaning dishes was like in a place like that. Dealing with half-eaten food sounded disgusting.

Scraps bucketed, he picked up the compressed air canister you could find in any kitchen and blasted away everything that wasn't plate. He'd kind of liked that part when he was little. He remembered it being satisfying. But that had been about, oh, eleven billion dishes ago, and blasting away food bits had long since lost its charm. He looked over at Xia, who was helping him that night. She was seven, and hadn't yet realised that getting to do grown-up things like dishes and pruning and floor cleaning was super boring. She stood attentively at his side, waiting for each plate he handed her, placing each one *just so* in the sanitiser. He had to admit, it was kind of cute.

He handed off the blasted dish to Xia, then picked up another dirty one, and scraped, and blasted, and handed off, and started again. Beyond the kitchen counter, everybody else from his hex was sitting in the same spots at the same tables, as they always did, having the same conversations they always had.

'The new algae pumps everybody's using, they're no good,' Grandma Ko said. 'You can feel it on the ferry. Anytime we push past the slow zone, there's this hum that starts up . . .' Grandma Ko – Kip's great-grandma, but that took too long to say – had been a freighter pilot back in the day and thought any tech that had been invented past, like, thirty standards ago was garbage.

'I'm telling you, we're going about the water budget all wrong,' M Nguyen said, on a tear about some political thing like always. 'If the other guilds got together and unanimously pushed for the growers to overhaul the farms, the growers would have to give in, and the council would *have* to fund it. But that'd mean the guilds doing something efficiently together, and we all know *that's* not going to happen.' Seriously, there was nothing more boring than politics.

'Did you see that new planter they've set up over in 612?' M Marino said. Kip took a wild guess that the next sentence would include the word *imports* or *creds*. 'Imported seedlings, all of it.' Bingo. 'They've even got jorujola in there. It's incredible – have you seen it? Those bio-luminescent leaves? But I don't know where they get the creds—' Double bingo.

'I hear Sarah's moved back in with the Zhangs,' M Sousa said in an excited hush to Kip's mom. 'Now, it's none of my business, but this isn't exactly the first time she's had things go south with a partner, and you have to wonder—' Kip's mom gave a nod that didn't really confirm anything, and she threw in an 'mmm' here and there for good measure. Kip knew she didn't care, and she didn't even like M Sousa much, but she pretended to, because that's how hexes worked.

'That reminds me of the time me and Buster let a whole tank of hoppers out,' laughed Kip's dad, talking to the Mullers. 'Have I told you this one before?' Stars, Dad. Yes, everybody had heard this one before. Everybody had heard this story twelve thousand times.

Kip thought about Solan restaurants, where people talked about murder and sex and left dishes full of food for someone else to deal with. He thought about the university exams looming on the horizon. He thought about his score on the last practice exam. Ras had told him it was no worries, that he'd do better next time. But Kip knew what was what. He was going to fail, and he'd live here in the same hex forever, cleaning dishes and listening to his dad tell the same jokes over and over until one of them died.

Stars, he was stuck. He was so, so stuck.

Kip scraped and blasted faster now, knowing he'd left bits less than clean but hoping the heat of the sanitiser would burn away the evidence.

'You missed some,' Xia said, holding up the dish she'd been handed, pointing at a swatch of oily crumbs.

Kip sighed and took the plate back. 'Guess I did,' he said, giving the plate another scrape. How come lunch breaks never lasted this long?

At last, at fucking last, the stack of dishes ended. Xia looked satisfied; Kip was relieved. They both washed their hands. As they did so, a few bubbles appeared in the big clear cistern by the herb planters. Kip remembered one time when he was really little letting the water run and run because he liked the bubbles so much. His mom had given him a strong talking-to for that.

He looked at Xia, counting the seconds under her breath as she washed up, hurriedly turning off the faucet once she hit *fifteen*. Looked like somebody'd given her the same talking-to.

Kip started to head for home, but his mom stopped him, dead interrupting M Sousa. 'Kip?' she called, leaning away from the table. 'Did you empty the bucket?'

Kip shut his eyes. 'No.'

'Well?'

Kip sighed again, trudged back to the kitchen, picked up the forgotten bucket of crumbs and bug husks and veggie stems, lugged it to the garden, and dumped it into the hot box. He could feel Mom watching him the whole way.

'I don't understand why he can't come sit with us,' he heard Dad mumble. Dad never mumbled as quiet as he thought.

'He will when he wants to,' Mom said.

Kip did not want to. He wanted to go home, so he did just that. The front door slid closed behind him, and he exhaled. He kicked off his shoes and headed to his room, letting that door close behind him, too. A double barrier. He flopped down on his bed and shut his eyes. *Finally*.

He heard the sound of his scrib dinging, muffled under . . . something. He sat up and looked around his bed. Nothing. He rolled over, found his satchel on the floor, and dug around. Nothing. He rolled over the other way. There it was – on the floor, sticking out from the jacket he'd been wearing earlier. He picked it up, and found a blinking alert from Ras.

Ras (17:20): do you have any tethering cable

Kip (18:68): uh no

Kip (18:68): why

Ras (18:69): I have something really cool for us to do

Kip (18:70): what

Ras (18:70): it's a surprise

Kip (18:70): what kind of surprise

Ras (18:71): a tech project

Ras (18:71): trust me, it's going to be awesome

Ras (18:71): I can get the parts in a few tendays

Ras (18:72): so long as you're not studying

This was code. Kip's parents didn't read his scrib, as far as he knew, but Ras' had once, and they'd found out he and Rosie Lee snuck a couple bottles of kick out of Bay Twelve and got shit-faced together, and it had been a ridiculous mess. Like, completely ballistic. So now, if there was something Ras wanted to talk about but didn't want to put in writing, he said 'so long as you're not studying' instead of 'it's a secret, I'll tell you in person.' Studying was the perfect cover for anything. What was that if not responsible? What parent would read that and worry?

Okay, maybe Ras' parents. Ras never studied.

EYAS

Hopping between homesteaders was a beautiful thing. She'd taken the ferry more times in her life than she could count, and yet every time, she looked forward to those twenty minutes or so spent in transit. She could view the space outside anytime she pleased from a cupola, but it was easy to lose track of the fact that reality did not end with a bulkhead, that the starry black outside was not just a pretty picture framed below your feet. It was in passing beyond the hull, in travelling through the gap, that she was reminded of the true scope of things. The view out the window beside her passenger seat was a busy one (the window *beside her*, that was important – the confirmation that space existed not just below but *above* and *beside*). She could see public ferries, family shuttles, cargo ships, mail drones, nav markers, harvesting satellites. There were spacewalkers, out doing repairs or for the sheer joy of it, separated from the ship lanes by rows of self-correcting buoys. Behind it all was their adoptive sun, Risheth – a white sphere that deceptively looked to be about the size of a melon, shining softly through the ferry's filtered windows, scattering light among the dense plane of floating rock that gravity would gather up in time. No planets to speak of, though. Risheth didn't have any orbital bodies big enough to build on (hence why the Aandrisks hadn't felt much loss in shrugging off their claim to the system). Eyas had been planetside twice in her life, both times on short vacations, both times wonderful, yet nothing she needed to repeat. Planets were imposing. Impressive. Intimidating. Eyas preferred the open. It was easier for her to wrap her brain around. Even though it was dangerous. Even though she'd seen it at its worst. But that wasn't something she needed to dwell on right then. No point in spoiling the view.

The ferry docked at the *Ratri*, and Eyas took her place in the exiting shuffle. Most people had made the trip for trade or friendly visits, and carried goods or luggage accordingly. Eyas was there for neither, and so carried neither. She had only a satchel of personal effects and the clothes on her back – the latter of which she wouldn't need for long.

Eyas hadn't had sex on her home ship since her thirtieth birthday, two standards prior. It had been even longer since she'd done so with anyone who wasn't a professional. The combination of those decisions was the best thing she'd ever done for herself (well, second maybe to moving out of her mother's home and in with friends). People got weird around caretakers. That was part and parcel of the job, and she'd long been accustomed to it. But it did get in the way of relationships, especially the kind where clothing was optional. Whenever she told a potential partner what she spent her days doing, the reaction was either one of stumbling deference – which invariably led to the exhausting business of guiding them to the conclusion that she was just an ordinary person who wanted an honest, uncomplicated hookup – or discomfort, which shut the whole thing down. Her choices were then either her peers – and yes, the caretaking profession was pretty incestuous that way, but she didn't have any workmates she thought of in those terms – or the tryst clubs. She'd learned that her use of the latter benefited from a bit of distance. The last time she'd visited a club on her own homesteader, the host whose room she'd been sent to had been one of the family members present at a laying-in she'd conducted the tenday prior. He'd realised who she was before they'd gotten much of anywhere, and she'd spent the next two hours helping him tearfully talk through the death of his uncle. Not an activity she minded, but definitely not the one she'd been after. Since then, she visited clubs off-ship, where nobody knew her face or what she spent her days doing, and nobody would start crying when she took her pants off (she knew the crying hadn't been in response to her lack of pants, but still).

She took the exit ramp to the dockway, the dockway to the transport deck, and the transport deck to the plaza, which led her, at last, to the club. All clubs had fanciful names – Daydream, Top to Bottom, the Escape Hatch. The establishment she entered now was called the White Door; she'd never been to this one before (she was pleased to note the door matched the name). She left the dimming artificial light of the plaza for a very different kind of illumination: dim, yes, but with a welcoming warmth as opposed to a sleepy absence. The decor was classy and simple, like the others. She'd noticed supposedly similar establishments on her one teenage trip to Mars, but she hadn't been able to get past their appearance: windowless shop fronts that popped up around bars and shuttledocks, painted slippery red and emblazoned with disembodied mouths and muscles. She had a hard time imagining anybody finding such a place appealing, let alone *paying creds* for it. Creds weren't part of the exchange in the tryst clubs, nor was barter. They provided a service, not goods, and their hosts fell into the same broad vocational category she did: *Health and Wellness*. The clubs were an old tradition, a part of the Fleet practically since launch, one of many ways to keep everybody sane during a lifelong voyage. Hosts took that tradition seriously, as seriously as Eyas did her own. Plus, they were often some of the loveliest folks she'd ever met. It went without saying that to work in a club, you had to *really* like people.

The hallway opened into a large lounge, filled with flowering vines, hovering globulbs, and comfortable furniture. A welcome desk stood at the entrance, staffed by a friendly-looking woman with ornately braided, electric blue hair. Eyas approached the desk, feeling a crackle against her skin as she passed through the privacy shield that blocked any conversation from those outside its radius. One of the many touches Eyas appreciated.

'Welcome,' the woman said with a kind smile. 'I haven't seen you here before, have I?'

'No,' Eyas said. 'I'm from the *Asteria*.'

'Oh, well then, doubly welcome, neighbour!' She gestured at the discreetly shielded pixel projector in front of her. 'You'll be in your ship's system, then?' The woman nodded toward the patch scanner bolted to the edge of the desk. 'Do the thing, and I'll get your info transferred over. Just needed a change of pace?'

Eyas swiped her wrist. 'Yes.'

'I hear that,' the woman said as she assessed the new pixels conjured up by Eyas' patch. Some of the information there Eyas had submitted herself – what she liked, what she didn't, that kind of thing – but she imagined there was more in her file than that. Health records, probably. Maybe some kind of note that she'd always followed the rules. 'All right. Are you looking to take a chance, or for a sure thing?' This was the option always given at the entrance. Were you interested in meeting a fellow visiting stranger and seeing where the night took you, or . . .

'The latter,' Eyas said. Not that it was a *sure thing*. The host could decline service, for any reason, and she could leave at any time. Neither party was pressured to do anything, and mutual comfort was paramount. But being matched with another walk-in would've defeated the entire purpose of her being there.

A polite nod, a bit of gesturing. 'Are you interested in a single partner, or multiples?'

'Single.'

'Any changes to your usual preferences?'

'No.'

'And how long of a visit would you like? Overnight, a few hours . . . ?'

'I'll take a half night.' Long enough to make the trip worth it, but with plenty of time to get back home and sleep in her own bed. And that, right there, in addition to everything else she'd been asked, was why the *sure thing* was the better option by far. She saw so many similarities between this kind of work and her own, polar opposites of the life experiences spectrum though they were. She, too, had strangers' bodies placed in her care. They couldn't speak, but they'd been assured their whole lives that when the time came, they'd be treated with gentleness and respect. Nobody would find them odd or ugly. Nobody would do anything unkind. They'd be handled by someone who understood what a body was, how important, how singular. Eyas undressed those bodies. She washed them. She saw their flaws, their folds, the spots they kept hidden. For the short time they had together, she gave them the whole of her training, the whole of her self. It was an intimate thing, preparing a body. An intimacy matched only by one other. So when she placed her own body in someone else's hands, she wanted to know that her respect would be matched. You couldn't make guarantees like that with a stranger at a bar. You couldn't know from a bit of conversation and a drink or two whether they understood in their heart of hearts that bodies should always be left in a better way than when you found them. With a professional, you could. And you'd know, too, that their imubots were up to date, that the kind of sex that could lead to pregnancy carried no such risk, that there wouldn't be any dancing around whether or not to stay the night or see each other again or if it *meant* something. Of course it always meant something. But you couldn't know if that something was the same. In Eyas' opinion, going to a club was the safest way to have sex, both physically and emotionally. The alternative was a minefield.

The pixels behind the counter filtered themselves as the blue-haired woman entered Eyas' answers. 'Okay,' she said. 'I've got eight guys free this evening who fit the bill. Would you like to go through the list, or—'

Eyas realised, in that moment, that she didn't want to make any more decisions. She hadn't thought about it when she'd headed out for the *Ratri*, but she was *tired*, tired in a quiet way that had become an everyday thing for reasons she couldn't point to. The tenday hadn't been bad, but it had been long, and she'd grown weary of decisions. 'Surprise me,' she said. She paused in thought. 'Whoever you think the nicest of them is.'

'Ha! You're going to get me in trouble.' The woman tapped her lips, then made a definitive gesture at the pixels. 'All right, you'll be in room fourteen. Your host will be there in about twenty minutes. You're welcome to wait in there, or you can relax in the lounge. If you feel the need to clean up, there are showers to the right of the bar. You're welcome to go there with your host as well. If you don't go straight to your room, we'll call you when it's time.' She gave Eyas an amused smile. 'And do *not* tell him how I picked him, or I will never hear the end of it.' Eyas thanked her, and walked on through. The lounge was inviting, and the aforementioned bar was laden with colourful bottles of kick, a menu of snacks, and short, clear jars displaying varieties of redreed and smash. Another time, she would've treated herself to something spicy to snack on and something sweet to drink. She would've chatted with the bartender, contemplated the clientele (which, as always, was as varied as varied could be), maybe played a round of flash with someone else waiting their turn. But Eyas looked at the crowd, and all she wanted was to be behind a door.

She found room fourteen, waved her wristwrap over the lock, and entered. Just the sight of the room felt like she'd taken a sip of water after several hours without. Everything looked soft – the bed, the couch, even the table, somehow. There was a thumpbox for music, a chill box for drinks, a storage compartment full of other things the host could introduce if desired. All clean, all inviting. All for her.

She sat down on the couch, closed her eyes, and let twenty minutes slip by. She barely felt them.

There was a soft chime at the door before it opened. A man entered, carrying a bottle of something amber brown. He was tall, but not too tall. Fit, but not too fit. His hair was thick and his eyes were kind. 'Hey,' he said. 'I'm Sunny.'

Of course you are, Eyas thought. 'I'm Eyas.'

'Eyas,' he repeated, the door closing behind him. 'I haven't heard that one before.'

Her mouth gave a scrunch as it prepared to offer an explanation given a million times. 'It's an old word for a hawk.'

Sunny leaned against the bedframe. 'What's a hawk?'

'Earthen bird. Bird of prey, apparently. Very striking, very fast. My mother' – she tried to find a tactful way to explain the most incongruous person in her life – 'she's a romantic.'

'Clearly. That's a poetic name.'

'Yes. Granted, she didn't dig deep enough into the language files to figure out that an eyas is a *baby* hawk, not a hawk hawk. So, I'm a scruffy baby bird that hasn't learned to fly. Not the best sentiment to carry around as an adult.'

Sunny laughed. 'You're not the only one with a name like that. I know a guy named Walrus.'

'I don't know what that is.'

'You know what a wolf is?'

Eyas thought back to school trips to the Archives. 'It's a . . . oh, I know this.' She frowned, rifling through neurons that hadn't been needed in a while. 'Some kind of carnivore, right? Or am I thinking of something else?'

'No, you're right. Like a wild dog. Beautiful, powerful, all that good stuff. That's what his parents were going for. Only, they got mixed up and didn't double-check, and went with Walrus.'

'And what's a walrus?'

Sunny raised a finger and pulled his scrib from his belt holster. He gestured at the screen, then turned it her way. The Archives helpfully displayed his friend's namesake – a sack-like water beast with ludicrous tusks and unfortunate whiskers.

Eyas laughed. 'Okay, that's worse than mine.'

The host chuckled as he set his scrib on the table. 'Hey, if it's any consolation, I don't like my given name, either.'

'You mean it's not Sunny?' Eyas said with a smirk.

The host winked. 'So, I heard you've had a long day.'

Eyas raised her eyebrows. 'Did you?'

'That was Iana's guess, at least. Did she get that wrong?'

Assuming Iana was the blue-haired woman, Eyas mentally gave her a few points for perception. 'No. It has been a long day.'

Sunny held up the bottle. 'Do you like sintalin?'

'I've never had it.' She considered the name. 'Aeluon?'

'Laru. It's . . . well, it's what I pour myself on long days.' He picked up two glasses, asking her a silent question. She nodded. He poured.

Eyas examined the glass placed in her hand. The liquid within had a caramel warmth, and the colour got darker and darker the deeper the glass went. It smelled unlike anything she'd ever had. A good smell, at least. A rich, spiced smell. She took a sip, and shut her eyes. 'Wow.'

'It's something, right?' Sunny sat next to her on the couch – close, but not too close. Close as good friends might sit, and just as easy. He took a sip from his own glass.

'That's . . . wow.' She laughed.

'I've got a friend who's a cargo runner, makes a lot of stops in Laru space. She always brings me a case of this when she's back home.'

'This isn't from the bar?'

'Nah, this is my stash.'

Another point to Iana. It was entirely possible Sunny pulled this bit with everybody who came to room fourteen, but even if it was fiction, it was very nice.

Sunny looked at her seriously. 'Eyas, I'm here to give you a good night, and that can be whatever you need it to be. If you need to just talk, have some drinks, chill out – that's fine. I'm happy with that.'

Eyas was sure he'd said those words before, but she also got the sense that he meant them. She studied his face. His lips looked soft. His beard was perfect, almost annoyingly so. 'No,' she said. She put her hand on his chest. She set her glass down, ran her palm up his throat, over his neck, into his hair. Stars, it felt good in her fingers. 'If it's okay by you,' she said, as his hand greeted her thigh, 'I'd rather not talk much at all.'

ISABEL

Dinner had been chaos, as per usual, and at one time in Isabel's life, this would have aggravated her. She would've wanted to put on a good face for an academic guest, particularly an alien one. But Isabel loved the nightly feeding frenzy, and at this point, she wouldn't have wanted it any other way. They hadn't done anything special, not even shifted the cooking order. Ninth day was her cousin's family's night to cook, and cook they did (albeit with some quiet instruction from Isabel, who'd sent them a list of common ingredients Harmagians could not digest – heavy salt being the trickiest one). There had been kids running around everywhere, a misunderstanding about how gravy worked (namely: not as a drink), a broken dish, a few translation errors, a bombardment of questions in both directions, and three dozen people tripping over themselves to look good in front of a fancy visitor. It was real. It was honest. It was so very Exodan.

Her hex was quiet now. Ghuh'loloan had departed for her guest quarters – not for sleep, as her species did not have that need, but to take comfort in a space designed for Harmagian merchants and diplomats, rather than incompatible Human physiology. The kids, in contrast, were (mostly) sleeping, and the grown-ups had retreated to the sanctuary of their homes. It was always such a sharp change, the switch between daytime and night-time. Not that the view outside changed. But the lights did, and the clocks did, and as much as Isabel seized upon the bright energy of the bustling hours, she always cherished restful dark.

She made her way through the courtyard, a mug of tea in each hand as she passed through her well-worn environment. In structure, every hex was the same, but once you got past the standard kitchen-garden-cistern setup, the hex was whatever you made of it. Isabel and her neighbours liked plants and they liked kids, so their shared space was a haven for both. They had an herb garden, where her wife's parents and *their* neighbours had grown vegetables once. The current eldest generation was content to leave farming to farmers, though there was a patch of climbing beans studiously tended by her grand-nephew Ollie, age six. He was much more at ease tending his tiny crop and whispering secret stories to his toys than joining in with the rest of the roaring, shrieking, giggling pack. Whenever his harvest was ready, he went from home to home, hand-delivering bundles tied with bits of string – usually no more than ten beans in a bunch. Isabel always treated this occasion with the same seriousness he did. She would unwrap each bundle, snap a bean between her teeth, chew thoughtfully, and after a moment of consideration, inform Ollie that this was, without a doubt, his best batch yet. This was not always true, but what kind of monster would say otherwise?

Aside from the herbs and Ollie's bean farm, the other greenery in the hex was decorative, from the blankets of vines encasing the walkways, to the orderly flower pots arranged around front doors. Isabel never had time for gardening, but Tamsin's brother did enough of that for everyone. That was the best thing about having hexmates. Everybody had tasks they were good at and ones they weren't, chores they didn't mind and chores they loathed. More often than not, it balanced out. Everybody pitched in, leaving plenty of time for rest and play. Humans were, after all, a social species – even the quiet Ollies, or the thoughtful, shy types that gravitated toward work in the Archives. There was a difference between being shy and being sequestered. Rarely in history had things turned out well for people who chose to lock themselves away.

Beyond the plants was the workshop – a three-sided area framed by workbenches and filled with larger shared tools. Isabel knew without asking that she'd find Tamsin there. She was seated in the back corner, at ease in the big soft chair their hexmates had jointly given her for her birthday. The years had been hard on Tamsin's body, and workstools didn't suit her like they used to. She'd been a zero-g mech tech once – life support maintenance, specifically – and like so many of her profession, the cumulative decades spent in a different realm of physics had played hell with her skeleton. She walked with a cane now, and had left her previous career to younger bones. Her days were now spent leading classes at the neighbourhood tech shop, where she taught basic everyday systems repair, or at home, where she'd make metal art or fix too-loved toys – anything that kept her hands occupied. Like Isabel, she was happiest when busy. It was why they'd hit it off so well, over fifty years before.

'What've you got there?' Isabel asked, entering the inner sanctum.

Tamsin had a box of fabric at her feet and a sewing kit perched on the closest shelf. She held up a small pair of trousers. 'Sasha wore the knees out.'

'Again?'

'Again.' Tamsin picked up her needle and resumed patching. 'She's an active kid.'

There was no argument there – of their five grandkids, Sasha was the biggest handful, always bruised or bleeding or stuck in a storage cabinet somewhere. *Menace* wasn't the right word for her. She was too agreeable for that. *Scamp*. That fit the bill. Sasha was an absolute scamp, and though Tamsin showered all the grandkids and hex kids with equal amounts of teasing and candy, Isabel knew she had a special soft spot for the little cabinet explorer. Tamsin had never said so, but she didn't need to. Isabel knew.

She set Tamsin's mug of tea within easy reach, pulled up a workstool facing her, and sat. 'You should've made Benjy do it. He's started stitching, he could use the practice.'

'Yeah, but then she'd be running around with lame practise

patches.' Tamsin spoke, as always, flat and factual, the kind of voice that hid its owner's perpetual good humour beneath a dry disguise. 'You get patched-up duds from *me*, you're gonna look real cool.'

Isabel laughed into her tea. 'So, tonight went well.'

'It did.'

Tamsin said the words in a neutral tone, but there was a line between her eyes that made Isabel ask: 'But?'

'No buts. Tonight went well.'

'But?'

Tamsin rolled her eyes. 'Why are you pushing?'

'Because I can tell.'

'You can tell *what*?'

Isabel poked the spot in question. 'You've got that crease.'

'Oh, stars, you and your magical crease. I don't have a crease.'

'Yes, you do. You're not the one who looks at you every day.'

Tamsin squinted at Isabel as she knotted a thread. 'And what does the magical crease tell you?'

'That there's something you want to say.'

'If I wanted to say something, I would've said it.'

'Something that you're *not* saying, then.'

'You're such a pain,' Tamsin sighed. 'It just . . . felt kind of . . . I don't know. I don't know what I'm saying. It was fine, you're right.'

Isabel sipped her tea, watching, waiting.

Tamsin set down her stitching. 'She's condescending.'

'You thought so?' This came as a genuine surprise.

'Didn't you?'

'No, I—' Isabel replayed the events of the evening as quickly as she could. Ghuh'loloan had been delighted to meet the hex. She'd brought gifts and stories and a wealth of patience. Isabel had thought it a rousing success on both sides of the exchange, right up until now. 'I had a really good time. It felt like we got things off to a great start.'

'See, and that's why I didn't want to say anything. This is your work, your friend. I don't know her like you do, and I don't want to ruin this for you.'

'You're not. This is your home – our home – and if something in it bothers you, you have to say.'

'Can I tell our neighbours to knock off their brewing experiments then? That scrub fuel they cooked up last time was *awful*.'

'Tamsin.'

Tamsin picked up her tea. 'She just came across so . . . so sugary. Everything was *wonderful* and *fascinating* and *incredible*.'

'That's just how Harmagians are. Everything's couched in hyperbole.'

'Yeah, but it makes it hard to trust them, y'know? If *everything* is wonderful and fascinating . . . I mean, everything *can't* be those all the time.'

'But it is to her. This is her . . . her passion. She's curious. She wants to learn about us.'

'I get that, I do. And I don't want this to sound like a bigger deal than it is. It's . . . I just felt like I was on display. Like some kind of exhibit she's visiting.' She shook her head. 'I don't know. I'm probably being unfair.' She paused. 'I know this isn't a nice thing to admit,' she added slowly, 'but it's hard to have her here saying these sugary things, poking our tech, touching our kids, and not remember how it was.'

Isabel didn't need to ask what she meant. She remembered. She remembered being not much older than Sasha and hearing the adults in her hex talking about the growing push for GC membership. She remembered the news feeds, the public forums, the pixel posters with their catchy slogans. She remembered being a little older, when the Fleet and the Martian government were in the thick of smoothing out relations so as to join as a unified species, and everything felt like it was one spark away from a flash fire. She remembered being in her teens and watching the parliamentary hearings, listening to the galaxy's most powerful debate whether her species had merit enough to go from tolerated refugees to equal citizens. She remembered the hopes everybody had pinned on it – Grandpa Teyo, with his medical clinic badly in need of new tech and proper vaccines, Aunt Su, with her merchant crew hungry for new trade routes. Everybody who had ever been to a spaceport and felt like they were a subcategory, a separate queue, an other. And she remembered the Harmagian delegation in those hearings, fully split on the issue of whether Humans were worth the bother, unable to vote in consensus. They hadn't been the only species with objections, but that wasn't the point. Every voice that got up there and spoke against Humanity stung as if the words were being said for the first time.

Isabel laid her hand on her wife's knee. 'That was such a long time ago,' she said. 'So much has changed.'

'I know.'

'Ghuh'loloan wasn't around for any of that. She wasn't even born yet.'

'I know.' Tamsin thought. 'They're born underwater, right?'

'Yes.' Isabel smirked. 'I'm sure she'd be happy to answer your questions about it. Seeing as how you're curious about her species.'

Tamsin stuck out her tongue. 'It's not that I don't understand curiosity. It's that . . . it's like you said. She wasn't even born yet. She missed out on all of that ugliness, and yet we're kind of *quaint* to her, it feels like. Yeah, it was forever ago, but those Harmagians who said those things are still around, right? They had kids, and those kids would've learned—'

'They don't raise kids like we do.'

'Well, *somebody's* raising them, right? Somebody's teaching them, somebody's telling them how the galaxy works. So what was your pal Ghuh taught about us? What do they say about us when we're not around? In some ways, they were right. We *don't* have much to offer. We build off their tech, and we get the planets they've decided are too crummy to live on. And *our* kids see that. They all want to go to Central space and mod their bodies and get rich. Did you hear Terra at dinner tonight?'

'You'll have to be more specific.'

'She was talking about the ferry ride she went on last tenday, and she said, "we flew past a big *yelekam*". I asked her what the word was in Ensk. She didn't know. She didn't know the word for *comet*.'

Isabel blinked. The younger generation, she knew, was mixing Klip and Ensk in ways hers never had, and they tended to lean heavily on the galactic language when speaking among themselves. But Terra was five years old. She would've barely started being taught Klip at school. Clearly, she'd been learning elsewhere. 'Languages adapt.' Isabel exhaled. 'That's the way of it.'

'Stars, you are the worst person to sympathise with about change being scary,' Tamsin said with a crooked smile. She set both stitching and mug aside, and leaned in to Isabel, lacing the hand on her knee into her own. 'I'm not saying I hated it tonight, or that I don't want her here. I'm saying I felt like I was on display, and it was weird. I expect that if I'm elsewhere. I don't expect that here. That's all.'

Isabel cupped Tamsin's face with her free hand and leaned forward to kiss her. 'I'm sorry you felt that way,' she said after their lips parted. 'That isn't fair to you.'

Tamsin rested her forehead against Isabel's for a long moment, the kind of moment that made everything else hold still. She pulled back just a touch. 'So since I've been so emotionally wounded in my own home—'

'Oh, stars.' Isabel sat back, letting the roll of her eyes lead the way.

'Can you go fetch the leftover custard out of the stasie?' She gave her lashes an out-of-character flutter.

Isabel sighed in acquiescence. 'Did you not get any at dinner?'

Her wife looked at her seriously. 'I am seventy-nine years old. If I want dessert twice . . . I get dessert twice.'

TESSA

This was a battle of wills, and Tessa was going to win. She was sure of that, sure in her bones, even though the scene before her was a daunting one.

'Ky,' she said. 'You need to lie down now.'

Her toddling son stood atop his cot in her room, all tummy and gravity-defying curls. He was the cutest thing in the universe, and she would've given anything for him to be someone else's kid right then.

'No,' Ky said with simple conviction. 'Up now.'

'It's not time to be up,' Tessa said. 'It's time for sleep.'

'No.'

'Yes.'

'*No*.' His knees wobbled, but they held steady. Ky presented his argument: 'Mama up now. Aya up now.' He raised his voice. 'Ky up now! All fixed!'

'Your sister is not up, either. She's asleep.'

'No!'

Tessa looked over her shoulder, across the living room toward Aya's door. It was closed, but . . . *but*. A new uncertainty needled at her. She wondered what little ears could hear that hers couldn't. Tessa ran her hand through her hair and let out a terse sigh. She looked Ky in the eye as she started to exit the room. 'When I come back, you need to be lying down.'

'No!'

Tessa crossed the living room, trading one battle for another. She opened Aya's door, and – well, she had to give the kid credit.

She was tented under her blanket, which would have hidden the light of her scrib were it not for one traitorous hole created by an errant foot.

'Hey,' Tessa said sternly.

Her daughter froze, an *oh shit* rigor that might've been funny if Tessa hadn't been so sick of this. 'I was just—' Aya began.

'Bed,' Tessa said. That would've been that, were it not for a creeping suspicion. She pulled the blanket up and away. Aya scrambled to shut off her scrib, but she was too slow. An image of neon weapon blasts and campy explosions lingered in the empty air.

Tessa frowned. 'What were you watching?'

Her daughter pouted at the bed.

'Aya.'

' . . . *Cosmic Crusade.*'

'Are you allowed to watch *Cosmic Crusade*?'

'No,' Aya said, mumbling so low her lips barely moved.

'No,' Tessa said. Stars, but she was over fighting to keep that Martian trash out of her kid's head. She took the scrib.

The protest was immediate and indignant. 'Mom! That's not *fair*!'

'It's totally fair.'

'When do I get it back?'

'You're not really in a negotiating position here, kiddo.'

'When?'

'When I say so.' She pointed. '*Bed.*'

She heard her daughter let out a long-suffering sigh as the door closed. One down. Tessa forged ahead, back to her room. She walked through the open door and . . . she blinked. 'Ky, where are your pajamas?'

Her naked son slapped his torso with twin palms. 'All fixed!'

Everything was *all fixed!* with him these days, and she had no idea where he'd picked it up from, no more so than she could figure out where his pajamas had gone. She looked around the bed, beside it, under it, under blankets, under pillows, feeling ridiculous at being outwitted by a two-year-old who was placidly watching her with a finger up his nose. This was one single room. How many places could there . . . she paused. It wasn't one room, technically. She walked the short distance to the attached lavatory, and opened the door. The light switched on. Tessa closed her eyes. 'Come here, please.'

Silence.

'Ky, *come here.*'

Ky padded over. He looked at her with his lips pulled inward, rocking slightly as he stood in place. It was an expression that would have been the same on any person of any age – the unmistakable dread of someone who knew they'd fucked up but wanted to see how it would play out.

Tessa put her hands on her hips. 'Why are your pajamas in the toilet?' she asked.

'Don' know.'

'You don't know? Who put them there?'

'Daddy.'

Tessa bit back a laugh. 'Your daddy's not here.'

'Yes, he – he put 'jamas. And – and then bye. Bye Ky, bye Aya, bye Mama.' He put his hand on his mouth and made kissing sounds. 'No 'jamas. No way.'

'I don't think so,' Tessa said, tugging the discarded footies away from the vacuum pulling them toward the sewage line. 'I think you put them here.'

'No, I don' think so,' he repeated while giggling. 'You – you put them here.'

Tessa imagined, as she put her kicking, now-crying boy back into another pair of pajamas, this same script playing out in this same room with herself and her parents. It had been their room once, and their parents' before that, and their parents' before that, and on and on. Generation after generation of wriggling toddlers and weary adults. She remembered waking in what was now Aya's room and hearing tiny, tubby Ashby shriek with laughter across the way. It was fair, she supposed, this cycle of aggravation. Payback for the days when you threw your own jammies in the toilet.

After two more false starts, three sung rounds of 'Five Baby Bluefish', and ten minutes of hand holding and hair stroking, the kid was down. Tessa tiptoed out of the room, holding her breath. She didn't exhale until the door closed behind her and she had waited long enough to confirm that the sound had fallen on unconscious ears. *Whew.*

Usually, she didn't fly solo for bedtime. But Pop was out that evening – off at the waterball game with his cronies, like he did every pair of tendays. He'd be home in a few hours, tipsy and ornery and no help whatsoever. She could've asked the Parks for a hand. They didn't have any kids, and they often helped out around the hex in terms of bathing and bedtime stories, but both Paola and Jules were going through that temporary period of punkiness everyone went through after bot upgrades, and Neil had had a rough shift at work – yet another water main was about to bust, he'd said at dinner – so Tessa hadn't wanted to bother any of them. No, better to brave bedtime alone and savour the reward of a few sweet, sweet moments all to herself.

She surveyed the living room. It was a wreck, as always, a carnage of toys and laundry and stained furniture even the cleanerbots couldn't keep up with. She considered the nearly-full bottle of kick sitting on the shelf, a gift from her workmates the standard prior. A few warm sips before bed sounded awfully nice, but . . . nah. If Ky woke up, she wanted to be clear-headed, and these days, even one drink was enough to make her start the next day with a headache.

Somewhere within, her teenage self was screaming in horror.

She poured herself a glass of water instead, and sat on the sofa, letting her body fall back like a bot that'd had its signal cut. Her head sank blissfully into the balding fabric. She closed her eyes. She listened. Quiet. Beautiful, sweet quiet. Nobody crying, nobody complaining, nobody needing her for anything. Just air filters sighing from above and the distant whoosh of greywater pipes below. She'd go to bed before long, but first, she was going to just *sit*. She was going to sit and do n—

Her scrib pinged. Somebody was making a sib call. If it had been anybody else, she would've thrown the thing across the room, but when she saw the name, she relented. With a sigh, she hauled herself up, sat back down at the ansible desk, and answered.

'You just missed 'em,' she said.

On screen, George sighed. 'Yeah, I thought I might've. Damn.' He was unsurprised, but still disappointed. Tessa couldn't help but smile. His skewed frown looked just like Ky's.

If you'd told eighteen-year-old Tessa that she'd have kids with George one day, she would've thought you were insane. George had been the friendly guy, the low-key guy, the guy you might trade a word or two with at a party before you each went off with your respective friends. George was nothing like gorgeous Ely, with a body straight out of a sim and the emotional intelligence of fish spawn, or charismatic Skeet, whose ambitious dreams were so easy to become smitten with until you realised there was no work ethic to back them up. It wasn't until she and George were both in their thirties that something clicked. He was on leave from his latest mining tour, Tessa was the bay worker who noticed the discrepancy on his formwork. Not exactly the most romantic of reunions, but it had led to drinks, which led to bed, which led to days of more of the same, which led to a fond and noncommittal farewell, which led to two idiots having a panicked sib call – 'Wait, did you not get dosed?' 'I figured you had!' – which led, in turn, to Aya.

At first, George had talked about leaving his job for something that would keep him around, but asteroid mining was valuable work, and Tessa hadn't seen any reason to disrupt things more than a kid already would. George made sure he was around the first half-standard of Aya's life, then went off again to the rocky orbital edges, with the baby in Tessa's care and the hex looking after both. Mining tours were long hauls, so Tessa and George conducted themselves how they liked during the interim, each keeping their own schedules and having the occasional fling (the highs and lows of which were always shared with the other). They were, in most ways, their own people with their own lives. But whenever George's ship came home with a haul of ice and metal, he stayed in the Santoso home, wrestling with Aya, chatting with the neighbours, sharing Tessa's bed. They always got their doses now, except for that one time three years prior, when they'd decided the first accident was worth repeating. They'd also decided, without much fuss, that since the whole arrangement suited them both fine, they might as well get married – nothing fancy, no big party or anything. Just ten minutes with an archivist and a nice dinner at the hex. None of it was love as her younger self had imagined. It was so much better. There was nothing frantic or all-consuming about her and George. They were grounded, sensible, comfy. What more could you ask for?

George's on-screen image crackled with distance. 'Well, if they're down, that means more time for us,' he said. 'Though you look pretty tired.'

'I *am* pretty tired. But I've always got time for you.'

'Aww,' he simpered.

'Aww,' she repeated, making a face. 'So? How's the edge?' This was always her first question.

George shrugged, looking around his cabin. 'Y'know. Rocks. Dark. The usual. We've got a big ol' ore ball we're headed for now. Take us about two tendays to get there. Should be a good haul.'

'Teracite?'

'Iron, mostly, looks to be. Why? You going into comp tech?'

'Not me. Everybody else, though. I can't tell you how many queries we get about teracite stores.' She leaned her jaw on her palm. 'How's the ship?' This was always her second question, the one spacers were forever asking each other.

'Fine, fine,' he said. His eyes shifted away from the screen. 'Still kicking.'

Tessa squinted. 'Don't bullshit me, George.'

'It's nothing, and definitely nothing you need to worry about.'

'You know that's a great way to make someone worry, right?'

'We had a minor – *minor*, Tess – hiccup in life support today. Air not filtering right, CO_2 got a little high for a couple hours.'

That *was* minor, in the grand scheme of things. But the *Rockhound* was an old ship even by Exodan standards, and this wasn't the first time there'd been 'hiccups' in their patched-up life support. 'Did Garren get it fixed?' Their mech tech.

George gestured to his door. 'Would you like me to get him up here?' he asked with a teasing look. 'Have him walk you through it?'

Tessa eyed the screen flatly. 'I'm just saying, Lela' – his captain – 'should talk to the mining guild about replacing it already.'

'You know as much as anyone there's a list as long as my leg for ships that need upgrades, and we are not at the top, I assure you.' He smiled in a way that was meant to soothe. 'Worst case, we'll head home if we start coughing.' His smile went wistful, and Tessa could see the tangent at work. An unexpected trip home meant he could hug the kids sooner, which meant they'd have grown a little less since the last time he saw them. 'How're they doin'?' he asked.

'Your son—'

'Uh oh.'

'—stuffed his pajamas down the toilet and told me you did it.'

George guffawed. 'No! I'm innocent, I swear!'

'Don't worry. You have a solid alibi.'

'That's a relief. My own son, throwing me out the hatch like that.'

Tessa shook her head. 'It's like family means nothing.' She paused. 'He's on this kick lately – "all fixed". He says it *constantly*. Any idea where he got it?'

George stroked his thick beard. 'I dunno.' He squinted at the ceiling. 'Isn't that a Big Bug thing?'

Tessa had never been into *The Big Bug Crew* as a kid, and she hadn't played any of the new ones with her daughter. 'Is it?'

'Maybe I'm remembering it wrong, but I swear it's Big Bug. Whenever something on the ship breaks down and you repair it, there's this, like . . . fanfare and confetti, and the kids yell, "All fixed!"'

'But he hasn't—' Tessa stopped. Ky wasn't old enough to be playing sims yet, not by a long shot. Anybody who'd only figured out his knees a standard ago didn't yet have the mental chops to distinguish between virtual reality and *reality* reality. She knew this. Aya knew this. Aya had been *told* this. And yet, Aya had also recently been deemed responsible enough to look after her brother unsupervised for a few hours. There'd been a few of those afternoons where Tessa had come home to find Ky wound up like she'd never seen. She'd chalked it up to his sister's overly liberal forays into the cookie box, or him just being excited about time spent playing with the coolest person in his little world. But Tessa put herself back in her childhood big sister shoes. She remembered the times her parents left her alone with Ashby. She remembered how annoying he'd been sometimes, how impossible to please. She remembered trying to find something, *anything* that would keep him occupied for more than ten minutes. She wondered, if they'd had a sim hub at home then, if she might've stuck a slap patch on his head, leaned him into a corner of the couch, and pumped sims into his brain while she did whatever she fancied. Watched forbidden Martian vids, maybe.

'Uh oh,' George said again.

'What?'

'Your face.' He made a circular hand motion around his own. 'It went super scary.'

She glared at him. 'I don't have a scary face.'

'You do. You do, sometimes, have a scary face.'

'If I have a scary face, it's because *your daughter*—'

'Ohhhh, boy.'

'—is in big trouble.' And stars, was she ever. Tessa had half a mind to wake her up right then. She would've, too, if getting her to sleep hadn't been such an odyssey.

'Sounds like everybody's in trouble. Am *I* in trouble? I swear to you, Tess, I didn't have anything to do with the toilet thing.'

She rubbed one of her temples and gave half a laugh. 'I still have to review the evidence on that. You're not out of the open yet.'

'Shit,' George said, with a sad shake of his head. 'Maybe it'd be best if I *didn't* come home early.'

Tessa looked at him – his broad chest, his big beard, his perpetually sleepy eyes. He was greyer than he'd been once, and fuller, too. He was a kind-looking man. A normal-looking man. George wasn't the sort of guy she'd once dreamed about. George was just George, and George never changed.

She knew that wasn't true. Nothing was permanent, especially out in the open. But when she was with George, even just on opposite ends of a sib call, it was nice to pretend, for a little bit, that this one thing would never end. It didn't matter that it wasn't perfect, or wasn't always exciting. It was hers. There was one thing in this universe that was wholly, truly *hers*, and always would be.

It was the cosiest lie she knew, and she saw no reason to stop telling it.

Part 2

· · · · · · · · · · · · · · · · · · · ·

WE HAVE WANDERED

Feed source: Reskit Institute of Interstellar Migration (Public News Feed)
Item name: The Modern Exodus – Entry #4
Author: Ghuh'loloan Mok Chutp
Encryption: 0
Translation path: [Hanto:Kliptorigan]
Transcription: 0
Node identifier: 2310-483-38, Isabel Itoh

[System message: The feed you have selected has been translated from written Hanto. As you may be aware, written Hanto includes gestural notations that do not have analogous symbols in any other GC language. Therefore, your scrib's on-board translation software has not translated the following material directly. The content here is a modified translation, intended to be accessible to the average Kliptorigan reader.]

———

At the heart of every district is a four-story cylindrical complex, stretching through the layered decks like a dowel stuck into a disc. The complex is made of metal, like everything else, and has no windows. The exterior is covered in muted murals of varying age, the details often obscured by the climbing vines growing from planters that encircle the base of the building. There are two entry-points at the neighbourhood level – an unobtrusive door used by the people who work there, and a larger archway used by those going through the most difficult days of their lives.

The complex is, in function, a corpse composting facility. Exodans do not call it that. They call it, simply, the Centre.

I admit I felt trepidation as I passed through the archway. This is an area of Exodan custom I was unschooled in, and I was unsure what I would find. I braced myself for the sight of rotting flesh, the air of decay. I found neither. The Centre does not feel like a place of death.

The lights are kind. There are planters everywhere, but they are tame and controlled, just as the entire process within this place is. The air surprised me the most: a slight hint of agreeable humidity, coupled with an utterly pleasant warmth (in truth, it was the most comfortable environment I've been in since arriving in the Fleet). There's a strange feel to it, yes, but it is inoffensive, reminiscent of a forest after a rain. I wondered if Humans – with their notoriously poor olfactory sense – could detect it at all.

The professionals who tend this place are known as caretakers, and one named Maxwell met me near the entrance. I knew his clothing was ceremonial, but you would never know it, dear guest, if you had not been told in advance. He wore no ornamentation, nothing that communicated pomp or importance. Just loose-fitting garments made of undyed fabric, cinched around his forearms and ankles to prevent dragging in the dirt. The outfit was a reminder that my visit that day was on a strict schedule. Maxwell was to conduct a burial – a 'laying-in', they call it – and though I was welcome to see the preparation, I would not be permitted to attend the ceremony itself. It was a 'family matter', he said, and studying the events from the sidelines would not be well received. Exodans tend to express strong emotions quite freely – brashly, even – but I have observed a general (though not universal) dislike of doing so around strangers. I struggle with this idea, but I respect it all the same.

'So,' my host said, gesturing to the chamber before us. 'This is the main event.'

The space we occupied was as tall as the exterior suggested. Stretching up before us was an enormous cylinder, unchanged since the days of the Earthen builders. A ramp spiralled around the cylinder, all the way to the top, wide enough for several Humans to walk side-by-side. At the base were several well-sealed hatches, from which the final product could be retrieved. Another caretaker was engaged in this very activity, filling metal canisters with what could easily be mistaken for nothing more extraordinary than dark soil. I was imme-diately filled with questions, but Maxwell had other ideas. 'We'll come back to this,' he said. 'We can't go out of order.' He paused, studying me. 'Are you comfortable seeing bodies?'

I answered honestly. 'I don't know. I have never seen one.'

He blinked – a response that indicates surprise. 'Never? Not one of your own kind?'

I gestured in the negative before I realised he wouldn't understand. 'No,' I said. 'I'm not in a medical profession, and am lucky enough to have never witnessed serious violence. I have lost connections, and have grieved them with others in a ceremonial sense. But we do not grieve with a corpse present. We do not see the body that remains as the person we have lost.'

Maxwell looked fascinated, as one could rightly expect from one of his profession. 'What do you do with them, then?'

'They're cleanly disposed of. Some still practise the old way of leaving them just beyond the shoreline, where the waves cannot reach them. Mostly, though, corpses are dissolved and flushed away.'

'Just . . . with wastewater?'

'Yes.'

Maxwell visibly wrestled with that. 'Right. That sounds . . . efficient.' He gestured for me to follow him. 'Well, if you *do* feel uncomfortable, just let me know, and we'll leave.'

I followed him through a staff door and down a corridor until we reached his preparation room. The difference between this place and the main chamber could not have been starker. My tentacles reflexively curled with chill, and the air was irritatingly dry.

It is difficult for me to distill all I felt as we entered the room. If I were to describe the moment with pure objectivity, I stood at a table looking at a dead alien. She was old, her body withered. I related to nothing of her anatomy, laid bare and unshrouded. I realised my declaration to Maxwell that I had never seen a dead body was untrue. I have seen dead animals. I have eaten them. I have walked past them in food markets. I have fished expired laceworms out of my beloved swimming tank at home. In some ways, observing the Human corpse on the table was no different than that. Please understand, dear guest, I do not mean that I believe Humans are equivalent to lesser species.

What I mean is that what lay before me was a species other than myself, and so any connection to my own mortality, my own eventual fate, was at first safely distant.

But then I began to think of the dead animals I have seen and disposed of and consumed, the ended lives I did not grieve for because I did not understand them fully. I did not see myself in them, and therefore it did not matter. I looked to this former Human – this former sapient, with a family and loves and fears. Those things I *could* understand, even though the body was something I could not. Nothing in the room was moving, nothing was *happening*, and yet within me, I felt profound change. I grieved for the alien, this person I had never known. I grieved for my pet laceworms. I grieved for myself. Yet it was a quiet grief, an everyday grief, a heaviness and a lightness all at once. I was overwhelmed, yet there was no way to express that beyond silence.

I do not feel I am explaining this experience well, dear guest, but perhaps that is appropriate. Perhaps none of us can truly explain death. Perhaps none of us should.

———

TESSA

Tessa stood in the doorway to her workroom, lunch box in one hand, the other hanging at her side. She'd had a bad feeling since the moment she'd discovered that the staff door opened for her despite the lock being offline. In the workroom, poor Sahil lay with his head on the desk, snoring and drooling without a care in the world. She looked out to the endless shelves. Everything appeared just as it had when she'd left the day before. She knew it wasn't. Somewhere, something was missing. Probably a lot of things were missing.

She did not need this today. She really, really did not.

She crouched down beside her colleague. 'Sahil?' she said, giving his shoulder a shake. 'Sahil? Dammit.' She gave him a once-over, just to make sure nothing was bloodied or broken, then turned to the vox. 'Help,' she called.

The connection was instant. 'Patrol dispatch,' a voice said. 'Is this an emergency?'

Tessa was pretty sure she knew the speaker. 'Lili?' she said. 'It's Tessa, down in Bay Eight.'

'Ah, jeez.' Definitely Lili. 'Again?'

Tessa wasn't sure whether to laugh or sigh, so she did both. 'Again.'

'Anybody hurt?'

'No, but looks like they hit my coworker's bots.' It was a mean but easy exploit, if you could get your hands on a med scanner. Trigger the imubots' suppression protocol, like a doctor would before a minor surgery, and say goodnight. 'I think he's just asleep, but—'

'Yeah, I gotcha. You've got two patrollers and a medic headed your way. Ten minutes, tops.'

'Thanks, Lili.'

'You got it. If you come by Jojo's tonight, I'll get you a drink.'

Tessa laughed dryly. 'I just might take you up on that.' The vox switched off. Tessa sat on the desk. She set her lunch down and studied Sahil, her hands folded between her legs. His sinuses roared. She thought about wiping up the drool, but no. She did enough of that kind of thing at home.

She glanced up at the clockprint on the wall. *Ten minutes, tops*, dispatch had said. So, rounding up to ten, that meant it was in her best interest to wait five minutes before calling Eloy, who would take twelve to get from home to work. Technically, she was supposed to call the supervisor the second something like this happened, but Tessa found the idea of delaying the inevitable headache until she had patrollers there much more palatable. Eloy was easier to deal with if another person of authority was there to balance him out.

One minute passed. Tessa opened her lunch box and removed the cake she'd packed for the afternoon. It was only eighth hour. It was warranted.

Four minutes passed. The cake had been pretty good. A little stale, but then, it was two days old. She brushed the remaining crumbs off her knee. Sahil snored.

Five minutes passed. She took a breath. '225-662,' she said to the vox.

A second went by. Two. Three. 'Yeah,' Eloy's marginally awake voice said. Great. Just great. This was the start of his day.

'Eloy, it's Tessa,' she said. 'We've had a break-in.'

'Ah, *fuck*,' he snapped. She could practically hear him rubbing his hands over his face. 'Fucking again?'

Sahil shifted in his sleep, his lips folding unflatteringly against the desk. 'Fucking again,' Tessa said.

ISABEL

When dealing with other sapients, issues of compatibility were difficult to anticipate. Isabel's go-to example of this was the first meeting between Exodans and Aeluons. The Exodans, overjoyed by what felt like a rescue, exhilarated by the confirmation that their species was not alone, predictably assembled in their festive best, and decorated the shuttledock in streamers, banners, bunting. There were recordings of the scene in the Archives – an over-whelming array of every colour the dyeworks could cook up, hung and layered like confetti frozen in time. To Exodan eyes, the display was ebullient, effusive, a celebration like no other (not to mention an extravagant use of cloth). To the chromatically communicative Aeluons, it was the equivalent of opening a nondescript door and finding a thousand screaming people on the other side. The Aeluons, well familiar with the more colourful habits of other species, dealt with it as gracefully as they could, but as soon as some Klip/Ensk translation wrinkles had been ironed out, a gentle request was made to please, *please* put the flags away.

Such misalignments were unpredictable, and blameless. Nothing that could've been foreseen. Nothing that could've been prevented. Isabel told herself that as she stood helplessly at the transport pod platform as . . . *something* nearby kept shutting down Ghuh'loloan's cart. She'd been fine on the elevator, fine as they crossed the platform. As soon as she approached the trans-port pod, though, the cart stopped in its tracks, as if someone had thrown a switch. Isabel had tugged her backward, and the cart had come back to life. But as soon as Ghuh'loloan drove herself across some invisible line, the wheels froze and the engine audibly slumped. None of her colleague's increasingly agitated flicking of switches had any effect.

'Weird,' the transport attendant said in schoolroom Klip. He scratched his head. 'It's got to be . . . I don't know.' He switched over to Ensk and gave Isabel an apologetic shrug. *'Some kinda signal interference from the pod. I'm sorry, M, I don't know where to start.'*

Isabel glanced around as she mentally scrambled for a solution. A small crowd had gathered, because of course they had. They kept their distance – out of respect and wariness in equal measure, no doubt – but their interest was unapologetic, and anything but subtle. How often did you get to go home and tell the dinner table about the alien you saw stuck on the transport deck? Isabel was aware that they were watching herself as well, the obvious responsible party, the one who would come up with something clever.

She did not.

'I do not hold you at fault,' Ghuh'loloan said to the attendant. 'Nor you, dear host. These things happen!' Her tone was bright, but her tentacles still flicked switches in fading hope. She pulled in her tendrils, and her eyestalks shut for a moment. 'M Transport Attendant,' she said, perking back up. She had yet to get a proper hold on honorifics, and the overdone result was often charming. 'Do you think you are capable of carrying my cart? It weighs approximately sixteen kems.'

The transport attendant – clearly tickled at being called 'M' by an alien visitor – nodded. 'Yes, I can lift. But, um . . .' He paused, searching for words. 'I'm not sure I can carry it and you same. Together?'

'Together,' Isabel said.

He nodded again. 'It and you together.'

'Oh, you won't need to worry about that,' Ghuh'loloan said. 'Isabel, would you—?' She gestured at her cart, and Isabel caught on. She grabbed the edge of the cart and dragged Ghuh'loloan a short ways backward. Right on cue, the cart hummed to life again. Ghuh'loloan pressed a few controls, and a compact ramp extended slowly from the side.

Understanding her colleague's intent, Isabel looked at the floor. Smooth, dry metal plating, just like everywhere else. Clean, but hard to say what had been on it, or what it had been cleaned *with*. A bit of solvent residue, a bootprint with traces of fertiliser, or an unseen patch of spilled salt were all enough to make a Harmagian itch for the rest of the day. Isabel frowned with concern. 'I'm sure one of us can carry you.'

'No,' Ghuh'loloan said. 'You can't.' She angled her eyestalks toward Isabel's bare forearms. *Right*, Isabel thought. Soap. Skin oil. Lotion. And you couldn't forget the clothes, either, undoubtedly still dusted with detergent. Stars, but Humans made a mess of getting clean.

Isabel looked to the crowd. *'Does anyone have any water with them?'* she called out in Ensk. *'A canteen, or . . . ?'*

The faces in the crowd looked surprised to be addressed, as if they'd just discovered they were playing a sim instead of watching a vid. But they responded to the question, opening satchels and digging through backpacks. Bottles, bags, and canteens were raised up.

'I'm sorry to ask this,' Isabel said. *'But we need to rinse off a path for her.'*

Ghuh'loloan wagged her facial tendrils. 'What are you saying?'

'I'm asking them to clean off the floor for you.'

'Oh, dear host, I'll be all right, really—'

'Don't be silly,' Isabel said, and turned again to the crowd. *'Any volunteers? Clean water only, please, no tea or anything flavoured.'*

Isabel hadn't expected differently, but was pleased to see everybody with water come forward to help. She knew a good deal of the motivation was self-serving – not only did they see an alien in a pinch on the platform, *but they got to help*. Still, the unquestioning willingness to pitch in made her proud. The onlookers emptied their drinks, tossing the water in forward-moving splashes.

One small girl upended her equally small cup straight down in front of her. It did little for the task at hand – most ended up on the girl's shoes – but she got the point. Every bit counted.

After a minute or two, a glistening path stretched from the Harmagian cart to the Exodan pod. '*Thank you, friends,*' Isabel said. '*And thank your families for us, too.*' That water had come from many, after all.

'Yes, yes,' Ghuh'loloan said, having caught a familiar word. Her dactyli unfurled like waking leaves. Had she continued in Klip, she likely would have delivered a truly Harmagian declaration of gratitude, but instead, she exercised one of the few Ensk phrases she knew: '*Thank oo mutsch.*'

The crowd was delighted.

Ghuh'loloan's eyestalks shifted to the ramp. 'Now, if you will forgive me further, this will take some time.'

And with that, Ghuh'loloan began to crawl.

There were a few muffled sounds from the crowd – a smothered gasp, a nervous laugh. Isabel looked sharply to them, giving everyone the same look her grandkids got if reaching for something forbidden. But in truth, she was one with the crowd, choking back her own instinctive yelp. She'd never seen a Harmagian leave xyr cart. She knew, logically, that vehicle and rider were two separate entities, but the visual confirmation was cognitively dissonant. She had imagined, given the Harmagian lack of legs, that Ghuh'loloan would simply slide, like the recordings she'd seen of slugs, or perhaps snakes. But instead, Ghuh'loloan's smooth belly began to . . . stars, what was the word for it? Grab. Pull. It was as if Ghuh'loloan's stomach was covered with a thick swath of fabric – several bedsheets, maybe – and behind the bedsheets there were hands, and the hands pushed against the sheets, curling, grasping, dragging the rest of the body forward. *Dough*, Isabel thought. *Putty*. There was no symmetry to it, no pattern easily discernible to a bipedal mind. And the result *was* slow, as Ghuh'loloan had intimated. Isabel imagined trying to walk alongside her like this. She'd have to take two short steps, then wait two beats, then two steps, then two beats, on and on. This was why Harmagians had spent so much of their evolutionary history enjoying the quickness of the sea before adapting for the riches of the land. It was why they'd invented carts. It was why their tech was so incredible. It was why they'd become so good at defending themselves – and at taking from others.

Ghuh'loloan heaved herself forward, a lumbering mass inching across the wet patch of already clean floor that had been rinsed with pure water for the sake of fussy, fragile skin. Isabel watched, and marvelled.

The former conquerors of the galaxy.

EYAS

'Need a hand?'

Eyas stopped spreading compost and turned her head. A man was there – younger than her, but not a kid, either. She looked him in the eye, thrown by his question. 'Sorry, what?'

'Do you need a hand?' he asked again in an accent she couldn't place. It was rough and bright and thick as pudding. He gestured to her cart. 'Looks like you have a lot to get through. I can't say I've ever really gardened, but I'm sure I could chuck dirt around.'

Eyas slowly brushed off her gloves and stood up. 'I'm—' She tried to straighten out her baffled brain. 'You know this is compost, right?'

'Yeah,' he said.

They stared at each other. 'You know what compost *is*, right?'

'Sure.' His face suggested he was starting to doubt that.

'Are you a trader, or—?'

The man laughed. 'No. The accent gave me away, huh?'

'Yeah,' she said. *That, and other things.* She knelt back down to the compost she'd been distributing, waiting for him to leave.

He did not. 'Do you sell it?'

'Do I *what*?'

'Do you sell this stuff? Or is it just something you make at home?'

Eyas lidded her canister, walked to the edge of the planter, and looked seriously at the man. 'These are Human remains,' she said in a low voice. 'We compost our dead.'

The man was mortified. 'Oh. Wow, I'm . . . jeez, I'm sorry.'

He looked at the cart full of canisters. 'These are all . . . people? Like, individual people, or . . . oh man, are they all mixed together?'

'If you have questions, I'm sure someone at the Centre would be happy to give you a tour.'

'The Centre. That's where you . . .' He gestured vaguely to the canisters.

'Yes.'

'And that's . . . your job.'

'Yes.' She threw a pointed glance back at the plants. 'Which I am not doing.'

The man held up his palms. 'Right. Sorry. Really sorry.' He turned to leave.

Eyas turned back to the plant and began to crouch down. For reasons unknown, she turned back. 'Where are you from?'

The man stopped. 'Mushtullo.'

'And you're not a trader.'

'No.'

She squinted. 'Do you have family here?'

'Heh, everybody asks that. No, I'm just trying something new.'

Oh, stars, he was one of those. She'd heard others complaining about said same, but never encountered it herself. Young grounders had made a thing of showing up on the Fleet's doorstep hoping to find kin or connection or some other such fluff, succeeding at little except treating everyone's home like a zoo before learning there wasn't any romance in it and heading back to cushier lives where every problem could be answered with creds.

Except here was this one, standing there with his hands in his pockets and an irritatingly eager smile. She should have let him walk away, but . . . he'd asked to help. He'd offered to help.

'Do you have work?' she asked.

'Not yet,' the man said. 'I went to the job office and everything, but they said the only openings they had were for sanitation. And not to be picky, but—'

'But you were picky.'

The man gave a guilty shrug. 'I'm just hoping something else will open up. I'm good with code, I'm good with customers, I could—'

Eyas removed her gloves, folded them over her belt, and sat at the edge of the planter, bare hands folded between her legs. 'Do you understand why they tried to give you a sanitation job?'

'They said—'

'I know what they said. There were other openings, I promise you.' Lots of them, she knew. 'That's not the point. Do you understand why they tried to give you *that* job?'

The last traces of his easy grin evaporated. 'Oh.'

Eyas sighed and ran her hand through her hair. He thought this was a matter of bigotry. 'No, you still don't get it. They tried to give you a sanitation job because *everybody* has to do sanitation. Everybody. Me, merchants, teachers, doctors, council members, the admiral – every healthy Exodan fourteen and over gets their ID put in a computer, and that computer randomly pulls names for temporary, mandatory, no-getting-out-of-it work crews to sort recycling and wash greasy throw-cloths and unclog the sewage lines. All the awful jobs nobody wants to do. That way, nothing is out of sight or out of mind. Nothing is left to *lesser people*, because there's no such thing. So you, coming in here at – how old are you?'

'Twenty-four.'

'Right. You've got ten years of potential sanitation shifts to make up for. You're here eating the food we grow, sleeping inside a home somebody worked hard to maintain, drinking water that is carefully, carefully managed. The people at the job office knew that. They wanted to see if you were actually willing to live like us. If you were more than just a tourist. They wanted to know if you were serious.'

The man straightened up. 'I'm serious.'

'Well, then, go muck out a sewer like the rest of us have to. Do that, and they might let you put some code to use.' Eyas was sure they would. There was need for that kind of skillset, no question. It just needed to be in the hands of someone with the right principles.

'Okay,' the man said. 'Yeah, okay. Thank you. Thanks very much.' The smile returned. 'I'm Sawyer, by the way.'

She gave him a polite nod. 'I'm Eyas.'

'Eyas. That suits you.'

'No.' She got to her feet and put her gloves back on. 'It really doesn't.'

KIP

'Trust me,' Ras said. 'This is totally safe.'

Kip wasn't so sure. His friend was smiling his usual smile, but he had a bunch of weird shit spread out on the floor between them – a patch scanner, some complicated cables, an info chip labelled 'BIRTHDAY.' All of it looked hand-hacked, and none of it was anything Ras had ever given any indication he knew how to use. 'Where'd you get this stuff?' Kip asked.

'Mail drone. I had some creds saved up.'

'Yeah, but from *where*?'

'You remember that job I worked for M Aho—'

'Not the creds. This . . . hackjob stuff.'

Ras lowered his voice, even though they were safe in his room. His mom had ears like you would not believe. 'Have you heard of this feed called Picnic?'

'No.'

'It's like . . . *serious* black market modder shit. Implants, code, ships even. You name it. Whatever you want, somebody there has it, or knows where to get it. And it's totally off the map. You can't find Picnic in public searches.'

Kip wasn't super comfortable with the sound of that, but he didn't want to look like a wuss. 'So how'd *you* find it?'

'Toby told me about it. It's where his sister gets all the gear she needs to make smash.'

'Wait, Una? She makes smash?'

'Do you not know that? I thought everybody knew that. How

do you think she bought her own skiff? Anyway, the supplier I got this from, xe told me—'

'Who?'

'What?'

'Who's the supplier?'

'Just . . . you know, it's anonymous, everybody's got codenames and—'

Kip leaned forward. '*Who?*'

Ras cleared his throat. 'Xe's called fluffyfluffycake.'

'Fluffyfluffycake.'

'Xe really knows xyr shit, man, I'm telling you—'

'You bought a hack kit from somebody called *fluffyfluffycake*.'

Ras rolled his eyes and pulled back his wristwrap, exposing the implant beneath. 'Look, I already did me.' He picked up the patch scanner – definitely hand-hacked, there were two different colours of casing fused together – and swiped it over his wrist. He turned the scanner screen toward Kip so he could read the ID data it had just pulled. 'See?'

Kip read, blinked, raised his eyebrows. 'Huh.'

'Yeah, *huh*.'

'And it's . . . okay?' Kip remembered the standard before, when the *Newet* had gone under quarantine because somebody came back from some neutral market with a bot virus – Marabunta, they called it. Hijacked your imubots and gave you seizures, then hopped to anybody you brushed your patch against, whether it was a hug or a handshake or a crowded transport car or whatever. Kip remembered seeing pictures of the victims on the news feeds – folks tied down in hospital beds, mouths strapped shut so they wouldn't break their own teeth. Everybody'd been really freaked out. At school, they'd gotten a big long boring talk about how you should never, ever get unlicensed bots and you should never, ever go to an unlicensed clinic. He could hear that lecture playing dimly in the back of his head, but the reality of his friend sitting in front of him was much louder. 'You feel okay?' Kip asked.

'Stars, I get us something awesome, and you turn into my mom. Yes, I feel fine. I did it yesterday before I asked you over. What, did you think I was gonna test it out on you first? C'mon, I'm not *that* much of an asshole.'

Kip's pulse thudded in his ears. If Ras'd done it, and he was okay, and the hack hadn't messed up his bots or anything, then . . . it was okay, right? He stared for a second, then pushed up his own wristwrap – blue and green triangle print, frayed around the edges. The one his dad had given him last Remembrance Day. 'All right,' he said.

Ras grinned. 'Only takes a sec.' He connected one end of the cable to Kip's patch, then the other end to his scrib. He popped the info chip in an empty port and gestured at the screen. 'You want to keep your actual birthday, yeah? Easier to remember.'

'Yeah,' Kip said. He shifted his weight as Ras worked. 'What if somebody we know sees us?'

'Well, if we're not stupid about it, they won't. We can go to one of the other districts and it'll be fine.' He waved his hand, and the scrib made a completed *ding*. 'All right, let's see what we got.'

'That's it?' Kip asked.

'That's it,' Ras said, picking up the scanner. 'I told you, fluffy-cake knows xyr shit.' He swiped the scanner over Kip's wrist, gave a nod, then handed the scanner over.

Kip took it and looked down at the screen.

GC citizenship record:
ID #: 9836-745-112
GC designated name: Kristofer Madaki
Emergency contact: Serafina Madaki, Alton Madaki
Next of kin: Serafina Madaki, Alton Madaki
Local name (if applicable): Kristofer (Kip) Madaki

Locally required information:
Ship: *Asteria*, Exodus Fleet
Address: 224-324
Standard date of birth: 23/292
Age: 20

'There we go!' Ras said. 'Damn, *finally* you look like you're having fun.'

Kip couldn't help but smile. He could get in so much trouble for this, and yet . . . yet he felt like he'd cut the line, like he'd been granted a reprieve from the agonising wait between birthdays. 'Do I look twenty, though?'

Ras pursed his lips and nodded. 'Totally.' He cocked his head. 'Maybe don't shave.'

Kip didn't have much to shave yet except his upper lip and a patch on his chin, but he didn't feel like sharing that. 'So, now what?' he said. Now that the scary part was over with, the lack of plan felt kind of anticlimactic. 'We could go get some kick, or . . . redreed? Do you wanna get some redreed?' Kip had tried it once and didn't like it, but he could get it now, and that was the important thing.

But Ras shook his head. 'I have a way, way better idea.'

SAWYER

Compared to the brightness and bluster of the rest of the plaza, the job office was a rather humble spot. Still, it was welcoming in its own way. There were benches outside where people could skim through listings on their scribs, and calming plants in neat boxes, and pixel posters cheering the reader on. *Need a change? We can help!*, read one, the letters glowing above a loop of a relieved-looking man setting aside a vegetable-gathering basket and picking up a stack of fabric instead. Another poster featured a teenage girl standing in a semblance of a hex corridor, surveying doors printed with various symbols – a leaping fish, a magnified imubot, a musical instrument, a shuttle in flight. *You never know where a job trial will take you*, the pixels read.

Sawyer took a seat on the bench beside the girl with four lives ahead of her. He'd just left the office, and done what the compost woman had suggested. Going back in armed with advice had put a spring in his step. Coming back out . . . he wasn't sure what he felt. He hadn't talked to the same clerk as before, so he'd missed out on the satisfaction of returning to say *aha, look, I have passed your test!* Learning that there was an expected order of vocational initiation had felt significant to Sawyer. The clerk hadn't conveyed the same, but why should he? What was *significant* about filling out the same formwork he probably filled out dozens of times a day? What had Sawyer expected? A knowing nod? An approving smile?

That's exactly what he'd wanted, he knew, and he felt stupid about it. But then again, he'd been given no next step, no direction beyond 'thank you, we'll contact you when a shift becomes available.' When would that be? Tomorrow? A tenday? More? In principle, Sawyer didn't mind downtime, especially when he didn't have to worry about food or a roof, but the idea of rattling around that big empty home until some nebulous point in the future arrived didn't sit well.

He set his jaw. Getting down about everything he didn't know yet wouldn't do any good. Maybe he could try making inroads with his hex neighbours again. Maybe they'd be more than distantly polite if they knew he was going to clean up the same messes everybody else did. Maybe he'd go out there at dinnertime today instead of going to a cafe or hiding out insecurely in his room. He'd never really cooked before, but he could chop stuff, at least. He could help. He could—

'Working up some courage?' a friendly voice said.

Sawyer found the speaker: a stocky man with an infectious smile and a mech arm. Such implants were common among Humans back home, but Sawyer hadn't seen many in the Fleet. 'I've already been in,' he said.

'Needing some comfort, then, judging by your face.' The man raised up a canteen, signalling the intent to share. 'Want some in liquid form?'

Sawyer smiled and put up his hands. 'I better not,' he said. 'I'm kind of a lightweight.'

'Then you've got nothin' to fear here,' the man said. He waggled the canteen. 'Just tea. Lil' sugar boost, that's all.'

Sawyer's smile grew, and he nodded. 'All right,' he said, joining the man. 'That's very kind.'

'I've been in your shoes,' the man said. He filled the canteen lid and handed it over. 'Not a comfy thing, having idle hands, huh?'

'No,' Sawyer said, nodding in thanks as he took a sip of tea. Stars, but this guy wasn't kidding about the sugar. He could already feel it clinging fuzzily to his teeth.

The man stuck out his hand. 'I'm Oates,' he said.

Sawyer returned the handshake, a kick of happy adrenaline coursing through him. 'Sawyer,' he said.

'And where are you from, Sawyer?' He pointed toward Sawyer's mouth. 'We don't grow Rs like those in the Fleet.'

Sawyer laughed. 'Mushtullo.'

'Long way from home.' Oates pulled a redreed pipe and a tiny bag out of his jacket pocket. Sawyer knew what was coming next: 'You got family here?'

'Nah.' He had the reply down pat by now. 'Just trying something new.'

Oates nodded as he filled his pipe – redreed in the hand he'd been born with, bowl in the one he'd chosen. 'Good for you.' He hit his sparker and took one puff, two puffs, three. The smoke rose steady. 'You been here long?'

'Two tendays.'

'How's it treating you so far?'

'Great,' Sawyer said, a little too fast, a little too loud. 'Yeah, it's . . . it's been great.'

Oates eyed him through the pipe smoke. 'Bit different than home, huh?'

Sawyer took another sip of the sickeningly sweet tea. 'Still finding my footing, I guess. But that's normal, right?'

'I'd say so,' Oates said. He offered his pipe; Sawyer declined. 'So what kind of work did they hook you up with?'

'I put my name in for sanitation.' Sawyer tried to look casual as he said it, but he was keen to see how that answer was received.

Oates did not disappoint. 'Sanitation,' he said with a favourable look. 'A time-honoured gig.' He took a long drag and let the smoke curl slowly from his nose. 'That's good of you. But tell me honestly, now that we're tea buddies and all – that's not really what you *want* to be doing, right?'

'Well . . .' Sawyer laughed. 'Does anybody?'

Oates chuckled. 'No. That's why the good ol' shit lottery exists in the first place. What kind of jobs did you do back on Mushtullo?'

'Lots of stuff – uh, let's see . . . I've worked at a cafe, a fuel depot, a stasie factory—'

'So, you can lift stuff and follow directions and be nice to people. Good, good. What else?'

'I can write code.'

'No kidding.' Oates looked interested. 'What kind of code?'

'I'm not a comp tech or anything. I didn't go to school for it. But I can write Siksek and Tinker, and—'

'Tinker, huh?' Oates rolled his pipe between his metal fingers. 'What level?'

'Four.'

Oates studied Sawyer. 'Listen, I know we've known each other for all of three minutes, but I can tell you're a good dude. If you really want to start with the sewers, I won't bother you further. But if you're interested in something more . . . *dynamic*, I'm on a salvage crew, and we're looking for some extra hands. Specifically, someone who knows Tinker. I've stopped a few others today, and you're the first I've chatted with who's got that skill.'

Sawyer had started to take another sip of tea, but the cup froze halfway there.

'Now, lifting shit and following directions is the main part of the job,' Oates went on. 'But we use Tinker more often than not. You know how it is with busted tech – sometimes you can't get a panel to work or a door to open, and it's always faster when we've got people who can just get in there and force code the thing. That sound like something you could handle?'

'Yeah, definitely,' Sawyer said, loud and fast again. 'I've never done it before, but—'

'If you're level four, it'll be cake.' Oates folded his lips together and nodded. 'All right, well, if you're interested, come meet me tonight at shuttledock twelve, after twenty-half. I'll take you to meet my boss.'

Sawyer's heart was in his throat. This was it. A friend. A *crew*. Holy shit, the compost woman had been right! Five minutes out of the job office, and just putting his name on that list had changed things. 'I mean—' Sawyer stammered, 'that would be awesome. I can just go find the listing, if that's easier, I don't want to take up any more of your time—'

'Not at all,' Oates said. 'Besides, my boss doesn't use listings. Personal recommendations only. She's a face-to-face kind of person.' Smoke escaped from between his smiling teeth. 'Great judge of character.'

TESSA

There had been a time, once, when Eloy hadn't been a bad boss. Or maybe he always had been, but he just hadn't yet been given the opportunity to let that quality shine. In any case, he'd been Tessa's vote for Bay Eight supervisor last standard, when Faye stepped down and left for the independent colonies. Tessa missed Faye. She got shit done, but you could go have a drink with her at her hex in off-hours and forget that she was in charge. Tessa had never been buddies with Eloy, but he was a reliable worker, and absurdly organised. He had that no-nonsense edge you needed when you had to go speak for everybody else at cargo guild meetings. But as soon as he got his stripe, he turned into one of those people who equated *being in charge* with *being outwardly stressed out*. He hadn't broken any rules or disrupted workflow enough to justify the workers voting him out yet, but it was coming. Tessa knew it was coming, and it was going to be ugly, but . . . well. That was the way stuff worked.

Eloy paced around the workroom, fingers tapping against his pockets. 'And you guys have no idea who's responsible for this yet,' he said, tossing the words at the patroller without looking at her.

The patroller – Ruby Boothe, from the Santosos' neighbourhood – was keeping it cool, but her patience was visibly running thin. 'That's why—'

'Because this is the fourth,' Eloy said. 'The fourth theft since I took this job. The sixth in a standard. And you haven't caught anyone. Not a one.'

'That's why we're asking questions,' Ruby said, her grip on her scrib tightening *ever* so slightly. 'And why we're out there inspecting the scene.' She pointed with her stylus toward the storage racks, where her volunteer second was walking with the now-awake Sahil – no worse for wear – trying to figure out what had been taken.

'Questions.' Eloy shook his head. 'You'd think with all the questions, you'd have some damn answers by now.'

'Eloy, come on,' Tessa said. She knew he wouldn't like her taking the patroller's side – and the terse look he threw her confirmed that – but this wasn't helping. 'How many people do you know who could do with some extra scrap to melt?' She nodded at the patroller. 'She's got a hell of a list to narrow down.'

The patroller gave her a thankful glance. 'Precisely,' she said. 'And there's no telling if the culprits are the same as the previous times. Nothing we've found here so far can tell us if this is an organised group, or a copycat, or a first-timer. Someone hit your worker's bots, and they made off with some scrap. That is not a lot to go on, but we're doing our best here.'

'Yeah, well, while you're doing your best, we're falling behind. I have to go to *my* supervisors and make excuses for why you can't keep this from happening to us.' Eloy gestured at Tessa. 'She can't do any of the shit she needed to do today because of this.'

Tessa rankled at Eloy using her as fuel for berating the patroller, but there was a kernel of truth in there she couldn't argue with. The crime at hand had a stupid irony: someone had been impatient enough with cargo bay processing times that they'd resorted to theft, thus setting the processing schedule back further for everyone. That was the part that really pissed Tessa off, more than falling behind in her work, more than finding Sahil knocked out, more than having to spend what should've been a quiet morning listening to Eloy take things out on people who didn't deserve it. The theft benefited the thief, and maybe the thief's friends or family, but that was it. They'd taken things out of the hands of people who *also* needed them, who had grit their teeth and followed the rules and made do without.

Sahil and the volunteer patroller came back. Eloy looked over. 'What'd they get?' he asked.

Tessa squinted. 'You feeling okay?' she asked.

Sahil was still looking a bit rough from his bot hack – dark around the eyes, paler in the cheeks. But he nodded. 'Just groggy,' he said, giving her a faint smile. 'Medic said it'd be like this for a few hours.' He turned his attention to the boss. 'So, teracite, mostly. Looks like they grabbed a few handfuls of sixtops, too, but not much. Just whatever they could put in their pockets as they left, I guess.'

'How much teracite?' Eloy said.

'A good amount,' Sahil said. 'I'd say . . . about a hundred kems, give or take.'

'Oh, fucking hell,' Eloy snapped. Tessa said nothing, but she felt the same. A lot of good things could've been done with that. Medical equipment. School computers. Shuttle upgrades. But instead, somebody was either going to melt it down for home use – personal smelters were everywhere these days – or sell it for creds. She hoped the thieves would go for the former option. The idea of somebody using the stolen stuff to repair their hex was easier to stomach. The latter meant luxuries that were nice but not necessary, and that . . . that was worth an Eloy-style rant or two.

'They'd need an autocart for a haul that size,' Ruby said, tapping her chin with her stylus. She looked to her second. 'What does that tell you?'

'A merchant,' the volunteer said. Tessa had missed his name, but he was older, and had the look of someone who had been excited to get his name pulled for this job. She didn't blame him. Tagging along after full-time patrol to keep them honest beat the pants off sewer duty. 'Either that, or someone who had access to bay-to-bay transport.'

'Yup,' Ruby said.

Eloy frowned. 'That is not much to go on.'

'No,' the patroller said, gathering her gear bag. 'But it's something, and it's more than we had when we walked in here.' She picked up the empty tea mug resting on the desk beside her. 'Where should I . . .'

'Just leave it,' Tessa said. 'I'll take care of it.' She smiled – the kind of smile you gave someone when the circumstances sucked but you appreciated them being there. 'Thanks for the help.'

The patrollers said their goodbyes and left. A silence sat uncomfortably in the workroom.

'I'm sorry, Eloy,' Sahil said. 'If I'd—'

Eloy put up his hand. 'Shit happens,' he said.

Tessa frowned. 'It wasn't your fault,' she said, speaking the words *someone else* should have. 'You sure you're okay?'

'I'm okay. Really.'

'I'm gonna come check up on you at home later.'

'Fine, fine,' Sahil chuckled. 'Eloy, do you need anything else from me?'

Eloy was somewhere else. He gave Sahil's question a half-hearted headshake. He seemed to have barely registered it.

'What's up?' Tessa asked.

Eloy let out a sigh that frayed around the edges. 'I was going to bring this up at the next bay meeting, but you might as well know now. The board's talking about AIs.'

Sahil looked confused. 'AIs for what?'

'For us,' Eloy said. 'AIs instead of us.'

'Wait, what?' Tessa said.

'They think it'd do away with the *Oxomoco* backlog. Sort through everything we've been trying to, get it recycled faster, have it done in a fraction of the time, keep it from happening again.'

Tessa laughed. 'We don't have the infrastructure for that. Do you have any idea the . . . the heavy duty gear you need to run one of those?' Her brother had one on his ship, and it was one of the most expensive things he had to maintain. Had to hire a separate tech to look after it and everything. AIs were long-haul stuff, big-creds stuff. There were AIs in the Fleet, sure, but they weren't the thinking kind. Just public safety systems, the kind who could recognise fire or turn off gravity if you fell a long way. Not the kind that watched everything and were programmed to sound like people. Not the kind that could do a Human job.

Eloy stuck his hands in his pockets and shrugged tersely. 'Yeah, well, apparently labour oversight has been on their ass about our processing times, and the idea's been floated that the cost of building a . . . I don't know what the terminology is here – building the shit you'd need to run a bunch of AIs – is less of a pain in the ass than doing things like we do them now. So they say.'

'That's . . .' Tessa shook her head. It was insulting, to say the least. 'They're not serious, are they?'

'I don't know,' Eloy said. The words indicated nothing, but the look on his face said he'd be worrying about it.

'They can't be,' Sahil said. 'There are so many higher-priority projects floating around. They'd never tag the resources for it.'

Tessa stared off into the cargo bay. She remembered, when she'd been in her teens, how M Lok next door had left one morning to go test the oxygen mix and came home that afternoon having been told that, thanks to the new monitoring systems his supervisors were going to install, he wouldn't need to do it anymore. The job office got him new training and a new profession, of course, but it was a hard switch for a man of forty-five, and all the harder because he didn't like his new career in aeroponics the way he had his old one. He was still at it, to this day. She wondered if he still thought about taking air samples in life support.

'Sahil, go home,' Tessa said. 'Get some rest.'

'I had plenty of that already,' Sahil said with a grim smile.

She laughed. 'Some real rest.' She looked to Eloy. 'And if it's all the same to you, boss' – she looked out to the overflowing racks of things people needed, the dormant liftbots awaiting her command – 'I need to get to work.'

KIP

Kip remembered how to speak, but it took him a minute or two to get there. 'I don't know,' he said slowly.

Ras placed a hand on his shoulder. 'Aw, come on,' he said. 'Don't be nervous.'

In front of them stood a doorway like any other. A panel. A frame. Plants and globulbs arcing up around it. But the sign on the door . . . that made all the difference.

THE NOVA ROOM
Age 20 and over

Kip swallowed. His palms started to sweat. This was Ras' grand plan, why he'd saved up those creds, why he'd found some random modder to help him hack his patch. Ras wanted to go to a tryst club. And being the good dude that he was, he'd brought his best friend along. Kip should've felt grateful. He should've felt excited – and he did, maybe? But it wasn't excited like finding a plate of jam cakes in the kitchen or trading in your old clothes for some crisp new ones. This was the other kind of excited. *Broken artigrav* excited. *Rattle in the shuttlecraft wall* excited. The kind of excited that occurred when the chances were good that everything would be okay, but you were still going to hold your breath until said okayness was a done deal.

'I don't know,' Kip said again. 'I— I haven't showered, I—'

'They've got places you can clean up,' Ras said.

'How do you know?'

'Omar told me. He goes to the one in our district, like, every day.'

Kip looked at his friend, all confidence and smile (and fresh shirt, too). His hair still had too much goo in it, but he at least looked like he *belonged* in a place like this. Ras'd had sex before – once with Britta, who he couldn't even be in the same room with now, and lots with Zi before her family moved to Coriol and Ras moped around for, like, ever. Kip had . . . well, Alex had kissed him at that party that one time, and he'd . . . um . . .

He hadn't.

Ras gave him a friendly slap on the chest. 'Trust me,' he said. 'You're gonna have a good time.' He strolled through the door, hands in his pockets, looking like he'd done this a million times.

Kip stood frozen. 'Shit,' he whispered, and hurried after.

The hallway beyond the door was nice – like, *really* nice. Little lights, big flowers, and something that smelled *awesome*. He'd seen places like this in vids and sims and stuff, but this was the real thing, and . . . and stars, he felt out of place. He could feel every stray hair on his chin, every zit on his face. He knew the clubs were a public service and all, but would anybody even *want* to have sex with him? He thought about the guy he'd seen staring back in the bathroom mirror that morning. That skinny torso. That beard that wasn't. *Nobody* would have sex with that.

Ras was already at the front desk, chatting with the receptionist. 'Two hours each for me and my buddy,' he was saying. 'Not together, I mean. We're not together.'

The receptionist looked between them, squinted, then craned his head toward the patch scanner without taking his eyes away.

Moment of truth. Ras swiped his wrist.

The scanner chirped, and the pixels in front of the receptionist rearranged themselves. His eyes moved as he read, but his face didn't change. 'And you?' the receptionist said, eyes flicking up toward Kip.

Kip felt like he might throw up. He could get in so much trouble, and he wasn't even sure he wanted to go in, but – but

Ras had done this for him, and spent all those creds, and if he just stood there and did nothing, then they'd *definitely* be in trouble. He swiped his wrist. The scanner chirped. The receptionist read, paused, and smiled.

'Okay, gentlemen,' he said. 'I've got some good news for you. Since it's your first time visiting us, we've got an extra special welcome package for you. If you'll follow me, we'll set you up with free drinks in the lounge, then send over some of our most requested hosts to take care of you this evening.'

'Ha! All right!' Ras said, grinning at Kip.

Kip managed a weak smile. Was this happening? Was this his life?

'Don't we need to fill out a survey or something, so you know who to send?' Ras asked the receptionist. 'I like ladies, and he—' He turned to Kip. 'Which way you wanna go tonight?'

'We'll take care of the preference questionnaire in the lounge,' the receptionist assured him. He stood and gestured toward a door. 'If you'll come this way?'

Ras followed the receptionist. Kip followed Ras.

The lounge was, no doubt, the coolest place Kip had ever been to. He turned this way and that as he walked, taking it all in. The ceiling was painted like a sunset – or at least, what he was pretty sure a sunset looked like. There were crazy drinks stuffed with fruit and leaves and flowers, and floating globulbs shining through the dim. There were all kinds of people in there – people alone, people together, people waiting, people headed elsewhere. There were some old people, too, which he hadn't imagined at all and thought was kind of weird, but all right, okay. At the bar, he saw a super fit dude in a too-tight shirt and perfect trousers murmuring to a lady wearing short-sleeved coveralls like they did down at the farms. The dude touched her hair. He pressed his palm against the small of her back. The woman laughed and ran her hand down the dude's chest as he whispered, down his stomach, down to – holy shit. She squeezed, and Kip tripped, running into an unseen table, rattling the flowery drinks perched on top, startling the kissing couple on the other side. 'Sorry,' he said. 'Uh – sorry.'

Ras glanced back. *What the fuck are you doing?* his face said. Kip hurried after. Cool. He was already looking stupid.

'Right here, if you would,' the receptionist said. He held out a gracious palm toward a table next to a fountain with a trio of globulbs slowly dancing above it.

'Thanks very much,' Ras said brightly, as if he went to places like this all the time. He sat. Kip joined him. The receptionist left toward the bar. Ras turned toward Kip, triumph written across his face. 'Worth. Every. Cred.' He glanced out at the room, and his mouth went slack. 'Holy *hell*,' he said, gaping at a pair of women at the bar. 'Stars, they're hot.' He elbowed Kip. 'See anybody you like?'

Kip didn't know how to answer that. He saw lots of people that yeah, he did like the look of, but the idea of having *actual sex* with any of them was making his foot tap and his mouth dry.

The receptionist came back with a drinks tray. 'Oh, nice!' Ras said, and Kip had to agree with the sentiment. The drinks were . . . what even *were* they?

'Two tropical twelves,' the receptionist said, placing a tall, thin glass in front of each of them. Kip inspected the contents – layered greens and yellows, ice spheres *that were glowing*, a rim of sparkling sugar around the top, a blue and flowery plume crowning the whole thing.

Ras raised his drink. 'Cheers, buddy.'

They clinked glasses, and sipped. 'Wow,' Kip said. Whatever was in a tropical twelve was pretty damn incredible. Kick usually tasted terrible, but there wasn't anything bitter or rough about this. Just sweet and cool. If it hadn't come from a bar, Kip would've sworn it was just juice.

Ras slapped Kip's arm. '*Finally* you look like you're enjoying yourself.' He took another sip. 'Damn, that's good. Seriously, that's the best drink I've ever had.'

The receptionist beamed. 'I'm so glad. Now, you might have a bit of a wait ahead of you. We're a little busy tonight. But we'll send over some snacks, and if you need another round or two, we'll keep them coming. Just wave at the bartender.' He turned and waved at the lady behind the bar, who did the same. She was laughing about something. A conversation they couldn't hear, Kip figured.

'Thanks very much,' Ras said. 'And no worries, we've both got free days tomorrow.'

That wasn't even remotely true. Ras had another round of shuttle licence practice, and Kip had math class. *Shit*, Kip thought. Did he have practice problems he was supposed to do? If he did, he hadn't done them. Shit.

But he looked at Ras, leaning back so chill in his chair. He looked at the receptionist, bowing his head to both of them like he was there for no other reason than to make their lives easy. He looked at the fancy drink, the fancy room. He looked at the polished people milling around, leaving in twos or occasional threes, holding hands or other things as they headed down mysterious hallways. Kip set his jaw. Okay. He could do this. He could be Kip Madaki, age 20, drinker of tropical twelves and expert at sex. He could have sex. He was *going* to have sex. Yeah. *Yeah*. He ran his hand through his hair, trying to knock it into something . . . good. 'Do I look okay?' he asked.

Ras gave him a thumbs-up and a nod. 'You look real cool.'

'You sure?'

'One hundred percent.'

They drank their drinks, ate a bowl of spicy fried peas, got more drinks, and . . . they waited. They waited and waited and waited.

'Should we go ask what's up?' Kip asked.

'Relax,' Ras said. 'He said they were busy.'

More time passed. More drinks were consumed, and more snacks, too. The novelty of the place wore off, and Kip's worries gave way to boredom. Even Ras looked unimpressed after a while.

Two women approached their table. Kip and Ras straightened up. The women passed them by for the next table over, and the boys slumped back down, returning to their drinks. A man headed toward them. They straightened up. He went elsewhere. They slumped. The pattern repeated, again and again. Straighten, slump, sip a drink. Straighten, slump, sip a drink.

The lift at the far end of the room opened, and Kip saw the woman in the farm coveralls walk out. Her hair was different. She was alone. She was smiling.

'How much longer, do you think?' Kip asked.

Ras shrugged. Kip could tell he was trying to look casual about it.

Kip swirled his glass. The ice had melted into the last sips, and the cool layers had fallen into each other and gone kinda pale. It didn't even really taste good anymore. 'Do you feel drunk?' he asked. He didn't feel drunk at all.

Ras shrugged again. 'I've got a high tolerance.'

'Do you think they forgot about us?'

'They've been bringing us drinks.'

'Yeah, but like—'

Kip felt a hand drop hard on his shoulder. He saw the same happen to Ras. They turned, and— oh no. Oh *no*.

'Fuck,' Ras groaned.

'So!' boomed Ras' dad, loud enough that half the lounge turned to look. 'You boys lookin' to get laid, huh?'

It wasn't just Ras' dad. It was his mom, and Kip's mom, and the swift, cataclysmic end of Kip's entire life.

ISABEL

'Buzz buzz,' Tamsin said, sticking her head through the open doorframe.

Isabel looked up over the cacophony of pixel displays and data tables wallpapering the air above her desk. 'What are you doing here?'

'What are *you* doing here?' Tamsin ambled in, cane in one hand, cloth bag in the other. 'Did you forget about your other home?'

What time was it? Isabel tapped the control bar on the side of her hud, bringing a clock up. She blinked. How was it twenty-half? She shut her eyes and shook her head. 'I'm so sorry, I—' She gestured wordlessly at the desk.

'I figured,' Tamsin said. She plunked the bag on the table and herself in a chair. 'That's why I brought dinner.'

Isabel peeked into the bag. A couple small storage boxes and a fork lay waiting. 'You sweetheart,' she said.

'Crispy fish, bean salad, and a slice of melon for after. It's not the best.' Tamsin leaned back and folded her arms over her belly. 'It was the Thompsons' night to cook. You know how Dek is about spices.'

'You mean, he forgets them?'

Tamsin winked. 'But, y'know. Food.' She eyed the pixels. 'I thought your minions were taking care of things while you're busy with M Tentacles.'

'Don't call her that.'

'Why? Is she here?'

140

'That's not the point.'

'You're ignoring my question.'

Isabel sighed. 'Everybody else *has* been taking care of things, but there's a question of recategorising that's come up.'

'Oh, stars,' Tamsin said knowingly. 'Uh oh.'

If you were to ask someone of another profession what archivists spent the most time fretting about, the assumption might've been restoring old corrupted files, or maintaining backup systems. But no. No, there was nothing nearer and dearer to the average archivist's heart than *categorising*, and it seemed like every standard an argument broke out over some file that belonged to too many categories, or too few, or some visitor who hadn't found what they were looking for because the tags weren't responsive or efficient or thorough enough, and nobody could get anything done until the matter of *everything being in the right place* was settled. Isabel opened her mouth, about to detail the issue – this one had to do with Earthen historical eras, which was always a thorny thing to delineate – but she took one look at Tamsin and changed her mind. Her wife's face was one of *look interested at all costs*, and she appeared to be bracing herself for an onslaught of archival minutiae. 'I'll spare you the details,' Isabel said.

Tamsin smiled. 'Big project,' she suggested.

'Big project,' Isabel confirmed.

'The kind of thing you're gonna get done in one night?'

The projected data tables stared imposingly down at Isabel. 'No,' she sighed, tucking an errant lock behind her ear. 'No, I suppose not.'

Tamsin cocked her head. 'I kinda miss you at home.'

'I'm sorry,' Isabel said. 'She'll only be here for a few more tendays, and then—'

'No, no.' Tamsin put up her hand. 'What you're doing with M— with Ghuh'loloan is good, and I know you're excited about it. And I know this kind of thing' – she pointed to the desk – 'is *your thing*, and that it's important. I care. It's good. You're doing cool stuff. But, also, I miss you.'

Isabel reached her foot beneath her desk and found one of Tamsin's. 'I miss you, too.'

Tamsin scrunched her lips so high, they nearly touched her nose. 'Wanna go do the Sunside?'

The suggestion came from out of nowhere and was the last thing Isabel expected to hear that day. She couldn't help but laugh.

'Come on,' Tamsin said with a grin. 'I'm serious. We could make the night flight if we go right now.'

'We haven't done that in ages.'

'And?'

'And I'm still working.'

'And?'

'And you just brought me dinner.'

'Psh,' Tamsin said, narrowing her eyes. 'Put it in the stasie, have it for lunch. I'll get you a stuffer on the way.' She patted the side of her jacket. 'I got a whole pocket of trade, and all you've got is weak excuses.' Her grin spread wider. Every line in her face took part.

Isabel was incredulous, but enchanted, too. The latter won out. 'All right,' she said, throwing up her hands. 'All right, let's go.'

'Ha!' Tamsin said, clapping her hands together and collecting her cane. 'I thought you'd punk out on me.' She extended her hand once she'd made it to her feet. Isabel took it without even thinking. The best kind of habit.

'Deshi,' Isabel called as they left her office. The junior archivist looked up from his desk. 'Please let everyone know I'm leaving the pre-spaceflight project until tomorrow. I'm—'

'She's being kidnapped,' Tamsin said, marching them toward the exit. 'Better call patrol.'

Deshi laughed and nodded. 'I dunno, M,' he said. 'I saw the one who did it, and she looked like bad news.'

Tamsin gave a deep, short chuckle. 'Smart man,' she said. She gave him a threatening squint worthy of any festival actor. 'Nobody likes snitches.'

Isabel rolled her eyes. 'Have a good night,' she said.

They made their way to the shuttledock as the globulbs began to dim. They made a short stop at the closest marketplace, where Tamsin made good on her word and traded a round of striped ribbon for two big pocket stuffers – toasted golden on the outside, packed with spicy shreds of red coaster meat and sweet onions. Isabel's stomach growled in anticipation as she raised it to her mouth. It was hardly a balanced meal, and had she seen any of her grandkids trying to argue the same for dinner, she'd have foisted a few vegetables on them first. But stars, it was good. The dough crunched at first bite, then bloomed into airy fluff, then gave way to the fiery centrepiece. Perfect.

She glanced over at Tamsin, who tore into her own stuffer as they walked. 'Did you not have dinner?' Isabel asked.

Tamsin swallowed. ''Course I did,' she said. 'But why should you be the only one to benefit from my good idea?' She took a large bite, *mmm*-ing appreciatively.

They continued their walk, relaying the events of the day between bites of bun until they arrived at their destination. The shuttledock stretched out before them, less crowded than in earlier hours. Beyond the entryway, a team of sanitation volunteers swept the floor, gaining nods and *thank you*s and short bursts of applause from the few passersby.

'Hi there.' A dock attendant appeared – a young teen, probably new to the job. He was short and well-groomed, and his polite alertness made it apparent that he took his role seriously. 'Can I help you find any particular vessel?'

'Have we missed the Sunside?' Tamsin asked.

The kid looked surprised, but recovered quickly. 'Let me check, M.' His eyes darted and blinked with practised purpose as he accessed information on his hud. 'You've still got time. Leaves in ten minutes.' He looked between the two old women before him, a slight anxiety creeping in. 'Have you done the Sunside before?'

Tamsin *tsked*. 'Kid, I was there for the *first* Sunside.' She smiled wickedly. 'And that was before they put in seatbelts.'

That last detail wasn't a bit true, but Isabel didn't dare call her out. The look on the kid's face was too hilarious. She leaned in. 'Is it still dock thirty-seven?'

The attendant gave a smart nod. 'Dock thirty-seven, yes, M.' He pointed the way with a flat, business-like hand. Isabel could feel him watching them leave with the air of someone who'd had their sense of balance thrown slightly askew. She couldn't help but smirk. Tamsin had always had a flair for ruffling strangers.

Dock thirty-seven was empty, save for the skiff waiting at the ready and a young woman leaning against the safety rail outside, playing a pixel game on her scrib. She was the pilot, as the multiple certification patches stitched onto her jacket indicated, and her uniformed appearance was every bit that of her profession, from her practical bamboo-fibre slacks to the resource-heavy boots that had probably belonged to another pair of feet first. But there were other details that would've been out of place on a pilot back when Isabel had been her age. The hypnotically shifting bot tattoos that danced up and down her forearms, for one. The thick Aandrisk-style swirls painted on her nails. The tiny glittering tech ports embedded near her temples, whose purpose Isabel could only guess at. She was an Exodan pilot, yes. But also . . . more.

The pilot glanced up as Isabel and Tamsin approached. 'Hey, M Itoh and M Itoh!' she said. 'How's it going?'

Isabel didn't know the girl well, but she knew her name, that she was from neighbourhood five, and that she sometimes came into the Archives to look at records of old Earth architecture. Isabel had done the naming ceremony for her niece earlier that standard. 'Hello, Kiku,' she said warmly. 'Are you our pilot this evening?'

Kiku looked delighted. 'You two here for the Sunside?'

'It appears that way,' Isabel said, throwing a look in Tamsin's direction.

Tamsin looked around the empty walkway. 'Do we have it to ourselves?' she asked, pleased with the possibility.

Kiku switched off her game, and the pixels scattered away. 'Not many folks go for a night flight on a work night,' she said, holstering her scrib and stepping toward the shuttle door. 'Just kids on dates, mostly.' She winked at them, and politely gestured toward the door. 'Come on in.'

The shuttle had six pairs of passenger seats in a straight line, and a clear, domed roof that began at seat level and arched all the way around. Walking through the door, you could tell the roof was as thick and sturdy as any bulkhead, but sitting next to it, you'd never know it was there.

'Anywhere you'd like,' Kiku said.

'What about that one?' Tamsin pointed at the pilot seat, serious as could be.

Kiku played right along. 'Can't have that one,' she said without cracking a smile.

'You sure?'

'Super sure.'

'*Tsk,*' Tamsin said, shaking her head. 'Well, this was a bust.' She started to head back toward the door, then chuckled, scrunched her nose at Kiku, and picked the second row behind the pilot's seat. Far enough to not be crowding the pilot, but close enough to give her a hard time.

Kiku started her prep, and Isabel took the seat beside her wife. Tamsin leaned over, speaking in a low whisper. 'Y'know, if she's used to kids on dates, I bet she won't mind if we make out.'

Isabel smothered a laugh and slapped Tamsin's leg. 'We'd traumatise the poor kid.'

'What? No. We're gorgeous.' Her eyes narrowed in thought. 'Didn't we make out on the Sunside once?'

A very old memory dusted itself off: a pair of women, younger than their pilot was now, drunk on bartered kick and eyes full of nothing but the other, cosied up in the back row of a shuttle as if no one else was there. 'That was the ferry, not the Sunside,' Isabel said.

'You sure?'

'I'm sure.'

'Okay. You're the archivist.'

Isabel leaned a little closer. 'How would you make out on the Sunside anyway? You'd knock your teeth in.'

Her wife snorted. 'But if you didn't, you'd be a legend. I'm surprised that's not a thing.'

'What? Go to town as long as you can without needing medical attention?'

'Yeah,' Tamsin laughed heartily. 'The Sunside challenge.'

The sounds of conspiratorial merriment made Kiku look back. 'You two gonna be trouble?'

Tamsin sat up straight and folded her hands across her lap. 'No way, M,' she said, like a school kid caught with cheat codes. 'No trouble here.'

'Mmm-hmm,' the pilot said, returning to her switches and buttons.

Isabel reached over and held Tamsin's hand. 'No trouble from me, anyway,' she said.

'Traitor,' Tamsin said. She gave her fingers an affectionate squeeze.

Kiku slipped on a navigation hud. 'Oh,' Isabel said. She reached up to her face, remembering that she'd been wearing her own hud since work. She removed it, and gave Tamsin a facetious glare as she slipped the device into a pocket. 'How long were you going to let me run around wearing this?'

Tamsin shrugged. 'Until now, I guess.'

The engines outside whirred, their ion jets starting to glow. 'All right,' the pilot said. 'Everybody ready?' She paused. 'I assume you two don't need the safety lecture, yeah?'

Tamsin tugged on her fastened seat restraint in response. 'Sit down, strap in, hang on.'

'And let the pilot do her job,' Isabel added.

Kiku pointed a finger back toward Isabel as she began to pull out from dock. 'I like that bit,' she said. 'I'm adding that bit.' She switched and pressed and made adjustments. 'You two want grav or nah?'

Isabel raised her eyebrows. 'You're allowed to switch it off?'

Kiku gave a mischievous shrug. 'Not officially.'

'We'll stick with grav,' Tamsin said. 'I like to feel like I'm actually upside down.'

'You got it,' Kiku said. She leaned into the vox. 'Sunside One, requesting a spot in line.'

'Granted, Sunside One,' the traffic controller replied. 'Have fun.'

The skiff pulled out and headed for the nearest airlock exit. A queue of private shuttles and long-haul transports each waited their turn. 'It'll be about half an hour until we reach the course,' Kiku said, easing into the queue. 'So just kick back and relax.' She took a hand away from the controls and dug around in a storage box strapped to the side of her seat. 'Either of you like salt toffee?'

Tamsin and Isabel spoke in tandem: '*Yes.*' Kiku grinned, retrieved a tin, and gestured at her controls. A cleanerbot deployed itself from its dock in the corner of the craft, its tiny stabiliser jets firing friendly green. It hummed over to Kiku, who balanced the tin on its flat housing. 'Second row,' she commanded, and the bot complied, uncaring of the extra cargo.

'Now that's a creative use for a cleanerbot,' Tamsin said, retrieving the tin from the idling machine.

'Works, yeah?' Kiku said.

'Sure does.' Tamsin looked at Isabel as she opened the tin. 'I'm never getting up to fetch you something ever again.'

The queue moved forward without much wait, and the skiff entered the airlock. One gate slid shut behind them, another opened ahead. Metal made way for space and starlight. Tamsin held her hand a little tighter, and Isabel didn't need to look at her to know she was smiling. She shared the feeling. The open was always beautiful.

And so they made their way to that old classic: the Sunside Joyride. A break-neck, full-throttle, sun-facing jaunt through whichever designated patch of rock the Fleet was orbiting closest to. A just-for-fun extravagance unveiled after GC citizenship expanded trade routes, and maintained by private donations after it became obvious that resources weren't as freely flowing as hoped. The courses were safe, obviously. They were mapped out well in advance, and every rock was equipped with proximity alarms and *backup* proximity alarms and stabilisation thrusters that kept them from straying into the track. The pilots were exhaustively trained, and traffic control back home watched their every move on the tracking map. But none of that changed the way it felt to be strapped into a small craft, looping and leaping in three dimensions, the clear wall around you playing the convincing trick that there was nothing between you and open sky. Some people hated it. Some people tried it once and decided they preferred keeping their lunch down.

Some people were no fun.

'What course are we hitting tonight?' Isabel asked.

'The Ten-Drop Twister,' Kiku said.

Tamsin looked at Isabel. 'I don't remember that one.'

'It's new,' Kiku said. 'Replaced the Devil Dive.'

'Aw, really? That one was *great*.'

The pilot nodded with sympathetic agreement. 'Yeah, but they found tungsten in that one.'

'Hard to argue that,' said Tamsin.

'Don't worry,' Kiku said. She put on a pair of pilot's gloves, the kind you only wore for manual control. Isabel's heart raced with anticipation. 'The Ten-Drop's a real kick in the pants. You won't be disappointed.'

The skiff pulled up to an asteroid patch, filled with tell-tale lights and markers. A big circle of light buoys wreathed the entrance point, blinking in an assortment of colours. Kiku activated her hud. The engines burned loud and hot. 'You two strapped in?'

Isabel tugged on her restraints, and her wife did the same. This had scared Tamsin the first time, Isabel remembered. She remembered a row of painful semi-circles embedded in her palm, where Tamsin had gripped tightly in fear. She remembered rubbing her then-girlfriend's back as she threw up on the dock the second they left the skiff. And she remembered the next day, when she awoke to find Tamsin's open eyes looking back from the pillow beside her, a who-cares grin in her voice as she asked Isabel if she wanted to go again.

Isabel had. From then on, if Tamsin was there, she'd be right alongside.

The engines roared, and the skiff ripped forward. 'Ohhhhhh nooooo!' Tamsin yelled, the last vowels blooming into a cackling yelp. Isabel yelled too, a screaming, living laugh as their skiff ducked and slid and jived.

'Faster!' Tamsin called.

'Faster!' Isabel echoed.

From behind, Isabel could see Kiku's cheeks pull into a huge smile. 'You got it,' she said, and they went faster, louder, upside down and circling sharp. Giant rocks floated beyond the windowed walls, looming one moment, then behind them in a blink. Stars flew by in a confettied blur. Tamsin was laughing so hard she was crying, and it was impossible not to laugh along. Isabel could feel nothing but motion, joy, heartbeat. It was as good as it'd been the first time, as good as it had always been. She shut her eyes, and she cheered.

EYAS

A canyon rose up around her, arches crumbling and rocks stained red. The sky was so far away, a swath of intangible blue beyond the grass-tufted clifftops. Below, birds nested in whatever cracks and crevices they could find. They darted around the shady space with breathtaking speed, turning to catch beakfuls of the insects that filled the hot air.

Presumably hot air, that is. The theatre did not include sensory input beyond sound and sight. This wasn't a sim. The theatre pre-dated that technology – or, to put it more accurately, pre-dated contact with species willing to share that technology. Every Exodan district had a theatre, and they still used the same anti-quated tech, patched up a thousand times over, and the same recordings, taken by Eyas' ancestors' ancestors when it became clear that collapse was unavoidable. It was an old tradition, viewing the last scraps of a living Earth. There had been a time when going to the theatre was something you did every tenday – every *week*, then – or more. Every day, for some. You and your hexmates put on comfortable clothes, you brought some floor pillows, and you sat alongside other families on the floor beneath the projector dome, surrounded by all-encompassing images of a canyon, a beach, a forest. It was time made for reflection, for reminding. People laughed, sometimes, or wept, or sang quietly, or had whispered conversations. Anything beyond that was frowned upon. The theatre was a sacred place. A quiet place, even when any given day found it packed from end to end.

Eyas had never seen a theatre that crowded. The need to

acquaint oneself with what a planet looked like had faded more with each generation after the real thing had been found. She'd never seen more than ten people in a theatre at once, and not all the theatres were in use anymore. They weren't a vital system, and they didn't get resource priority unless the surrounding district voted otherwise. Hers always had. Eyas sympathised with people who wanted their stores to go to more practical uses, but she was glad the majority of her neighbours shared her view that practicality became dreary if you didn't balance it out properly.

Her primary reasoning for loving the theatre was selfish, and she knew it. She could've cited tradition and culture – and no one would've questioned her, given that her work embodied said same – but no, Eyas was glad to have a functional theatre nearby because it was one of the few places she could just *think*. Her work might've seemed quiet to some, but there were always families involved, and supervisory meetings like everyone else had. And even on the days when her only company was someone dead, she was focused on the task at hand. As for home – home was a place of rest, sure, but more chiefly distraction. Chores to do, friends to chat with, conversations leaking through closed doors. There weren't many places in the Flect you could be alone. While she very much enjoyed being around the living, sometimes her own thoughts were noise enough. The theatre wasn't private. It was as public as could be. But it was a different kind of public, the kind of place where you could be alone around others.

She lay down on the floor, resting her head against the cushion she'd brought from home. The ghost of a wind rustled the scrappy canyon plantlife, and she imagined she could feel it coasting over her skin. She had no strong yearnings for wind and sky, but they were fun to think of anyway. Imagine: the intense vulnerability of an unshielded space. The wild chaos of atmosphere. Such thoughts were soothing and thrilling in equal measure.

Eyas folded her hands over her stomach, letting them rise and fall with each breath. She let her mind drift. She thought about the laundry she needed to do at home. She thought about her mother, and knew she should summon the fortitude to visit her one day soon. She thought about Sunny, and a hidden place inside her kicked with remembrance. She thought about dinner, and her empty stomach growled. She thought about work the next day, and she felt . . . she felt . . . she wasn't sure.

She shifted her weight, the floor now less comfortable than it had been a few breaths before. There it was again – that tiredness, that nameless tiredness. It wasn't lack of sleep, or overwork, or because anything was wrong. Nothing was wrong. She was healthy. She had a good home with good friends, and a full belly when she remembered to feed it. She had the profession she'd wanted since she was a little girl, and it was a valuable thing, a meaningful thing, a thing she believed in with all her heart. She'd worked hard for that. She had the life she'd always wanted, the life she'd set out to build.

Maybe . . . maybe that was the problem. So many years of training and study, always striving, always chasing the ideal at the end of the road. She'd reached that end by now. She had everything she'd set out to do. So now . . . what? What came next? Maintaining things as-is? Do well, be consistent, keep things up for however long she had?

She pressed her back into the metal floor, and felt the faint, faint purr of mechanical systems working below. She thought of the *Asteria*, orbiting endlessly with its siblings around an alien sun, around and around and around. Holding steady. Searching no more. How long would it stay like that? Until the last ship finally failed? Until the last Exodan left for rocky ground? Until the sun went nova? Was there any future for the Fleet that did not involve keeping to the same pattern, the same track, day after day after day until something went wrong? Was there any day for *her* that would not involve the same schedule, the same faces, the same tasks? What was better – a constant safeness that never grew and never changed, or a life of reaching, building, striving, even though you knew you'd never be completely satisfied?

A bang broke the stillness, startling everyone present. The

canyon gave a seizing shake, froze, and went dark. The audience collectively held their breath. Someone turned on a handlight and ran around the theatre's edge.

'Sorry, folks,' the theatre attendant called out, to a chorus of disappointment (but also, relief). 'Looks like we've bust a projector. I'll get the techs up here right now.'

Eyas got to her feet and picked up her pillow, knowing maintenance had a thousand more important things to fix *right now*. Besides, her stomach was growling louder. She'd never solve anything hungry.

KIP

This was, hands down, the worst night of Kip's life.

He sat in the living room, opposite his parents at the low table. Grandma Ko was doing whatever in the background. Messing with plants. He didn't care.

'We're not mad, Kip,' Dad said.

'I'm mad,' Mom said. She stirred a steaming mug of tea.

'Okay, your mom's mad. I think it'd be a good idea—'

'No, wait, he needs to understand why he's in trouble.' She set down her spoon. 'It's not because you went to a club. It's really important that you understand that.'

'That's right.' Dad did that dorky pointing thing with his index finger that he always did when he thought he was saying something smart. 'We're not mad because you wanted to have sex.'

Kip would've given anything in that moment – anything – for an oxygen leak, a stray satellite, a wormhole punched in the wrong place. Anything that would swallow him up and bring a merciful end to this conversation.

But instead, Mom *kept talking*. 'That part's okay. That's normal.'

'Absolutely,' Dad said. 'I remember what it was like to have all those hormones going around, all those urges – I couldn't stay out of the clubs when I turned twenty.'

'Me neither,' Mom said. 'Twice a day, sometimes.'

Kip buried his face in his hands. 'Can we . . . maybe . . . not?'

Grandma Ko looked over from her plants and laughed. 'It's not like you and your friends invented sex, kiddo,' she said. She pointed back and forth between his parents with her gardening clippers. 'You wouldn't be here otherwise.'

A rogue comet. A Rosk battlecruiser. A face-eating alien plague. *Anything.*

'The reason you're in trouble,' Dad said, 'is because you lied and you broke the rules.'

'He broke the *law*, Alton,' Mom said. 'Not just Fleet law. GC law.' She looked at Kip with that look that meant the next tenday or so was really going to suck. He could already picture the lengthy list of chores that was going to appear on his scrib after this. 'The only reason you're talking with us and not a patroller right now is because that host at the club cut you and Ras a break. Tampering with your patch is not a joke, Kip.'

'I know,' Kip mumbled. The faster he agreed with them, the faster this might be over.

'That hack you boys used could've uploaded *anything*. It could've carried a virus that messed with your bots. You know that's what happened to those people on the *Newet*, right?'

'I know, Mom.'

'One person went to an unlicensed mod vendor, and the next thing you know—'

'My patch is fine,' Kip said. 'You made me scan it, like, five times.'

'That's not the point,' Mom said. 'The point is, you did something illegal and dangerous. You got *lucky*.'

'Not in the way he was hoping,' Grandma Ko laughed.

'Grandma,' Mom said. 'Please.'

Grandma Ko put up her hands in surrender and kept working.

'*Tika lu*, okay?' Kip said.

The look on Mom's face somehow got even frostier. 'In Ensk.'

Oh, stars, was she really going to get on his ass about *that*? Fine. Fine, whatever it took to get him out of there. 'I'm sorry. All right? I don't know how many times you want me to say *I'm sorry*.'

'We know you're sorry,' Dad said, 'and we also know you want to get out of here. But you need to know the score, son.'

'I get it,' Kip sighed. 'I do, okay? I get it.'

Mom tapped her fingers against her mug. 'When do you start your next job trial?'

Ah, shit, Kip thought. He mumbled a response under his breath.

'What was that?'

'I haven't signed up for one yet.'

The look on Mom's face got worse. Kip could see three more to-dos being added to his list. 'You were supposed to sign up for another before your last one ended,' she said.

'I forgot.'

'Kip, we talked about this,' Dad said.

'Okay, so, first thing tomorrow, you're signing up for a job trial,' Mom said. 'And until it starts, you come straight home after school so you can help your hex. No sims, no cafes, no hanging out wherever it is you hang out. There are a lot of projects in the neighbourhood that need some extra hands right now.'

Kip reeled. 'But I probably won't start another trial for a tenday.'

'Yep,' Mom said.

No way. *No way.* 'That's not fair!'

'You're home instead of in detention. You don't get to complain about *fair* right now.'

Dad put his hands flat on the table. 'All we're asking is for you to clear your head and get focused,' he said, his voice irritatingly mellow. He often did this thing where he wanted to sound all reasonable and cool even though he was just agreeing with Mom. It drove Kip nuts.

He tried to negotiate. 'Ras and I are going to the waterball game on second day. We have plans.'

Mom's mouth tightened. 'We think a break from Ras might be a good idea, too.'

That did it. Kip exploded. 'This wasn't his fault!' he said. It was totally Ras' fault, but that wasn't the point. 'Stars, you guys are *always* hating on him.'

'I don't hate Ras,' Mom said. 'I'm just not sure he's—' She looked up at the ceiling, thinking. 'It'd be wise for you both to take some time to think about the kinds of choices you've been making.'

'This is bullshit,' Kip muttered.

'Hey,' Dad said.

'No, it is,' Kip said, getting louder. 'It *is* bullshit. Look, I'm sorry I messed up tonight, but the only – the only reason I went along – the only reason we went there is because *there's nothing to do*. It sucks here. What am I supposed to do? Go to school, do chores, learn how to do a job that's basically more chores?'

'Kip—'

'And now you don't even want me to have *friends*.'

'Oh, come on, Kip.' Mom rolled her eyes.

'Of course we want you to have friends,' Dad said. 'We just want you to have friends that bring out the best in you.'

'You guys don't understand,' Kip said. 'You don't understand at all.' He pushed away from the table and walked off.

'Hey, we're not done,' Mom said.

'*I'm* done,' Kip said. He went into his room and punched the door switch behind him.

'Kip,' Dad called through the metal wall.

Kip ignored him. Stars, fuck this place. Fuck these stupid rules and stupid jobs and fuck being sixteen. He was getting *out*. The day – no, the *second*, the very second the clock hit his twentieth birthday, he was hopping on a transport, and he'd be *gone*, university or not. He'd find a job somewhere. He didn't care where or what. Anything was better than this. Anything was better than Mom's lists and Dad's stupid voice. Anything was better than here.

Behind his door, he could hear them still talking. Kip knew listening in would only make him madder, but he put his ear up anyway.

'Maybe I should go talk to him,' Dad said. 'Y'know, just me and him.'

'He doesn't want to talk to either of us,' Mom said. 'Or were you not here for this conversation?'

'But—'

'Let him be,' Grandma Ko said.

Mom sighed. 'He's so impossible right now.'

'Yes, well,' Grandma Ko said. 'You were a dipshit at that age, too.'

Kip snorted. 'Love you too, Grandma,' he grumbled. He flopped down onto his bed and buried his face in his pillow, wishing he could erase the entire day. *Dammit, Ras*, he thought, but he wasn't mad at him. Well . . . kind of. But not, like, a forever kind of mad. He knew Ras hadn't meant for it to go wrong.

He rolled over onto his side and groaned. Seriously. Zero hour on day 23, standard 310. Once that hit, he was *out*.

SAWYER

'Nervous?' Oates asked as they headed down the walkway.

Sawyer gave a sheepish smile. 'It's a job interview. Have you ever *not* been nervous at one?'

Oates chuckled and clapped Sawyer's shoulder with his mech hand. 'Don't worry. The boss is gonna love you. I mean, unless she hates you.' He winked. 'She'll tell it to you straight if she does.'

They continued along. Ships of varied size coasted slowly by. The shuttledock was a complicated stack of layers and levels, all built over a century prior, once Exodans found themselves with *other places to go*. Sawyer felt as if he were standing in the middle of the sea, watching creatures migrate past – little lively ones, modest middling beasts, and ponderous behemoths everything else made way for. He remembered his mom taking him to the planetside docks on Mushtullo, making up stories about where each ship had gone and was going. The memory came with a familiar sting, but it was a hurt he'd long ago learned to shelve.

Oates led him to a dock designated for mid-size ships – merchant vessels and small cargo, mostly. They walked past thick bulkheads, slim atmospheric fins, hand-hacked tech upgrades, every design as different as the last. Sawyer eyed the names with enjoyment. *Out of the Open. Take-A-Chance. Good Friend. Quick and Easy. The Better Side of Valour.*

'Here we are.' Oates gestured Sawyer ahead. 'Home sweet home.'

Sawyer looked up at a nondescript freighter – dull grey plating, big engine, somewhat rough around the edges. It wasn't as flashy or added-to as some. It didn't stand out. But to Sawyer, that was a good thing. Flashy tech would've been intimidating, and too much of a penchant for modding would've worried him. This ship appeared solid, functional, and looked-after. All you wanted in a spacecraft, really.

He spotted the ship's registry info, printed by the open entry hatch.

THE SILVER LINING
Registration No. 33-1246
Asteria, Exodus Fleet

'Do you live on this ship?' Sawyer asked.

'Pretty much,' Oates said. He walked through the hatch; Sawyer followed. 'I see my folks when we're docked, but it's easier to keep all your stuff in one place, y'know? Nyx, though – that's our pilot – she splits her time between this home and a home-home. Her ex's hex. They hate each other, but they've got a kid, so. Y'know. You don't have kids, right?'

'Uh, no,' Sawyer said. He ducked, avoiding a low string of festival flags stretched across a doorway. The internal structure of the *Silver Lining* was as standard as the outside suggested, but it was crammed to the gills with crates, boxes, and barrels, sealed and stamped with the same multilingual export permits you'd find on any goods that had to cross a territory or two. On top of that, this ship was unmistakably a home, with all the weird decor and knick-knacks that implied. There were pixel posters of musical acts he'd never heard of, globulb strands wrapped around doorways, failing herbs planted in old snack tins and struggling up toward a grow lamp. It wasn't a mess, exactly, but it was a *lot*. 'What do you guys trade in?'

'Oh, a little of this, a little of that. We're not picky. If it'll fetch good creds, we'll haul it.' He rounded a corner, and ran smack into the tallest, burliest woman Sawyer had ever seen.

Whoa, Sawyer thought. Was this the boss? Was *this* who he'd have to impress?

'Whoops!' Oates said with a laugh. 'Sorry about that, Dory.'

Dory squinted wordlessly at him with her one organic eye. The plex lens in the other audibly clicked into focus. Her head was only about a hand's length away from the ceiling, and her broad arms looked as though they resented what short amount of sleeve they'd had to push themselves through. Sawyer waited for her to smile, to offer her own cheerful apology, to do *something* resembling friendly Human behaviour. But no, instead, she moved her eye – and only her eye – to Sawyer. The squint evolved into a full frown.

'This is Sawyer,' Oates said. 'He's here about our empty spot. Sawyer, this is Dory. She's terrifying.'

Dory let out . . . not so much a laugh, but a short chuff. And that was it. She pushed past them and continued on her way.

'A real bundle of sunshine,' Oates said. 'Come on, let's find some better company.' He went a short way further, and they entered a kitchen. Three people were present there, two in conversation across a table. A clean-shaven man leaned against a storage cabinet, eating a large jam cake. He, too, was broad and muscled, but something about his stature – or maybe the sticky pastry he held – made him look far more approachable than his one-eyed crewmate. He nodded congenially at Oates, then continued to watch as the other two spoke.

'You said nine hundred last time,' one said in a testy tone. She was around Sawyer's age – twenty, tops, he guessed.

The other was at least twice that, and cool as rain in her reply. 'Last time, you brought me better merchandise. Nine hundred is what you get for quality. Not for this.' She gestured dismissively at an opened box on the table between them.

Sawyer no longer wondered who was in charge here.

'That's not *fair*,' the girl said. 'We made a *deal*.'

'Yes, and you're the one who isn't delivering, Una, not me. You can either take three hundred a pop now, or come back with something better. Or find another buyer, if you really feel you're being treated unfairly.' Her eyes flicked over to Sawyer and Oates. 'My next meeting is here, so I'll let you settle this with Len.' She gestured to the cake-eating man. 'He'll let me know your decision.'

The man – Len, apparently – folded the last of his pastry into his mouth, brushed the crumbs from his hands with a neat *one-two*, and stepped forward to escort the young woman elsewhere. The woman sulked, but she grabbed her box of . . . whatever it was, and followed.

The boss put her hands on her hips and sighed at Sawyer with the sort of knowing smile he might expect if they'd already met. 'Business,' she said. She waved him over. 'You must be Sawyer.'

Sawyer approached the table. 'And you must be the boss.'

She laughed – a rich, honest sound. 'Muriel,' she said. She looked to Oates. 'I like this one already.' She made a short tipping gesture toward her mouth as a means of request. Oates went about fetching some mugs. 'I have to say, it's a trip hearing that accent on this side of the galaxy. Central space, Oates said?'

'That's right.' Sawyer took a seat. 'Mushtullo.'

'I haven't been myself, but I have a friend who's done business there. A bit rough, is what I heard.'

The words came across as a question. 'A bit,' Sawyer answered.

Muriel leaned back in her chair. 'So. You're here after Livia's job.'

Sawyer was confused. 'Sorry, I don't—'

Oates leaned over from the counter, where he was pouring water from a kettle. 'I don't think I mentioned Livia.'

'Ah,' Muriel said. 'Livia was – let me back up. How much has Oates already told you about this job?'

'I know it's a salvage job,' Sawyer said. 'Recovering scrap, that kind of thing.'

Muriel gave a thoughtful nod. Despite her friendly demeanor, Sawyer couldn't help but feel that every word that left his mouth was being weighed, measured, and scored. 'Exactly,' she said. 'And the trick with wrecked ships is, sometimes both they and their cargo pose challenges that require a bit of code.' She turned her palm to Sawyer, silently adding: *and that's why you're here.*

Oates handed both her and Sawyer a mug overflowing with spicy steam. 'Thanks,' Sawyer said, setting it down before his fingers scalded. 'What kind of challenges?'

'Let's say . . .' Muriel considered. 'Let's say we're talking about a cargo ship. Medical supplies, going from here to there. Now, any merchant worth xyr salt is gonna have xyr crates locked up, and xe's not going to hand over the key code until creds are exchanged. But our poor merchant met the mean side of an asteroid patch, and now xe and xyr crew are dead, and nobody knows the cargo key.'

'Ah.' Sawyer got it. 'You need somebody who can open doors so the rest of you can do your job.'

'Bingo. Because otherwise, nobody can get those goods to where they were going.'

'I see.' This sounded like kind of a cool job, now that Sawyer thought about it. Opening doors, salvaging goods, making sure nothing went to waste. Nothing went to waste in the Fleet.

'So Livia.' Muriel's eyes rolled. 'She did stupid during our last planet stop.' She waved her hand. 'Not worth getting into. Kick and poor decisions. Anyway, her dumb ass is now in an Aandrisk jail, and I'm stuck here without a comp tech.' She sighed at Oates.

'I hear Aandrisk jails are nice,' Oates said over the rim of his mug. 'Y'know, far as jails go.'

'She doesn't deserve it,' Muriel said dryly.

A flicker of concern shot through Sawyer. 'Just to be totally up front,' he said, 'I'm not a comp tech. I'm not certified or anything, and I don't have a ton of experience. I just know mid-level Tinker.'

'So Oates told me,' Muriel said. 'Though I appreciate your honesty. Certifications don't concern me. What I care about is skill, and a willingness to learn. You have a scrib on you?'

Sawyer reached for his holster. 'Yeah.'

Muriel reached elsewhere, and came back with a lockbox. 'Think you could get this open?' She slid the box across the table.

Sawyer picked up the box and wet his lips. 'I've never done locks before.'

'What have you done?'

'Input pads, gesture relays, that kind of thing.'

Muriel looked less than impressed, but she shrugged and tossed over a tethering cable. 'Hook it up, take a look. And take your time thinking about it.' She blew over the top of her tea. 'I'm in no rush.'

You can do this, Sawyer thought. He connected scrib to cable and cable to lock jack. He gestured at his scrib, and a flurry of code appeared. *All right*, he thought. He spoke this language. He understood these puzzles. *If, then.* He scrolled through, minutes ticking by. Every second that passed pressed down on his neck. He could feel Muriel watching him as she sipped her cooling tea. He wondered if this was part of the test, too, if he was taking too long, if the bit of sweat forming on his brow was giving her second thoughts. But all he could do was his best. He'd been honest with her. He had to expect the same. She said take time to think about it, so he did. It was, in a way, not too different than his trips to the commerce square back home, demonstrating his skills for judgey Harmagians, impressing by doing rather than writing the right words. Only, this was so much better. This wasn't a judgey Harmagian watching him work. This was a cool lady and a nice guy who were as Human as he was and didn't hold it against him. These were people who wanted him to succeed. His nerve steadied as he realised that, and, at last, words and strings began to reveal themselves to him.

Sawyer pieced the logic together. He tweaked here, added there. The box stayed shut.

He glanced up. Muriel was nearly through her mug of tea. *Shit.*

He grit his teeth, and he wrote, and he read, and he wrote some more, and—

There was a sound – a dull click. It wasn't much of a sound, but to Sawyer, it was sweet victory. He pulled the lid open and swung its empty inside around to Muriel.

The boss nodded with a quiet smile. 'Found him outside the job office?' she said to Oates.

Oates gave a happy shrug. 'It's a talent, what can I say.'

'I don't pay you enough.'

'I know.'

Muriel studied Sawyer. 'I'd want you to do that faster. But now that you've done it once, you have a better idea of what to do next time, right?'

'Right. I can practise before the job, no problem. I mean . . . if I got the job.'

Muriel smirked. 'Let's talk about the job. We're heading to the *Oxomoco*.'

'Wow,' Sawyer said. 'Okay. Wow.'

Muriel leaned forward and rested her chin on her laced fingers. 'What does that mean to you?'

'Well . . . jeez, everybody heard about that. What happened to it, I mean. That was a huge thing. And horrible. Really horrible.' He processed this new info. 'Must be a ton of scrap that needs sorting, huh?'

The captain considered him in silence. Something satisfied her, and she sat back up. 'It's a trial run, you understand. Right now, all you and I have is one gig we're going to work together. If either of us is unhappy with how it goes, we walk away, no hard feelings, and no further obligations. But if it goes well . . .' She made a *let's see* motion with an opened palm. 'I do have an empty set of quarters open to the right person.'

Sawyer wasn't sure when he'd last felt so determined. He was the right person for this, he knew it. He was going to rock this job. He was going to give it one hundred percent. One hundred and *ten*.

A part of him, though, was hesitant. This wasn't what he'd imagined. He'd imagined a hex, an address in the Fleet. But then again . . . A warm thought cut through the caution. This was the Fleet, too. He'd read the Litany they recited at ceremonies. *We are the homesteaders*, yes, but also: *We are the ships that ferry between.* Well, here he was, on a ship, ready to do some spacer recycling. That sounded pretty Exodan to him.

Muriel reached her hand across the table. 'We got a deal?'

Sawyer took her hand and shook it firmly. 'We got a deal.'

. . . .

Part 3

TO THIS DAY,
WE WANDER STILL

Feed source: Reskit Institute of Interstellar Migration (Public News Feed)
Item name: The Modern Exodus – Entry #6
Author: Ghuh'loloan Mok Chutp
Encryption: 0
Translation path: [Hanto:Kliptorigan]
Transcription: 0
Node identifier: 2310-483-38, Isabel Itoh

[System message: The feed you have selected has been translated from written Hanto. As you may be aware, written Hanto includes gestural notations that do not have analogous symbols in any other GC language. Therefore, your scrib's on-board translation software has not translated the following material directly. The content here is a modified translation, intended to be accessible to the average Kliptorigan reader.]

––––

It is without question that there are many ways in which Exodans have benefited from GC influence. Imubots, artigrav, algae fuel, tunnel access – and of course, mek, which Exodans drink in quantities on par with the rest of the galaxy. But cultural exchange is never without its disruptions, and while the elder Exodan generation frowns over the younger's preference for Klip and penchant for Harmagian charthump (why that genre of music in particular, I can't say), I submit that there is one introduced factor more divisive than any other: the Galactic Commons Commerce Credit.

To understand the conundrum created by the humble cred, you must first understand how Exodans manage labour and resources – and indeed, how they have done so for centuries. To begin, the basics: if you are physically present within the Exodus Fleet, you receive lodgings, food, air, and water. You have access to all public services, and you are granted the same sapient rights as any. No exceptions, no questions asked. There are limits to how much an individual can receive, of course – finite stores within a closed system can only be stretched so far. But Exodan life support capacity has been greatly expanded by the upgrades they've implemented over the standards (again, thanks to GC tech), and they take careful count of each person who enters the majestic homesteader shuttledocks. Were Fleet systems or supplies to become taxed, all but citizens would be systematically deported. This has yet to become an issue. In fact, if anything, the decrease in Exodan population since their admission into the GC has made the Fleet more capable of welcoming others.

You may be wondering, dear guest, as I did, how labour is compensated if your base needs are met. This is the part that's hard for many – non-Exodan Humans included – to understand: it's not. Nor do some professions receive more resources than others, or finer housing, or any such tangible benefits. You become a doctor because you want to help people. You become a pilot because you want to fly. You become a farmer because you want to work with growing things, or because you want to feed others. To an Exodan, the question of choosing a profession is not one of *what do I need?* but rather *what am I good at? What good can I do?*

Of course, some professions are more glamorous than others – a pilot, it's safe to argue, has more dynamic days than a formwork clerk – but this ultimately comes down to personal preference. Not everyone *wants* a busy, exciting profession that requires long hours and specialised training. Many are content to do something simple that fulfils the desire to be useful but also allows them plenty of opportunity to spend time with their families and hobbies. This is why professions that *do* require rigorous schooling – or pose inherent risk, either physically or emotionally – are so highly respected within Exodan society. I witness this often in the company of my dear host, Isabel, who receives gifts and deference wherever she goes (you may be wondering how *gifts* work in a society with no native currency; I will come to that). I have seen this behaviour as well with caretakers, miners, and council members. This is not to say that other professions are unvalued – far from it. There is no such thing as a meaningless job in the Fleet. Everything has a purpose, a recognisable benefit. If you have food on your plate, you thank a farmer. If you have clothing, you thank a textile manufacturer. If you have murals to brighten your day, you thank an artist. Even the most menial of tasks benefits someone, benefits *all*.

Perhaps it is their very lack of planetary scale that makes this kind of inclusive thinking possible. Societal machinations and environmental stability are not abstract concepts for the Exodans. They are an immediate, visceral reality. This is why it is rare for able adults to eschew a profession entirely (though this does happen, to considerable scorn), and why youths are under intense scrutiny from their elders as to which line of work they will apprentice in. A job is partly a matter of personal fulfilment, yes, but also – and perhaps chiefly – *social* fulfilment. When an Exodan asks 'what do you do?', the real question is: 'What do you do *for us*?'

This is not a wholly communal society, however. The concept of personal belongings (and living space) still exists, and is quite important. A canister of dried beans, for example, is a public resource, until said canister is allotted to a family. The family trades nothing for this item, as access to it is their right as citizens. But once the canister crosses from storeroom to home, it now belongs to the family in question, and another family taking it would be a punishable act of theft (not to mention unnecessary, as the thieves would have their own beans to start with). Let's now imagine that a member of this family decides to become a baker. Xe takes xyr family beans, makes them into dough, and creates delicious confections (or so I am told; as with so many Human foods, bean cakes are one of the many staples I cannot consume). Unless this individual is extremely generous, xe will not distribute these goods for free, as this is food now absent from the family pantry. Xe will instead engage in that most Exodan of traditions: bartering. Were I an Exodan with want of cake, I could offer vegetables from my home garden, or a selection of spare bolts, or any such offering that both the baker and I deemed a fair and acceptable trade.

If the baker is successful enough in bartering xyr wares, xe will have a surplus of bartered items that can then be traded with the public food stores in exchange for surplus allotments of beans, at which point the herbs and bolts and whatnot re-enter the realm of public resource and become available to the general populace. Or, the baker can simply hang onto xyr bartered items in lieu of having a full cupboard at home, if the family decides they prefer bolts to beans. So even though all resources are rigidly controlled and meted out on a public level, there is profound freedom in what each family decides to do with their share.

Perhaps it has already become obvious how this delicate balance was disrupted the moment Exodan forebears crossed paths with an Aeluon research probe. Exodans are not impoverished (a misconception I encounter constantly back home). They are healthy and housed, and experience no extraordinary stress. But it is true that if you were to pick up an Exodan home and place it in the middle of, say, Sohep Frie or the residential edges of Reskit, that home would appear jarringly meagre. It is not that Exodans are lacking; it's that the privileged of us have so much more. A canister of dried beans is well and good, but it's not as nutrient-packed as jeskoo, not as tasty to a Human palate as snapfruit, not as exciting as *something new*. Yes, an Exodan might say, the shuttle engines built in Fleet factories are perfectly adequate, but have you seen what the Aandrisks are flying these days? Have you seen the latest sim hubs, the latest implants, the latest redreed hybrids? Have you seen what wonders our alien friends have?

I should note, in case you're getting the wrong idea, that Exodans have been steadily innovating and inventing throughout their history. The Fleet is one enormous tinkerer's workshop, and the equity with which goods are accessible means that anybody with a new idea – mechanical, scientific, artistic, what have you – has the resources to bring it to life. The only limit to what an Exodan can create is what xe has on hand. The fact that Humanity has been liberally implementing GC tech (and building off of it in ingenious, locally specialised ways) does not mean that the Fleet has been technologically stagnant since leaving Earth, nor does it mean their system of labour management is insufficient in driving creative minds to improve upon the old. Dear guest, I cannot impress strongly enough how important it is that we understand the current Exodan state of affairs. It is not that the Exodans were standing still. It is that the rest of us were so far ahead.

Which brings us to those who keep the treasures the average Exodan cannot resist: GC merchants. Non-Human species in residential areas are so rare as to be effectively hypothetical, but the merchant-facing shuttledocks are relatively diverse. Multilingualism is a job requirement for today's import inspectors, as is interspecies sensitivity training. But while the Exodans working the docks have made efforts to adapt to alien custom, the merchants they so eagerly welcome have neglected to adapt in one crucial respect: payment. This is hardly surprising, nor is it unfair. A GC trader has no use for beans or bolts. Xe wants creds, plain and simple. If the Exodans want their imports (and they badly do), they must pay up.

On a galactic scale, a unified currency makes sense. The alternative would be madness. But in a society as small as the Exodus Fleet, the mixture of creds and barter has yet to gel. The Exodus Fleet produces virtually no trade goods of outside interest, which means creds can only come from elsewhere. For generations, more and more Exodans have left to do work in other systems, in search of wealth, adventure, or simply a broader variety of occupational options. These individuals are Exodan through and through, however, and they do what any community-minded citizen would: they send creds home. Who wouldn't do this? Who wouldn't want their families to eat better, to be more comfortable, to have more conveniences and delights? How could this act of sharing be born of anything but kindness?

Imagine now that our baker has been given some creds. Now xe no longer needs to wait for beans to become available, or to carefully save up the right number of bolts. Xe can instead put in an import order for suddet root – not the same as beans, but usable in the same way, and more valuable for its exoticism. The creds then leave the Fleet, nothing re-enters the public stores – beans, bolts, or otherwise – and other bakers who once comfortably traded bean cakes in nearby neighbourhoods now find their customers making longer walks elsewhere for the sake of alien novelty. A seamless harmony that was maintained for centuries has been thrown off-key, and it remains unclear how the song will end.

This is not a new problem. The Fleet has been struggling with creds since the days of first contact. At first, participation in the galactic economy was perceived as a harmful acquiescence to foreign values – not alien, interestingly, but *Martian*. Contact with the GC in turn enabled Fleet contact with the Sol system for the first time since the Exodans left, and the reunion was not a cordial one. Much has been written on this topic elsewhere, so in the interest of brevity, I will mention only that in the early days of the post-contact Fleet, anything coded as Martian – money, war, extreme individualism – was understood to be dangerously incompatible with Exodan morality. This sentiment still lingers (unwaveringly so in military affairs), but in matters of economy, there has been a slow, steady shift. There are Exodan merchants who, to this day, steadfastly refuse to accept creds out of cultural pride, and there is a social righteousness I've observed in individuals who, in turn, choose to only interact with such establishments. But these principled people live next door to others who *do* have the newest implants and the trendiest food. While our resolute barterers may not be tempted by flash and fashion, while they may be content to live with amenities that are *suitable* and *adequate* and *just enough* . . . their children are still making up their minds.

———

SAWYER

Sent message
Encryption: 0
Translation: 0
From: Sawyer (path: 7466-314-23)
To: Eyas (path: 6635-448-80)

Hi Eyas,

I hope you don't mind me sending you a note. I found your scrib path in the ship's directory (you're the only one with your name!). Anyway, I wanted to thank you again for your advice the other day. I'd just signed up for sanitation work when I met somebody outside the job office looking to hire workers for a salvage project. It's just a gig right now, but it might be more. Plus, this crew's been the only group of people other than yourself to offer to show me the ropes. They seem like fun folks. So I'm on board with them now, but don't worry! My name's still in the sanitation lottery. I took what you said seriously, and I'll help out when I'm needed. Thanks for steering me in the right direction.

Sawyer

———

He should've been sleeping. Sleep was the smart thing, the responsible thing. He was worried about not screwing things up that day, and he knew that if he was smart, he'd still be in bed, because being well-rested would help him actually accomplish that. But instead, he was up during the artificial dawn, standing in his bedroom in the otherwise unoccupied home, turning this way and that in front of the mirror, cycling through the five shirts he owned and liking none of them. They didn't look like what Exodans wore. They were too bright, too crisp. They lacked that degree of sincere, inoffensive wear that Exodan clothing always had, that reminder that new cloth only came around every so often. His clothes, cheap though they'd been, simple though he'd thought them, were made too well. He hadn't known that when he'd packed his bags back on Mushtullo, but he knew it now, just like he knew that his accent put people off, and that even though he shared the same DNA as everybody else here, they saw him as something other.

I should've bought new clothes, he thought irritably as he pulled off his shirt with a sigh. He'd meant to, but he'd been so busy brushing up on Tinker that he'd run out of time. He backed up to the edge of his bed and sat down, holding the garment in his hands. Red and brown threads, woven together in a breezy fashion, perfect for the sticky days back home. He'd bought this shirt at Strut, one of his favourite shops down in Little Florence. He'd been with friends at the time – Cari and Shiro and Lael, blowing their creds and getting drunk in celebration of yet another payday at the shitty stasie factory.

Of all the things he'd anticipated in leaving Mushtullo, homesickness hadn't been one of them. He didn't feel it with a pang, but with an ache – a dull, keening ache, the kind of thing you could ignore at first but that grew less tolerable every day. There was a lot about his homeworld he didn't miss. The crowds. The grime. The triple dose of daylight that made shirts like the one he held a necessity. But he missed the people. He missed Lael, with her incessant puns. He missed Cari, always good for the latest gossip. He even missed Shiro, the cranky bastard, garbage taste in music and all.

He'd left for good reasons, he told himself. He'd left for the *right* reasons. What was there for him on Mushtullo, beyond working jobs he didn't care about so he could buy drinks he'd piss away and shirts he wouldn't like later? What was there beyond a drab studio in a drab residence block, in a neighbourhood where people shoved guns in your back and took your creds? What meaning was there in that? What good?

Even so, he missed his friends. Stars, he missed having friends.

He wondered, cautiously, if he'd made a mistake. If he was still making one. Maybe Eyas had been right. Maybe the folks at the job office had been trying to tell him that he didn't have the right stuff to become part of the Fleet. He knew where the transport dock was. He only had five shirts. It wouldn't take him long to pack.

Sawyer shook his head. What was wrong with him? He was starting a job today! A job! With people! With Oates, who'd liked him! Muriel seemed to like him, too, and Len seemed all right, and . . . okay, Dory was scary, but maybe she'd come around. Maybe he was what they were looking for. Maybe they'd welcome him in.

Sawyer realised that was what was scaring him. He was afraid of getting his hopes up, of putting too much stock into this new thing. He'd learned, in the past few tendays, that deciding ahead of time how a thing was going to go was setting yourself up for a faceplant.

So, fine, he didn't know how it would go . . . but he knew what he wanted from them. A posse. A crew. A real crew, like he'd seen in vids and sims. People who looked after each other. People who were messy sometimes, but could pull together when stuff got tough. People who would laugh at his jokes, and give him a nickname, maybe, who would knock on his door late at night because they knew where they could go with their problems. People who always had a spot at the table for him. People to whom he mattered.

It was too big of an expectation to put on one job offer, he knew that. But he looked at himself in the mirror, and he felt some confidence creep back in. If it was a matter of either getting

his hopes up or glooming himself to the edge of going home –
well then, hopes up it was. He took a breath and put on his shirt.
His clothes were fine. They would do. The crew of the *Silver
Lining* would like him. He'd do a good job. He'd use the last of
his creds and buy everybody a drink after. He'd be cool and
funny, and they'd want him to come back again.

Sawyer stood and examined himself. *Red looks good on you*,
he could hear Cari saying, the payday kick making her loud. *You
should definitely buy that.*

He nodded. He smiled. He was gonna do great.

TESSA

'Aren't you supposed to be at work?' Pop grumbled, slumped and spread-legged in the clinic waiting room. They were the only ones there, thank goodness. The last thing this ridiculous to-do needed was an audience.

'Nope, I'm here,' Tessa said, idly scrolling through a news feed on her scrib. Stars, was there ever a day when the news was good?

'Don't you have a shift?'

'I swapped with Sahil for the afternoon.'

Out of the corner of her eye, Tessa saw his arms cross and mouth scowl. 'I would've gone,' Pop said.

'You haven't gotten a checkup in six tendays. You're supposed to go every three.'

'I'm *fine*.'

Tessa's eyes shifted to the wall across from them. 'Can you read that sign?'

'What sign?'

She nodded at the assertive yellow notice on the wall, informing people about the new imubot models that had become available. '*That sign*.'

'Oh, so *you're* my doctor now?'

'Pop.'

'Sorry, but only a medical professional can ask me those kinds of questions.' He looked her up and down. 'And I don't see your credentials.'

A twinge appeared in Tessa's left temple. He was acting infant-ile, but she was also fairly certain he *couldn't* read the sign, and that meant she had to stick this out.

The office door opened, thank goodness, and Dr Koraltan stood waiting with a broad smile. 'M Santoso, at last!' he said in a tone that suggested he knew exactly what the score was. 'I was beginning to think you didn't like us.'

Pop stood; Tessa did the same. 'You're not coming with me,' Pop mumbled.

'Oh, yes, I am.' She put her scrib in its holster and gestured toward the door. 'After you.'

Dr Koraltan's smile grew larger. 'Nice to see you as well, Tessa. How's your back?'

'Behaving,' she said, following her defeated father onward to the examination room. 'Amazing how not twisting my spine while lifting my toddler has helped.'

The doctor laughed as he waved the exam room door closed. 'Up on the table, please, M. Tessa, make yourself comfortable.' He gestured at his scrib. 'All right, M, it looks like it's been . . . wow, almost nine tendays since you were last here.'

Tessa's head snapped to her father. 'Nine, huh.'

Pop scowled at the floor. He looked for all the world like Aya when she'd gotten into something she shouldn't. It might've been funny if it weren't so damned embarrassing.

Dr Koraltan cleared his throat. 'I really do recommend coming by every thirty days, M. I know it's not fun, but—'

'I'm not having another surgery,' Pop blurted out. 'I'm fine.'

The doctor exchanged a glance with Tessa. 'Do you think you need one?' he asked.

Pop was quiet a beat too long. 'How should I know?' he said.

The twinge in Tessa's temple made its way to her eye socket.

'Well, let's see if I can settle the matter,' the doctor said. He wheeled over a bot scanner; Pop placed his wrist in habitually. For all his protesting, he was entirely compliant as the doctor performed the exam. Tessa had seen this play out many times, but there was always something disquieting, something sad about watching Pop submit to the pokes and prods. In childhood, he'd been awesome, invincible, the guy who could pick you up and spin you around and make your fears melt away. Superhuman, him and Mom both. It had been an eternity or two since Tessa had thought of Pop like that, but he was, after all, still her dad. And while her mother's too-soon death had been a brutal confirmation of mortality, it had also been fairly quick. Watching someone succumb to an unexpected disease over the course of a few tendays wasn't the same as standing witness to decades of decline. Pop wasn't ill or anything. He'd be a pain in everyone's ass for a good while yet. But she looked at him now, wrinkles and spots and hunched shoulders, here because of problems that kept coming around. She thought of her back, which *was* better, but still woke her up in the night sometimes. There were lines in her face that weren't getting shallower. Grey highlights were taking over her black curls. She looked at Pop, entropy incarnate, and wondered if his present would be her future. She wondered which of her kids would sit in the extra chair in the exam room and lament the days when she'd been awesome.

Dr Koraltan studied the live feed from the imubots reporting within Pop's eye, and he sat back with a neutral look. Tessa held her breath. Their doctor was an affable sort, and the only time he didn't show his cards was when the news was going to suck. 'I'm sorry to say it, M,' he said. 'But the growth around your cornea's come back.'

Pop didn't look overly surprised, but his mouth twisted. He said nothing.

'This is the trouble with Kopko's syndrome,' the doctor said. 'We can remove the errant tissue, we can have your bots clean out the remnants, but this is about your genes. You didn't get the prenatals that your kids did, and performing gene therapy on someone your age is often too much of a system shock. It's not worth the risk.'

'We got new lights at home,' Pop said. 'The good ones.'

The doctor looked sympathetic. 'Modern globulbs do decrease the risk of Kopko's coming back. But it's a *decrease*, not a guarantee. You – and I see this in so many patients your age – you spent decades rolling the dice with the old sun lamps down at the farms. Once that switch gets flicked, it's so hard to turn off. We can try, but . . .' He sighed. 'I'm sorry, M. Kopko's is a bastard.'

'So, he needs another surgery,' Tessa said.

'I'm afraid not,' Dr Koraltan said. 'And I'm sure *you're* happy to hear that, M, but . . .' He pressed his lips together.

Uh oh, Tessa thought. This really wasn't good.

'Every time we go in there to clean things out, we do damage. Tissue scars. Things wear out. Can't be helped. We've gotten to the point where your eye can't take much more.'

Tessa frowned. 'What are our options, then?'

The doctor made an empty-handed gesture. 'We either do nothing, and he loses sight in that eye, or we do another surgery, and there's a good chance that he loses sight in that eye. Honestly, I don't think the modest chance of benefit is worth the trouble of surgery.' He nodded at Pop. 'But that's up to you.'

'What about an optical implant?' Tessa said.

The doctor looked at her with interest. 'Is that on the table?'

Pop stared. 'We can't afford that.'

Tessa braced herself, knowing what she was about to say wouldn't go over well. 'Ashby sent me some creds, specifically so we could order you an implant.'

Pop glared as he realised he'd been ganged up on. 'If he's sent you creds, you should spend them on the kids.'

'The kids aren't our only family, Pop.'

'M Santoso,' Dr Koraltan said seriously. 'I understand that this isn't what you want to hear. I also can't force you to receive treatment. But replacing your eye with an optical implant would solve the problem. No more surgeries after installation. If repairs need doing, we can undock the main attachment without any pain. I know the implants back in your day were unreliable, but modern biotech is incredibly comfortable and easy to maintain. Your vision would be good as ever. *Better* than ever.'

'And I'd look like one of those modder freaks,' Pop said. 'No thanks.'

The doctor was careful with his words. 'Getting used to the look of a new implant can take some adjustment, yes,' he said. 'Especially if it's on your face. But you *would* adjust.'

Pop looked at the floor. He was quiet for a moment. 'I don't want to lose my eye.'

A sliver of sympathy pushed past Tessa's frustration – not enough to erase it entirely, but she did *care*. She wouldn't want to lose an eye, either.

Dr Koraltan's voice was gentle, but direct. 'M Santoso, if something doesn't change, you're going to lose your eye one way or the other. It'll still be in your head, but it won't work. I'm sorry. We did everything we could do with what we have here.' He gestured at his scrib. Pop's scrib dinged in response. 'I've sent you some reference docs on implants. They're good, M. If you have the means, I really do recommend it.' He stood and gestured toward the door. 'Go home, take some time to think about it. Let me know what you decide.'

Pop exited the room without a word.

Tessa sighed, and stood. Stars and fire, he was such a child. 'Thank you,' she said on her way through the door. He gave her an understanding nod.

Her father was old, but he was still fast, and already out into the courtyard by the time she got out of the clinic. 'Hey,' she called. She quickened her pace until she fell into step beside him. 'Where are you going?'

'I'm goin' to Jojo's,' he said. His face was grim, but he strode forward purposefully. 'It's second day, and that means fish rolls. If I get there before eleventh, they'll still be warm.'

'Pop.'

'Plus, Micah owes me trade. We bet lunch over flash last tenday, and he hasn't made good yet.'

'*Pop.*' She took his arm.

Pop shrugged her off and kept walking. 'You've got two kids at home,' he said. 'I'm not one of 'em.'

Tessa stopped, a swell of anger ballooning in her chest. She'd switched her shift for this. She'd upended her *whole day* for this, and . . . and . . . what a stupid, stubborn jackass. *Fine.* Fine, he could go to Jojo's, and play his stupid games, and let his eye kill itself. It was his fucking life. She was only the one who had to live with him.

She turned away and stormed off toward the transport deck, where she could catch a pod to Bay Eight. *Someone* had to be an adult that day.

ISABEL

'So it's true, then,' Ghuh'loloan said with delighted disgust. 'You expel organs during live birth.'

Isabel laughed as they made their way down the ramp to the viewing area. 'We expel *one* organ, yes. But it's a disposable one. We don't have it the rest of the time, and we only need it during pregnancy.'

The Harmagian's tentacles rippled. 'You'll forgive me, dear host, but to me, the idea is . . .'

'Horrifying?'

'*Yes.*'

'You're not alone in that. Explaining the business to kids always results in a raised eyebrow or two.'

'A raised . . . ah, yes, yes. Is it not painful?'

'... giving birth, not raising eyebrows, correct?'

Ghuh'loloan laughed. 'Correct.'

'It is. But not the . . . the discarding of an organ. That part's not so bad, or so I hear. Everything else is, though.' She spread her arms as they came to the end of the ramp. 'Here we are,' she said. They'd come to a broad platform, fitted with benches and picnic tables, guarded with a waist-high railing around the edge. Below the platform lay a fibre farm, overflowing with thickets of bamboo standing in orderly rows under a ceiling painted with blue sky. The tall plants had plenty of room to stretch up and up and up until finally bowing under their own leafy weight. Farmers made themselves busy in the walkways between, some harvesting, some testing the soil, some planting new seedlings. A caretaker was at work as well, pulling her heavy wagon behind her.

Isabel kept waiting for something that did *not* elate her colleague, but that moment had yet to arrive. 'Oh, marvellous!' Ghuh'loloan cried. 'Stars, look at them! What curious trees!'

'Grass, in fact,' Isabel said.

'No!'

'Yes. That's what makes it a much better crop for us. It reaches full height quickly.'

Ghuh'loloan's dactyli undulated in a gesture Isabel had come to learn meant *appreciation*. 'A grass forest,' she said. 'Ahh, I can smell the new oxygen. Wonderful.'

Isabel sat on a nearby bench and considered the Harmagian's phrasing. 'Does your species have a sense of smell?' She could've sworn she'd heard they didn't.

Ghuh'loloan parked alongside her, so they were both facing the farm. 'Well caught, dear host,' she said. 'We do not, not in the same manner as you. You know that we do not breathe, yes?'

Isabel turned that statement over. She'd never thought about it before, but . . . but yes, other than their mouths, Harmagians didn't have visible breathing holes. 'Then . . . how . . .' She searched for the right words. 'You're *speaking*.'

Had she not been in alien company for several tendays, what happened next might've sent Isabel running – and even so, she had to steel herself through it. To say that Ghuh'loloan opened her mouth wide was an understatement. There was no word Isabel knew that could properly describe what she saw. Not a gape, not a yawn, but an unfolding, an expanding, a hideous extension of empty space. Ghuh'loloan pointed one of her tentacles toward her gullet, and with a smothered shiver, Isabel understood. Ghuh'loloan wanted her to look inside her throat. And so Isabel did, with all the grace she could muster, leaning forward – not into her mouth, of course, there were limits – and spotting an unfamiliar structure at the back. A large, fleshy sack, unconnected to what was presumably Ghuh'loloan's oesophagus (or equivalent thereof), every bit as yellow as her exterior.

Thankfully, Ghuh'loloan closed her mouth, and Isabel leaned back. 'Now watch carefully,' Ghuh'loloan said, pointing at her mouth again. She formed each word that came next with exaggerated precision, as a teacher might speak to a child. 'Watch – what – is – happening – in – my – throat.'

Isabel could see it, though she wasn't sure that she wanted to. The oesophagus did not move, but the sack did, expanding to give the words life, contracting to push them out. 'So you don't . . . you don't use that to breathe.'

'No,' Ghuh'loloan said, speaking normally now. 'It is my *kurrakibat*, a wholly self-contained organ. An airbag, in essence. It pulls in air and it makes sounds. That is all.'

Isabel tried to imagine how she was going to relay this part of her day to Tamsin when she got home, and came up empty. 'Then how do you breathe?'

'Through my skin. All over, front to back. And in the same manner, I can detect chemicals in the air around me, and this produces . . . it is difficult to explain. In Hanto, the word is *kur'hon*.' She considered. '"Air-touch" is a rudimentary translation, but it does not envelop the full meaning.'

'I understand.'

Ghuh'loloan curled her front tentacles. 'It is a full-body sensation, and much like smell – or, that is, what I understand of smell – it can be pleasurable or distasteful. It is easier, then, for us to use words like *smell* or *scent* in Klip, as the end effect is the same.'

'I see.' A question arose in Isabel's mind, a childish thing she wasn't sure she wanted the answer to. 'I have . . . I have heard that other species often . . .' She sucked air through her teeth with an embarrassed smile. 'I have heard that other species sometimes find the way Humans smell to be . . . unpleasant.'

Ghuh'loloan's entire body gave way to a mighty laugh. 'Oh, dear host, do not ask me this!'

Isabel laughed as well. 'I'm so sorry.'

'Do not be,' Ghuh'loloan said, her skin rippling with mirth. 'And please do not take offence.'

'I won't.'

'If it is any consolation, I stopped noticing it within a few hours of arriving.'

Isabel groaned. Poor Ghuh'loloan. 'You got used to us, eh?'

'Well . . .' Ghuh'loloan gave a quieter laugh. 'Stars, this is a horrible thing for a guest to say. But in the interest of cultural exchange: the Human *kur'hon* in these ships is so overpowering that not only have I become numb to it, but I cannot "smell" much of anything else.'

'Oh, dear.' Isabel put her palm to her cheek. 'On behalf of my species, I apologise.' She paused. 'But you could smell – you could—' She wrapped her lips around the unfamiliar word. *'Ker-hone.'*

'You are very close. *Kur*. Our word for both air and vapour. *Kurrrrr'hon.'* The Harmagian gave the R a mighty, over-exaggerated trill.

Isabel couldn't duplicate the sound, but she gave it a valiant attempt. *'Ker'hon.'* That would have to do. 'You could . . . you detected the oxygen here.'

'Yes, it is very strong here, and it's wonderful. I could stay here all day.'

Isabel had no argument there. The fibre farms were peaceful, and sitting on a bench and discussing differences of biology sounded like a marvellous way to spend an afternoon – provided Ghuh'loloan did not invite her to inspect her innards again. Isabel's disquiet from the experience was still ebbing away, and she found herself with an impish desire to return the favour. 'So you were asking about Human birth.'

'Yes, indeed.'

'Do you know,' Isabel said with a grin, 'that during late pregnancy, sometimes you can see the baby's features pressing through the mother's skin?'

The Harmagian's eyestalks gave a slight pull downwards. '. . . not the face.'

'Sometimes the face.'

Ghuh'loloan made a sound of good-humoured revulsion. 'My dear Isabel, I really do recommend that your species try spawning like normal people do. It is far, far less disturbing.'

SAWYER

The vox snapped on with a loud scratch, waking Sawyer with all the courteousness of being dropped into a pond. 'One hour to go time,' Oates announced. 'Up and at 'em, folks.'

Sawyer processed the message, processed his surroundings, and processed the fact that he felt wholly like shit. 'Ugh, stars,' he moaned, rubbing his face with his palms. He was hungover, and how. Len had presented two bottles of Whitedune after dinner the night before, and every memory Sawyer had retained after that point was hazy at best. A bellyful of corrosive kick should've been enough to make him sleep through the night, but it turned out that Oates, who had the room next to his, snored with a vigour and volume that could pull even the drunkest punk into a queasy, half-awake limbo for cumulative hours.

And yet, in between the heavy pulses in his temples, he remembered other things. He remembered the table cracking up at his lousy imitation of a Martian accent. He remembered Len jamming on his lap drum and cheering loudly when Sawyer proved he could sing along to 'Go Away Away' – the Exodan pop song of the standard – in its entirety. He remembered Dory roaring with laughter and thumping him across the back after he choked on one shot too many and felt it exit his throat by way of his nose. He remembered Muriel saluting him with a raised glass.

They like me, he thought as he threw up in the washbasin. He spat, smiled, and half-laughed at himself. What a great look for his first day. He'd laugh in full about this, at some point, that first job on the *Silver Lining* when Len got everybody shitfaced the night before. Yeah, that was the kind of story you'd tell fondly a few days down the road.

He washed himself up and found his last clean shirt. It had been four days since they'd left dock and headed into the open. He could make out the Fleet in the distance, just barely – a bright cluster of lights that didn't match the stars. But he couldn't see the *Oxomoco* yet. He didn't know much about navigation, granted, but he was kind of confused by the direction they were heading. He thought he'd heard that the wreck had been put into orbit in such a way that it and the Fleet were always on opposite sides of the sun, so nobody would have to look at it. If he could still see the Fleet, then . . . then maybe he'd got that wrong. He'd misunderstood. Wouldn't be the first time.

He headed to the kitchen. No one else was there, but some saintly person had put out a big hot pot of mashed sweet beans, a bowl of fruit, and – best of all – an open box of SoberUps. He availed himself of everything, plus a giant mug of water.

'Hey hey, grounder,' Nyx said, entering the room. The pilot delivered the dig with a friendly grin, then spotted the items on the counter. 'Oh, thank fuck,' she said, reaching into the box of SoberUps. She had a packet open and its contents crunched between her teeth in seconds flat. Nyx grimaced. 'I hate the taste of these.'

'Me too,' Sawyer said.

She flipped the packet over and squinted at the label. 'Snapfruit flavoured, my ass. More like . . . snapfruit's ghost. Like a really sad ghost.'

Sawyer navigated a chuckle around his mouthful of mash. The magic combo of carbs and medicine was already doing its trick, and his temples throbbed less forcefully now.

Nyx helped herself to breakfast. 'You ready for the hop?'

Sawyer wasn't sure what she meant. A tunnel hop? That couldn't be right. He was pretty sure they weren't anywhere near the Risheth tunnel, and they couldn't have got there in four days anyway. Besides, they weren't leaving the system for this job, so

– hmm. Whatever. He chose ignorance over sounding stupid, and replied: 'Yeah, totally.'

'Good good,' she said, fetching herself a spoon and heading for the door. 'You can ride it out anywhere you like. Bed's best for it, though, if you're not flying. Doesn't take long, but most folks like to lie down.'

'Okay, cool,' Sawyer said, having even less of an idea of what was going on now. 'Is there . . .' He had no idea what they were talking about, much less what to ask. 'Is there anything I can do to help?'

'Nah,' Nyx said, grabbing a spoon. 'Muriel or Oates'll call you when it's your time to shine. Go put your feet up.' She winked. 'Let the snapfruit ghosts do their job.'

Sawyer chuckled and nodded, feeling utterly lost as she left the room. Well, it was his first day. Feeling lost came with the territory, right?

He headed back to his room and lay down, as instructed. His body sank into the bed with gratitude. SoberUps were great and all, but he still felt like he was balancing his brain on stilts. A bit of rest, and he'd be good to go.

He passed the time quietly, skimming through feeds on his scrib and letting the helpful drugs smooth out his edges. He'd almost forgotten about all his questions until another one appeared: *What's that sound?*

It was a sound he knew, but he couldn't place it. A mechanical sound. An engine sound. Something that had been activated. Something . . . different. He started to sit up, but the vox stopped him. 'Hop time, everybody,' Oates said. 'Sit down or lie back.'

Sawyer lowered himself back down. His heart quickened. His head puzzled. And then – *oh fuck*.

Space disappeared. Time disappeared. For how long or how far, nobody could say, because neither of those things meant anything anymore. Everything doubled, tripled, folded in on itself. Sawyer tried to look out the window, but his vision swam and his head begged to hold still, *hold still, everything's wrong*.

Then, just as abruptly, everything was fine.

Sawyer sat bolt upright and held onto the edge of the mattress. Nausea – a whole fun new version of nausea – pushed at him in waves. He knew that feeling. Not well, but he knew it. He'd felt it once on a trip to Hagarem, when his sedatives hadn't quite kicked in before the deepod got going. That's what had happened. That's what the sound had been.

They'd punched through the sublayer. The *Silver Lining* had a pinhole drive.

Sawyer knew, as any kid who'd taken a shuttle licence lesson did, that pinhole drives were dead-ass dangerous, that making tiny collapsing holes in the space between space was risky business, that doing so outside of designated transport lanes was illegal in the GC. He frowned. Well, it was illegal in Central space, anyway. Was it in the Fleet? He didn't know.

There was nothing to worry about, he told himself. These folks were professionals. They had a clean ship, a registry number, kids and families back home. Besides, he didn't know jack about scavenging. He didn't know—

Something tugged at the edge of his vision. He looked up. He froze. Slowly, he got to his feet and approached the window. 'Stars,' he whispered. In the blackness hung what was left of the *Oxomoco*. A shell. A corpse. A ruin clasped in a sphere of flotsam. He'd seen pictures. He'd known where Muriel and her crew were taking him that day. None of that had prepared him for it. Nothing had made him ready for the tangible presence of this once-mighty homesteader, torn to shreds by something so seemingly simple as one moment of air meeting vacuum. Sawyer stood at the window, awed and shaken.

What was he doing here?

The sound of the vox switching on made him jump. 'All right everybody,' Oates said. 'You know what to do. Sawyer, meet us at the airlock. Time to suit up.'

Sawyer didn't waste a moment. He headed down the walkway, getting his head on straighter with every step. This was new, and he was just nervous. Time to shove that aside. He had a boss to impress. A crew to join, maybe. There'd be plenty of opportunity for questions later. For now, he had a job to do, and dammit, he was going to do it right.

KIP

Kip knew, theoretically, that things weren't always going to be like this. He knew that he wasn't going to be sixteen forever, that exams would be a memory one day, that if other people lived away from their parents, he could, too. He *would*.

But right then, it sure as shit felt like life was never, ever gonna change.

Bored wasn't even the word for it anymore. There was something biting inside him, something shouting and endless sitting right at the bottom of his rib cage, pressing heavy with every breath. He wanted . . . he didn't know *what,* even, but he was always reaching, always waiting, and not knowing how to fix it was making him crazy. He thought about the vids he watched, where everyone was cool and clever and knew how to dress. He thought about the sims he played, where jumping meant flying and punches exploded. He thought about the spacers he'd see in the shuttledock sometimes, coming home with armfuls of expensive shit for friends and fam, handing their belt guns over to patrol before crossing that invisible line between *out there* and *in here*. Squish all of that together, and that's what he wanted. He wanted aliens to nod hello to him when he walked through spaceports. He wanted to look in the mirror in the morning and think something other than *well, I guess that's as good as it gets.* He wanted. He *wanted*.

Yet he knew, as he made his way to his usual bench after trading for his usual lunch, that he was full of it. He was still seething at his parents after the whole patch thing – which, of course, had gotten around school, too, and was doing such fucking wonders for his social life – but deep down, there was some snivelling, traitorous part of him that . . . *ugh* . . . that had been glad, kind of. Glad that his parents had showed up at the Nova Room. Glad that he'd been given an out. And that was his whole problem, really, more than parents or job trials or the slow crawl between birthdays. The problem was that what he wanted, more than anything, was to fuck someone or fight something, and he knew – from experience, now – that if given the opportunity, he'd be too scared to do either.

Cool. Real cool.

A group of his schoolmates walked by, on their way to Grub Grub for hoppers of their own. He didn't look at any of them, but he could hear whispers, giggles, a pack passing him by.

Stars, he sucked. Everything sucked.

He saw Ras approach out of the corner of his eye. He had a spring in his step, a look that said *I've got an idea*. Kip took a long sip of his choko and sighed. He was still kind of pissed at Ras, but at the same time, there was nobody else coming over to sit with him.

'*Tek tem*, man.' Ras took his place on the bench and reached for Kip's drink. 'You look like shit.'

Kip let the bottle go without a fight. 'Yeah, well, I spent my night boxing up all the food compost in the whole fucking hex, so . . .' He let a shrug serve as the end of the sentence.

Ras winced. 'They are really on your ass about this, huh?'

'Are yours not?'

Ras shook his head as he drank. 'They keep giving me shit, but I'm not in trouble-trouble.' He handed the bottle back over. '*Tika lu*, man. I feel kinda responsible.'

Kip looked at his friend and felt some irritation slip away. Ras cared, and that . . . that felt pretty good. 'Nah,' Kip said. 'It's cool. *Semsem*.'

The smile returned to Ras' face. 'To make sure that it is, I wanna make it up to you. You think they'll let you come out soon?'

Kip considered. It had been a tenday since it had all gone down, and Mom was being more reasonable. 'Maybe. I got a job trial—'

'Where at?'

'Tailor shop. Y'know, stitching socks, whatever.'

Ras rocked his head, trying to look positive but undoubtedly unimpressed. 'Cool.'

Kip gave a short laugh. 'It's not.' He took another sip.

'Well, here,' Ras said, handing over his satchel. 'You'll feel even better about this, then.'

Kip looked at the bag, then looked at Ras.

'Open it, dumbass.' Ras turned his head toward another group from school. 'Hey, Mago!' he called cheerfully. *'Porsho sem!'* Nice ink.

'Go fuck yourself,' came the inevitable reply. Mago had gotten a cheap bot tattoo on vacation and it looked straight up *dumb*. Like, the lines didn't even move at the same time.

Kip unclasped Ras' satchel as the sparring continued. Just school stuff, it looked like. Scrib, stylus, some pixel pens, a bag of candy, a lunch tin, an info chip, a— *wait*. He rifled back to the bag of candy. He wasn't sure that it *was* candy.

'Dude,' Kip said, starting to lift the bag out of the satchel. 'Is this—'

Ras pushed Kip's hand down into the satchel without looking. 'Stay stylish, man,' he called after Mago's back. Ras snapped to Kip. 'What the hell,' he whispered, more amused than mad. 'Don't let people see.'

That clinched it. This was *not* candy. Kip dropped his voice to match Ras', his heartbeat kicking up several notches. 'Where did you get this?'

'Toby's sister, remember? I told you.'

Kip looked at the clear pack, full of non-threatening bundles, each wrapped in a colourful bit of throw-cloth. He'd never smoked smash before, but he knew what it looked like. He'd played sims. Smash wasn't illegal or anything – not in the Fleet, anyway – but you could only get it and use it in special cafes with bouncers at the door and patrol always hanging around outside. It was also yet another one of those things locked away behind the *When You Turn Twenty* seal, and he didn't know any adults who were into it. His mom definitely wasn't. She said it was 'a waste of time, trade, and self-respect.'

'Don't worry.' Ras gave him a reassuring look. 'It only lasts a few hours, and it's not like we'll be sitting around your kitchen. We'll go park ourselves in a garden somewhere after lights out, and it'll be a real good time. And besides, Una makes solid stuff.'

'Have you tried it?'

'Well . . . no, but everybody says. You should've heard her explaining it to me as she packed it up. It's some serious science. Look, if you don't want to, it's cool—'

'Nah,' Kip said. He closed the satchel definitively. 'Let's do it.'

Ras blinked, then laughed. 'All right, man!' He clapped Kip on the shoulder. 'I thought you were gonna take more convincing than that.'

Kip swallowed the last of his choko, heart still quick but head as steady as could be. He shrugged again, as if he did this every day. 'Something to do, right?'

TESSA

Somewhere in her head, she knew that she'd left the cargo bay, that she'd found someone to cover for her, that she'd taken a transport pod, that she'd walked (and run, in spurts) through the crowded plaza and into the entry doors of the primary school. She'd felt nearly none of it. Nothing but a furious blur existed between getting a vox call at work and her bursting into the admin office, where Aya sat sobbing on the couch, untouched tea and cookies on the table in front of her, a pair of concerned adults on either side.

'Tessa, I am so sorry,' one of them said, standing to make way for her. M Ulven, Aya's teacher. 'I don't know how they got away from the group, it happened so fast—'

In the same distant part of her head that held the memory of getting from there to here, Tessa knew that the teacher wasn't to blame, that field trips were frantic and kids were unpredictable, that her daughter would be okay. But all of that was shadowed behind a raw animal fury, something that wanted to roar at everyone who'd let this happen.

She took her place beside Aya and pulled her close. Aya trembled, her face burning red and her nose pouring down her lip. There was a throw-cloth clutched in her hand, unused. Some part of her head was distant, too.

Tessa glared at the people who were supposed to keep her kid safe. 'Give us a moment,' she said from behind her teeth.

M Ulven started to say something, but the head teacher laid her hand on his arm. He nodded guiltily – *good* – and they exited the office. Aya clutched Tessa's shirt as the door slid shut, sobbing all the harder.

'It's all right, honey,' Tessa said, hugging, rocking. The girl in her arms was so big, and yet still so small. 'Here, blow your nose.' A sizable portion of Tessa's shirt was already soaked with snot. No matter. Ky had done the same to another corner that morning. Her definition of *clean* hadn't been the same since the moment a night-shift doctor had placed a blood-smeared newborn in her arms.

Tessa took the throw-cloth from Aya's hand and pressed it to the kid's face. 'Blow.'

Aya did as told, and continued to sob. 'I was so scared.'

'I would've been, too.' Tessa rubbed her daughter's back with the palm of her hand for a few minutes, waiting for Aya to quiet a bit. The sobs slowed, hiccuping out weakly every few seconds. 'M Ulven told me what happened, but I want to hear it from you. Tell me how it went.'

Aya sniffed. 'Am I in trouble?'

'No.' Under different circumstances, she would have been, but that was a bridge too far right then.

Aya swallowed hard and began to speak. 'Everybody age nine went on a field trip to water reclamation today.'

'Mmm-hmm,' Tessa said, handing her the wet cloth. That part she hadn't needed a recap of, but okay.

'And Jaime, he – he said – it wasn't my idea, Mom—'

'You guys snuck off on your own,' Tessa said. A pack of four or five of them, was what she'd gotten over the vox.

'Yeah.'

'Yeah,' Tessa echoed. She was sure that her daughter had leapt at the chance to abandon a dull field trip for a de facto obstacle course. That was a talk for another day. 'And then what?'

Aya's lower lip quivered. She wiped her nose with the back of her hand.

'Use the cloth, please.'

Aya gave her nose a perfunctory rub. 'I don't know why they

– why they – I *hate* Opal. I hate her!' Her words were ragged now. Angry.

Tessa raised her eyebrows. 'Opal was involved in this?' She didn't even try to keep the edge out of her voice.

Aya nodded hard. 'Palmer, too. I hate him also.'

Aya's most frequent playmates – or they had been, before this. Their parents were going to get hell incarnate on their doorsteps before the day was out, but for the time being, Tessa put her arm around her daughter's shoulders and squeezed. 'Tell me what they did,' she said.

'Opal told everybody that I'm scared of – that I'm scared of outside. Etty told me that was stupid, and Palmer said I was a baby, and – and they kept being mean, and I told them to stop it but they didn't, and then—' The sobs started again.

Tessa put both her arms around Aya now, and let her cry. She knew what had come next. The little bastards had shoved her in a cargo drone port, closed the door, and made her think they were going to pop the hatch. They didn't have the auth codes for it, but Aya didn't know that. Her screaming was what brought one of the nearby mech techs running.

'I hate them,' Aya said again. 'I'm not going to school anymore.'

That . . . okay, *that* wasn't on the table, but Tessa didn't think it was the time to argue. 'They did a horrible thing to you, honey,' she said. 'I am so, so sorry.'

'Why did they *do* that?' It was a genuine question, brittle with betrayal.

'I don't know. Sometimes . . . sometimes kids think it's funny to be mean to each other.' Tessa reached back to the times she'd been teased, to the times she'd teased in response or for no reason at all. 'I don't know why.'

'It wasn't funny.'

'No, it most definitely was not funny.'

'And I hate living on a ship.'

Tessa blinked. This turn wasn't entirely unexpected, but it surprised her nonetheless. 'I know you're scared of outside, but our home is so good. Yeah? It's safe here. You're safe with me, and your grandpa, and our hexmates, and our friends—'

'I *hate* it.'

'You know those kids couldn't have opened the hatch, right? There are codes that—'

'I don't want to live on a ship anymore. I want to live on a planet.'

Tessa sighed. 'Planets have dangerous things, too.'

Aya wiped her nose with her sleeve. She pulled close to her mother, away from the walls, away from the emptiness outside. 'Not like here.'

Tessa searched for the right response, the right comfort, some of that motherly instinct bullshit you were supposed to just *have*. She found nothing.

Aya sniffled mightily and said: 'Can I say a swear word?'

Tessa remembered a couple tendays prior, when she'd knocked a mug of mek onto her workbench while repairing a cleanerbot. A cascade of profanities had exited her mouth before she'd noticed the kids had entered the room. *Don't say stuff like that*, Tessa had told them at the time. *I only said it because I was mad*. She'd spent several days after trying to make Ky stop gleefully chanting 'son of a *bitch*' – and had won that particular skirmish – but hadn't realised Aya sponged up a lesson from the exchange, too. 'Yes,' Tessa said. 'This is a time when a swear word is entirely appropriate.'

Aya took a breath. 'I fucking hate them,' she said. 'I'm gonna kick all their asses.'

Tessa smothered the laugh pressing against her lips. She gave a serious nod. 'That was two swear words.'

'Well, I'm really mad.'

'And you know fighting solves nothing, right?'

'Ugh, Mom.' Aya rolled her bloodshot eyes. 'I didn't mean like that. I just meant . . . I meant . . .'

'I know.' Tessa put her arm around her daughter and kissed the top of her head. 'I want to kick all their asses, too.'

EYAS

Sunny had become a habit, and Eyas didn't know what to make of that. It wasn't romance, she knew that much. Romance had never been her thing. She watched him as he traced the path back from the bed to where his pants had ended up. He picked up the rumpled pair and dug around in a pocket. 'Do you mind if I . . .?' he asked, holding a retrieved redreed pipe and an accompanying tin.

Eyas shook her head. 'Not at all.' He'd never done this before, and she found it endearing. This wasn't part of a seductive script. There was nothing in this *for her*. The man wanted a smoke. On the clock though he was, something had shifted enough for him to feel comfortable not spending every second entertaining her. They were just . . . hanging out now. She liked that.

He returned to bed, leaving the pants where they'd been. 'Do you want some?'

'Not really my thing.' She reached for his bottle of Laru kick, an ever-present part of these evenings. 'This, however, is.'

Sunny nodded as he filled his pipe. 'Help yourself.'

He puffed; she poured. They sat side by side, leaning against propped pillows, close enough to feel the warm brush of the other's bare skin but nowhere in the realm of a cuddle. Eyas felt perfectly at ease. No pretence, no bullshit. No 'M.' She felt like herself, nothing more or less. Judging by the content neutrality on Sunny's face, he felt the same.

It was really nice.

'Is this what you always wanted to be?' Eyas asked, cupping

her glass in the palm of her hand. Sintalin benefited from a bit of warmth, she'd learned.

Sunny exhaled. The smoke twisted up toward the air filter above. 'You mean, a host?' His face shifted into a far-away smile. 'Not my first choice. I was going to be a Monster Maker.'

'A what now?'

'A Monster Maker! Didn't you play that sim?'

'Oh, stars.' Eyas shut her eyes and laughed. 'I'd forgotten about that. Where you go around the galaxy scanning different animals to . . . collect their DNA, or something.'

'Yeah! And then you smash them together to make hybrids!'

'This was for some superficially educational purpose, right?'

'Yeah, yeah, you did it to solve *problems*. Say, like – say you've got to cross a flooded area. You've got DNA scans for something with long legs, and scans for something that can move through water. You punch 'em both into your Monsteriser—'

'Your—'

'Your *Monsteriser*. Eyas, please, this is serious technology we're discussing.'

'Of course, I'm sorry.' She swallowed her smile. 'Please explain how a Monsteriser works.'

'Well . . . I can't, but that's beside the point. The point is, it makes a monster. It is the most crucial tool a Monster Maker has.' He bowed his head. 'It was a very, very hard day when my dad broke the news that none of it was real.'

Eyas patted his shoulder. 'My condolences.'

Sunny scrunched his face into a parody of grief. 'Thank you.'

'So once you got over the shock,' she said, 'you decided the only thing left for you was a life of getting people off.'

Smoke shot out of Sunny's nose as he laughed. 'There were a few more steps between that and this. I bounced around for a while. I thought about being a doctor, but I'm a lazy student. I spent some time in one of the festival troupes—'

'You play music?'

'No, I sing. It was fun, but . . . I dunno. Wasn't what I wanted to do forever, y'know? Then one of my friends, she started her host training, and she was telling me about it – not just the physical side of it, but all the ethos and whatnot. I was like, hey, that sounds pretty cool. And it was, and here I am.'

Eyas sipped her drink. 'You found something that incorporates everything else you tried. You perform, you make people feel better.' She took another sip and smiled. 'And maybe sometimes you help people with their monsters.'

Sunny's pipe paused on the way to his mouth. 'Huh,' he said, seeming pleased. 'Huh.' He took a drag and angled himself toward Eyas. 'So what about you? I mean, seems fair to ask, but I know you don't like talking about work, so it's cool if—'

'No, I don't mind,' she said. *I don't mind talking about it with you*, she meant. It was different with Sunny. Backwards. Usually, people had to get past what she did in order to get to know her. Sunny had come at it the other way around. Explaining her work wasn't a chore with him. She wasn't teaching; she was sharing. 'I always wanted to be a caretaker. Seriously. I went to my aunt's laying-in when I was six. She died very suddenly. Exosuit accident.'

'Stars. I'm sorry.'

Eyas nodded in acknowledgement. 'The caretaker who conducted the ceremony, he was so kind and so . . . *impressive*. I was upset and confused, and the adults around me were a mess, but he was this . . . this *calm* in the centre of it. I remember watching him, watching the ritual, absorbing everything he explained to me – me, directly – about the science of it. It was beautiful. Magic, almost. That was it for me. That was what I wanted to do.' She took a pensive sip.

Sunny watched her even though she wasn't looking at him. 'And?' he asked.

'And, nothing. It's what I always wanted to do.'

'Is it exactly what you'd thought it would be?'

She glanced at him. 'Perceptive,' she said, surprised but unbothered.

'Literally part of that training I mentioned.'

Eyas leaned her head back into the pillows, taking her time. 'The caretaker I encountered that day, he was a . . . a symbol to me. This symbol of fearlessness, of . . . harmony. He took a terrifying thing I barely understood and he showed me it was okay. It was normal. And that feeling was reinforced by the way adults treated him. They didn't pull away. They weren't repulsed. They embraced him – in both senses of the word. He was life and death walking as one, and they wrapped their arms around him and gave him gifts, and by extension, showed me I did not have to be afraid of our reality.' She paused again. She'd never talked about this with someone outside of her profession, and certainly not to this degree. 'I am that, now. I am that symbol to others. It's exactly what I wanted, what I worked for. But there's this other side to it I didn't expect. I'm a symbol, yes, but a symbol wearing my face and my name. Myself, but also not. Mostly not. People know, when I walk through my district, who I am, what I do. Doesn't matter if I've got my wagon or am wearing my robes. They know. And so I always have to be Eyas the symbol, the good symbol, because I never know who's looking at me, who needs to see that thing I saw in a caretaker when I was six. It doesn't matter if I'm having a bad day, or if I'm tired, or if I'm feeling selfish. They look to me for comfort. I have to be that. And that *is* me, in a sense. That is a genuine part of me. But that's just it – it's a part. It's not—'

'It's not the whole,' Sunny said.

Eyas nodded. 'And that aspect of my work, I wasn't ready for. I never thought about who my aunt's caretaker was when he went home.'

Sunny held the bowl of his pipe in his palm. The smoke ascended as if he were conjuring it. 'Sounds lonely.'

Eyas weighed that word. *Lonely*. Was she? She pursed her lips. 'Not exactly. It's not like I work alone, or live alone. It's more that I feel . . . I feel . . . incomplete. Or stuck, maybe. Like I can only ever be this one thing. Like this is the only side of myself I'll be able to express. Like there's something more I could be doing.' She shrugged and sipped. 'But then, I've never wanted to do anything else, so I have no idea what it is I want to change.' She paused, her mouth twisting.

'What?'

'That's not entirely true.'

'What's not?'

Oh stars, was she really going to tell him this? *Why not*, she thought. She was already naked as naked could be. Eyas looked away with an embarrassed smile. 'There was a brief period in my teens when I went off on a Gaiist kick, but *other than that—*'

'Wait, wait, wait.' Sunny laughed. 'You can't fly past that. You. You went on a Gaiist kick.'

Eyas laughed right along with him. 'I did. Drove my family crazy.'

Sunny was gleeful. 'Were you going to go to Earth, or . . .'

'No, it's so much worse than that.' She made an exaggerated grimace. 'See, I got this info chip at a spaceport—'

He cracked up. 'Oh, stars, you were going to be a *missionary*. Oh, fuck. That's so much dumber than Monster Makers.'

Eyas flicked his thigh. 'Shut up,' she said. 'I was fifteen.'

'And that's why it's forgivable,' he said. He took a deep breath. '*Hoo*. Congrats on growing out of it.'

She raised her glass in salute.

'So what steered you away from that truly amazing life goal?'

'I don't know. Not one specific thing.' She pursed her lips. 'The problem with Gaiist philosophy is . . . well, my work.'

He spread out his hands, inviting her to continue.

Eyas considered. 'You're fine with me digging into what I do? It won't ruin the mood?'

'Yeah, it's cool.' He rearranged himself on the mattress, facing her fully now. 'It's interesting. Just . . . part of life, right?'

Eyas studied him. 'Yeah.' She smiled. 'Okay. So. Gaiist philosophy. "Our souls are tied to our planet of origin." That's their central tenet, yeah? Our souls are tied to Earth, and they essentially get sick if we go elsewhere. Since there's no hard-and-fast definition of *soul* anywhere, we'll go with what I interpret that to be: the quality of being alive. The thing that separates us from rocks or machines. By my definition, every organic thing has a soul – it's not just for sapients.' She gestured around the room. 'According to Gaiists, the Fleet should be a place chock-full of diseased, malnourished souls. This is as far from organic as it gets. We live inside machines. We've replicated the systems on Earth. There is no wind to move our air, there is no water cycle, there is no natural source for photosynthesis. This is a lab experiment. A biologist could make no real conclusions about our natural behaviour. They'd have to add the caveat "born in captivity" to everything they recorded.'

'That's . . . oof. Okay.'

'See, I told you I was going to ruin the mood.'

'You haven't, but I would like some of *that*,' he said, nodding at the bottle. 'Seriously, I want to hear this.'

'Okay.' Eyas poured him a glass. 'I promise things look up from here.'

He nodded. 'I trust you.'

Eyas inwardly noted that, and kept going. 'So, despite everything about our environment, there *is* a natural cycle that remains, and it's one that we can't escape, that we couldn't leave behind. It's completely beyond our technological grasp to alter or replicate.'

'You mean death.'

'I mean life *and* death. Can't have one without the other. If my work has taught me anything, it's that death is not an end. It's a pattern. A catalyst for change. Death is recycling. Proteins and nutrients, 'round and 'round. And you can't stop that. Take a living person off Earth, put them in a sealed metal canister out in a vacuum, take them so far away from their planet of origin that they might not understand what a *forest* or an *ocean* is when you tell them about one – and they are *still* linked to that cycle. When we decompose under the right conditions, we turn into soil – something awfully like it, anyway. You see? We're not detached from Earth. We turn *into* earth. And it's an entirely organic process. We can't substitute anything artificial. I can't make a corpse compost without adding batches of bamboo chips to get the carbon–nitrogen ratio right. If I don't remove the corpse's bots, they'll disrupt the bacteria the entire process relies on. Likewise, I have to take out any implants or mods the person had installed, or they'll contaminate the finished product.'

'But isn't the core artificial, too? I'm not being contrary, I'm just trying to understand.'

'It is,' Eyas said. 'But think about it: it's an artificial system set up to accommodate something *that would happen without it*. We would still die and rot if the core wasn't there. We'd rot *differently*, yes, but you could say that about someone who died in a desert versus someone who died in a swamp. In both cases, rot is inevitable. So all we've done is provide conditions that encourage the kind of rot we want, and facilities that ensure we're not tripping over corpses all day. Sorry for the visual.'

'That's okay.'

Eyas nodded. 'Despite growing up in an environment that is utterly artificial, we default to the rawest, purest state at the end. So you can't tell me that our souls are sick and broken when they're inextricably linked to a force that powerful. Whatever soul we got from Earth – whatever that even means – we took it with us when we came out here. And that's why I do what I do. Yes, I'd love to see a forest, a real forest. I'd love to stick my hands down into the humus and touch saplings growing out of stumps. I'd love to see a system of decomposition and growth that just *happened* without any need for Human tending. But the system we built here *does* need tending, and that means it needs caretakers who understand the magnitude of that.'

'It needs you.'

Eyas paused, considering the line between hubris and honesty. 'Yes,' she said. 'It needs me. And I do believe that. I do love what I do. So I don't know what this . . . this discontent is. I don't know why I'm conflicted about it lately.'

Sunny swished his drink around. 'Can I ask you a weird question? And I'm not trying to be disrespectful or negative, honestly. I just want to pick your brain.'

'Go ahead.'

Her companion shifted his jaw in thought. 'Is it the most efficient thing? Composting, I mean. In terms of resources, is it still the best thing for us to be doing?'

Eyas had been preparing herself for a question about funeral preparation, or states of decay, or what bodily functions a corpse can still perform. Those questions, she was used to. This, she was not. 'What alternatives are there? You want to just space them?'

'Of course not. You could fly people into the sun, though, right? Like we did after the *Oxomoco*. Wouldn't that be easier? Less work?'

Eyas continued to feel thrown. She remembered the announcement that the *Oxomoco* victims would be flown *en masse* into their sun, and the second grieving that decision had prompted – the disbelief, the backlash, the endless requests for personal exceptions, the crowded lines at counselling clinics and emigrant resource centres and neighbourhood bars, the exhaustion, the resignation, the popular justification that the bodies would fuel the sun, and the sun fuelled their ships, so a similar end would be achieved. And now here they were, just a few standards later, talking about that recourse as matter-of-fact as could be. 'You're forgetting resources,' she said, speaking words she'd never thought an Exodan would need to be reminded of.

'That was true for old folks,' Sunny said. 'That's why we did composting while we were still drifting around the open. It's different now.'

'We . . . we still have to manage metal and fuel. They're less rare than before contact, yes, but the . . . the need to be frugal hasn't changed. You can't fly bodies anywhere without metal and fuel.'

'But does the math work out that way? Is it *actually* less of a drain on resources anymore to keep the Centres working than it would be to kit out a busted old skiff sometimes?'

Eyas stared at him. That wasn't math she'd ever done, ever *considered* doing. She had a dozen polished responses to the question of *why* the tradition she oversaw existed. But Sunny wasn't asking *why*, he was asking *why now*, and that . . . that she didn't know how to answer. She emptied her glass down her throat and tried to think.

Sunny cringed apologetically. 'So, what I was *trying* to do was push you into some kind of epiphany and help you untangle this thing . . . but it looks like I maybe messed you up further.'

She sputtered. 'How was this supposed to help?'

'You were *supposed* to say that the math doesn't matter. Because you love it, and because it's our way, and that's reason enough. And then, see, you'd feel like your *job* was enough, and you wouldn't feel conflicted anymore.'

'You asked me a practical question!' She hit him with a pillow. 'Not an emotional question! Those two never have the same answers!'

'Well, fuck, sorry!' he laughed, fending off her attack, holding his pipe well out of harm's way. 'You called me perceptive, and I got cocky.'

Eyas shook her head with a smile. 'That's the last time I pay you a compliment.'

'Probably for the best.' Sunny gave a low whistle. 'Stars, I am sooooo glad I picked an easy job. I am not used to getting this existential.'

She chuckled. 'I wouldn't call your job easy.'

He gestured to his reclining, naked frame. 'I am in the middle of a shift, right now.' He took a long drag of his pipe. 'I am on the clock.' He sipped the last of his drink and swallowed with an indulgent exhale. 'Oh, what a difficult profession.' He set the pipe and glass aside and rolled over onto her, far more goofball than alluring, and planted his face smack between her breasts. 'Look at me, serving the greater good,' he said, nuzzling appreciatively. He sat back as Eyas laughed. 'I guess I kinda am, huh?' he said, his voice more serious. He gestured at her. 'You're the literal greater good here.'

Eyas raised an eyebrow. 'Do you get this sappy with all your clients?'

Sunny grinned broadly. 'I wouldn't have gotten very far in this job if I didn't.' His eyes softened – not worryingly so, but enough to make her stop teasing. 'I meant it, though.'

Eyas held his eyes for a moment. She squeezed his hand, and poured them both another drink.

SAWYER

'Boss, we got a problem.'

Everybody in the airlock paused their suiting up. 'Do tell,' Muriel said, continuing to wake the four empty autocarts that would be joining them.

Nyx cleared her throat over the vox. 'We've got company. The *Neptune.*'

Muriel paused. 'How long?'

'Three hours, maybe four.'

Sawyer stood awkwardly, helmet in hands, not sure what that meant or why the mood in the airlock had changed. 'Ah, shit,' Oates said. He frowned at everyone present. 'Who got drunk and told someone where we were going today, hmm?' His eyes lingered on Sawyer.

Sawyer swallowed. He was pretty sure he hadn't said anything to anybody other than that he had a salvage job. He hadn't known he wasn't supposed to talk about it, but who would he even have talked to?

'It doesn't matter,' Muriel said. She fastened her suit latches in sequence, one, two, three. Methodical. Matter-of-fact. 'Is what it is.' She looked around at her crew. 'This just became a rush job. Grab and carry first. Tear-downs if you can.'

Sawyer cleared his throat. 'I'm sorry, I don't— what's going on?'

Muriel clicked her helmet into place, and the vox below the seam switched on. 'We've got competition. Another salvage crew. Think of it like a race.'

A competition. Sawyer hadn't planned on that. 'Do you guys – do the salvage crews not keep a schedule?'

Dory laughed and shook her head, walking toward the hatch. 'Salvage is a more . . . independent line of work,' Oates said. 'First come, first serve.'

The airlock remained tense, so Sawyer decided to save the rest of his questions for later. Still, his list was growing. If retrieving salvage was competitive, there must be some kind of special compensation given by the Fleet to salvage crews, but that didn't mesh with . . . well, with how everything else worked. Maybe it was dangerous, or messy? You could say the same about asteroid mining, though, or zero-g mech work, or sanitation. Sanitation. Maybe he *should* have stuck with that, started there. He didn't understand enough about anything else yet. Maybe . . . maybe the race Muriel mentioned was purely a matter of pride. A race to see who could bring the best stuff back home. Yeah, that made sense. He put on his helmet and got ready to follow.

That is, he *thought* he was ready. He'd been outside before, tethered and on a guided walk, but that was different; he wasn't floating now. He could feel the sudden lightness of everything in and around him, but his cling boots held his feet firmly to the ruined shuttledock they walked out onto. He'd never worn cling boots before, and he found them . . . not uncomfortable, exactly, but more challenging than the others made them look. A little like walking through wet sand. It'd take practice, he assured himself. After all, this crew had probably been wearing them since they were kids. One step at a time.

Sawyer looked up from his feet and met the *Oxomoco*. He shuddered. He swallowed. Around them were the same features he'd seen in the *Silver Lining's* dock four days prior – walkways, railings, directional signs – but this was a fever dream, a rent and twisted mirror image. The vacuum occupying the space around them glittered with dust and dreck. It would've been almost pretty, were it not for the violently wrenched metal everywhere else.

Sawyer turned to look around, and even in the regulated warmth of his exosuit, the sight made him go cold.

There was no wall on the other side of the dock. Just a gaping hole into empty space, the edges surrounding it bent outward. He knew the decompression had been quick, but stars, he hoped it had felt that way, too.

'All right, three hours,' Muriel said. 'We should split up. Oates, head to the hexes. Dory and Len, let's go to cargo. It's bound to be even more picked over than the last time we were here, but we gotta give it a shot. Sawyer, you're with Oates. More code that'll need tweaking where he's headed. Nyx, you'll keep us posted?'

'You know it,' Nyx's voice said inside their helmets.

Muriel nodded at the group. 'Let's move.'

They split as directed, autocarts trailing after. Sawyer followed Oates, and tried his best to look nonchalant.

He failed at that, apparently. 'Don't worry,' Oates said, pushing his big bag of tools along. 'Fucks everybody up the first time.'

Sawyer felt embarrassed at that, but relieved, too. 'I've seen pictures, but—'

'Yeah, pictures don't cut it. I always need a good, stiff drink to get me to sleep after we make a run here. Speaking of – you holding up okay?'

The slightest echo of a headache was all that remained of Len's Whitedune. 'Yeah,' Sawyer said. 'I'm good.'

Oates gave him a solid pat on the back, his thick glove landing dully against an even thicker oxygen canister. 'See, you'll be great. We got about an hour's walk there, and if we've gotta be back in three, we need to keep a good pace if we're gonna have any time to actually work. If you gotta piss, well – you've worn a suit before, right?'

Sawyer hadn't ever used that particular exosuit feature, but he nodded.

Oates grinned. 'It's a fancy job, what can I say.'

The walk was tiring, thanks to the boots, but Oates made for good chatter. After an hour and change, as had been predicted, they arrived in a residential corridor. 'Okay, a lot of these will be empty already,' Oates said. 'I'll know a good one when I see it, though.'

Oates' quarry was found a few minutes later, though Sawyer couldn't see what had drawn him to this particular spot. The centre of the hex was empty. No toys or tools littered the floor. No dishes lined the table. No plants remained in the hollowed planters. Everything that wasn't bolted down had been sucked away through a gash in the floor that split the hex in two. Sawyer could see the remaining edges of the sewage deck below and the stars beyond.

'Hmm,' Oates said, as if he were picking apart a pixel puzzle. He eyed the front doors. 'That one. We'll start there.' He pointed to a door that was open about a hand's width, on the other side of the gash.

Sawyer hesitated. 'How do we . . .'

'Ah,' Oates said. 'Here, I'll show you.' He reached down and hit the cling boot controls on his ankles. With a low buzz, Oates was unanchored. 'Okay? And then—' His suit thrusters activated, and he flew forward at a cautious speed, drifting over the tear in the floor, then reactivated his boots once he reached the other side. 'See? Nothin' to it.'

Sawyer repeated each step. Detach, thrusters, forward, anchor. There wasn't anything to it, now that he'd done it, but he felt pleased anyway.

The autocarts flew themselves across the gap as well, and the small party stood at the cracked-open door. Oates reached into his tool bag and retrieved a power pack and a pair of cables. He popped open a service panel by the doorframe, connected the pack, and gestured at the door. Nothing happened. He ran his hand inside the open space between door and frame. 'Nothing blocking it,' he said. He rattled the door itself. 'And it's not off-track. It's just locked itself in a weird spot.' He nodded at Sawyer. 'This is where you come in.'

On cue, Sawyer hooked up his scrib to the control panel and dove into the code. It was a different setup than the lockbox code, naturally, but the territory was more familiar now. He tweaked and teased, coaxing the commands to do what he wanted. Sure enough, five minutes in, the door slid open.

'Hey, hey!' Oates said. He rubbed his hands together as he entered the home. 'We're in business. Nice work.'

A smile briefly formed on Sawyer's lips, then disappeared. Eerie as it was to see a hex without any stuff in it, a home still full to the brim with belongings was worse. Free of gravity, every piece of furniture and everything that had been on them was afloat, drifting in a bizarre jumble. Oates pushed things out of his path as he walked through, like a parody of a man wading through water. The objects tumbled into each other, set in motion by the intrusion.

A sock floated past Sawyer's face. He saw a fork, a kettle. A frozen, dilapidated piece of fruit. A horrible thought struck him. 'Are there any . . . um . . . there aren't still . . .'

Oates looked at him. 'What?'

Sawyer wet his lips. 'Bodies.'

'Oh, stars, no.' He made a face. 'Couldn't pay me enough to come here if there were. No, after it happened, the Aeluons, they've got these . . . I dunno what they're called. Some kind of bots that detect whatever organic form you tell 'em to look for. They use 'em to retrieve their dead after battles in zero-g. You know what I'm talking about?'

'No.'

'Well, anyway, the Aeluons gave us a bunch for clean-up. They can bore through walls and whatnot, so if you're in a closed-off space like this and you don't see a big hole in the wall, it means there was nobody in here, and nobody's been in since.'

There was nobody in here. A small comfort, but Sawyer took it.

'Okay,' Oates said. 'Cloth and metal, those are always good to grab. Anything that can be made into textiles or melted down.'

He grabbed a floating storage crate, put it beneath one boot, and began to pry the lid up. 'Tech takes priority over everything. Broken is fine, intact is better, functional is best. We can't grab everything, so use good judgment. Find things people can make use of.'

Sawyer looked around. Everything in there had had a use, once. Everything in there had been brought in for a purpose. He shook his head. Job. He had to do his job. *Okay*, he thought. He reached out and grabbed the floating kettle. 'Like this?'

'Yeah. Someone can smelt it, if nothing else. Remember, we're on the clock. Grab and go.'

Sawyer grabbed. Utensils, tech bits, blankets. He brought handful after handful to one of the autocarts, steadily filling its enclosed compartments. The grimness of the place was starting to ebb into the background. Instead there was just the work, the task at hand. There were creds to be made, and crew to win over, and – he paused. He'd opened a decorative box – no, not a box. An old cookie tin someone had painted. The contents inside drifted up to greet him. Sawyer's chest went tight. There wasn't much in the box, nothing that Oates would want, nothing that was of any use. There were kitschy figurines, a pair of Aandrisk feathers, an info chip, a handful of yellow stones washed smooth by an alien sea. He took the info chip, which had a name printed on it. *Myra*, it read. He turned his attention to the wall of painted handprints, which he'd been steadfastly ignoring since the moment they walked in. *Okoro*, it read. The hands reached nearly to the ceiling. He wondered which of them was Myra's. He wondered where she'd been during the accident, if she hadn't been here. He wondered if she'd made it.

'Hey,' Sawyer said. 'What about things like this?' He gestured to the floating mementos.

Oates was busy carving hunks of stuffing out of the sofa with his knife. 'Like what?' He looked over. 'Just junk. Leave it.'

'It's got a name on it. If she's still around, she'd be in the directory, yeah? Doesn't weigh much, and I bet she'd be happy to get her stuff back.'

Oates paused. He lowered his knife. 'We're here for salvage,' he said. 'Not lost and found.'

'But—'

Oates' voice changed. Sawyer couldn't put his finger on what it was, but he didn't like it. 'On the clock, remember?' Oates said. 'You pick up every piece of junk you find, and we'll be here forever.'

Sawyer frowned. An uneasiness filled him, the same feeling he'd gotten after the tunnel hop, the same he'd gotten in the airlock when competition arose. Competition. He looked at Oates, speedily tearing away hunks of fibre as if someone might take it away at any moment.

'Oates,' Sawyer said slowly. His tongue felt thick. He knew what he wanted to ask, and he knew how stupid it was. He knew he'd sound like an idiot, that it was probably nothing to worry about, that this might take him down a few points in the eyes of the man who'd picked him out of a crowd. But the needling grew stronger, and his stomach felt sour, and . . . and he had to. 'Are we allowed to be here?'

Oates sighed, his helmet angling toward the floor. 'Can we have this talk once we get back to the ship?'

'Um—' Sawyer shook his head, a bright panic growing in his chest. 'No, I want to talk about this now. Are we allowed to be here?'

Oates gave him a look of pure exasperation, then returned his attention to the sofa. 'You're a grounder, so you'll understand this analogy. Imagine you're with a bunch of people wandering out in the desert. I mean a *real* desert, nothin' anybody can use. There are jungles nearby, but you can't go there. The jungle will eat you up. You'll get lost in there. You'll disappear. Now, sometimes, the people in the jungles will throw you a bag of food, but it ain't much. Not like you'd get if you actually lived in there. But you're desert people, and you're not goin' anywhere. One day, you stumble across a big, dead animal. Like a . . . I dunno, I was never good at animals. What's a big one?'

'I—'

'A horse. That's big, right? You stumble across a dead horse. Biggest horse you've ever seen, and it's freshly dead. You could cut it up and eat it right now. It's there for the taking. But the leaders of your group, they say, no, no, we need to talk about this. We can't do this now. We need to talk about how to do this fairly. We have to make sure everybody's getting the exact same amount of horse. We're going to cut just a *little* bit of horse off, but oh, wait, no, now we need to reorganise all our satchels so we have room for the horse bits. And while we're doing that, we should really talk about which of us could use some horse more. So everybody sits in the sand, doing fuck all but talk about the horse instead of actually using it. Meanwhile, everybody's hungry, and they're getting hungrier. Your *family* is getting hungrier, and that horse isn't getting any better as the days go on. So some of your group, they decide to just cut up the damn horse already, because the people in charge are going to talk forever anyway, and you can feed a few mouths in the meantime.' He shoved an armful of sofa stuffing into the nearly-full autocart. 'What's the harm in that?'

Sawyer stared at him. 'That's . . . this isn't a horse. The *Oxomoco* isn't rotting. And nobody's starving. Nobody's gonna die without . . . without . . .' He gestured emptily at the cart.

Oates opened a closet and began working his way through the floating clothing. 'I didn't say it was a perfect analogy. But we're getting people the things they need. We're not hurting anybody. We're helping. If the council's gonna sit on its ass, somebody else is gonna step in.'

'But you're . . . you're . . .' Sawyer tried to work some moisture back into his mouth. 'You're stealing.'

Oates laughed. 'You've filled half this cart yourself, kid.'

Sawyer's head swam. He pulled his fingers into his gloved palms. 'I – if I'd known—'

Oates' expression grew serious. 'You heard the boss. If you're not happy, you walk away after this. *After this.* We are your ride home. We put food in your mouth and air in your lungs.' He took a step forward, knife still in hand. 'Right now, you owe us.' He smiled as if nothing were wrong. 'Now, we've eaten up a good chunk of time with this. To make up for it, I want you to take the other cart and check out the other homes while I finish up here.' He clapped Sawyer's shoulder. 'Are we good?'

Sawyer would've given anything in that moment to be a stronger person. A smarter person. He wanted to tell Oates to fuck off, he wanted to run out of the room, he wanted to get back to the ship and into an escape pod and beat them back to the Fleet, where he could tell patrol what had happened, and they'd understand, they'd know he hadn't known, they'd be reasonable and fair and . . . and . . . would they? Or would they scoff at him for being stupid? Would they lock him up? Would they kick him out?

The moral high ground didn't look any safer. What would happen if Sawyer simply did nothing, if he refused to help any further with this? Would they leave him? Would they . . . He looked at Oates' knife. Stars, they wouldn't, would they?

Would they?

Sawyer couldn't see any path of refusal that ended well. He didn't have any clue what he'd do when they got back to the Fleet, but Oates was right. They were his ride home. He had four more days with these people. There wasn't much else he could do.

He looked at the floor, and nodded.

'Good,' Oates said. He handed Sawyer his satchel of tools. 'Go quick, and holler if you need a hand.'

Sawyer gestured for the cart to follow. He left the home. He walked to the next home over. There was nothing else he could do. Nowhere else he could go.

The front door was firmly sealed, and as unresponsive as the first had been. There was no big hole made by Aeluon bots. No one had opened this place up since the accident.

Sawyer stood motionless for a moment. He didn't want to do this. He didn't want to be there. *Sanitation*, he thought. That's where he should be. Maybe he'd tell that to patrol when he got back. Maybe if he mentioned that he was in the sanitation lottery, they'd go easy on him, they'd see that he was serious about being there, that he hadn't come all this way to cause trouble. Or would he go to patrol? Maybe it was better to do like Muriel had said – shake hands, walk away, no problem, never speak of it again.

'Shit,' he said. He leaned his forehead against the inside of his helmet and shut his eyes. He had to do this. He had to get back home. Back to the Fleet, anyway. He wasn't sure he had a home. At the moment, he wasn't sure he deserved one.

Sawyer reached into Oates' satchel and found another power pack. He gestured. Nothing happened. He connected his scrib, like he had before. He went through the code, like he had before. This one was the same as the other had been, and he blazed through it in a blink. It was keyed differently, that was all. Keyed for someone else. Another family. Another wall full of hands.

Focus, he thought. *C'mon, don't fuck this up even more.*

He punched in the last command.

Sawyer would never be sure of what came next. The sealed door slid open, and with it came force, and fear, and pressure, and Sawyer was in the air – no, that wasn't right, there wasn't air in space, there was – there *was* air, all the air that had been behind the door, and it was carrying him, and the contents of the home, all the things Oates wanted, all the things that family had needed, rushing, rushing, flying, thudding, falling. Then there was a bulkhead, and a split second of pain, pain everywhere, an inescapable shatter. But that was all. He didn't have time to process what dying felt like.

Part 4
· · · · · · · · · · · · · · · · · · ·

BUT FOR ALL
OUR TRAVELS

Feed source: Reskit Institute of Interstellar Migration (Public News Feed)
Item name: The Modern Exodus – Entry #11
Author: Ghuh'loloan Mok Chutp
Encryption: 0
Translation path: [Hanto:Kliptorigan]
Transcription: 0
Node identifier: 2310-483-38, Isabel Itoh

[System message: The feed you have selected has been translated from written Hanto. As you may be aware, written Hanto includes gestural notations that do not have analogous symbols in any other GC language. Therefore, your scrib's on-board translation software has not translated the following material directly. The content here is a modified translation, intended to be accessible to the average Kliptorigan reader.]

————

Where would you begin, dear guest, if you wanted to venture out into the galaxy? Would you talk to a friend? A trusted person who had made the journey before? Would you reach for a Linking book, or test the waters with a travel sim? Would you study language and culture? Update your bots? Purchase new gear? Find a ship to carry you?

Every one of these options are on offer at the emigrant resource centre, a relatively new fixture you can find in most homesteader districts. Some are set up at existing schools, others fill unused merchant space. All serve the same purpose: to prepare GC-bound Exodans for life beyond the Fleet.

Scroll through a workshop listing for any centre, and you will find an exhaustive array of topics. Here is a sampling of the current menu at the resource centre my dear host Isabel took me to visit yesterday:

- *Conversational Klip: What You Didn't Learn In School*
- *Interspecies Sensitivity Training 101*
- *Weather, Oceans, and Natural Gravity: Overcoming Common Fears*
- *A Guide to Human-Friendly Communities*
- *Trade Licence Advice Forum (ask us anything!)*
- *The Legal Do's and Dont's of Engine Upgrades*
- *How to Choose the Right Exosuit*
- *Introduction to the Independent Colonies*
- *Those Aren't Apples: Common Alien Foods You Need To Avoid*
- *Imubot and Vaccination Clinic (check calendar for your desired region)*
- *Ensk Six Ways: Making Sense of Humans from Elsewhere*
- *Ground Environment Acclimation Training (sim-based)*
- *Ground Environment Acclimation Training (non-virtual discussion)*
- *Tunnel Hopping for Beginners*

The list goes on.

I sat in on 'A Guide to Human-Friendly Communities.' Neutral market worlds were prominently mentioned, as were Sohep Frie and, I was pleased to note, my own adopted home of Hashkath. Harmagian territories, depressingly but unsurprisingly, were presented as hit-or-miss. Quelin space was vehemently discouraged, to no one's surprise.

'People's biggest fear is getting kicked to the margins,' said Nuru, the course instructor, who graciously took time to speak with me afterward. 'Everybody's got a great-aunt or uncle sitting around the hex, grumbling about how their parents were sidelined when they made market hops in the pre-membership days. Everybody hears horror stories about Human slums or whatever, and they come in here with exciting ambitions but a huge fear of ending up homeless or mistreated. Life outside the Fleet isn't like that anymore, not if you're smart about it. Times have changed. There are rough places in the galaxy, yeah, but that's what my class is for. That's what this whole centre is for. We want to give people the best start we possibly can.'

I asked Nuru why he spends his days training people for life elsewhere when he himself lives in the Fleet. 'I lived on Fasho Mal for ten years,' he said. 'I loved it, every second. I loved the sky, the open space, the dirt, all of it. But I came home when my mom got sick last standard. Our hex was taking good care of her, but . . . how could I not? So, now I help people get ready for *their* lives on Fasho Mal, or wherever it is they're headed. It's the next best thing to being there myself. At least someone gets to go, right?'

Not everyone agrees with that sentiment. The majority of my time spent in the Fleet has been a delight, but I have, on rare occasion, encountered individuals less approving of my presence. I crossed paths with one of these on my way to the resource centre – not an elderly person, as you might have expected, but a man somewhere in his middle years.

'We don't need you,' he shouted at me as Isabel and I approached the centre. It was clear from the way my skin puckered as he came close that he was intoxicated.

At first, I was not sure if he was addressing me. In hindsight, Isabel knew, as she began to walk more quickly, but in my ignorance, I stopped my cart to make sense of the situation. 'Are you speaking to me?' I asked.

The man did not answer my question, but continued on as if that point were obvious. 'We're Exodans. We belong *here*. You get that? You're not like us. You don't understand what we need.'

Isabel tried to get me to move away, but I assured her I was fine. 'I want to hear what he has to say,' I said. I gestured my willingness to listen to the man, even though he would not understand, even though I believe it only agitated him more. 'I do not understand why you are angry at me.'

'Whatever you're here to teach, take it home,' he said. 'Take it home. We don't need you.'

'I'm not here to teach,' I said. 'I'm here to learn.'

The clarification confused the man, and I admit that I cannot relay what his reply was, for the remainder of it did not make much sense. The underlying intent was anger, though. That much I can say for certain.

'You're embarrassing yourself,' Isabel said curtly. 'Go sober up.' My host is gracious and kind, dear guest, but even to my alien ears, she can be quite assertive when the situation calls for it. I thought it best to follow her into the resource centre at that point, as it was clear nothing else of value would be gained from the exchange. Isabel apologised for the encounter (which was hardly her fault or that of her people, but I understood her embarrassment all the same). I told her it was nothing. I have weathered far worse in academic review. But the exchange did colour my time at the resource centre, and I was thinking of it still as I spoke with Nuru later on. I asked him if this was a sentiment he encountered often.

He replied, with weariness, that it was. 'I get told that I don't deserve the food in my mouth and the walls around me,' he said, 'because I'm taking away instead of giving back. I'm taking away the people who grow the food and maintain the walls, is how they see it. Look – there's no denying that more Exodans are leaving than coming back, but we're hardly in danger of dying out. Farms are still working. Water's still flowing. The Fleet is fine. The people I teach, they'd leave whether or not classes were available to them. But if they left without taking a class or two, they won't know what's what out there. That way lies trouble. All we're doing is giving them the tools they need to stay safe. Exodans helping Exodans. Isn't that what we're supposed to be about?'

I asked Isabel her opinion of the centre once we had left – as an elder, as someone who had watched friends leave and trends unfold across decades. My host was noncommittal.

'Knowledge should always be free,' she said. 'What people do with it is up to them.'

————

KIP

Everything was tingly. Kip had thoughts beyond that one, amazing thoughts that people probably needed to hear. Toes were weird – like *really* weird, if you thought about it. Thinking was weird, too. He could think about what he was thinking about. Did that mean that there was a separate part of him? A thinking part and a . . . thinking thinking part? That was a super good idea, but first: cake. Man, he loved cake. He wished he had a cake. He imagined a cake so big he could put his face down into it and the frosting would rise up and up around him, like the waves of seafoam in the theatre vids, only thick, dense, enveloping him, taking the place of air, sliding in closer and closer and – and no, no, that was scary. He didn't like cake. Cake needed to stay small and manageable and away from his nostrils.

Kip had those thoughts, and more besides, but as soon as they'd bubble up, they were drowned out, washed away by the thought – The Thought – that dominated all others.

Everything was really, really tingly.

'Do you ever wonder,' Ras said. He was tapping the tip of his nose with the tip of his finger, drumming, pulsing. Kip watched him do so for a short eternity. Tap. Tap. Tap. 'Do you ever wonder about, like – okay, you're sitting here.'

'Yeah.'

'And I'm sitting here.'

'Yeah.'

'We're sharing this . . . this moment.'

'Yeah.'

'But *are we really*?' Ras looked deeply concerned. 'Because think about it. I'm seeing *this*, right?' He gestured at the oxygen garden, tracing angled lines outward from his eyes. 'But you – you're seeing *this*.' He touched the sides of Kip's face and drew a different set of lines.

'Whoa,' Kip giggled. 'Your hands are so *weird*.'

'Dude, listen, this is – this is important. What you see is different from what I see. And nobody's ever seen this before. Nobody's ever seen the oxygen garden exactly like I'm seeing it, but it's – it's not like you're seeing it. Kip, we're – we're not sharing anything. Nobody has ever shared anything.'

Kip looked at Ras for a long time – or maybe a short time? A time. He looked at him for a time. He blinked. He laughed, but quietly, because he remembered they were supposed to be quiet, and that part was very important. 'I have no idea what you just said.'

Ras stared at Kip, and he started laughing, too. 'You're such an idiot.'

Kip shut his eyes and nodded, still laughing. He fell back into the grassy bed. He could feel every blade of grass, bending to hold him like a million caring hands. They were in the centre of the garden, the best place in the garden, the quietest, tallest, most hidden place, the place where you could actually *lie down* surrounded by bushes and little trees and leaves leaves leaves. Plants were good. Plants were so good. He loved plants, and he loved smash, and he loved Ras, and he loved life. He loved himself. Wow. He loved *himself*. Everything was . . . was so . . . tingly.

Ras grabbed Kip's shirt. The move was intense and hurried, out of place among the grassy hands and quiet laughter. Kip didn't like it. 'Someone's coming,' Ras whispered.

Kip sat up, abandoning the grass. 'Are you sure?'

They froze. Everything froze. Everything except the unmistakable sound of footsteps. Movement. Invasion.

'Fuck,' Ras whispered. 'I think it's patrol.' He scrambled. 'C'mon!'

They scurried behind a large bush, and everything was bad now, loud heartbeat and metal muscles and screaming edges. The footsteps got closer. With every step, Kip willed himself to be more still, more invisible. He would turn into stone, and they'd never find him. They couldn't find him. Shit, they couldn't find him. They couldn't.

He wished the tingles would go away for a minute.

He could feel Ras beside him. They weren't actually touching, but he could *feel* him, buzzing like a living thing. Ras was wrong. They *were* sharing this. It wasn't a good thing to share, but it was better than being alone.

Someone was in the grass now, the sounds told him. Someone was standing in the grass, turning in a careful circle, looking around. Someone was sitting down, coughing, opening a bottle, drinking. Staying put. Kip was sure the someone would know he and Ras were there, that xe'd hear their breath, their blood. But the someone surprised him. The someone didn't notice. The someone waited.

Then, all at once, there were two someones. The new one spoke. 'Looks like you've been hitting that hard,' she said.

'I'm surprised you haven't,' the first someone said – a male someone.

The woman sat. 'I know this shit's been rough—'

'Rough? *Rough?* Rough is when you haven't been laid in a while, or when your engine breaks, or . . . I fucking killed that kid, Muriel.'

Kip and Ras looked at each other. The ground fell away. Everything was wrong.

'Keep your voice down,' the woman said calmly.

'There's nobody here.'

'Still,' she said. 'Keep it down.' She sighed. 'How could you have guessed he'd do something that stupid? Stars, my niece knows not to open a sealed door in a vacuum, and she's *six*.'

'I should've said something, I was distracted, I—'

'You should've, yes. But it was an accident. Accidents happen.'

'Somebody ever accidentally die on you?' There was a long pause. 'Yeah. I thought not.'

'Oates. It happened. It's done. All we can do is clean up and move forward.'

Kip felt like the giant cake was back, only now it was the air itself, pressing in and smothering. 'Is this real?' he mouthed to Ras.

Ras said nothing, which said everything.

Beyond the bush, the bottle glugged. 'You got everything ready?'

'Yes,' the woman said. 'Food, fuel, every favour I had. We can be out of here this time tomorrow.'

'Thank fuck. Every time I see a patrol, I nearly shit myself.'

'Just keep your head down and your mouth shut, and it'll be fine.'

The bottle glugged again. 'Where'd Dory put him?'

'Do you care?'

'Yes.'

The woman was silent a little too long. 'We didn't have great options.'

'*Where?*'

'Cloth processing. Bottom of the pile.'

'Cloth processing? Are you fucking high? They'll find him in a—'

'—in several days, which is all we need to get gone. Look, where could we have put him where they *wouldn't* find him? We couldn't space him or leave him there without those fuckers on the *Neptune* finding him – and you know they wouldn't hesitate to use that against us one way or another. We couldn't risk a second punch, especially a blind one. We couldn't keep him on the ship, because there's no chance import inspection would overlook a body, no matter how many creds we sent their way. The gardens aren't deep enough, he's too big for a hot box chute without us getting disgusting about it, the foundry's always got people there, cargo bay's too closely patrolled these days – and where do you get off, anyway? We clean up, and you complain about the details?'

'I'm sorry. I just—' The man's voice broke. 'I didn't mean it. I really didn't—'

'I know. And that is why we're doing this for you. Because you're crew, and shit happens. If you'd *meant* to hurt that kid, we wouldn't be busting our asses to make this right.'

'I'm sorry. I'll make it up to you, I—'

'I know.' There was a touching sound, a friendly pat. 'Now are you going to share that kick, or what?'

Kip shut his eyes. He tried to ignore the voices. He tried to ignore everything. He wanted to go back to the grass and the weird toes, but that was gone now. Lost. Now everything was sharp and hot, and – and he didn't want this. He didn't want his brain to be like this anymore, but he was pretty sure he was stuck this way forever, and someone had *died*, and oh stars, what if *he* died? What if he was going crazy and then something went wrong in his brain and he *died*? He looked down at the dirt he was crouching in, the dirt smeared across his palms, the dirt staining his knees. There were dead people in that dirt. Lots and lots of dead people. They were dead, and he'd be dead, and he'd be dirt, too. He didn't like smash anymore. He didn't want to feel like this. He wanted to be okay. He wanted to live. He wanted to live so badly.

TESSA

She heard him, despite his best efforts. Stars, he really was giving it his best. She heard the rustle of his sheets as he tossed them aside, then a slow, deliberate crossing of the floor and ascent of the mattress. He wiggled under her sheet. She did not respond. He thought she was sleeping, and she wanted to see where that would lead. With what must've been agonising self-control, Ky lay alongside her, touching but only barely, silent except for his breathing. He held himself with a two-year-old version of stillness – a tortured rigidity that gave way to a stray twitch and wiggle every few seconds or so.

He was trying – trying *very hard* – to snuggle without waking her up.

Tessa scooped the kid up and covered his tangled scalp with kisses.

'You 'wake!' he squealed.

'Yes, buddy,' she said between one kiss and another. 'I've been awake a while.'

'Good morning!'

'Good morning, Ky.' She waved at the bedside lamp, and a soft glow spread through the room. Ky's hair was a portrait of chaos, and deep pillow lines crossed one of his chubby cheeks. Tessa sat up with her boy in her arms and caught a glimpse of herself in the wall mirror. Her hair and face weren't in much better shape than his, and she didn't have the free pass of toddlerhood. But who cared, at this hour? Certainly not her son, who had inserted a finger a worrying ways into his ear canal.

'Mama, no breakfast,' Ky said. He raised his voice in a shout: 'No breakfast!'

'Shh,' Tessa whispered, pulling his twisting hand away from his head. 'We don't want to wake everybody up. Okay? Can you be quiet? Can you whisper?'

'*Yes.*' Ky's whisper could've been heard from the opposite side of the room, but it was an improvement.

'Do you want to go see the stars?'

'No.'

Everything was *no* these days. He'd put precisely zero effort behind this particular one, so Tessa paid it no mind. 'I think you do. Let's go see the stars.'

Ever-growing boy on her hip, Tessa walked into the living room. A few nightlights and the emergency arrow pierced the darkness, but otherwise, it was pitch dark. She could hear Pop snoring, and nothing from Aya's room. Good. Tessa tiptoed forward, anticipating the couch, the table, the— '*Motherf*—' Tessa hissed, and swallowed the rest in a muffled groan. She hadn't anticipated the stray toy that had found its way into the bare sole of her foot.

'Shh!' Ky breathed loudly. 'Quiet!'

'Yes, thank you,' Tessa said. *Smartass*, she thought.

She reached the ring of tiny floor lights that marked the edge of the shaft down to the family cupola. She'd thought, once, that the reason homes had cupolas in common spaces was because the architects had tried to parcel out window resources as economically as they could. That was true, but only the half of it. Apparently, the shared portal was an intentional design. Her ancestors had worried that if people could lock themselves away and look outside in solitude, they'd lose a few screws. They'd get scared, lose hope. It was a mixed bag, the view of the open. Breathtaking beauty and existential dread all mixed together. Far easier to focus on the former and avoid the latter, the thinking went, if you sat at the window with friends ready to hold your hand or listen or just share company with. That, Tessa thought dryly, or you'd go buggy as a group. Either way, you weren't alone.

Her eyes adjusted to the negligible light. She opened the railing gate, sat on the bench with kid firmly in grasp, and pushed the down button. Home slid away, and for a second or two, the only sounds were the pulley turning and her son sucking his fingers. Then: a rushing, strangled roar behind thick walls. 'Ky, can you tell me what that sound is?'

'Don' know.'

'Yes, you do. What goes through the deck under ours?'

Even in the dim, Tessa could see her son's blank stare.

'Water,' she said. 'Remember? All the water we use goes through big pipes in the floor.' She'd save *filtration tanks* and *settlement ponds* for another year.

'Can have cookie?'

Tessa looked forward to the day when linear conversations became a thing. 'Not for breakfast.'

'What 'bout . . . what 'bout cookie to lunch?'

'*Maybe* if you're good this morning, Grandpa will give you a cookie at lunch.'

Ky looked around as the background noise changed. 'Where water?'

So he *was* paying attention. 'It's up above us now. We're about to stop.'

'Oh boy, get ready!' he said.

'Get ready,' Tessa said with a laugh. 'Aaaaand – stop!'

The bench settled into place. At their feet was a shallow window sticking into the empty space outside. It was different than the one her family'd had when she was a kid. They'd had one of the old ones then, polygonal in shape, made of thick glass as old as the Fleet itself, the view cut in segments by thick metal frames. Ashby had bought them one of the nice new plex ones after his first tunnelling gig – no angles, no inner frame. He was always doing stuff like that. She'd once worried that he was treating them at the expense of getting things for himself, but once he'd bought his own ship, she didn't feel as bad about it. She was just glad he kept them in mind.

She thought about how much she liked the things he sent them – the plex window, the sim hub, a box of spices from some alien port. A guilty, toxic idea surfaced, the same one that had awoken her hours before. Tessa shoved it away before it could make itself plain. She focused on her son.

She slid off the hanging bench onto the cupola seating area. It wasn't much, just a shelf around the edges. The view wasn't much either – at least, not compared to the big, broad starscapes you got at the plazas. But this was her own corner of sky, and she liked that. She'd always liked that.

Ky wriggled against her grasp. She let him go. He toddled out onto the plex, brown feet against black sky. He sat, all at once, unceremoniously. 'Stars!' he said, looking down through the gap between his bent knees.

'Yep,' Tessa said.

He pointed a chubby finger. 'Is five stars.' With his other hand, he held up two fingers and a thumb.

'It's a bit more than five, baby.'

The stars darkened as a hefty transport shuttle sailed past, docking lights blinking, hull crusty with tacked-on tech and repurposed siding. Ky shrieked with glee. 'Oh man!' He looked to her, his eyes and mouth perfect circles. 'Mama, did you see?'

'Yeah!'

'Wow! Did you – did you see?'

'Yeah, I saw.'

'Dat's my ship.'

'Wow, that's *your* ship? Cool.'

''s my ship. 's all fixed.'

Aya had lost dessert privileges for a tenday over the origin of *all fixed*, but even though the illicit sim babysitting sessions had ended, the vocabulary addition remained. Tessa sighed, hoping her eldest hadn't irrevocably mixed up the younger's brain.

She let him play on the window, automatically responding with stock affirmations as he babbled on and on (he was on about . . . pillows? She'd lost the plot, and so had he, it seemed). Her mind was on the sky at her feet, which was to say she wasn't thinking about much at all. Something about that view always set her right, even though she'd seen it a million times. She thought back to the first time she'd been planetside, on a family trip to Hashkath. Ashby hadn't been much older than Ky. Mom was still with them. Their first night, Pop called Tessa out to the courtyard by their bunkhouse. 'Look at that, kiddo,' he'd said. She'd tilted her head up to match his. As an adult, she remembered how different the stars looked in that moment, how muted, how fuzzy. Her father had wanted to share something special with her, she knew in hindsight, but her immediate impression then was one of fear. There was no plex, no frame between her and that sky. She felt that any second, someone would switch the gravity off, and she'd float up and up, out forever. She'd stayed outside for all of two seconds before running back in and clinging fast to her bewildered mother, sobbing that she wanted to go home.

That experience still lingered on the few subsequent vacations she'd taken in adulthood, even though she knew nobody could turn off a planet's gravity, even though she knew her walls were less reliable than grounders' atmospheres. She knew that at home, she wasn't really looking *down*. She was up, sideways, all around. She was looking in the direction the artigrav nets told her to look, the same direction the old centrifuges made her ancestors look (and their view, of course, had always been spinning). But she could know that and still feel in her gut that stars lived below her feet. That was normal. That was where they belonged.

She thought, though, of visitors she'd had from somewhere else. The last time Ashby had been there with his crew – Ky had been tiny then, she reflected, remembering him kicking his untrained legs in her brother's arms – those two odd techs and the Aandrisk had parked themselves in the cupola for hours, sitting on the floor like Ky was now, freaked out and fascinated, never tiring of the novelty. A person's view of the stars was, ultimately, a matter of perspective. Of upbringing.

Tessa wondered how Aya would do with a planetside sky. She never came down to the family cupola – or any cupola, for that matter. These days, wherever she was in a room, she strategically placed herself as far from walls as she could manage. Would she mind being close to a wall if her feet were always held fast to the ground? Would she look out windows if she could trust them to not suck her through?

As for Ky, he was small. The sky was just another constant to him, like cookies and pajamas and family. He wouldn't care one way or the other for a few years yet. He'd absorb whatever environment you stuck him in. *All fixed.*

The guilty idea began to surface again, and Tessa knew it was time to get about her day. 'Come on, baby,' she said, gathering Ky, wiping his spit off the plex where he'd been licking it. 'I gotta get to work.'

They returned to the bench and headed upward. He looked up, watching the cable carry them. Tessa looked down just in time to see the stars darken again. 'Hey, Ky, look! There's a skiff!'

Ky nearly threw himself out of her arms, doubling over at the waist, pointing his head toward the cupola. But he was too late. The ship had already passed.

'Aw, bummer,' Tessa said. 'It's gone now.'

Her son looked at her, stricken, betrayed. His eyes widened. His lip trembled. The entirety of his face collapsed into itself, and he wailed with bitter injury.

Dammit. Well. Time for everybody else to wake up anyway.

ISABEL

Isabel hurried through the door as soon as she saw Ghuh'loloan through her office window, patiently waiting in front of her desk. 'Good morning,' Isabel said. She tapped her hud to bring up the time. 'I'm sorry, were we supposed to meet early?' She didn't recall that they'd arranged that, but then, she had so much on her plate that things were starting to fall off the edges.

'No, no,' Ghuh'loloan said. She stretched her dactyli reassuringly. 'I simply had much on my mind and wished to speak with you.' She pointed a tentacle at Isabel's desk, where two mugs of mek stood waiting. 'I managed to brave that contraption of yours, but I'm afraid I was too cowardly to try for a brew as hot as you make.'

'That's not cowardly.' Not at all, Isabel thought, considering the Ensk-labelled temperature dial and smooth knobs built for human hands. 'That was very kind.' She rather disliked starting her day with mek, but she wasn't about to turn down a drink made by someone who'd risked a nasty burn. She sat, and sipped. Stars, but Ghuh had made it strong. 'So, what brought you here?' She put her scrib on the table, ready for whatever questions about musical traditions or food storage or toilet technology her colleague had today.

But the Harmagian surprised her. Ghuh'loloan did not have her own scrib out, and she did not launch forth with a ravenous barrage of queries. Instead, she did something Isabel had never seen: she hesitated. 'Dear friend, I'm not sure how to begin,' Ghuh'loloan said. Isabel took immediate note of the change in address. Not *dear host*. *Dear friend*. 'The topic I wish to discuss is positive, but I worry it may cause difficulty, or worse, insult.'

Isabel set down her mug. She knew Ghuh'loloan understood smiling, and so she smiled. 'Dear friend,' she said, hoping her echo of the phrase came across as sincere. 'I very much doubt you'd insult me, especially since you've told me at the outset that it's not your intent. You trust me to be honest with you, right?'

Ghuh'loloan's tentacles relaxed. 'Indeed. Still, if my profession has made me aware of anything, it is that cultural bruising is often worst when done accidentally.' Her body quivered from front to end – her species' equivalent of a shrug. 'But now, at least, if insult occurs, you will know it was not by design.'

Isabel sipped her lukewarm mek and nodded, patiently awaiting the end of the Harmagian song and dance.

There was a great sucking sound as Ghuh'loloan filled her airsack. 'You know my writings of my time here have gained a sizable audience.'

'Yes.' Isabel didn't know how she could've responded otherwise. Ghuh'loloan had been downright euphoric over the messages she'd received from her readers. Modern life in the Fleet, it seemed, had struck a chord in the niche world of ethnography, and her colleague was happily spending her sleepless nights responding to as many questions as she could until Isabel woke up.

Ghuh'loloan forged ahead. Her friendly concern was absent now, having given way to matter-of-fact explanation. If there was one thing a scholar was good at, it was laying out a case. 'There has been a particularly strong reaction to my mentions of the Fleet's technical capabilities and resulting challenges. I'm sure you can imagine the sort I mean.'

Isabel gave a tight smile. 'They think we're a little backward, hmm?'

'To some, yes. Please do not take it personally. Cultural arrogance is depressingly universal, particularly among my people.' Ghuh'loloan paused, waiting.

It took Isabel a moment to catch on. 'I don't take it personally,' she said. 'Not to worry.'

The Harmagian was satisfied. She continued. 'Those responses, I pay no attention to. But there are others . . .' The hesitance returned. 'Others who wish to help. Not because you are incapable of helping yourselves,' she added quickly, 'but out of a real desire to provide resources that would be of benefit.'

Isabel leaned back in her chair. 'We're still a charity case,' she said. She felt that twinge of ego once more.

'Again, to some. But I wouldn't look at it as an act of pity. For many, it's out of a genuine wish for you to gain equal footing.' She wrapped a tentacle around her own neglected mug of mek. 'The reason I have decided to share this with you is that I have had a few letters that offer some intriguing possibilities.'

'Such as?'

Ghuh'loloan conducted the retract-face-open-mouth-pour-liquid manoeuvre, then cradled the mug against her porous bulk. 'Such as oshet-Tasthiset esk-Vassix as-Ishehsh Tirikistik isket-Haaskiset.'

Isabel blinked. Full Aandrisk names were nothing if not a mouthful. 'Who's . . . that?'

'Have you heard of Ellush Haaskiset?'

'No.'

'It's a comp tech developer, based in Reskit. Their entire managing council is comprised of a single feather family, and they represent a staggering amount of wealth. Tirikistik is one of the more public faces in their circle. She's also an amateur enthusiast of alien cultural study, and I've seen her in attendance at various symposiums at the Institute. It was quite exciting to receive a letter from her directly.'

Ghuh'loloan paused again, and Isabel took the cue to compliment her on a prestigious happening. 'That does sound exciting,' Isabel said. 'It speaks well of your work.'

Her colleague twisted her dactyli with pride. 'Thank you,' she said. 'Tirikistik has read all my writings on the Fleet to date, and she is understanding of the problem creds have created. She said she initially considered opening a trade line here, but my piece on your economic imbalance made her reconsider.'

Isabel gave a slight frown. Was Ghuh'loloan's work inadvertently discouraging outside trade? Were alien merchants reading her essays and becoming concerned that their business was doing more harm than good? The creds-or-barter issue required some serious ironing out, yes, but . . . but they did *need* that stuff. She wondered, with a sudden heaviness in her midsection, if this cultural exchange would hurt them in the end.

Ghuh'loloan continued her thread. 'Instead, she's interested in making a donation.'

'What kind of donation?'

'Well, she mentioned ambi storage facilities—'

'That wouldn't be of much use here.'

'That's what I said. I suggested that rather than her deciding what would be of help from an outside perspective, I could perhaps open a line of communication to the Fleet itself to see what would be of most use.'

'I can tell you exactly what the labour guilds' consensus would be,' she replied. 'Exodan problems require Exodan solutions. They'll say we've already relied too much on alien charity.'

'Charity from the GC parliament, and from Aeluons collectively. But this is a representative of a civilian business offering what amounts to a personal gift. A potentially enormous gift, but a gift nonetheless.' Ghuh'loloan took another disquieting gulp from her mug. 'The thing about gifts is, with correct, careful phrasing, they can always be turned down. Plus, you have me as an . . . an ambassador of sorts. I can easily deflect her if this offer would be poorly received. But I felt obligated to, if nothing else, pass the message along.'

Isabel tapped her fingertips together as she thought. A personal gift. Yes, *that* might open some doors. 'I could set up a meeting with the resource oversight council,' she said. There was no harm in a conversation, right? Like Ghuh'loloan said, they could always say no. But you couldn't know what you were declining until the option was at least on the table.

'Splendid,' Ghuh'loloan said. 'I'll hold off on my reply to Tirikistik, then.' She raised her mug in a mimicry of a Human cheer.

Isabel returned the gesture with a smile. As she drank, she thought of the artigrav nets beneath her feet, the solar harvesters orbiting outside, the limited-cognition AIs installed in public corridors for safety's sake. All gifted in decades past by species who couldn't imagine life without such things. Now, it was her own species who couldn't imagine life without them. She wondered what else could – and would – be replaced. What essentials would disappear.

KIP

Kip (10:13): are you awake

Ras (10:16): yes

Kip (10:16): can we meet up

Kip (10:16): I need to talk

Ras (10:20): I can't, I have chores

Kip (10:20): I really need to talk

Ras (10:21): there's nothing to talk about

Kip (10:21): uh yes there is

Ras (10:21): no

Kip (10:21): Ras come on

Kip (10:22): this is serious

Ras (10:23): I have to study

Ras (10:23): like actually study

Kip (10:23): okay fine I can come over

Kip (10:23): we could study together

Kip (10:25): and I could help with chores

Kip (10:30): Ras?

Kip (10:42): come on man

Kip (10:48): stop ignoring me

Kip (10:54): stop

Kip (10:54): ignoring

Kip (10:54): me

Kip (10:75): Ras please I just want to talk

Bastard.

Kip had hoped Ras would change his tune after they'd both slept and sobered up – both of which had been a profound fucking relief. Or at least, it *had* been a relief, until Kip had awoken enough to realise that everything that had happened really *happened*, and that the conversation they'd overheard wasn't a dream or a trip or anything so convenient.

Somebody had hid a body. It wasn't exciting, like it was in vids. This was terrifying. This was real.

As soon as the garden had cleared out, Ras had made it clear that he got how fucked up this was, but that they weren't going to say anything. They didn't know who those people were, and if they told someone, those same people might come after them. They might end up down in cloth recycling, too. Ras had left no room for argument. End of discussion. *They didn't hear anything.*

Except they had. They *had* heard it, and there was no forgetting it. There was no wishing it away, no matter how hard Kip tried.

He lay in bed, staring at the ceiling. He was starving, and his mouth was so dry his tongue felt sticky. But he hadn't left his room, even though he'd been awake for hours. The thought of facing family was too much. He couldn't put on an easy face. There was no pretending with something like this.

He was really hungry, though. Like, really hungry. He had a weird headache, too, and he felt tired to his bones. He was never doing smash again, he decided. Not fucking worth it.

Maybe somebody's already found him, he thought. Yeah. Yeah, that was comforting. If those people had stuck the – stars – the body down in cloth recycling . . . well, there were lots of people who worked there, right? Somebody would have to find him. Even the people who'd put him down there knew that. Yeah, somebody else would find him – had found him already, probably. Somebody had found him, and the patrols would take care of it, and Kip didn't have to worry about it. Nobody would know that he knew.

He wondered if someone was looking for whoever it was. His hex had to have noticed that he hadn't come home. The dead guy had been a bad dude, if he was working for those folks. But . . . he'd been someone, right? He'd been someone. They'd called him 'kid'. Someone else had to be looking.

Kip dug around the clothes lying by his bed and found his scrib. He did a skim through the news feeds. Bot upgrades, council meetings, Aeluons at war, Toremi at war, boring Human politics, boring alien politics – nothing about a body down in cloth recycling.

Shit.

He rubbed his face. Maybe they just hadn't found it *yet*. They'd find it today, though, definitely. Kip thought back to the time he'd won the shit lottery and spent two tendays in the recycling centre. He'd been on food compost, not cloth, but he'd walked through there, and seen all the folks washing and folding and stitching, all the folks walking by the . . . the . . . the giant piles of cloth. The piles you'd never get through in one day.

Kip thought about what it would be like to pick up an armload of everyday laundry and discover something horrible shoved underneath. A dead face lying silent. Cold eyes staring still. He wondered how it would be – how it would *look* – if the body lay there for a few days. His empty stomach knotted. He didn't want to think about that. He didn't want to, but now that he'd started, he couldn't stop.

Someone else would find the body, yeah. Someone else would find it, and xe wouldn't expect it, and it'd be the worst day of xyr life.

And those people he'd heard the night before . . . they were gonna get away. Throw a person away like it was nothing and hop to some planet where no one would ever find them. That wasn't okay. That wasn't right.

That wasn't right.

Kip thought about what Ras had said – how those people in the garden might come after them. He thought a lot about that. That thought made his stomach hurt, too. But he also thought about the opposite: what if they went after someone else? What if they did this again? Could he sit with that? How would his stomach feel if he read the feeds one day and . . . and . . . 'Fuck it,' he muttered. He sat up and searched for some trousers. His head tightened, the last remnants of smash sleep still making him feel crunchy around the edges. His heart hammered, too, but *that* wasn't because of the smash. That, he'd done on his own.

He stood at his bedroom door for a while before waving it open. Mom and Dad were in the living room, reading their scribs, drinking tea. The scene was so normal, so boring. So comforting. His heart beat harder, and even though there was nothing in his stomach, he wanted to throw up.

'You came home late,' Mom said. Her voice was annoyed, and her face was, too, right until she looked at Kip. The lines around her eyes let go. 'Kip, what's wrong?'

Kip had barely realised that he'd started crying. Stars, he was such a fuck-up. His parents were dumb, but they *cared*, in their own dumb way, and they'd *always* cared, and then he went and did shit like this. He stood there stupidly, hands in his pockets, trying to pull the tears back. He failed. Fine. He failed at everything else anyway.

He cleared his throat and frowned at the floor. 'I need to tell you guys something.'

EYAS

Eyas sat in her chair and stared at Sawyer's corpse, lying ready on her worktable. This was a typical sight, an everyday tableau, and the tasks ahead were normal as could be. But nothing about this body was normal. Nothing about this was okay.

She sat for half an hour before she finally got to her feet. She walked to her cabinet, opened the top drawer, and took out a belongings bag. The bag was made of throw-cloth, clean and well-stitched. A neutral way to contain objects that were anything but. She turned to the body, hesitant like she'd never been. Knowing him in life wasn't what troubled her. She'd prepared corpses of people she'd known, and known far, far better than a one-time acquaintance such as this. Hexmates' family members. Her favourite childhood school teacher. Her grandfather, which had been bitterly difficult. No, her reticence came from elsewhere. This wasn't a heartbreak. This was a desecration.

Her nose itched beneath her heavy breathing mask. She rarely wore a mask at work, not even when the person had been old or the death had been gruesome. But then, she'd never worked with a corpse in this state. It wasn't dangerous, of course – it had gone through a decontamination flash on arrival like all the rest. However, it *was* in the early stages of unchecked decay, and neither Eyas nor any of her colleagues encountered that regularly. This corpse hadn't been brought to the Centre on the day of death, accompanied by a grieving family and sombre medical staff. This corpse had been brought in by a patrol team, still retching and moaning over what they'd found hidden away.

Are you sure you want to take this one? her supervisor had asked. They'd been assembled that morning, every caretaker and apprentice, sitting in shock as it was explained what had been left for them.

I'm sure, Eyas said. She'd volunteered, and no one had argued. Everyone knew it was right. She was the one who'd gasped when the patroller displayed a picture of the corpse's face. She was the one who'd known the deceased's name.

Someone had thrown Sawyer away. Like garbage. Like a thing unwanted, used up. The thought filled Eyas with silent rage. The feeling smouldered in her chest as she removed a soiled shirt, a pair of thick socks, a trinket ring of alien make. It rattled her hands as she washed the body and saw flecks of trash floating down the drain. It wrenched her jaw as she reset visibly bent bones. She hoped whatever happened had been quick. Stars, she hoped it had been quick.

Sawyer was just one death, but the indignity, the aberrance, the slackness brought on by improper storage made her think of the tendays following the *Oxomoco*. She remembered cleaning body after body after body, laid out not in the seclusion of her workroom, but in the chill of a repurposed food storage bay. She remembered the day spent aboard the *Oxomoco* itself, when it had been her turn to take a shift cleaning out the abandoned Centres. She remembered learning what bodies looked like when they'd only composted halfway, remembered the smell that lingered on her exosuit in the airlock, remembered spending a standard afterward hand-grinding bones that hadn't disintegrated properly after exposure to air.

That time had been worse than this. An exponential amount worse. And yet, tame as Sawyer's corpse was in comparison, she knew the details of this day were going to bolt themselves to a similar spot in her mind. She didn't know this man, really, but he'd . . . he'd trusted her. Blindly trusted her, just like he'd blindly trusted the people who had led him to this table. If she'd been more patient with him, if she'd answered his letter and become his friend, if she'd given him a few more than five minutes of her time, would he – no, no, no. She knew better than to get dragged along by *if*s in situations like these, and she shut that line of questioning down. The guilt lingered, even so. Ghosts were imaginary, but hauntings were real.

She turned over the corpse's right arm, studying the hole where his wristpatch had been. The removal had been rushed and clumsy, and there wasn't much she could do about the damage. She wrapped it with a cloth bandage, for decency's sake. She'd read about patch thieves who prowled the grittier sides of spaceports, but – even though she had no experience with such things herself – her gut said this wasn't that. She'd never heard of that flavour of crime in the Fleet, and she doubted, under the circumstances, that someone had jumped on that particular bandwagon *now*. No, someone didn't want anybody to know who this corpse had been. But she knew. She'd given patrol a name, a place of origin, and a scrib path. *We can work with that*, the patroller had said, visibly grateful. That was a shred of comfort, at least. That was something.

She lifted the corpse's arm and inserted a length of thin, fluid-filled tubing connected to a bot reclaimer. She hit the switch and heard a mechanical hum as the reclaimer activated Sawyer's imubots, directing them to parade up the tube and into the soon-to-be-sealed receptacle. Eyas would then send them along to the hospital, where they'd be sterilised and reset and injected into someone else. Nothing went to waste in the Fleet.

She looked at the thrown-away corpse, the skin bruised and blue. Nothing was *supposed* to go to waste.

The reclaimer finished its task. Sawyer's body was ready for storage. Eyas wheeled it into the stasis chamber and shut the door. The corpse was gone, but she could still feel it in the room with her, a mess that would never be clean. She looked at the bag she'd put the clothes and trinkets in. There was a delivery label printed on the front of it, waiting for a name and family address. She found a heat pen, and wrote the only piece of information she had. She hoped the patrollers would fill in the rest.

She removed her mask, washed herself as hastily as good hygiene would allow, and left the room in a hurry, taking the belongings bag with her. She passed colleagues in the hall, but didn't meet their eyes.

'Eyas?' someone called. 'You okay?'

Eyas said nothing. She continued to the main chamber and took the elevator down to the cupola. She kept everything placid, everything *inside*, just in case there were any families down there, seeking the same quiet she was.

The elevator came to rest. Thankfully, thankfully, Eyas found herself alone.

She sat on one of the benches surrounding the domed window in the floor. Stars spilled out beneath her feet. The Centre wasn't sunside, but it was right on the cusp. Bright fingers of light teased past the thick windowsill, upstaging the delicate glitter beyond. The constellations changed as the *Asteria* continued its unending orbit, but the view from this spot always felt the same. The constancy was a comfort, a reminder that whatever unpleasantness you'd just been through was only a moment, only a blink within a vast, slow splendour.

Or it *was* a comfort, most days. All Eyas could feel now was the smouldering, the shaking, the wrenching. Assured of her solitude, she did something she hadn't done in a long time, not where bodies were concerned. She held the belongings bag in her lap, and she wept.

Part 5

WE ARE NOT LOST

Feed source: Reskit Institute of Interstellar Migration (Public News Feed)
Item name: The Modern Exodus – Entry #14
Author: Ghuh'loloan Mok Chutp
Encryption: 0
Translation path: [Hanto:Kliptorigan]
Transcription: 0
Node identifier: 2310-483-38, Isabel Itoh

[System message: The feed you have selected has been translated from written Hanto. As you may be aware, written Hanto includes gestural notations that do not have analogous symbols in any other GC language. Therefore, your scrib's on-board translation software has not translated the following material directly. The content here is a modified translation, intended to be accessible to the average Kliptorigan reader.]

Before I was Ghuh'loloan, my body belonged to someone else. Something else. By definition, I cannot remember this time, but I can tell you, from having visited my own offspring while they were in development, what it would've been like. The Being That Was Not Ghuh'loloan had no name, no identifying distinction beyond parentage. Xe was a polyp, an unfeeling mass anchored to a rock face alongside a hundred or so siblings. That being had the beginnings of the tentacles I do now – tiny buds waving in the simulated tides, pulling in the nutrient mix the minders routinely pour into the nursery pools. All Harmagians begin this way. For the first ninety tendays before we become ourselves, the polyps do nothing but hold fast and eat while engaged in the taxing business of growing a brain.

When the brain is sufficiently formed, the polyp detaches from the rock. Xe floats freely in the water for another tenday at least, wriggling constantly and without direction. Slowly, slowly, the new brain masters locomotive control, and the swimmer becomes strong enough to navigate around the pool. It is marvellous, dear guest, to watch the near-instantaneous shift from hapless writhing to purposeful experi-mentation. The child – for it is a child, now – does not have fully formed eyes or dactyli yet, nor is xyr gut developed, nor will xe venture out of the water for another eight tendays. But xe has control. That is when a Harmagian begins life. That is when I became Ghuh'loloan.

Biologically, I find that other species understand this phase of transition quite readily. What they do not understand is that culturally, we consider the moment of the polyp's detachment to be a death. To a Harmagian, this is obvious. What else could it be? The form and behaviour of a polyp are so different from that of a mature Harmagian that they can only be seen as separate entities. How could I have been Ghuh'loloan if I did not have a brain to understand what Ghuh'loloan was? How could I claim that polyp as a part of myself if I have not even the faintest recollection of that experience? (I do of swimming in the nursery pools: a hazy memory of a dash around a very tall rock, an image of an adult's enormous tentacle reaching underwater to fix an oxygen filter). Remember, we are a species that does not sleep. Our lives are defined by the aggregate of all that happens during the waking.

I used to assume, when I first began to study the lives of my sapient neighbours, that perhaps sleep would better prepare those species for death. Sleep sounds quite like death to me, a strange temporary death, complete with an afterlife of surreal visions. I have heard both a Human and an Aandrisk, on separate occasions, posit that death must feel like nothing more than a 'dreamless sleep'. You would think, then, that these species are less fearful of the inevitable end. If one experiences oblivion daily – and for an enormous portion of the day, at that – should it not be familiar territory?

I was wrong about this, of course. Some species have a more passive reaction to death than others – I am thinking here of the Laru, with their total lack of funerary customs – but sleep or no, all fear it. All spend lifetimes trying to outstretch its grasp.

In a highly social species such as my Human hosts, a death is keenly felt, even if it is that of a stranger. Certainly, I have been moved by the end of those I did not know – please read my fourth essay on this feed, dear guest, if you have not already – but Humans habitually react in a way that members of my own species might find extreme. A single death, regardless of relation, can dominate conversation for tendays upon tendays. It takes over news feeds, workplace chatter, decisions about the day. A death always fixates Humans in one direction or the other. They either talk about it at any given opportunity, or doggedly avoid the topic. I did not have a good hypothesis as to why this might be until I joined my dear host Isabel for dinner at her hex tonight. There has been an unusual death in the Fleet – accidental or purposeful, no one yet knows – and the families could speak of little else. All species emote around death, but there is an intensity of mood here I am unaccustomed to. I cannot stop pondering it.

As I sat witness to this behaviour tonight, two individuals caught my eye: Isabel and Tamsin's son, Miguel, holding his young daughter Katja on his lap. His embrace was snug, and he was stroking her hair as the others spoke and argued. At first, I thought the gesture was in order to calm or reassure her. Perhaps consciously, that is why he did it. But Katja was paying no attention to the conversation. She was fully engrossed in building a fortress out of mashed vegetables on her plate. If she registered the topic at hand, I do not think she understood much of it. But still, her father held, and stroked, and the longer the conversation went on, the more affectionate he became. I thought then of the means of Human reproduction. It is an intense process, an internal process. Even though her father did not go through this process himself, he was close audience to it (as is commonly the case, he is romantically partnered with Nina, Katja's mother). Human infants are famously frail, and the amount of time they remain dependent on adults for needs as basic as eating or locomotion makes me wonder how the species didn't give up on the whole prospect millennia ago.

Perhaps I am completely wrong about linking these two behaviours, dear guest, but I find it likely that there is a connection – even if only a tenuous one – between Humans' heavy parental involvement in child-rearing and how socially unsettled they become around death. Were I among my own kind and had someone met a sad end, it would be discussed, certainly. If I knew the deceased, I would visit their family to recite my praise of their life, as is proper. But I would not think of my offspring in that time. This would not occur to me. My offspring are not the ones who have died. I would know them to be well. Depending on age, I would know them to be swimming safely in their ponds, or being mindfully reared by their tutors, or living in homes of their own. I would not imaginatively transfer the misfortune of another onto them. I would not worry about them unless given reason.

Human parents always worry. Their offspring developed while attached not to rocks, but to themselves. And unlike Harmagians, who bid farewell to polyps and welcome new children in their stead, their progeny have but once to die.

——

TESSA

There was never a day when Tessa's home wasn't a mess, but the one she walked in on now was of a different kind. Cupboards were open, drawers were empty, and things she was sure she'd tidied up had found their way elsewhere. She might've thought the break-ins at work had moved to her home, were it not for Pop sitting on the couch in the middle of it, smoking his pipe and observing.

'What is going on?' Tessa asked warily, hanging her satchel by the door. Elsewhere in the home, she could hear industrious movement.

Pop raised his chin. 'Aya,' he said, 'is packing.'

Tessa had long ago stopped trying to predict anything that was likely to be waiting for her at home. She might as well write a bunch of nouns on some strips of cloth, add an equal number of verbs, shake them up in a box, pull two of each out, and pair them with her kids' names. *Ky eating paint. Aya breaking bots.* That system would be closer to the mark than anything she could come up with on her own.

Still. *Packing.* That was new.

She made her way to Aya's room and leaned against the open doorframe. Yes, indeed, there was her daughter, sitting by several old storage crates and everyday satchels stuffed with clothes and sundries – a pack of dentbots, Tessa could see, and a tin of tea as well. Her son was present too, kneeling on Aya's bed and trying his darnedest to put on one of her shirts. He was attempting to stick his head through the sleeve, but hey, points for effort.

Tessa surveyed the goings-on. 'Hey,' she said. 'What's all this?'

Aya looked up from her concentrated work. She took a large breath. 'Mom,' the nine-year-old said in a serious voice. 'I know this might be hard for you to hear.'

Tessa kept her face as straight as possible. 'Okay.'

'I'm moving.'

'Oh,' Tessa said. She gave a thoughtful nod. 'I see. Where are you moving to?'

'Mars. I know you don't like it there, but it's better than here.'

'Sounds like you've made up your mind about this.'

Aya nodded and resumed emptying her dresser into one of the crates.

Tessa watched for a moment. 'Can I help?'

Her daughter considered, then pointed. 'You can put my toys in this box here.' She pointed again.

As directed, Tessa sat on the floor and began to gather figurines and model ships. 'So, how are you getting to Mars?'

'I wrote to Uncle Ashby,' Aya said. 'He's going to pick me up and take me there.'

'Really,' Tessa said. 'Did he say that to you, or is that what you asked him?'

'That's what I asked him. He hasn't replied yet, but I know it'll be fine.'

'Hmm. You know, he's pretty far away right now. Why not take a transport from here?'

'I don't have trade good enough for a ticket.'

'Ah. Yeah, that's a problem.'

Ky wriggled his way off the bed and marched over to the boxes. 'I help!' he said. He grabbed a battery pack out of one of the crates, put it on the floor, then reached for something else to remove.

'Ky, stop it,' Aya said, not a trace of patience in her voice.

'No,' Ky said. He threw a bundle of socks with a laugh. 'No!'

'Mom,' Aya whined. 'Make him quit it.'

Tessa pulled her son into her lap. 'Ky, come on, don't throw,' she said. She handed him the least fragile of the toy ships in order to keep him busy. 'Aya, be nice to your brother.'

'He's so annoying,' her daughter muttered.

'You were annoying when you were little, too.'

'Was not.'

Tessa laughed. 'All toddlers are annoying, baby. It's the way of the universe.' She kissed her son's hair as her daughter continued packing. 'So, once Ashby drops you off on Mars, what's your plan?'

'They have bunkhouses at the docks,' Aya said. 'I can stay there until I make enough creds for a house.'

Tessa smothered a smile. Whatever vids Aya had picked up *dockside bunkhouses* from hadn't driven home the fact that nobody on Mars would give her a room *without* creds. She was from the Fleet, through and through. She wondered what other facts about grounder life her daughter hadn't gleaned. 'You know Martians don't live under open air, right?' She said the words strategically, trying not to scare *too* much.

Aya paused. 'Yeah, they do.'

'They don't. Humans can't breathe the outside air on Mars. Every Martian city is under a big shield dome.'

'What? No.'

'Yep. Here,' Tessa said, handing Aya her scrib. 'You can look it up on the Linkings.'

Ky dropped the toy ship and reached for the device as it was handed off. 'Mine!' he said.

'That's definitely not yours,' Tessa said. 'And your sister's using it now.' Ky started to fuss, so she grabbed the pair of socks he'd thrown earlier and put it in his stubby hands. 'Here, show me how fast you can make this into two socks.'

Ky plucked at a random patch of fabric. He'd be at it a while.

Aya, meanwhile, was frowning in a way that said she expected parental trickery. She looked down at the scrib and made a few practised gestures. The screen responded with pictures of Florence, Spirit's Rest, Perseverance. All glittering, all metropolitan, all . . .

corralled behind barriers against the harsh red dust outside. Aya visibly wilted. Tessa felt a little sorry for her. Adventures were a hard thing to let go of.

'Did something happen at school?' Tessa asked. The bullying had ended – as far as she knew – but Aya had been playing solo since then.

'No,' Aya said, annoyed at the question.

'You sure?'

'*Yes.*'

'Okay.' Tessa raised her palms. 'Why do you want to move, then?'

Her daughter's bravado was shrivelling before her eyes. 'I don't know,' she mumbled.

'That's not what you told me,' Pop said. Tessa craned her head back to find him standing in the doorway. How long had he been watching? 'Go on, bug,' he said kindly.

Aya said nothing. She fidgeted.

Pop looked to Tessa. 'She's upset about that grounder they found.'

'Oh, honey,' Tessa said. A pang of jealousy blossomed in her, and she hated it, but she couldn't shake it, either. Why had Aya shared that with Pop over her?

Ky fell quiet, understanding as far as his baby brain could that something was up with the grown-ups. Pop reached over and picked him up, making distracting nonsense sounds, leaving nothing to get between mother and daughter.

'I'm upset about that, too,' Tessa said. 'Everybody's upset about it.' That was true, and how could they not be? Some grounder thief, murdered and tossed away. Murdered. In the Fleet. Was there anyone who wasn't rattled by that news, who wasn't still wrestling with the idea of something like that happening *here*? There wasn't much to the story yet, but that didn't stop everybody from talking endlessly about it. Tessa scolded herself for not bringing it up with Aya before now. She hadn't thought it was anything a little kid needed to concern herself with, but clearly, it was. Sometimes, she lost sight of how easy it was for children to absorb the things adults whispered about. 'That was an awful thing that happened,' she said. 'A really terrible thing. But the patrols are on it. They're gonna find the bad guys who did it, and it won't happen again.'

'How do you know that?' Aya said. It was a direct challenge, a question that demanded an answer.

'I—'

'She doesn't,' Pop said. 'She wants you to feel better.'

Tessa glared at her father. 'How is that helping?'

He shrugged. 'She wants the truth, Tess. She's old enough to understand what happened, so she's old enough for – hey, hey, quit it, buddy.' He turned his attention to his grandson, who was pulling hard at his remaining hair.

His refuting her in front of her daughter was irritating, but he was – all the more irritatingly – right. Tessa folded her hands together and spoke to her daughter, who was growing up too fast. 'I *don't* know that it won't happen again. I'm bothered by it, and I'm scared, too. But I also know that . . . that kind of thing isn't normal here. Our home is a safe place, Aya. It really is.'

'That's not—' Aya struggled. She understood so much, and yet, not quite enough to pick apart her feelings. 'I'm not scared about it happening again.'

'Then what?'

'I'm not scared.' She frowned harder. 'You said we can't go live on a planet because bad stuff happens there. But – but bad stuff *does* happen here. I don't understand why we can't live on the ground if bad stuff happens here, too. If it happens everywhere, then . . . then it's everywhere.'

Aya's words were clumsy, but Tessa understood. Every lesson she'd tried to impart was based in principle, rather than practicality. *No, we can't move planetside, because it's too dangerous. No, you can't have creds, because you need to learn to trade. No, you can't watch Martian vids, because they solve every problem with violence, and that's not our way. No, you can't keep all the cookies to yourself, they belong to the hex, and you have to share, because we share. That's what we do. That's who we are.*

But now there was one news story, one unpleasant headline, that had thrown all that out of whack. There was danger in the Fleet, and it came from people who hadn't cared about trade, who hadn't minded violence – and those people were Exodan. That was the part that bothered Tessa the most. Everybody was so focused on the grounder, they sidestepped the one sentence that had shaken her: the patrols were pretty sure the dead guy's crew was Exodan, and would anybody who knew anything please come forward?

She looked at her daughter, bags packed, brow furrowed. Her daughter, who didn't understand that rooms cost money, who had unabashedly called on extended family for help when she lacked the ability to trade. Fear was the primary driver for Aya wanting to be elsewhere, despite how *not scared* she claimed to be. But maybe there was more to it than that. Maybe it wasn't that Aya didn't want to be Exodan. She was Exodan already.

Maybe, in her daughter's eyes, it was the Fleet that wasn't Exodan anymore.

'I think,' Tessa said, getting to her feet, 'I think we could do with something out of the ordinary this evening. How about . . . fish fry for dinner?'

Aya looked suspicious. 'We only do that on birthdays.'

'Well, I want to treat my kid. Is that allowed?'

Tessa watched her daughter wrestle between a nagging existential problem and the promise of greasy, crispy, calorie-laden food. 'Can we go to the waterball game, too?' she said.

'Is there a game tonight?' Tessa asked her father.

He nodded. 'Fast Hands versus Meteors,' he said. 'Just a scrimmage, not a qualifier.'

'Still, that sounds fun,' Tessa said. She wasn't much for waterball, but for her kid, she'd put up with a scrimmage. She smiled. 'Sure. We can go to the game.'

'Looks like it's you and me tonight, buddy,' Pop said to Ky, who was dozing off on his shoulder.

'No,' Tessa said. 'No, we should all go.' She took in her family, the mess, the room that had been hers. 'It's more fun if we go together.'

EYAS

Eyas hurried into the Centre, her heart a touch lighter. Her supervisor hadn't said anything over the vox except that patrol was there and wanted to talk to the grounder's caretaker. That had to mean progress. The stasis chamber holding the corpse had been left undisturbed since she'd cleaned the body over a tenday ago. Finally, *finally* patrol had found something. They'd found someone to take him home.

She headed to one of the family waiting rooms, where she'd asked for patrol to wait for her. The door swung open at her gesture, and a woman wearing a distinctive shoulder patch sat on one of the couches inside.

The patroller stood. 'Hello, M. I'm Patroller Ruby Boothe,' she said. 'I understand you're the one looking after Sawyer Gursky.' She was full-time, her patch indicated, but oddly, she didn't have a volunteer second with her. Under any other circumstances, Eyas would've reported her, but in this case, she got the impression the absence was for discretion's sake. Perhaps the patroller didn't want to stoke the gossip further. If so, Eyas respected that.

The addition of a last name to Sawyer's first should've kept Eyas' mood aloft, but the grim look on the woman's face prompted a spike of concern. 'You found his family?'

The twitch of Patroller Boothe's mouth said otherwise. She gestured for Eyas to sit, then pulled out her scrib. 'Sawyer Gursky,' she read. 'Twenty-four Solar years of age, born on Mushtullo, no siblings. We had to do some digging, but he's a descendant of the Arvelo family on the *Al-Qaum*. Housing records say they left to grab some ground right after contact.'

'No relations here, then?' This wasn't a surprise, given what Sawyer had said during their brief interaction, but she'd been hoping she remembered wrong.

'No.' Boothe cleared her throat. 'We don't have much communication with anybody in Central space, so it took a while to find the proper folks to talk to. Local law enforcement helped us out in the end.' She was dancing around something. Whatever it was, it bothered her. 'There was an outbreak of saltlick fever that tore through the Human district on Mushtullo about thirteen standards ago.'

'I don't know saltlick fever.'

'Neither did I. One of those wildfire mutations you hear about from time to time. Some minor alien thing that jumps species and fucks everyone over for a few tendays until imubots can be updated. I'll spare you the details. It was . . . well, it was bad. He lost his whole family. Grandparents, parents, everybody. Sawyer was the only one that made it.'

Eyas converted standards to Solars. 'He would've been . . . what? Six?'

''Round about.'

'Stars.' She frowned. 'Why did he remain on Mushtullo, then? He must have had relatives elsewhere.'

The patroller shrugged. 'I have no idea. Maybe they weren't close. Maybe they didn't know. Maybe they didn't care. Grounders, y'know?'

Eyas didn't care for that assumption. She gave a noncommittal 'mmm' and waited for Boothe to get to the point.

'Anyway, we couldn't find much about him, but based on his bank records and known addresses, it looks like he bounced around until adulthood – some kind of foster home setup, or friends, maybe. I don't know. He worked a bunch of odd jobs, then he wound up here.'

Eyas sighed. *Trying something new.* 'So who'd he record as his next of kin?'

'That's the shitty bit,' the patroller said. She tossed her scrib onto the table between them. 'He didn't.'

Eyas stared. 'His emergency contact, then.'

'Nope.'

'All GC records have them. It's right there for you to fill out when you update your patch.'

'Yeah, well, apparently he missed that bit. Didn't think he'd need it, or something.'

How could you miss that bit? Eyas thought incredulously. *How could you—* She shook her head, ending the loop between scorn and pity. 'There has to be someone.'

The patroller shifted in her chair. 'I'm telling you, M, we tried. We tried to get on the local news feeds, we tried to get law enforcement to put out a notice or something. But they're not Human, and they don't get it. The way they see it, somebody with no family and no emergency contact is dead and has been identified, and their job is done. If he has friends, all we can do is hope they read Exodan news, because we don't know who to—'

'Are you saying,' Eyas broke in, 'that nobody's coming for him?'

Patroller Boothe nodded. She cleared her throat again. 'We might hear from someone. I don't know. I can't predict that. Could be tomorrow, could be next standard. But I also know that the, um . . . the stasies you guys use here aren't built for long-term storage. So you might . . .' She trailed off.

Eyas understood. 'I might want to take care of it sooner rather than later.'

'Yeah.'

The room fell quiet. Nobody was coming for him. Nobody was coming for him, and there was nothing more to say.

KIP

Feed source: The Thread – The Official News Source of the
Exodan Fleet (Public/Klip)
Item name/date: Evening News Summary - Galactic - 130/306
Encryption: 0
Translation path: 0
Transcription: [vid:text]
Node identifier: 8846-567-11, Kristofer Madaki

———

Hello, and welcome to our evening update. I'm Quinn Stephens. We begin tonight's headline summary with news from the Fleet.

The investigation into the body discovered aboard the *Asteria* last tenday is still unfolding. Five suspects have been apprehended and detained in connection with the untimely death of Sawyer Gursky, a Central space immigrant who recently took up residency in the Fleet. The crew of the *Silver Lining*, a registered Exodan cargo ship captained by Muriel Saarinen, are believed to have hired Gursky to assist with looting aboard the *Oxomoco*. Large stores of stolen and illegally obtained goods were found aboard the *Silver Lining*, in addition to drugs and small weapons. All five crew members have been charged with theft, smuggling, illegal salvage, possession of firearms, and unlicensed possession of a pinhole drive. No murder charges have been reported yet. Jannae Green, a member of the traffic control guild, has been arrested as well. Green allegedly accepted credits from the thieves in exchange for disabling the

Oxomoco's proximity alert system for several hours while salvaging took place.

The supervisory council for the Fleet Safety Patrol reminds all citizens that illegal salvage is a serious crime, and is punishable by imprisonment. Patrol also encourages any persons aware of such activity to make an anonymous report, and wants to remind the public that without such a report having been filed, today's arrests would not have been made so quickly.

———

There was a buzz at the door. Kip put his scrib down and raised his head up from the pillow. 'Yeah?'

The door spun open. His dad entered, wearing a dorky smile and carrying a shopping bag. 'Know what time it is?'

Kip shook his head. Shit, was he supposed to be somewhere?

'Almost three. You blazed right through lunch, buddy.' He lifted the bag. 'Hungry?'

A tantalising, familiar smell drifted its way to Kip's nose. He sat up. 'Yeah.'

The dorky smile intensified, and his dad produced the bag's contents: a wrapped-up hopper and a frosty bottle of choko. He tossed both to Kip, one at a time.

Kip turned the warm bundle over after he caught it. The order was quick-printed on the cloth. *2x pickle. Fried onion. Extra hot sauce. No greens. Toasted bun.* 'How'd you know?'

'M Rajan knows your order, apparently.' His dad shook his head. 'I weep for your stomach lining.'

Kip managed a small smile. 'Thanks, Dad.'

The meal had been exchanged, and Kip was grateful, really, but his dad just stood there awkwardly, hands in his pockets, bag hanging around his wrist. 'So . . . tailoring didn't work out, huh?'

Kip rubbed his face. Stars, but he did not want to talk about job trials. 'Please don't lecture me.'

'No lectures,' Dad said, holding up his hands. 'Just . . . curious as to what you're up to.' He paused. 'Any fun plans today?'

'No.'

'Nothing with Ras?'

Kip looked away. 'No.' He didn't want to hang out with Ras. Ras had been pissed at first that Kip talked to patrol, but once time went by and no trouble came with it, Ras started straight-up *bragging*. Everybody at school was talking about the body, and Ras was telling them, yeah, he'd overheard the scavengers who did it, they were a buncha mean motherfuckers, you should've heard the way they laughed about killing that dude. Kip hadn't talked to Ras since he heard him doing that, and he hadn't responded to any of his scrib messages, either. 'I don't want to talk about it.'

'Okay.' Dad nodded like he understood. Kip didn't know if he actually did or not. 'You know that if you ever do want to talk – about Ras, or work, or . . . or . . . you know your mom and I are here, right?'

Kip picked at the hopper wrapper. Dad going to Grub Grub was nice and all – like, really nice – and he knew Dad wanted him to talk. But Kip wanted to be alone. Alone was easier. Alone was safe. He didn't know what to say. He didn't know what he was feeling. The wanting was still there, but it was different now. It wasn't him and Ras wanting more together. It was just Kip, wanting alone. 'Yeah. Thanks.'

His dad nodded. He seemed disappointed, but he didn't push. 'I'll be in the hex if you need anything,' he said. He started to leave, then turned back. 'You know, might feel good to get out for a while. I can give you some extra trade. Y'know, if you want to go play a sim or pick up some vid chips or something. I heard there's a new vid out with – oh, what's his name, that Martian actor you like – Jacob something.'

Kip rolled his eyes. 'Jasper Jacobs,' he mumbled.

'That's right,' Dad said. 'He's not my type, but I get it, I really do. He's got those . . . those big arms, and—'

Kip's chest began to cave in on itself. Stars, of all the things he didn't feel like talking with his dad about, Jasper Jacobs' arms were in the top three.

Dad cleared his throat. 'Anyway, let me know if you want to do something fun.'

Kip squinted. 'I spent all my tenday trade already.'

'I know.'

His suspicion grew. 'Mom doesn't let me have more after that.'

Dad winked. 'Mom doesn't have to know.' He gave a half-wave. 'In the hex. Just holler.' The door slid shut behind him.

Kip sat cross-legged on his bed, gifted lunch in his lap, guilt gnawing at his empty gut. Dad was trying to be his friend, and he knew that. He sighed, unwrapped the hopper, and tucked in. '*Mmmmph.*' The moan was reflexive. He *was* hungry. He tore into the meal like somebody was going to take it away. M Rajan had made it perfect, like always. The fried grasshopper meal was satisfyingly crunchy, the twice-round pickle felt like a salty, sour hug, and the hot sauce skirted that line between *ow, this hurts, please stop* and *I want to eat this forever*. He swore she put more hot sauce on each time, like she was training him or something.

The knot in his stomach grew. He thought about M Rajan, who knew his order when he wasn't even there, and Dad, who'd thought to go pick it up for him, and Grandma Ko, who'd been offering to take him for 'an unofficial Sunside' even though she one-hundred-percent did not have a shuttle licence anymore – and even Mom, who hadn't given him any shit when he pulled out of the trial at the tailor shop.

He shoved the last of his hopper into his mouth. He kind of wanted another one, and he did kind of want to go out. Not to the sims or the vid shop or anything. He popped open the choko and washed the burn away from his mouth. He'd had a weird thought for the past tenday or so, one he couldn't shake and couldn't share. It wasn't bad or anything. It was just . . . weird. A weird thing he wanted to do, one he couldn't have explained to Dad or Ras or anybody. Definitely not to himself.

Kip folded the wrapper and picked up his scrib. He stared at it for a moment. Maybe this was stupid, but . . . nobody would know, right?

'Public feed search,' he said. 'Saved parameters.'

The scrib chirped and did as told. He'd run this search probably a dozen times by now, but this time, a new result popped up. It wasn't much – just three lines. He read them a couple times over. He took another swig of his drink, then thought for a minute, then took another. He noted the date (tomorrow) and the time (eleventh hour). He looked down at himself, wearing a holey shirt and pajama pants. He got up, opened his closet, and sighed. Most of what belonged in there was on the floor. Bit by bit, he gathered shirts and trousers and underwear, and threw them into the basket that often stood empty.

His dad – who hadn't made it to the hex yet – looked surprised as Kip exited his room with laundry in tow.

'Hey,' he said, sounding confused. 'You . . . doing laundry?'

'Yup,' Kip said.

'Need any help?'

'Nope.' He headed to the hex's wash machines without another word. If he was going to do this weird thing, he was gonna do it right.

ISABEL

Funerals were never an easy affair, but Isabel was hard-pressed to think of one as uncomfortable as this. Not in a personal way. That distinction belonged to the funerals of her parents, her sister, Tamsin's parents, close friends. This was a different sadness. A social sadness. It was a natural feeling to have when attending – or even hearing of – a funeral for someone you didn't know. But this . . . this was exceptional.

In attendance were herself, of course, to make record, and Tamsin, who insisted on joining her for this one. Eyas Parata was the caretaker that day. Isabel had done ceremonies with her before, and she knew her to be the sort of compassionate guide a grieving family would benefit from. But there was no family today. There were no friends. Just three strangers, a body that had been thrown away, and a story that elicited plenty of public thrill but little sympathy. People had been horrified by the discovery of the body, and satisfied when the culprits were caught. There was a general buzz in the air that something had gone too far, something had to be done.

When it came to the victim himself, however, feelings changed. Isabel had heard everything from apathy to blame to indignation. The victim was an outsider. A leech. *He'd come into their home*, the party line went. *He'd eaten their food. He repaid their welcome by attempting to steal.* There was more to it than that, Isabel knew, but that was the story being told over tables. Sawyer Gursky had become an abstraction, an evidence file for whatever societal shift you hoped for. You want to encourage your kids to lock down a profession instead of heading elsewhere? Look at that poor dead boy, born of people who'd left Exodan values behind. He hadn't had the sense to find honest work. You want resource management reform? Look at that guy who died on the *Oxomoco*. He wouldn't have been there at all if there wasn't demand on the black market. You want to tighten up entry requirements for non-citizens? Look at that thieving bastard who got himself killed. Why should we let people like that into our homes?

'Round and 'round the chatter went, at hundreds of tables with hundreds of families. Yet none of them seemed to care about the indisputable truth: a Human being was dead, and no one had come to mourn him.

Isabel and Eyas stood together in the privacy of the shrouding room, side by side next to the body. Neither said a word. Tamsin had pulled up a chair. Her legs were giving her extra trouble that day, so she was saving herself – 'preserving her batteries,' as she put it – for the walk up the ramp.

'This is so . . .' Eyas began. She shook her head. 'I know how to do this with families. I've done this a thousand times.'

'I know,' Isabel said. 'I'm feeling lost, too.'

They were quiet again, and still.

'Can I see him?' Tamsin asked, nodding toward the body.

'Are you sure?' Eyas said. In preparation, she'd made an understandable break with tradition: the body was already shrouded. Usually, that was part of the ceremony – the family lovingly wrapping the cloth together. In this case, though . . . 'He's not in the best of shape.'

Tamsin pursed her lips. 'Is it bad?'

'Not—' Eyas' face twisted as she thought, perhaps weighing the difference between what was 'bad' to her and what it was to people who didn't do this every day. 'Not gruesome. There's no blood or disfigurement. But we didn't receive him right away. He'd started to decay before I got him into stasis. I did my best with him, but he . . . doesn't look like they usually look.'

Tamsin took in that information. 'I'd like to see him.'

Eyas stepped forward and pulled the shroud from his face. She'd done her best with him, that much was clear. He was clean. He was peaceful. But yes, he was different, different enough to give Isabel a stab of adrenaline, a shiver of disgust. This wasn't right.

'Oh, stars,' Tamsin said. 'He's just a kid.' Isabel laid her hand on Tamsin's shoulder. Her wife grabbed it. 'I'm sorry,' she said, brushing at her cheeks.

'Don't be,' Eyas said. 'I'm glad someone's crying for him.' She paused. 'I did, too.'

Tamsin nodded. Her tears continued to flow. She stopped wiping them away.

'Do you want to read the Litany?' Eyas said. 'I wasn't sure which of us should do it, so if—'

The door to the shrouding room opened, and they all turned to look. A boy stood there, a teenage boy in fresh-pressed clothes that didn't fit quite right. Isabel didn't know him. It didn't appear that Eyas did, either.

'Are you lost?' Eyas said.

The boy's eyes fell to the body, and he stared. 'I, um—' He cleared his throat. 'I asked outside where to go, and uh, they said I should go here, and— I didn't know you'd already started—'

'Are you a friend of his?' Eyas said, her words rising with a sliver of hope. 'Did you know him?'

The boy continued to stare. 'No. I just, um, y'know, I heard about it, and I—' He tugged at the edge of his shirt. '*Tika lu—* I mean, I'm sorry, this is stupid, I—'

Eyas gave a puzzled frown. 'You're welcome to join, if you want, but—'

Two pieces clicked together in Isabel's mind – a sliver of gossip and an inexplicable hunch. 'Are you the one who told patrol?'

The boy swallowed, and nodded. Isabel watched him with interest. His eyes had yet to leave the table. Had he been to a funeral before? Had he seen a body? To him, the face on the table would not be young, but older and respectable, an ideal he could grow into, a stage he aspired to, a promise cut short.

'What's your name?' Isabel asked.

The boy finally made eye contact with someone other than the corpse. 'Kip,' he said. 'Uh, Kip Madaki.'

Madaki, Madaki. Her brain tossed the name around, seeking connection. 'Does someone in your family work in water?'

'My Grandpa Griff did.'

Another piece clicked. 'Yes, I remember him. Not well, but I remember.' Old memories surfaced. She remembered being an assistant, an extra pair of hands at a naming. 'He had twin girls?'

'Yeah. My mom and aunt.'

Her brain was satisfied. 'Well, then. Kip Madaki.' She nodded with confirmation. 'I'm Isabel, and this is Eyas and Tamsin. We're glad you're here.'

'Would you like a seat?' Tamsin asked, pointing toward the other chairs.

'I'm good,' Kip said, shuffling closer to the table. 'Thank you.'

Isabel continued to study him. 'How did you know this was happening today?'

The boy moved as if he didn't know where to put his limbs. Stars, Isabel didn't miss that age. 'I've, um, been checking,' he said.

'Ceremony schedules? The public feed?'

'Yeah.'

'You mean, since they found him?'

The boy shrugged.

Isabel felt her spirits rise. 'Kip, before you came in, we were discussing who should read the Litany for the Dead. Would you like to?'

Kip was taken aback. 'Me? Um . . . I dunno, I've never—'

'Is this your first laying-in?' Eyas asked gently.

'No,' Kip said, 'but – I've never read the . . . that.'

'It's up to you,' Isabel said. 'But you helped this man. You helped the right people find him. You're the closest thing he has to a friend.'

Eyas extended her scrib. Kip took it. 'I don't know,' he said.

'You can do it,' Eyas said with the sympathetic smile that went hand-in-hand with her profession.

He cleared his throat, then licked his lips, then cleared his throat again. He began to read. 'From the stars, came the ground. From the ground, we stood. To the ground, we return.'

Isabel bowed her head as he spoke, one hand on his shoulder, the other holding Tamsin's. This still wasn't right. But it was better. It was a little better.

'Here, at the Centre of our lives, we carry our beloved dead. We honour their breath, which fills our lungs. We honour their blood, which fills our hearts. We honour their bodies, which fuel our own. We honour you, son of, um . . .' Kip stopped. 'What's his homeworld?'

Isabel turned the question over a few times. She'd never heard this portion of the Litany for the Dead said with anything other than a homesteader name. She wasn't so rigid in her traditions that the idea of inserting the name of an alien planet bothered her, and yet . . . and yet. 'He's still Exodan,' she said. 'Just more distantly.'

The boy looked unsure. 'So . . . should I say the *Asteria*, or . . .'

'The *Al-Qaum*,' Eyas said. She looked at Isabel and nodded. 'Patrol said that's where he was descended from.'

Kip started again. 'We honour you, son of the *Al-Qaum*. From death, you took life, and from your death, we now live. Here you will stay, until we rejoin the stars once more.'

Isabel took her cue and gestured at her scrib. 'We record the laying-in of Sawyer Gursky, age twenty-three. His name will be remembered. For so long as the Archives remain, so shall he.'

Eyas turned to Kip. 'Will you help me with him?'

Kip nodded, his face unreadable, his heart unknowable. But he took his place at the head of the stretcher. He shared the caretaker's weight. He accompanied the stranger on the long walk up the ramp. He did these things, and it said all that needed to be said about him.

Isabel followed, Tamsin leaning on her arm. All unoccupied caretakers had gathered, as they always did, standing vigil along the pathway, each holding an item of their choosing – a globulb, a flower, a dancing ribbon, a gnarled root, a bowl of water.

'Thank you,' they murmured to the body as it passed by. 'Thank you.' *Thank you for what you will become,* they meant. *Thank you for what you will give us.*

They came at last to the top of the ramp, and reached the covering bed. To the untrained eye, it was nothing more than a flat layer of bamboo mulch, but Exodans knew better. There were walking paths raked by the caretakers around the unmistakable mounds. There were painted flags stuck in patches recently filled. There were shallow craters over patches ready to be filled again. And there was the warmth – a thick, earthy heat rising from the ground, almost too hot. A suggestion not of death, but of life, of energy, of birth.

Eyas led the way to an unmarked patch, then set down her end of the stretcher. Kip set down his as well. A set of shovels lay waiting. They both took one, and Isabel did as well, though she knew she wouldn't get as far as the other two. That wasn't the point. Everyone who was able had to turn the soil. Tamsin stood by the body, resting her weight on her cane, eyes closed as she whispered the Litany from memory, for no one's comfort but her own.

Isabel dug as best she could, and as she did so, her heart filled with a complicated tangle. Sorrow for Sawyer, whose time had been stolen. Anger for Sawyer, who'd been led astray. Respect for Eyas, and all of her profession. Respect for Kip, too, who dug vigorously, even as his face became covered in silent tears. Love for Tamsin. Love for her living family. Love for her dead family. Fear of death. Joy for life.

It was, in the end, a proper funeral.

They set aside their shovels and lifted Sawyer's body. Slowly, carefully, they laid him in. He was cold now, and heavy, but those things would soon change. He'd followed his ancestors. He'd rejoined their ancient cycle. They would keep him warm.

Part 6

WE FLY
WITH COURAGE

Feed source: Reskit Institute of Interstellar Migration (Public News Feed)
Item name: The Modern Exodus – Entry #18
Author: Ghuh'loloan Mok Chutp
Encryption: 0
Translation path: [Hanto:Kliptorigan]
Transcription: 0
Node identifier: 2310-483-38, Isabel Itoh

[System message: The feed you have selected has been translated from written Hanto. As you may be aware, written Hanto includes gestural notations that do not have analogous symbols in any other GC language. Therefore, your scrib's on-board translation software has not translated the following material directly. The content here is a modified translation, intended to be accessible to the average Kliptorigan reader.]

——

Imagine, for a moment, a Harmagian shoreline village of old. It is a busy place, but a simple one. The people there do little more than gather – river mud for building, ocean sand for resting, smaller creatures for eating. There is a world outside this tiny territory, but the villagers know next to nothing of it. There is no need for them to think beyond home and dinner.

Well past the beach, there is a wooded marsh, and in the marsh lives an animal. The villagers have never seen it, but they have heard its call – a strange hooting that pierces the dawning hours. There are many stories about the sound. Some say it is a monster that will prey on any children foolish enough to leave the safety of the village. Some say it is a being made of dead Harmagians, the amalgamation of each body left to disappear under the heat of the sun. But there are some who doubt these stories. How, they wonder, can you speak of what a thing is if you have never seen it with your own eyes?

One day, quite by accident, the question of the animal is answered. Its corpse washes downstream, and comes to rest in the very spot where the villagers gather mud. No one has seen anything like it before. This is a creature adapted not to water, but to trees. It is covered in hair – a feature no Harmagian has seen before. Much debate takes place over what to do with it, and, perhaps inevitably, one question dominates all others: *Can we eat it?*

When the beast is cut apart, a discovery is made. The poor thing's stomach is full of metal slag, which the villagers routinely dispose of in an out-of-sight heap on the edges of the beach. Undoubtedly, this was the cause of death. *Why was the animal eating this?* the villagers wonder. *Why did it continue to eat this?*

Why?

And so, they make the leap from people of superstition to people of science. A group of the village's bravest set out for the marsh, in search of the animal's kin. They discover much more than that, of course, and a frenzy takes hold of the explorers, a mad passion for wanting to unlock every secret the marsh holds. More expeditions are launched. Base camps are built, so they may journey farther and farther still. Trading posts are built near rivers, so as to not waste any time in back-tracking to replenish supplies. Their intentions are born of the purest curiosity, a trait no one can fault them for. But their quest for knowledge has an unfortunate side effect. The animal they were seeking – bal'urut, they have named it – is comprised of a devastating combination of traits. It is skittish to the extreme, instinctively afraid of anything travelling in a pack (thanks to the prowling kressrols, a predatory species our villagers will encounter in due time). If the bal'urut becomes scared enough, its drive for survival will cause it to flee the area – with or without the lengthily gestated young it has been caring for in its den.

The bal'urut is also a specialist. It eats only a specific type of insect that nests in a specific type of tree in this specific corner of the world. Migration to more tranquil territory is not an option, not in the time it would take their guts to evolve for more varied fare.

By the time the explorers realise their presence is what is driving the very creature they wish to understand to abandon its offspring, it is too late. Infant mortality has skyrocketed to the point that the species can no longer sustain itself. Within a Harmagian lifetime, the bal'urut is no more. Other species fall in its wake. Our plucky explorers have the dubious distinction of making the first Harmagian record of a trophic cascade.

If you have studied any scientific discipline through Harmagian instruction, dear guest, you already know the story of the bal'urut. It is one of our most enduring cautionary tales. Many a professor has relished frustrating students with the ethical quandary at its core. If the villagers had not ventured into the marsh to better understand the bal'urut, then its breeding behaviour would not have been disrupted. But had the villagers stuck to their beach and their narrow view, they would've continued to pile slag at the marsh's edge, and the bal'urut would've kept dying from eating it (archaeological studies suggest that bal'uruts found the salt deposits left behind in the metalworking process irresistible). My own research methodology professor phrased this concept succinctly: learn nothing of your subjects, and you will disrupt them. Learn something of your subjects, and you will disrupt them.

The bal'urut has been on my mind as of late. As an ethnographer, my role is to be a neutral observer. I cannot judge, I cannot suppose, I cannot fill in blanks with my own biases (as much as this is possible). And yet, my presence here has prompted change. I have not done anything harmful, to my knowledge. All I have done is talk. I ask questions, I give answers, I make connections. This is not much, and yet, I of all people should know that this can be everything.

I am being vague, dear guest, and for that, I apologise. I have set events in motion that will bring new technologies into the Fleet – namely, improved medical equipment, and sentient AI installations to facilitate resource management. I believe – or I sincerely hope, at least – these will be of great benefit to my hosts here. Given the letters I have received from many of you, I feel confident in assuming that you would agree. Indeed, I am humbled by the generosity that has made these donations possible. Truly, the name of our Galactic Commons was chosen well.

Still, I cannot ignore the fact that I came here to document the Exodan way of life, and as I near the end of my visit, that way of life is changing. This should not surprise me. I have ventured into the marshlands. I know this story well.

———

Received message
Encryption: 0
Translation: 0
From: Tessa Santoso (path: 6222-198-00)
To: George Santoso (path: 6159-546-46)

Well, they actually did it. Cargo bay jobs are going away. Not today. Not for a while. But they're going to install sentient AIs here on the *Asteria* as a pilot programme, and, if it goes well, kit out the rest of the Fleet as well. I would've told you differently a couple tendays ago, but today, my gut says that pilot programme is going to catch on quick. People love these things. My brother just had to get a replacement for his old one, and he's being very weird about it. It's like he lost a pet or something. I don't get it, but I've never worked with one, so who knows. Easier to deal with something that's always cheerful and there to help than with us slow, cranky people, I suppose.

Me and a few others have been asked to work with the incoming comp techs to figure things out or set things up or however it works. Teach the machines what we're doing so they can do it better. I've also been advised to start talking to the job office now, so I can figure out where I might want to go. Y'know, make time for classes. Make time to apprentice. Stars, George. I've been running job trials all standard, and now I'm the one who needs one.

I'm mad about it, and I know it's stupid. It's not like managing cargo is the most exciting job there is. But it was *my* job, and all I can think about are the projects I'm not going to finish and the systems I worked out and felt proud of that don't matter anymore. I don't know if this will make sense, but I keep wondering where we're going to draw the line. Nobody's talking about replacing pilots or bug farmers or teachers, even though AIs could do all of those, because those are *fun* jobs. Jobs that mean something, right? But *I* liked my job. There were things in it that I found fun. I thought what I did was meaningful. I thought I was doing something good. Who decides that? What if we decide that flying shuttles and raising red coasters aren't actually all that fun, and we get rid of those jobs, too? What do people do, then? I went for a drink with Sahil after we got the news, and I asked him that question. He thought it'd be great. He said he'd go be a perma-student at some university and learn all he could. But why? Why learn anything if you're not going to do something with it? Why learn anything if everything worth knowing is in the Linkings anyway, and you can ask your pet AI?

Sorry, I know I'm rambling. I just don't know where I want to go from here. Right now, I'm not sure I want to be here at all.

———

EYAS

Eyas fidgeted in the corridor outside the unfamiliar hex. What if this was a bad idea? What if this screwed things up? She'd entertained both those possibilities, and was entertaining them still, but this was the only course of action that didn't leave her feeling restless. This was the only thing, right then, that made sense.

She walked forward into the common area. Eyas had thought, on her way here, that she'd have to approach a stranger, introduce herself, bring a third party into this exchange. But her timing was perfect. Sunny was kneeling right there in a planter square, a gardening apron tied around his neck and waist, a palette of leafy starters abandoned by his knees, a young boy clinging to his back and wrestling him from behind. Sunny could've easily thrown the kid off, but he swayed and moaned in mock defeat.

'Oh, no!' Sunny yelled. 'Oh, no, you've got me! Help, someone help, there's a monster, a horrible monster's got me—'

The kid giggled. 'I'm not a monster,' the boy said. 'I'm a lion. I'm from Earth!' He made a . . . well, he made a sound. Whether it was actually lion-like was anyone's guess.

'I'm very sorry, I should have realised,' Sunny said. 'Please, M Lion, don't eat me.'

'I *am* gonna eat you!' the kid said, noisily play-biting Sunny's shoulder.

Sunny gave a wicked grin. 'Or maybe . . . I'm gonna eat *you*!' In one fluid sequence, he grabbed the kid, hauled him around to

289

his front, pinned him down, and made chomping sounds as he mercilessly tickled the now-shrieking boy's tummy. 'Oh, no, a dramatic reversal! Nom nom nom nom nom—' His eyes flicked up and saw Eyas for the first time.

Eyas had her knuckle against her mouth, a smile spreading behind it. She gave a little wave.

Sunny was surprised, no question, but took it in stride. The ticklefest ended abruptly. 'We gotta take a break, buddy. We've got company.' The kid looked over as Sunny stood up. 'This is my friend Eyas,' Sunny said, cocking his head. 'Hi.' It was a question.

'Hi,' Eyas said. She smiled at the boy. 'What's your name?'

The kid scrutinised her. 'Kirby.'

'My nephew,' Sunny said, pushing his own hair back into place, brushing his hands on his apron. Was he self-conscious? Did he mind her seeing him like this – unshowered, dirty palms, ratty work clothes? Had she crossed a line? Having sex was one thing; entering someone's home was another. Maybe this was an intimacy she shouldn't have assumed.

'I'm sorry,' Eyas said, 'I hope I'm not—'

'No.' He meant it. 'No, not at all. Please.' He gestured to one of the dinner tables. She followed.

'Hi there!' someone called. Eyas turned. An elderly woman had stuck her head out the front door of her home, no doubt curious about the newcomer. She waved as if they were fast friends.

'Hello,' Eyas called back.

'Friend of mine,' Sunny said. 'From the *Asteria*.'

'Oh, welcome!' the old woman said. She nodded with approval – approval of *what*, Eyas could only guess at – then went back into her space.

'That's M Tsai,' Sunny said, sitting at the table. 'She's very sweet, and very nosy.'

Eyas laughed as she sat opposite him. 'I gathered.' She looked around the hex. Kirby had abandoned lioning and was now digging haphazardly through Sunny's neat planter rows. If Sunny noticed, he didn't seem to mind.

'So.' Sunny looked at her, the question unanswered.

'Right,' she said. She'd had the entire ferry ride to think about this, but now she didn't know where to start. 'I was hoping I could – that is, if you have the time to talk—'

'Yeah, I'm not— hey, Kirby, you can play in the dirt all you want, but leave the shears alone, yeah? – sorry.'

'Don't be. Kids are kids.'

'I'm not busy, is what I was saying.'

'Cool. Okay, well . . . I've been stuck on this idea, and I thought—'

Her attempt was derailed by M Tsai, who had reappeared with offerings in hand. 'I thought you two might like some iced tea,' M Tsai said, setting down a full pitcher and a pair of glasses. 'My own special recipe. I always keep some around in case guests show up.' She filled Eyas' glass. 'Are you one of his clients?'

'M, you know you can't ask that,' Sunny said. 'That's confidential.'

'It's okay,' Eyas said. She smiled at M Tsai. 'I am.'

'But she's my friend, too,' Sunny said. He locked eyes with Eyas. Something passed between them. He'd seen her every which way, and yet, somehow, *this* – a shared pitcher of tea, a confirmation of friendship, a secret smile – this was the most vulnerable she'd ever felt around him.

'How nice,' M Tsai said. 'And what's your profession?'

Sunny transmitted an apology through his eyes.

'I'm a caretaker,' Eyas said.

'Oh! Oh, my goodness. Well.' She looked at the now-filled glasses, trying to find an excuse to stay now that her previous one had ended. 'You know . . . biscuits. I got a packet of quick dough as trade a few days ago, and a bunch of herbs in my home that aren't going to last much longer. I think this kind of company deserves a proper snack, don't you?'

'M,' Sunny said, 'that's really—'

'It's no trouble!' M Tsai said, already on her way. 'It won't take long!'

Sunny gave an apologetic sigh as soon as M Tsai's door shut. 'I'm sure this isn't why you came by.'

'Not quite,' Eyas said.

He folded his arms on the table. 'Start at the beginning.'

'I'm still thinking about Sawyer.' She'd reserved a whole night with Sunny after the funeral, instead of the usual half. Neither of them had commented on it, or needed to. She'd taken care of someone else. He'd done the same for her.

Sunny folded his mouth sympathetically. 'That had to be pretty . . . I dunno. Traumatic.'

'Not his body. It was . . . unpleasant, yes. But I don't mean that. I mean *Sawyer*. I mean the man I spoke with for five minutes.' She frowned. 'I wasn't very patient, and I wasn't very kind. But he was so grateful for what flimsy advice I gave him. He looked so happy. He wrote me a letter. I think I may have been more patient and kind to him than most, and that's . . . that's why he's dead. He got taken advantage of. He didn't know how things worked. But he *wanted* to. I know I only had that one short conversation, but . . . I think his heart was in the right place.' Eyas sipped her iced tea and paused. 'This is delicious.'

Sunny nodded. 'M Tsai is a legend in the kitchen. Used to work in imports, so she's got all kinds of spices and stuff. I'm honestly stoked she's making biscuits.' He sipped his own drink. 'But again, not why you're here.' He looked at her with kind eyes. 'It makes sense that you're still upset about it.'

Eyas shook her head. He was getting the wrong idea. 'I'm not here because I'm upset. If I needed a counsellor, I'd go see a counsellor.'

'Talking to friends is okay, too, y'know.'

'I didn't mean – I know. And I appreciate it. But I don't want to sit around and be sad. I want to do something about it.'

'Okay.' He leaned back thoughtfully. 'What'd you have in mind?'

'You know the emigrant resource centres, right? With their workshops and such. How to speak proper Klip, how to live alongside aliens. Everything you need to know before you move planetside. That's what our ancestors were trying to prepare us for, right? That's why the Fleet *exists*. Except that's *not* the point of the Fleet anymore, not entirely. I'm not here to shepherd people along to new planets. I care for the ones who made their lives here. And you – you're the same, only in present tense. We both want to make life good for the people who choose to stay. So . . . why don't we have the opposite?'

'The opposite of what?'

'Classes. Workshops. Resources for grounders who want to live in the Fleet. We have nothing for them right now. We have homes standing empty, and jobs unfilled, and we're . . . what? Hoping that the next generation will want to stick around more than the last? Look, if it was a matter of everybody wanting to leave here, fine. But that's not the case. People aren't just staying in the Fleet. They're *coming back*. We have such disdain for outsiders who come and act like this is a museum, but what about the Sawyers? What about the people who *don't* have a place out there, who think that our way of life has some appeal? We look at them and we say, oh, stupid city kids, stupid Martians, they don't know how things are. They don't understand how life works out here. So, let's teach them. Let's teach them, instead of brushing them off and laughing behind their backs. Let's bring them in.'

Sunny took that in. 'Huh,' he said. He took a long sip of his tea, looked over his shoulder to verify that his nephew had indeed left the shears alone, then set his drink back down. 'Huh. That is . . . not a terrible idea.' He paused. 'That's a great idea, actually.'

'Thank you.'

'You could totally get council support for it, too. They'd be all over it, especially given your . . .' He gestured. 'What you do.'

'My thinking exactly.' Some of the *Exodan resources for*

Exodan problems types might be harder to sway, but – come on. Who could argue with a caretaker who wanted some resource allotments in the name of *preserving tradition*?

He nodded. 'And you want to teach?'

'Not full-time, and not alone. Think about the resource centres. Most of those people put in an hour here, a day there. All sorts of different professions helping out. It has to be that way, if the centres want to give people a proper toolkit. So, we'd need to do the same. Get people with jobs you don't find elsewhere in the galaxy to explain what it is we do and why.'

'"We".'

'Yes. I want you to do it with me, if you're interested.'

'Wow, okay. Um . . . hmm. I'm not sure I'd be much of a teacher.'

'Why not?'

'I was an awful student. I've told you. The laziest.'

'Academic prowess and base intelligence are two separate things.'

'See? I could never make a sentence like that on the fly.'

'So? That's ideal, actually. That was a boring sentence, and the last thing we want to be is boring. You're charismatic. You know how to talk to people. You'd be great at this.'

'You're serious.'

'Completely.'

'Okay.' He crossed an arm over his stomach and scratched his chin with the other. 'Well . . . can I think about it a bit?'

'Of course. Take some time, see how it sits.'

'In the meantime, can I give *you* something to think about?'

'Always.'

Sunny stared up at the ceiling for a moment, as if the words he was looking for were up there. 'Obviously, I don't have plans on going anywhere soon, and I know we live on different ships, but whenever my time comes – how would you feel about . . . y'know. Taking care of me.'

Eyas set down her glass. 'Yes, absolutely. You can put in a

request for a specific caretaker at your deck's Centre. We're all part of the same guild, so they'd contact me.'

He laughed. 'So you *don't* need to think about that one.'

She paused. 'Sorry, I treated that like a practical question, didn't I?'

'Yep.'

She laughed as well. 'Sorry.' Stars, here he'd asked her something profound and she'd responded like a formwork header.

He folded his hands on the table. 'Treat it like an emotional question.'

She looked down at her drink. 'I'd be honoured,' she said. 'That means a lot to me, that you want that.'

Sunny smiled. 'And it would mean a lot to *me* to know that the person who will take care of me is a *whole* person. Not just a symbol.' He stopped, and his smile grew. 'You'll be happy to know we can stop being corny now, because I have some great news.'

'What's that?'

He gave a dramatic sniff and pointed at the air. 'Biscuits.'

ISABEL

Of all the places Isabel might've guessed Ghuh'loloan would want to make a repeat visit to, her hex was at the bottom of the list. The First Generation murals, perhaps, or a musical performance, or the plaza oxygen garden. But no, this distinguished academic from an equally distinguished species wanted to spend one of her final days in the Fleet in hex 224-613's common area. She was in their far more humble garden now, surrounded by shrieking kids. Shrieking, laughing, soaking-wet kids.

'Again! Do it again!' one of the relatively older kids cried in Klip. The others echoed him in tiny accents: 'Again! Again!'

'Again?' Ghuh'loloan said, her tentacles dancing with amusement. 'Are you quite sure?'

'Yes!'

'As you wish.' She gestured to her cart, and the kids flailed with knowing anticipation as a panel opened. Out flew Ghuh'loloan's mistbot, a floating globe filled with cool water, designed to refresh Harmagian skin whenever the need arose. Nothing about Ghuh'loloan's face approximated Human expression, but nonetheless, Isabel could discern the unbridled glee her colleague felt as she directed the bot to deploy itself, for the fifth time now, over the kids' heads. They screamed and giggled, running aimlessly in the steady drizzle.

'Again! Again!'

'I'm afraid that will have to do, dear children,' Ghuh'loloan said, 'or I will have none left.'

Isabel stepped in, venturing into the splash zone. *'That's enough now,'* she said in Ensk. *'Let's give Ghuh'loloan a break, hmm?'*

There was some mild protesting, but the kids were too wound up now to hang around doing nothing. They dispersed in bits and pieces, running off to play with toys or raid the kitchen or shake their soggy hair at their parents.

'It is a truly singular experience,' Ghuh'loloan said, 'living alongside your offspring *and* your offspring's offspring.'

Isabel took a seat on a nearby bench. 'An experience you wish you'd had?' she asked.

The Harmagian let out a rolling laugh. 'Oh, stars, no. This is madness. Wonderful, too, dear host, but I enjoy it for the novelty. I could not do this every day. I admire your species for its stamina in this regard. And your patience.'

'Oh, we run out of patience plenty,' Isabel said. She glanced aside. Tamsin was seated nearby, out of earshot, but within plain sight. Isabel had thought she'd been watching the mistbot shenanigans, but though they had ended, she remained, her hands busy with a broken vox, her eyes on the alien. Isabel caught her wife's gaze, waved her over, and continued speaking to Ghuh'loloan. 'You don't miss them? Your children, I mean. When they're growing up.'

'It is not the same for us,' Ghuh'loloan said. She bowed her eyestalks in acknowledgement as Tamsin joined Isabel on the bench. 'It is not an experience we have, so there is nothing to miss. Children are kept in nursery pools, tutelage villages, and universities. I was never in the homes of either of my parents until I was an adult, and I never lived there. It would not have occurred to me to want that.' She looked around the hex. 'You would think a communal home would not feel so strange to me, as I live in an Aandrisk city. But their homes are not like yours. You are different, dear hosts. You are unique.'

Tamsin leaned forward. 'But are we worth it?' She spoke the words without hesitation, as if they'd been sitting on her tongue for tendays.

Isabel knew they had been, and she couldn't believe they'd been let out. '*Tamsin.*'

Her wife was as unconcerned as could be. 'It's just a question.'

Ghuh'loloan looked puzzled. 'Forgive me, but I do not understand.'

'Do you think we're worthy of the rest of the galaxy's time?' Tamsin said. 'GC membership, donated tech, this star you gave us. Do you think we're worth it?'

Isabel looked away in embarrassment. She wasn't going to fight in front of a guest, but oh, it was happening later.

The Harmagian fanned her dactyli in thought. 'I am here, am I not? But that is not what you are asking. You are not asking if the Reskit Institute finds you worthy of study. You are asking what I, Ghuh'loloan, think of you.'

'Yes,' Tamsin said.

'That is a risky thing to ask, dear host, but I would not insult you with a dishonest answer.' Ghuh'loloan's eyes blinked and widened. 'Very well. You are a species of slim means. You produce nothing beyond extra bodies to perform labour, and you have contributed nothing to the technological progress of the GC at large. You value being self-reliant, and you were, once, but now you eat our food and harvest our suns. If we kicked you out now, it would be difficult for you to sustain yourselves as you did before. And even with our help, the age of these vessels means you are constantly, irresponsibly courting a disaster like the one you've already weathered. These are the facts. Now, let us discuss the facts of my own species. We are the wealthiest species alive today. We want for nothing. Without us, there would be no tunnels, no ambi, no galactic map. But we achieved these things through subjugation. Violence. We destroyed entire worlds – entire species. It took a galactic war to stop us. We learned. We apologised. We changed. But we can't give back the things we took. We're still benefiting from them, and others are still suffering from actions centuries old. So, are *we* worthy? We, who give so much only because we took so much? Are you worthy, you who take without giving but have done no harm to your neighbours? Are the Aeluons worthy? Are the Quelin? Show me the species that has never wronged another. Show me who has always been perfect and fair.' She flexed her body, her alien limbs curling strong. 'Either we are all worthy of the Commons, dear Tamsin, or none of us are.'

Tamsin said nothing for a moment. 'The first Harmagian I ever saw was on a news feed, talking about how Humans didn't belong.'

'The membership hearing.'

'Yeah.'

Ghuh'loloan stretched the dactyli around her mouth. 'The first Human I ever saw was at a spaceport, in the process of being arrested for selling unlicensed scrub fuel.'

Tamsin gave a short chuckle. 'Great first impressions, huh?'

'Indeed.'

Isabel looked between the two, still thrown by the turn the conversation had taken. Would Ghuh'loloan ever have said anything like this to her on one of their carefully chosen field trips, in one of their polite academic chats? Would her dear guest have been this candid if, for a moment, Isabel had stopped worrying about being a good host?

'You can't shake hands, right?' Tamsin gestured vaguely. 'I can't touch your tentacle with my hand, right?'

Ghuh'loloan reached for one of the storage compartments on her cart. 'If you give me a moment, I believe I have some sheaths with me . . .'

'Some what?'

'It's like a glove,' Isabel said.

'Oh, no, don't go to that trouble,' Tamsin said. 'How would . . . do you know what shaking hands means?'

'Yes,' Ghuh'loloan said. 'In essence.'

'Do you . . . have an equivalent of that? How would you communicate something like that to me?'

'It would help if I knew the specifics of what you wish to communicate.'

Tamsin looked at Ghuh'loloan seriously. 'Respect.'

The Harmagian rose up on her cart, holding her body like a wave frozen in time. Her tentacles shuddered, curling and unfolding in strange symmetry. 'Respect,' she said.

Tamsin took in the display, and gave a satisfied nod. 'Right back at you.'

TESSA

Received message
Encryption: 0
Translation: 0
From: George Santoso (path: 6159-546-46)
To: Tessa Santoso (path: 6222-198-00)

Tess,

I know you're running around like a headless hopper these days, but I've got a surprise for you. Go to our bench after dinner, or whenever you can manage. Leave the kids with the hex. It might take a while. And no, I won't tell you what it is. I think you'll like it, though.

George

———

Tessa would never disparage her husband for being cute, but stars, she didn't have time for this today. Aya needed help with her schoolwork – she was struggling with reading, just like her father had – Ky needed a bath, Pop needed . . . stars, what *didn't* he need. A swift kick in the butt was what he needed. Besides which, the laundry needed doing, the herb garden was wilting, and the cleanerbot had glitched out *again*. Whatever George was up to was probably very sweet, but did it have to be *today*?

She stepped off the transport pod and headed for the big plaza oxygen garden, not needing to follow the signs. She took a breath and tried to shift her mood. She was being ungrateful. Since that cargo guild meeting a tenday ago, she'd written George a half-dozen or so letters that amounted to nothing more than emotional ejection. He hadn't had the time to respond to any of them, which she'd expected. He was busy, and had never been one for writing. She hadn't really wanted a back-and-forth, to be perfectly honest. She'd wanted a recycling bin, a compost box, somewhere she could throw the junk cluttering her brain. But now he'd gone and arranged something to make her feel better – *what*, she had no idea. She considered the possibilities as she entered the garden and wound her way along the lush, familiar paths. A present dropped off by a friend, maybe. She hoped it was nothing performative. That wasn't his style, but then, he wasn't in the habit of sending her cryptic messages and making her trek through the district on a school night, either. She was being a jerk about the whole thing, she knew, but she hoped whatever it was was worth the bother. She hoped—

Tessa froze, mid-stride. There, on a bench, with his back toward her, was George. George. Her husband, George.

His head turned slightly at the sound of her, just a touch, no eye contact needed. 'There's room for two,' he said.

She walked up and faced him. 'What—' Her mouth could form no other words, and her brain was stuck on one thought and one thought alone. George. George was *here*. 'What—'

George looked around. 'Well, this is a canteen,' he said, lifting the container resting beside him. He patted the space to his left. 'And this is a bench.'

Tessa rolled her eyes. 'What are you doing here?' He wasn't supposed to be back for another three tendays, at least.

George took the lid off the canteen. A ribbon of steam unfolded as if it were alive. He filled the lid with tea and gestured for Tessa to sit. 'I got your letters.'

Tessa sighed and sat. 'Stars, George. I'm fine.'

'You didn't sound fine.'

'All right, fine, I'm *not* fine, but I've been not fine before without you – you running back home. You could've got on the sib.'

He handed her the cup. 'This seemed like it should be a face-to-face conversation.' He reached into his pocket, produced a flat packet of throw- cloth, and unwrapped two big spice cookies.

Tessa accepted both cookie and tea, but consumed nothing yet. She leaned back against the bench, a hand's-width apart from George, not ready to be closer until she'd processed the full scope of things here. He smelled great, though. He always smelled great. 'I don't know if I meant any of it,' she said. 'I was just . . . y'know. Mad. I don't know why you took it so seriously.'

'The way I read it, Tessa Santoso is considering the *mere possibility* of leaving the Fleet. That seems pretty damn serious to me.'

Thick steam drifted from the cup, but she braved a sip anyway. 'Is this your dad's blend? He added something.'

'Don't change the subject.'

'What is that? Cinnamon?'

'Don't—' He frowned and took the cup, taking a timid sip of his own. 'Huh. Yeah, I think that is cinnamon. Where'd he get cinnamon?'

'See,' she said. 'That's why I don't mean what I said.'

'I'm not following.'

'Why I don't mean what I said about leaving.' Tessa looked at the tea and shook her head. 'Your dad, your mom, my dad. Your brother—'

'You've got a brother, too. He left, and it was fine.'

'Yeah, and that's why I can't. One of us needs to be here.'

'Why?'

She looked him in the eye, disbelieving. 'Are you seriously saying I should?'

'No,' he said, taking a large bite of his cookie. 'I'm just asking questions.' He swallowed, sipped the tea, and handed the cup back. 'I don't believe for a minute that the sole reason you're here is because Ashby left and you feel obligated. That's never been the case.'

'I'm not saying it is. I'm just . . . I'm just saying. With the exception of Ashby, our family is here. Aya and Ky's family is here.'

'So then explain the letters you wrote me. Explain why you're entertaining this.'

'I already told you.'

He waved his hand. 'Tell me again. Tell me so I can hear how you sound when you say it. Come on, I'm missing out on cleaning drill bits for this.'

She snorted. 'You're having tea and cookies.'

'I've got both tea and cookies back on my ship. And honestly, scrubbing off ore bits is easier than getting anything out of you sometimes.'

Tessa ignored the comment and drank the tea. The added cinnamon was growing on her. She sat, thinking. She wasn't sure what to say.

A moment passed. George leaned forward and folded his hands together. Tessa knew that pose, the George Is Being Serious pose. 'How much of this is about the job?' he asked.

She relented. 'I was thinking about it – about leaving – before that. The job was just . . . I don't know, the last fucking straw, I guess.'

'So, this isn't solely because you don't want to learn a new job.'

'No. Well—' She sighed impatiently. 'There's a part of me that's scared about learning something new. Not because I don't think I can do it, but because this has been my job for twenty years. I hadn't ever pictured doing anything else. Not because it's my favourite thing in the world, but because I'm good at it, and because it's got things that are weirdly satisfying, and because I know – I *knew* what every day was going to look like. At least, as far as work went.'

'You liked the stability.'

'Yeah.'

'And now you're staring down a whole mess of instability and you're like, eh, fuck it, let's see how much of that I'm comfortable with.'

Tessa laughed. 'I guess.' Her face fell. 'It's the kids, mostly. I . . . I don't know. This doesn't feel like the same Fleet you and I grew up in.'

'That's been true with every generation.'

'I know, but . . . this is different. In my gut, this is different. We've had six break-ins in my bay in the past standard. Six. And that's just my bay. Then that whole business with that grounder – stars, *nothing* like that ever happened when we were kids.'

George flexed his eyebrows in acknowledgement. 'Break-ins, sure—'

'Not this many.'

'True.'

'And nobody died.'

'Also true. But bad shit happens everywhere.'

'That's what I told Aya, and she turned it around on me.' A weight pressed against Tessa's chest. 'She's not doing any better. She's getting worse, if anything. Those little bastards at school—'

'Have they kept at it?'

'No, but she's playing by herself.'

George frowned. 'That's not like her.'

'She's scared of them, George. She's scared of them, and she's scared of our home. And I don't know how to help her. I know we thought she'd grow out of it, and she's had counselling, but . . .' Tessa felt her eyes well up, and given the company, she didn't feel the need to hide it. 'She doesn't feel safe here. Do you know how awful that must be, to be a kid and not feel safe at home?'

George slid closer to her and put his arm around her shoulders. 'Almost as awful as being the parent who can't make that kid feel safe, huh?'

'Stars,' Tessa said, taking a shaky breath. 'I'm such a shit mom.'

'Oh, come on. You are not.'

'My mom – she always knew what to do. Whenever I got scared, all she had to do was *be there* and I knew I'd be okay.'

'Your mom didn't have to walk you through seeing a homesteader blown to shit.' He sighed. 'And you also had a dad who was around all the time.'

They both fell quiet.

George spoke, slow and kind. 'Let's say you did leave. Where would you go? Central space? Sol?'

Tessa gave him a sharp look. 'George Santoso, if you seriously think I'd raise our children on Mars, we are getting a divorce.'

Her husband guffawed. 'Well, hey, I didn't want to presume.'

'Sol,' Tessa snorted. 'I'm not freaking out *that* much.' She took another sip of tea. 'Honestly, I – and this is hypothetical—'

'Sure.'

'For the sake of argument.'

'One hundred percent.'

Tessa chewed the inside of her lip. 'The independent colonies. We know people who've gone there. I keep thinking about Seed.'

George made a thoughtful sound. 'Where Ammar went.'

'Yeah.' Ammar and his husband Nick had lived one hex over until three standards prior, when they'd packed up and headed for ground. Tessa had been friends with him through school, and though they weren't close, he was the type of person she imagined would be happy to hear about her moving nearby.

Hypothetically.

'They could definitely put someone with bot-wrangling experience to work in a place like that,' he said.

'That they could,' Tessa said noncommittally. 'If not cargo, then map drones, or . . .' She shrugged. 'I have to learn a new job either way, right?'

'True,' George said. 'I hear it's kinda rough out there, though. Terraforming's a long-game deal.'

'Yeah,' Tessa said, with a nod. 'But . . . is it so different from here? It's not as clean, sure. It's not as established. They're still figuring it out. But they have to ration their water and mind their food stores, and . . .' She shrugged. 'I don't know, I think I'd fit much better in a place like that than a city, or . . . a market stop, or something.'

'Stars, no, I couldn't see you in a market stop.'

She looked askance at him. 'But you could see me on Mars?'

'I didn't say – you're not going to let this go, are you?'

'Never.' She leaned into him, releasing some of her weight, taking on some of his warmth. 'But I love it here. I do. I love how we do things, and why we do them. I love Remembrance Day. I love the Bug Fry Festival. I love the gardens. So many people who left, they wanted *more*. I don't want more. I'm good with what I have. I don't need land or . . . or open sky, or whatever. So many people have left for the wrong reasons.'

George pulled in his lips, folding mustache into beard as he thought. 'Maybe that's why you *should* go. Go for the right reasons. Go for the reason the first of us left Earth – to find a better place for your family. Honestly, Tess, you're the best kind of person to join a colony, because you'd bring all those right reasons with you. You believe in our way of life here? Cool. Implement those ways planetside. Make sure people don't forget. Make sure people remember that a closed system is a closed system even when you can't see the edges.'

Tessa said nothing for a while. 'I don't want to leave you, either. Or take the kids away.'

'What makes you think you would?'

She shut her eyes. 'Don't be ridiculous. I couldn't – that is too much to ask.'

'So . . . what, I'm not allowed to want to do this with you if I think it's an okay idea?'

Tessa pulled back. 'I couldn't ask you to do that.'

George scoffed. 'I go where my family goes. End of discussion.'

'You have a job here. You have a life—'

'I have a skillset I can apply anywhere, and my life is ongoing until the universe says otherwise. I go where you and our kids go. And if you think you can give them a better life on the ground than you can here, then I believe you. You're with them every day. You spend more time with them than I do. There's no question in my mind that you know what's best for them.' He stroked his beard. 'And maybe . . . maybe it would be a good thing for me that way, too. Maybe if we found somewhere I could work planetside instead of hopping rocks all the time, maybe I could be a better dad. A better husband, too.'

'You're good at both of those.'

'If you say so. But I'm not an *always around* kind of guy, am I? I don't have any regrets about how we've been doing things, but it would be nice to . . . I don't know, not be surprised when Aya's grown a hand-length since I saw her last.'

'That'll surprise you even if you see her every day.'

'You know what I mean. I'm not saying this is what I want, definitively. I'm saying that if this is what *you* want . . . I might not be opposed, either.'

'You can't put this all on me.'

'I'm not. I'm asking you if you really – I mean, really, really, really – want to do this. And if you do, then we need to sit down and talk about it.'

Tessa took inventory of their situation. 'We're already sitting down and talking.'

George gave her a knowing glance.

Tessa thought about the letters she'd sent, full of cagey phrasing and danced-around ideas. She thought about the nights she'd lain awake, the long hours spent looking down at the stars. She thought about the whisper she'd been trying to ignore, the one that got a little louder every time she read the news, every time she patched up her home, every time she watched her kids. And here was George, calling the whisper out in plain speech, telling her what she already knew.

'Shit,' she said. She put her face in her palms. 'Oh, stars.'

KIP

System log: device unlocked
Node identifier established: 8846-567-11, Kristofer Madaki

——

Ras (18:62): tek tem dude

Ras (18:62): I know you're not talking to me or whatever, but I
wanted you to know exam scores are out

——

**Feed source: The Human Diaspora Centre for Higher Education
Student Portal**
Encryption: 0
Translation: 0
Transcription: 0
Password: accepted

Thank you for using the Human Diaspora Centre for Higher Education
student portal!

Your most recent exam was: HDCHE entrance qualification exam
Your score was: 803 (out of possible 1000)

Congratulations! You have qualified for admission into any Tier 2 member institution of the HDCHE.

Your options are as follows:
- Red Rock University (Spirit's Rest, Mars)
- College of the Rings (Silver Sea City, Titan)
- The Jovian School for Future Technicians (Jupiter Station, Jupiter)

The following schools require at least an 875 to attend. Should you wish to attend one of these schools, you will need to retake the entrance qualification exam.
- Alexandria University (Florence, Mars)
- The Solan Institute of Reconstructive Biology (Hamilton Junction, Luna)

If you accept admission to any of the schools listed here, you will still need to complete placement tests for any given academic track. Some academic degree programmes require an additional qualification test.

If you are interested in attending a school outside of Human territory, there are many GC educational institutions with reciprocal admission agreements with the HDCHE. Admission conditions vary greatly, so please contact an HDCHE adviser for information specific to your desired school.

Based on your listed location, your nearest source for HDCHE informational meetings is:
- *Asteria* Emigrant Resource Centre, Deck 2, Plaza 16

We highly encourage you to attend an informational meeting. All questions are welcome.

Happy studies!

———

Ras (18:80): how'd you do?

Ras (18:81): I got a 908

Ras (18:81): going to mars, baby

Ras (18:81): big cred time

Ras (18:94): dude will you please talk to me

Ras (19:03): whatever

Ras (19:12): I don't get why you're being such an asshole

Node identifier disconnected
System log: device deactivated

ISABEL

Isabel rarely went to the theatre in the dark hours, so she couldn't say what the usual crowd was during that time. There were a few people in the audience who were easy to predict. Old folks like her, scattered around the mostly empty hall. A young father, dozed off on the floor, his tiny child asleep on his chest, the exhausted conclusion to what had likely been a long night of walking the mostly vacant public corridors with a crying infant. But there was one member of the audience she did not expect. She sat down next to him, as she would with an old friend.

'Hello, Kip,' she whispered. 'Mind if I join you?'

Kip was taken aback. Wherever he'd been, he hadn't expected *her* to rouse him. 'Uh . . . yeah, sure, M.'

Isabel folded her arms across her lap and took in the view. The projected environment was a rich tapestry of thick reeds, waving sheets of grass, protective trees, scummy water, and the calls of chittering birds with pointed opinions. 'Wetlands,' she said. 'I haven't been to a wetlands recording in a while. I tend to favour deserts. This is a nice change.'

Kip was quiet – not a contemplative quiet, but the unsure kind of quiet that kids his age sometimes fell into when addressed by an adult. Maybe he was just shy. Maybe he wanted to be left alone.

Isabel kept talking anyway. 'Why aren't you asleep, Kip?'

Kip shifted. 'Why aren't you?'

She chuckled. 'Fair. My wife has a bad pair of legs. They wake her up a lot, and that woke *me* up enough times tonight that there wasn't any going back from it.'

'That sucks,' Kip said.

'That it does.'

He was quiet, again. The recorded trees rustled. The water lapped. 'I haven't slept great since . . . y'know,' Kip said.

'Understandable. Have you talked to someone about it?'

Another long pause. 'My parents won't *stop* talking to me about it. And I get they're just trying to help, but like . . . sometimes I *don't* want to talk about it.'

'Yes,' Isabel said, with a nod. 'I get that.'

Kip shuffled, as restless as the reeds. 'Sorry.'

'No, no, I asked. I appreciate you being honest.' She watched as a great grey and white bird – some kind of predator – glided past on motionless wings. 'So why here? Why not the sim hub, or the Linkings, or . . . ?'

'I dunno. It's . . . it's quiet. I like that.' He shifted again. 'I like pretending I'm somewhere else.' Isabel would've changed the subject at that, had he not continued: 'That's what the theatre's for, right?'

Isabel turned her head toward Kip, his face silhouetted against the bright muddy green. 'Is it?' she asked.

'Well, and so we know what it's like to live on planets. So the ancestors wouldn't freak out if they made it to the ground. They'd know what the sky looked like and . . . and yeah.'

Isabel looked back to the blue sky – that edgeless blue, streaked with clouds and birds whose names few knew off-hand. 'Do you have somewhere to be anytime soon?'

'Uh . . . no?'

'Come on,' she said, giving his arm a definitive pat. 'I want to show you something.' She stood. He hesitated. 'There's a bean cake in it for you.'

Kip got up.

The Archives were on the same side of the plaza as the theatre, so getting there took little time. Isabel swiped her patch over the locked entrance. Doors opened and lights bloomed awake. She looked around. None of her colleagues were there. Good. They would've gotten a scolding about still being up if they had been. No Ghuh'loloan, either, who was likely packing her things and preparing her goodbyes. Isabel and the boy were alone.

'You spend much time in the Archives?' Isabel asked as they took the lift down to the lowest level of her place of work.

Kip shrugged. 'Namings and stuff. Sometimes for school.'

'But never just to look, hmm?'

'Uh, not really. When I was little, I guess.'

That wasn't a surprise to Isabel. Why paw through boring old memories when you could go out and make your own?

The lift came to a halt, and Isabel led the way into the centre of the data room. Seemingly endless towers of globular nodes spiralled out around them, each pulsing with the soft blue light that meant all was well. Isabel smiled proudly. 'Beautiful, isn't it?'

Judging by Kip's expression, he was making a valiant effort to be polite – or maybe he just really wanted that bean cake. 'It's cool, yeah.'

Isabel folded her hands in front of herself and continued to admire their surroundings.

Kip waited. He shuffled. He stopped waiting. 'I've been down here before, M.'

'I'm sure you have. School visit?'

'Yeah.'

'Mmm. I'm sure you got a very technical explanation of how it all works, like I'm sure you did with water reclamation and engine tech and solar harvesters.' She sighed. 'Kip, what's the most important cargo the Fleet carries?'

'Um . . . food?'

'Wrong.'

He frowned. 'Water. Air.'

'Both wrong.' She pointed to the racks. 'This.'

Kip was unconvinced. 'We'd die without air, M.'

'We die one way or another. That's a given. What's *not* is being remembered after the fact. To ensure that, you have to put in some effort.' She reached out and touched one of the racks, feeling the warring balance of cold metal and warm energy. 'Without this, we're merely surviving. And that's not enough, is it?' Isabel looked at the boy, who was still confused. She patted the rack and began to walk. 'Our species doesn't operate by reality. It operates by stories. Cities are a story. Money is a story. Space was a story, once. A king tells us a story about who we are and why we're great, and that story is enough to make us go kill people who tell a different story. Or maybe the people kill the king because they don't like his story and have begun to tell themselves a different one. When our planet started dying, our species was so caught up in stories. We had thousands of stories about ourselves – that's still true, don't forget that for a minute – but not enough of us were looking at the reality of things. Once reality caught up with us and we started changing our stories to acknowledge it, it was too late.' She looked around at all the lights, all the memories. 'It is easy to remember that story here, in the Fleet. Every time you touch a bulkhead, every time you tend a garden, every time you watch the water in your hex's cistern dip a little lower, you remember. You know what the story is here. But *outside* of here, there's a different story. There's sky. There's ground. There are cities and money and water you can take for granted. Are you following?'

'Uh . . . I think so.'

Isabel nodded and went on. 'Comforts are not bad things, not by base. There's nothing wrong with wanting to make life easier. The Gaiists on Earth would have you think otherwise, but they're also dying of diseases that can be easily cured and leaving imperfect infants out to freeze, so no, I don't think technology is the greater evil here. The comforts we've invented – or that our neighbours have invented – can *become* bad if you don't always, always ask what the potential consequences could be. Many of our people skip that step. Many – not all, but many – leave here and are too eager to change their story. There's not just one planet with organic resources anymore. There are thousands. Hundreds of thousands. And if that's true, you don't need to worry so much, right? You don't need to be so careful. Use one up and move on to the next. The Harmagians were like that, once, until the rest of the galaxy got tired of their story. They changed. They learned. And that's why their society, and the Aandrisks, and the Aeluons, and everybody else – that's why they look so appealing to us. We're coming in at their happy ending and not stopping to think about how they got there. We want to take on their story. And we can, if we want to. But I worry about those who think adopting someone else's story means abandoning their own.' She turned to face the boy. '*That's* why the theatres are here, Kip. That's why we keep Archives, why we paint our hands on the wall. It's so we don't forget. We're our own warning. That's why the Fleet needs to remain. Why it *has* to remain. Without us out here, the grounders will forget within a few generations. We'll become just another story, and not one that seems relevant. Sure, we broke Earth, but we won't break *this* planet. We won't poison *this* water. We won't let *this* invention go wrong.' She shook her head. 'We are a longstanding species with a very short memory. If we don't keep record, we'll make the same mistakes over and over. I think it is a good thing that the Fleet is changing, that our people are spreading out. That's what we were meant to do. That's what our species has always, always done. But we must remember.' She contemplated Kip, as if he were a file that needed categorising. 'What are your plans for the future? Have you chosen a profession yet?'

Kip shifted his weight. 'I'm gonna leave the Fleet.'

Isabel waited for some specificity. None came. 'And do what?'

'I dunno.'

'Where will you go?'

'I . . . I'm not sure.'

'Are you going to university? Are you looking for work?'

'I don't know. I don't know yet.'

'Then why,' Isabel asked without judgment, 'do you want to go?'

Kip shrugged with agitation. 'I just . . . I need to get out of here.'

'Why?'

She'd hit the crack in the boy's patience. 'Because there's no point to any of this!' Kip blurted out, finally speaking with something other than a guarded drone. 'Seriously, what is the point to orbiting here forever? So we remember stuff? Why? For what? What are we *for*?'

'A fair question. You think you'll find the answer to that planetside?'

'It's . . . that's where we're supposed to be.'

Isabel laughed. 'That's a slippery slope you'll never see the end of. Head down the path of "how we're supposed to be", what we *evolved* to be, and you'll end up at "hunting and gathering in grassy plains". Maybe the Gaiists are right, and that is how we're *supposed* to be. I don't know. But if everything has to have a point: what's the point of hunting and gathering? How is that more meaningful than any of this?'

'I'm not talking about hunting and gathering, M.'

'Oh? Why?'

'Because . . .' He struggled. 'That can't be all there is, either.'

'So what you're saying is Humans aren't really *supposed* to do anything in particular, and we get to choose the kind of lives we have. But that doesn't mean any of it has a point, son. You think people born planetside don't wonder what the point of it all is? You don't think they know that their cities will fall and their houses will rot, and that somewhere down the line, their planet will get swallowed up by its sun? Spacers and grounders, we're riding the same ship. We both depend on fragile systems with a million interconnected parts that can easily be damaged and will eventually fail. Yes, we built the Fleet. The Fleet didn't just *happen* the way a planet does. But why does that matter? The only difference between our respective ecosystems is scale and origin.

Otherwise, it's the same principle.' She studied him. 'Have you ever gone through any of the Archives from the first days of Human spaceflight?'

'No.'

'I'd be surprised if you had. It's archaic stuff, and the Ensk translations aren't the best.' Yet another project, she thought, to keep some future archivist happy. 'Do you know why people – why Humans started heading out into the open? Oh, there was lots of military posturing involved, no mistake, but the true believers, the ones who couldn't bear the thought of *not* going out there – that's where they thought they'd find answers. They said, hey, we haven't got the context right. We need a sample size bigger than one lonely planet if we're ever going to understand any of this. And in many ways, they were right. We found other people out here, so that question got answered. We found out that life isn't rare. We've learned exponentially more about how planets work and how physics works, and the technology we have today would've blown their minds. We understand the galaxy in a way we never could have if we hadn't left. But the big question – the end-all, be-all question – well, that's still up for discussion. *Why?* What's the *point*? Kip, there isn't a sapient species living or dead that hasn't grappled hard with that. It scares us. It makes us panic, just like you're panicking now. So if the lack of a point is what's bothering you, if it's making you want to kick the walls and tear your hair out, well, welcome to the party.'

'But—'

Isabel put up her palm. 'Your ancestors thought they would answer the big question in space. Now here you are, out where they longed to go, looking back at the planets, trying to answer the same damn thing. You won't. You need to reframe this frustration you're feeling. If what you're saying is that you don't see a life for yourself here, that the kind of work you want to do or the experiences you want to have aren't available in the Fleet, then by all means, go. But if the only reason you want to do it is because you're looking for a *point*, you're going to end up miserable. You'll float around forever trying to make peace with that.'

Kip looked lost, but an entirely different kind of lost than he had moments before. 'I have no idea what kind of life I want,' he said at last. 'I don't know what I want to do.' He fell quiet, the blue glow of the data nodes highlighting his face.

Stars, he was young. He had so far to go.

'What do you like to do?' Isabel asked. 'What interests you?'

Kip gave a brittle laugh. 'Nothing.'

'There must be *something*. What do you do with your day?'

'Nothing important. Sims, vids, school.'

Isabel let the implication that school wasn't important slide. 'Job trials?'

The heaviest sigh in the world escaped the boy's lips. 'Yeah.'

'And nothing's stuck?'

'Nothing's stuck.'

'And you think something will out there?'

He looked at her as if that were obvious. 'Why else would so many people leave and not come back?'

'Again, that's fair. You're waiting for something to grab you, then. Something that feels like it's got a *point*.'

'Yeah.' Kip looked at her. 'What do you think I should do?'

'Oh, I can't tell you that,' Isabel said. 'I can only tell you what I *want* you to do, and that's based on my shallow impression of who you are and how I'd like your story to go. You can't operate by that. You're the only one who can think about what you *should* do.'

'Okay,' Kip said. 'Then what do you *want* me to do?'

Isabel paused. 'I'll only tell you if you understand that when a person tells you what they want of you, they're not deciding for you. It's their opinion, not your truth. Got it?'

'Yeah.'

'All right.' Isabel didn't need to think about what she was going to say next. She'd wanted to say it since the moment they'd started digging a burial trench together. With a sure step, she began to walk back out of the data chamber the way they'd come. 'I want you to apprentice with me.'

She could practically hear the kid blink. 'What?' he said.

'Not a job trial. A proper apprenticeship. Stripes and all.'

'Um.' Kip hurried after and fell alongside. 'Why?'

'Because of what you did for Sawyer.'

'What does—'

'—that have to do with anything? You tell me. Why wasn't it enough for you to simply report what you heard to patrol and have them deal with it?'

'I – I don't—'

'Yes, you do,' Isabel said firmly. 'Why?'

'It just . . . it bothered me.'

'Him being alone.'

'Yeah.'

'Him being thrown out. Him not getting a real funeral.'

'Yeah.'

'But you didn't just pay your respects. You weren't a passive mourner. You carried his body. You read the Litany for the Dead. You care about our ways, Kip, even if you think you don't. The idea of them not being performed shook you so hard, you had to do them yourself. And *that* – that's the kind of love the Archives needs. We won't survive without that.' She sorted her thoughts. 'I know that in this moment, you hate it here. I'm not belittling that. That's why I don't want you to apprentice for me *right now*.'

Kip was the picture of confusion. 'M, I'm sorry, but I . . . I really don't get it.'

Isabel smiled. 'I want you to leave the Fleet, Kip. For a little while. If you decide to stay wherever you land forever, so be it. But you can't apprentice with me until you see what's out there.'

'I don't—' Kip gave his head a short shake. 'You don't know me, M. You don't know me at all. I'd suck working here. I'm not smart.'

'What makes you say that?'

'I'm . . . I'm *not*. I suck at school, and—'

'What'd you get on your entrance exams?'

'803.'

Not amazing, true, but hardly a suggestion of *not smart*. 'That's an entirely decent score, Kip. That'll get you into everything but the top-tiers.'

'I barely made it, though. I busted my ass, and I got *entirely decent*. I'm not like . . .' He frowned. 'Like people who ace all their tests.'

Isabel gave a single nod. 'Good! Stars, the last thing I want is some cocky gifted kid who's never had to break a sweat. Give me someone who wants it and had to work for it any day.'

'But I don't know if I *want* to work here, M. I— I dunno, I've never thought about it.'

'You don't have *anywhere* you want to work, so having at least one option on the table can't hurt, hmm?'

'Wait, so . . . why would I have to leave first?'

'It's simple. If you never leave, you'll always wonder. You'll wonder what your life could've been, if you did the right thing. Well . . . scratch that. You'll *always* wonder if you did the right thing, no matter what the decision is, big or small. There's always another path you'll wonder about. But that wondering is less maddening if you know what the other path looks like, at least. So. You should go. Go to Hashkath. Go to Coriol. Go to Earth, even. Go wherever calls to you. And maybe you'll find out that life out there is good, that it suits you. Maybe you'll find that thing you're missing. Maybe not. What you *will* find, no question, is perspective. What that perspective is, I have no idea. But you'll find one. Otherwise, you'll only ever think about other people in the abstract. That's a poisonous thing, thinking your way is all there is. The only way to really appreciate *your* way is to compare it to somebody else's way. Figure out what you love, specifically. In detail. Figure out what you want to keep. Figure out what you want to change. Otherwise, it's not love. It's clinging to the familiar – to the comfortable – and that's a dangerous thing for us short-term thinkers to do. If you stay, stay because you want to, because you've found something here worth embodying, because you *believe* in it. Otherwise . . . well, there's no point in being here at all, is there? Better for everybody to leave, in that case.' She pushed the button to call the lift. 'Go out there and see what it's like to be the alien. Eat something weird. Sleep somewhere uncomfortable. Then, *if* you come back, and *if* you want to apprentice here, I want you to look me in the eye and tell me exactly why.'

Kip frowned. 'I don't know, M. This is kind of a lot.'

'Of course it is!' The lift arrived, and she stepped in. 'I wouldn't want anything to do with you if it felt otherwise.'

TESSA

The scene at home was the last thing she expected to find. Instead of discarded clothes and messy toys, there was only Pop, sitting on the couch in a tidied-up living room, a bottle of kick and two empty glasses on the table. He had been waiting, elbows on his thighs, hands folded between his knees. He smiled when she entered the front door.

Pop picked up the bottle. 'Don't worry about waking the kids. They're spending the night next door. Been a while since this home had only grown-ups in it, huh? Not since Aya was born.' He examined the label. He squinted, holding it at length, then up close, then farther out, trying to find the spot that fit his eyes best. 'You know, they don't make this stuff anymore.' He rotated the bottle for her to see: a bluefish, leaping its way into the stars. 'Farmer's Friend,' he said. 'They used to make it out of the fruit that wasn't good enough for the stores. Stopped making it after M Nazari died – must've been . . . well, let's see now . . . I guess forty-some years ago. She was the one who made the stuff. Sweet old lady, always nice to me and my brother. Whenever we'd go down to trade with her, she'd always hand us a bunch of fruit or something after the barter was done. And we'd always say, aw, c'mon, M, we didn't give you enough for that, here, take a couple extra chips. But she'd always say, no, no, and tell us we were her favourite customers. I think she said that to everybody, but she made you feel like it was true. After she went, though – well, none of her kids were much into brewing, so, the kick went, too.'

Tessa sat down, the back of her neck tingling, her stomach uneasy. She'd been holding the conversation with George in her stomach the whole way home, and the added uncertainty of wherever this conversation was going made her . . . not scared, exactly. But time had slowed, and she felt *awake*. *Present*. There was gravity centred around the table. Real gravity, not the conjured stuff in the floor. 'I remember the label,' she said. An old memory came back to life. 'You kept a few bottles on the shelf, over there.' She pointed. There weren't bottles there now, but tins of seeds and tech bits.

Pop nodded. 'For fun and company,' he said, pouring two generous fingers into the glasses. 'That's how your mother always put it. And you two weren't supposed to touch that shelf. You did once, though.'

'Oh, stars.' Tessa laughed. 'Oh, no. I forgot about that.'

'When your mother and I were going on a market trip—'

'The shuttle broke down half a day out, and you had to come home early.'

'Yeah, we came home to you two dipshits, puking your guts into a blanket.'

'Hey, that was Ashby, not me. *I* found a sink.'

Her father gave her a look that told her how little that distinction mattered. 'Couple of dumb teenagers who couldn't handle themselves.'

'I maintain that playing charthump all the next day was an asshole move.' Full volume drums, for hours and hours. She felt an echo of nausea from memory alone.

Pop laughed heartily. 'That was your mother's doing, and you deserved every second of it. Here.' He handed her a glass. 'For grown-ups.'

They clinked glasses and sipped. The kick was rough, but once she got past the edges, it warmed her all the way through. She didn't remember the taste – she didn't remember much of that adolescent night, honestly – and yet, somehow, it made her feel at home.

'Ahhhhh,' Pop said. 'Stars, that's fun.' He took another sip. 'Do you like it?'

'I do,' Tessa said honestly. She eyed the bottle. 'It's half empty,' she said.

'That it is.'

'I've never seen you drink this.'

'I've been saving it. Wasn't sure if I'd ever get to have any again.'

Tessa waited patiently. Pop didn't always make sense on the first go.

'I first opened this bottle,' he said, 'when your brother told me there was something he needed to talk about.' He briefly met her eyes over the rim of his glass. 'Would've been a good number of years ago now.'

Nobody said anything for a moment. 'You kept the other half for me,' Tessa said quietly.

'Yep,' Pop said. He drained his glass and exhaled appreciatively. 'Just in case. I didn't think I'd bring it out again, but – well, kids have a way of surprising you.'

Tessa stared into her glass, held with both hands low in her lap. She watched sediment drift and swirl in the decades-old kick. She raised the glass and tossed it back in one smooth swallow. 'We haven't made a decision yet.'

He refilled both their glasses. 'Uh huh,' he said. He left the bottle uncorked. 'Is George with his folks right now?'

'Yes,' she said.

'So, you've decided between yourselves, then.'

Tessa shook her head. She couldn't believe they were having this conversation. She couldn't believe anything about this at all. 'I don't know.'

'You don't know . . . what? Where you two left things?'

'No, I – I don't know. I don't know how to have this conversation.'

Pop sipped and exhaled, same as he had every sip before. 'One word in front of the other is how I do it.'

'Me and him and the kids . . . that's not our only family.'

'Obviously.'

'And we can't do this without talking to everyone else.'

'Define "this". Tessa, if you can't say it, you've got no business doing it.'

She shoved the words out. 'We're thinking about going planetside.' There. They were out now, out in the open, somewhere between treachery and relief.

Pop did nothing but nod. 'Colonies?'

'Yeah.'

'Good. It's hard work out there, and hard work keeps you honest. Keeps your head on straight.'

She waited for him to say more than that. She waited for him to get mad, to scoff, to tell her every reason why this was stupid, to be the outward confirmation of all the guilt and fear she felt within.

He did not.

'Is that all you have to say?' Tessa said incredulously.

'What do you want me to say? That I don't care? Of course I care. I'll miss you and the kids like hell. Or do you want me to get pissed and tell you no way, no how are you leaving home? That kind of thing didn't work when you were a teenager, and it sure as shit won't fly now.' He laughed. 'You're an adult. You know what you're about. Whatever you decide, I'm not gonna tell you otherwise. I'm too old for making big decisions. Had my fill of those.'

'But—' She scrambled, trying to find the trigger for the reaction she'd expected. 'But what about—'

'You know *I'm* not going, girl. I'll visit. But I'm not going anywhere.' He reached across the table and patted her hand. 'You don't have to worry about me. I got a good hex and the best friends a person could ask for.' His face scrunched into a worryingly pleased grin. 'Y'know Lupe from neighbourhood four?'

An image appeared in Tessa's mind: a tiny, white-haired old

woman, arguing with her son behind the seed shop counter. One of Pop's lunchtime cronies. 'Yeah.'

Pop replied with a waggle of his eyebrows.

The other shoe dropped, and Tessa recoiled. 'Ugh, Pop, I don't need to know.'

'It's nothing serious,' he said, relishing her discomfort. 'Just some casual fun—'

'Pop. I don't. Need. To know.'

Her father laughed and poured them both another drink. 'Here, I have something else to show you.' He unholstered his scrib, gestured at the screen, and slid it across the table.

M Santoso,

This is a confirmation for your ocular implant installation this upcoming second day.

Please arrive at the clinic at 10:00.

On a personal note, I'm very happy you've made this decision. I think you're going to be pleased with the results.

Dr Koraltan

'See,' Pop said, bringing his glass to his mouth. 'You don't need to worry about me.' He sipped and exhaled loudly. 'Though you are gonna have to send me those creds.'

Tessa truly, genuinely didn't know what to say.

Pop's gaze lingered on the wall of painted hands, reaching from floor to ceiling. 'Y'know, my great-granddad – we called him Great-pa, he thought that was funny – I didn't know him long, but I knew him.'

Tessa knew this much already, but she didn't interrupt.

'He remembered contact,' Pop said. 'He told me so often about that day when the Aeluons arrived. He was always pushing me to go. "Get out there, boy," he'd say. "That's what we're meant to do." I wondered, when I got older, why *he* didn't go, if he felt that way. I thought maybe he'd been scared, or set in his ways. But now I think it's because he knew that wasn't for him. Some of us have to go, yes. But some of us have to stay and kick the others out. Otherwise . . .' He scratched his chin. 'Otherwise all we know is the same place. My great-pa, he was right. We're meant to go. And we're meant to stay. Stay and go, each as much as the other. It's not all or nothing anymore. We're all over the place. That's better, I think. That's smarter.' He nodded. 'That's how we'll survive, even if not all of us do.' He looked up. 'You're gonna do great out there. I know you will.'

Tessa's first instinct was to protest. They hadn't made a decision yet, and here he was, talking like it was a done deal. But she looked again at the bottle, kept half full for her sake, an offering for a future her father had prepared himself for decades before she'd considered said same. She closed her eyes for a moment. She got up from her chair, sat down on the floor, and rested her head against her father's leg like she used to when she was small, like she used to when he was huge and handsome and knew everything there was to know. He pressed his palm into her curls, and she closed her eyes. 'I love you, Pop.'

'I love you, too, Tess.'

Part 7

· · · · · · · · · · · · · · · · · · ·

AND WILL UNDYING

Feed source: Reskit Institute of Interstellar Migration (Public News Feed)
Item name: The Modern Exodus – Entry #20
Author: Ghuh'loloan Mok Chutp
Encryption: 0
Translation path: [Hanto:Kliptorigan]
Transcription: 0
Node identifier: 2310-483-38, Isabel Itoh

[System message: The feed you have selected has been translated from written Hanto. As you may be aware, written Hanto includes gestural notations that do not have analogous symbols in any other GC language. Therefore, your scrib's on-board translation software has not translated the following material directly. The content here is a modified translation, intended to be accessible to the average Kliptorigan reader.]

———

When their planet could no longer sustain them, the waning Humans dismantled their cities. Down came the shimmering towers of glass and metal, beam by beam, bolt by bolt. Some of it was repurposed, but most was melted in noxious foundries hastily constructed on barren farmland. The Humans who did this knew they would not live to see the end result. Their years were almost universally cut short by famine and disease, but even if they had been as healthy as their ancestors, the work was too great for one lifetime alone. The scavengers made way for the builders, who poured and welded for the sake of children they would likely not live to see grown. Their completed efforts were launched into low orbit, and assembled there into thirty-two ships, each a city unto itself.

'A city made of cities,' my host told me during our first day. 'We took our ruins with us.'

I keep thinking of this now that I have returned to my own

adoptive city of Reskit. I look out at this sprawling architectural triumph, and I cannot imagine a Hashkath where this does not exist. I cannot imagine how this land looked when Aandrisks first arrived. I cannot imagine how it will look after they – and I – are gone.

Strange as it is to be back, I have slid effortlessly back into my usual patterns. I missed the length of a Hashkath day, the warmth of a brighter sun. I appreciate the open sky as I never have before, and will never again complain of days that are too windy. I spent an entire afternoon swimming at the Ram Tumma'ton Aquatic Park, and at one point, I could not help but sing for joy.

And yet, though I have travelled far from Risheth, I have brought the Fleet with me. There is no place I can go, no activity I can engage in without thinking of them. I can't see a garden without thinking of how theirs differ, nor can I watch a sunset without thinking of the mimicked rhythms of their abandoned sun.

'Night-time' in the Fleet is a curious thing. This is a people who have never lived on a planet – for some, never even *visited* a planet – yet they still follow an artificial semblance of a rotational day. I have experienced this environmental arrangement within long-haul ships built by a variety of species, but these have all been among crews with at least passing familiarity with life on the ground. Consider that the only generation of Exodans that would have truly needed an Earth-like environment would have been the first. It was they who needed night-time, who needed gravity, whose moods would've benefited from being surrounded by plant life rather than cold metal alone. And yes, the original intent of the Fleet was to seek out a terrestrial home, and they believed their progeny would adapt to that better if they were already accustomed to planetary norms. In that context, Exodan adherence to Earthen patterns is quite logical.

But imagine the alternative. Imagine if the Earthen builders had known their descendants would choose to remain in space, that this transitory life satisfied them even when empty ground lay within reach. What would the Human species look like today were that the case? Evolution is often thought of as a glacial process, but we know from countless examples that this is not always true. Rapid environmental change can prompt rapid physical change. What if the first Exodans had left their ornamental gardens behind? What if their lights did not dim? What if they had built homes designed for zero-g instead of gargantuan centrifuges filled with unsecured objects?

The first generation would have been miserable, no doubt. Health problems, both mental and physical, would have been rampant, especially when coupled with the unfathomable stress of leaving their planet for the unknown. But what of the second generation? What of the third, the fourth, the tenth? It is possible – likely, even – that my Exodan friends would look quite different today. Currently, there are small physical differences in modern Humans based on region. Centuries-old Solan populations based around the sun-starved Outer Planets are distinctively pale. Exodans, Martians, and independent colonists can sometimes tell each other apart (I have yet to grasp that nuance). So, imagine an Exodan people who had gone without gravity, without scheduled darkness. I find it likely that we would already see hereditary changes in bone mass, digestive process, eye structure. We would be present for the first days of a new species. Instead, we have space-dwelling Humans who get irritable if malfunctioning environmental lights prolong day or night beyond its time. They love their gardens, even if they have not seen wild plants. Chaos breaks out if local grav systems fail.

I must stress, dear guest, that I do not view the idea of a separate Exodan species as a missed opportunity – merely an intriguing road untravelled. I myself am bound by the pulse of bygone generations. I mist myself constantly, because my skin still requires an approximation of the steady sea breeze my people have not lived in since primitive times. I cannot digest the absurdly broad variety of foodstuffs that my sapient counterparts can, even though Harmagians have lived alongside such delicacies for centuries. For all my species' vast travels, our skin has not hardened, and our guts have not diversified. We, too, took the ways of our planet with us. And so, too, go the Exodans, a spaceborn people who balk at abandoning an environment inspired by a planet that, to most, may as well be myth.

Humans will never leave the forest, just as Harmagians will never leave the shore.

——

EYAS, HALF A STANDARD LATER

Every fourth day, she reviewed her lesson plans and practised her explanations, and every fifth day, she went to the spare classroom she'd reserved at the technical school, where no one but the other instructors – the other people *she'd asked* to do this – were waiting. Fifth day had become the most depressing day out of ten. Her usual work included.

She stepped off the transport pod, and, as she walked through the plaza, she did the necessary preparation of keeping her expectations low. *Nobody will be there*, she told herself. Maybe nobody ever would. Ten tendays, she'd told her assorted volunteers. If they tried this for ten tendays and nobody showed up, they'd call it quits. Well, this was the ninth tenday, and that meant she only had to sit around an empty classroom two more gruelling times before she could go back to her life and forget this whole idea. Just forget this whole thing ever—

Her interest piqued as she saw Sunny running out of the school and across the plaza toward her. He stopped a few feet in front of her, eager as a kid who'd flown his first shuttle. 'There's *people*,' he said.

Eyas' jaw dropped. 'What? No. Really?' She hurried along the way he'd come. 'How many?'

'*Three.*'

'Are you serious?'

'Dead serious. I guess those pixel posters Amad keeps putting up at the docks worked.'

Eyas tried to get her wits about her as they entered the school and walked down the corridor. Three people! It wasn't much, but it was a start. Finally, at last: a start.

'Oh, no,' she said. She came to a halt before they entered the classroom door.

'What's up?'

Eyas paused. 'We've never *had* people before.'

Sunny laughed. 'Are you scared?'

She cuffed him. 'Of course not. I'm just . . .' She took a breath. He squeezed her shoulder. 'Okay. People.'

The door spun open, and sure enough, there they were: a young woman, a middle-aged man, and . . . She turned and gave Sunny a secret, surprised look. An *Aeluon*.

Sunny raised his eyebrows and gave a nod of *yeah, I know*.

The other instructors turned to look at her, each as excited as she was. Eyas took a breath, and walked up to the teacher's station at the front of the room. The others sat in the chairs lined up alongside her, like they'd practised. 'Hello, everybody,' Eyas said to the attendees. 'Thank you so much for coming to our workshop.' She gestured at the assembled volunteers. 'We're the Exodan Cultural Education Collective.' She gave a slight pause, half expecting at least one of the attendees to realise they were in the wrong place and leave. None did. She smiled. 'Right. So.' This was harder than she'd anticipated. At the Centre, there were Litanies and traditions, set ceremonies to follow. She'd planned this class out, sure, but that didn't change the fact that she had made this whole thing up, and was making it up still.

She glanced over at Sunny. He winked. She steadied. 'This is a whole-day workshop, but if you need to leave at any time, feel free. We're hoping, at some point, to split this into individual classes – and more advanced classes as well – but we're new, and we're learning, too, so for now, you get all of us at once.' She paused, the presence of an alien prompting the realisation of something she should've thought of ahead of time. 'Does everyone here speak Ensk?'

The middle-aged man nodded. The Aeluon wiggled her hand.

'Yes,' the young woman said in some staggeringly thick fringer accent. 'But not much well.'

Eyas shifted linguistic gears. *'Klip remmet goigagan?'*

Everyone nodded, including the Aeluon. She'd clearly spent time around Humans. Eyas turned to the row of instructors. 'That okay with you guys?' she asked in Ensk.

'Mine's not great,' Jacira said. She was older, maybe fifty or so.

'That's okay,' Eyas said. 'Just do it in Ensk, and one of us will translate.' She switched back to Klip. 'This better? Okay, good. Our goal here today is to give you a good starting point for finding the resources and assistance you need to begin a life in the Fleet. We're going to cover a huge range of topics and services, and there will be plenty that we won't have time for. We're not here to teach you everything, but our hope is that you'll leave here knowing where to find the right answers. Let me introduce you to your instructors. Some of these professions won't be things you're familiar with. Others will be, and they're here to highlight some of the differences between our way of doing things and the ways you might be more used to. I'll start with myself, and we'll go down the line. My name's Eyas. I'm a caretaker for the dead. I conduct funeral rites and . . . well, I'll explain the specifics of it later.' She turned to the other volunteers. 'Let's focus on the living for now, yeah?'

'Hi, I'm Ayodeji,' the first said. 'I'm a doctor at a neighbourhood clinic. I'll be answering your questions about basic medical care.'

'Hi, I'm Tohu. I'm a ferry pilot. I'm gonna explain how to get around, both inside a homesteader and in between.'

'I'm Jacira. I'm a bug farmer, and I'll be talking to you about food stores and water management.'

'Hey there, I'm Sunny.' He smiled with all the confidence in the world. 'I'm a sex worker, and I'll be explaining where to go if you want to get laid.'

The young woman stared. The man laughed. The Aeluon looked at him, confused as to what was funny.

The instructors continued – a mural artist, a mech tech, a trade-only merchant – until there were no more names to give. Eyas turned to the class. 'Now, I'd like you three to introduce yourselves as well. Who are you, where are you from, and what brings you here?'

The students sat in silence for a moment, like all groups of strangers did. The man spoke first. 'I'm Bruno,' he said. 'I'm a spacer. From Jupiter Station originally, but that was a long time ago. I haul cargo – foodstuff, mainly. The Fleet's been one of my stops for six standards now, and I'm considering putting an end to all the back and forth. I like the people here, but I'm . . . I'm not quite sure yet.' He gestured to the instructors. 'I was hoping you could give me a better idea of what I'd be in for.'

Eyas smiled. 'We'll certainly try.'

'I'm Lam,' the Aeluon said. 'I am sure you weren't expecting me.'

The room chuckled. 'Not exactly,' Eyas said kindly.

'I'm from Sohep Frie, and I'm a textile merchant,' Lam said. 'I'm not going to relocate here, but I would like to understand the Exodans I work with better. They make great effort to make me comfortable. I'd like to be able to do the same.'

Eyas hadn't considered that other species might find value in a Exodan cultural crash course. Something to add to the workshop description, she supposed. Out of the corner of her eye, she saw Amad, the poster maker, already making a note on her scrib. 'That's wonderful,' Eyas said. 'We're delighted to have you here.' She looked to the woman. 'And what about you?'

The young woman swallowed. Eyas could tell she was shy. 'I'm Anna,' the woman said. 'I don't really . . . I guess I'm . . . I dunno. I guess I'm trying something new.'

There wasn't an encompassing word for what Eyas felt then. Tightness. Warmth. Pain. Clarity. She thought of the top of the cylinder, of one particular sunken crater she'd refilled with bamboo chips some tendays before now. She thought of the canisters that had rattled in her cart some tendays after then.

She thought of dirt, dark and shapeless, and of sprouts, tender and new.

Why now? Sunny had asked of her profession, right before giving her the answer she'd always had: *Because you love it, and because it's our way, and that's reason enough.* There wasn't maths or logic or any ironclad measure of efficiency to back it up. There didn't need to be. If *trying something new* was valid, then *keeping something old* was, too. No, this wasn't the same Fleet as that of their ancestors. Yes, things had changed, and would keep changing. Life meant death, always. But by the same token, death meant life. So long as people kept choosing *this* life, Eyas planned to be there – for as long as she could – guiding them through both sides of the equation.

Eyas looked Anna in the eye. She smiled, and said what she should've said the first time she'd heard a grounder speak those words. 'Welcome. Whatever questions you have, we're happy to help.'

KIP, ONE STANDARD LATER

Ever since he'd arrived on Kaathet, Kip had encountered so many things he'd never seen before that the phrase 'I've never seen anything like this' had almost stopped feeling like something worth pointing out. Nothing was like what he knew, not the food, not the crowds, and definitely not the school, which was the complete opposite of school back home in that *everything* was fun and interesting (and that was a whole new problem, because it was all so good, he didn't know what concentration to pick). To say 'I've never seen anything like this' was the same as saying 'I got up today'.

That said: he'd never seen anything like the Osskerit Museum, one of the biggest repositories of Arkanic artefacts in the GC. The inside of the building was decorated to look like one of their long-gone grand temples – or, at least, somebody's best guess as to how they looked. It was hard to say anything hard and fast about a sapient species that had gone extinct long before any of the ones around today had woken up. Still, if their buildings looked anything like the Osskerit, the Arkani had been damn impressive. Everything inside and out was harsh angles and reflective surfaces, a sharp, stabbing fractal of shimmering light. The visual effect felt violent, almost, and was nowhere Kip would want to live. He was wowed all the same.

'Hey, come look at this!' Tuumuu said. The Laru's body was facing a display, but her limb-like neck was stretched back around her foreleg so she could face the others. Kip was still getting used to that. He was also still getting used to having whole conversations in Klip all day every day, which he was getting better at. He wore a translation hud to fill in the gaps.

The rest of the group came over to Tuumuu's side, and Kip left the fossils he'd been looking at to drift their way. They were inseparable, the five of them, all first-year students, all interstellar transfers, all taking Introduction to Historical Galactic Civilisations. They were each from *somewhere else*, and even though the homegrown students at the Kaathet Rakas school were friendly (mostly), somehow it felt natural for the outsiders to stick together. Even if they were total weirdos.

Dron leaned toward the display, his cheeks swirling speckled blue. 'Huh,' he said.

Viola pointed at Dron's face. 'What's that one mean?'

The Aeluon gave Viola a tired look. 'Stars, you are not going to let this go, are you?'

'How else am I supposed to know what's up with you if you don't explain your colours? See, now there's some yellow in there. What's yellow mean?'

'Yellow means lots of things.'

'What's *this* yellow mean?'

'Annoyed. It means I'm annoyed.'

Viola cuffed the innocent Laru. 'Jeez, Tuumuu, stop bugging Dron. Can't you see he's yellow?'

'Kip,' Dron called. 'Will you please get over here and make your cousin behave?'

'And will you all please shut up?' Kreshkeris said from a bench nearby. She was taking furious notes on her scrib, like always. 'Some of us would like to actually do well on this assignment.' She was a lifelong spacer, too, and always acted like she had to prove herself to the grounder Aandrisks they went to school with. Some things weren't that different.

Kip walked up to Viola with his hands in his pockets. 'Hey, cousin,' he said. 'Behave.' He could hear his accent, his imprecise words. But it was cool. With this group, he knew it was cool.

Viola smirked at the joke. Their first day at school, Dron had asked if she and Kip were related, which was hilarious, because Viola came from Titan, and they looked nothing alike. At least, they didn't think so. Everybody else did. *'Bug-fucking spacer,'* Viola said in her weird, flowy Ensk.

'Cow-licking Solan,' Kip shot back.

'That's for Martians, you idiot. There aren't any cows in the Outers.'

'I dunno, I'm looking at one right now.'

They both grinned.

'They're talking shit about us again,' Dron said in the others' general direction.

'You have no idea what we're saying,' Kip said.

An elaborate explosion of colour danced across the Aeluon's face. 'And neither do you.'

'Oh, *come on*,' Viola said.

'You guys,' Tuumuu said, the fur on her neck waving in the air as her big funny feet danced impatiently. 'Look at this.'

They leaned in to see what had gotten their fuzzy history nerd so excited. On the pedestal before them rested an ancient lump of metal, smashed in on itself, worn down by time.

'It's a star-tracker,' Tuumuu gushed. 'It's what they used to study the sky. Think about it! They were trying to find people out there, too. Only . . . only we showed up too late.' Her head sagged. 'Stars, that's sad.'

They leaned in closer. 'Doesn't look like much,' Dron said.

'That's 'cause it's old, dummy.'

'How'd it work?' Viola asked.

Kip cocked his head. 'Looks like there was a switch here.' He reached out and picked up the star-tracker.

Everything went batshit at once. An alarm went off. Previously unseen lights started flashing. His friends yelled in unison.

'Kip, what the fuck?!'

'Dude, what are you—'

'Put it back!'

A shout in Reskitkish came from behind. A line of translation shot across Kip's hud: *Put the object down.*

He turned to see an Aandrisk security guard standing behind him. She was about two heads taller than he was, and had a stun gun at the ready.

Kip stammered. 'I – what—'

The Aandrisk repeated herself in hissing Klip: 'Set the item down.'

Kip looked down at the lump of metal he was still holding stupidly. He had no idea what he'd done wrong, but he did as told. 'I – I wasn't stealing—'

The guard glared at him, and everyone else. She looked straight at Kreshkeris as she walked away. *'Mind your foreign friends,'* she said.

Kreshkeris got up from her bench and stormed over to Kip, her feathers on end. She was tall, too. 'What were you *thinking?*'

Kip looked at his friends – Tuumuu an anxious puff from front to back, Dron red as a bruise, Viola laughing with her forehead in her palm. What was he thinking? He had a better question: what had he *done?* 'I wasn't stealing,' he said again.

'Kip, you – you know you can't touch stuff at a museum, right?' Dron said.

Kip blinked. 'Why not?'

'Oh, stars,' Viola said, laughing harder.

Tuumuu stepped in. 'These are priceless things,' she explained. Her fur started to settle. 'This star-finder might be the only one left. If you break it, that's . . . that's it. There are no more, and we can't learn anything.'

'If you break it, why not fix it?' Kip frowned. 'You can't learn anything like – like this.' He gestured to the trouble-making metal. 'You can't learn how it works if it's broke.'

'I – well – you should take an archeology class,' the Laru said, her tone brightening. 'Professor Eshisk is great. You'd learn all about restoration techniques, and preserving context, and—'

'The point, Kip,' Kreshkeris said, 'is that you can't touch. That's the rules.'

'Okay.' Kip put his palms up. 'Okay, that's the rules. I'm sorry.' He surrendered the argument, but he didn't understand. He tried to imagine the same situation playing out back in the Fleet. *This is a First Generation telescope, and you can't attempt fixing it, you can't recycle the metal and glass, and you definitely can't touch it. We're just going to put it here on the shelf, spending space and fuel on something nobody can use.*

Tuumuu seemed to read his mind. She fell alongside him as the group continued through the hall, walking on four legs and keeping her neck down so as to match his height. 'Don't you have museums in the Exodus Fleet? You obviously don't have *buildings*, but collections or . . . or museum *ships* maybe, or . . .'

'No,' Kip said. 'We have the Archives, I guess.'

'What's that?'

'They're like a library. All on servers though, no paper or tablets or anything. Just recordings of . . . of . . .' The Archives were such a basic thing to him, such an everyday given. He'd never had to sum them up before. 'Of everything. Earth, the Fleet, families. Seriously everything. We don't need to carry museum stuff around.'

'But you – you don't have any physical artefacts of your history. None at all.' She looked bothered by that idea. Tuumuu lived and breathed for artefacts.

Kip started to say no, but realised that wasn't true. He thought about his hex, where he'd watched Mom melt down old busted tools, where he'd watched Dad refit an exosuit that was still good and sealed after three generations. He wondered how Tuumuu would react to that. If she freaked out over him just *picking up* an old thing, she'd lose her mind at a neighbourhood smelter. 'We . . . use stuff,' Kip said. 'If we can use it, we use it, and if we can't, we make something else.' He thought for a moment. 'I guess everything is an artefact, kind of. Like . . . I dunno, a plate. A plate wasn't always a plate, see. It could've been a bulkhead once, or . . . or flooring, or something. Or maybe it *was* a plate all along, and my great-great-great-great-great-grandparents ate off of it. I'm still going to use it.'

Tuumuu got that cute fold in her face that happened when she was putting ideas together. 'And that plate would've been something else down on Earth first. A machine, or a house, maybe.'

'A house?'

'Well, because of the metal foundries, right? Where they took apart the cities.'

'I guess so,' Kip said. The Laru beside him had a better grasp on Earthen history than he did, and he was kind of embarrassed about it. He'd been meaning to get a Linking book.

'Wow,' Tuumuu said. 'Wow. So you *can* touch everything. You're touching your artefacts all the time.' She let out one of her weird alien chuckles. 'So that star-tracker, you would've just . . .'

Kip shrugged. 'Made a plate.'

'Made a plate,' she repeated, disbelieving. She pushed her face a little closer to his. 'Can I come visit some time? Can I stay with your family?'

Laru, Kip had learned, didn't find it rude to ask for exactly what they wanted, be it a favour or part of your lunch or, apparently, a cross-galaxy trip to stay with your parents. 'Yeah, sure,' he said, and as he said it, he realised that he really, weirdly, *did* want Tuumuu to visit. He thought about the Fleet through her eyes, and it wasn't the same Fleet he knew at all. He thought about the murals he walked past every day without a second thought, the theatres he went to because it was something to do, the farms that were just farms until you saw farms on the ground. He imagined how Tuumuu would see those things, what they'd mean to someone who never shut up about *artefacts*. He imagined saying, 'Go ahead, touch anything you want.' He imagined her fur fluffing and her big feet bouncing and her face folding and folding until she exploded from excitement. He thought, for a second, about taking her to the Archives so she could meet M Itoh, who would totally be able to tell Tuumuu anything she wanted . . . but that imagining wasn't as good. *He* wanted to be the one to tell her. He wanted to know stuff, like Tuumuu knew stuff. He wanted to hang out in his district with her and have the neighbours come stare. He wanted to teach her things. He wanted his alien friend to think the Fleet was cool.

And maybe . . . maybe it was.

'Hey, hurry up!' Dron called back to them. The rest of the group was rounding a corner. 'I'm not coming back if you get lost.'

Kip followed along. He moved through the museum, passing intangible history and thinking of home.

TESSA, TWO STANDARDS LATER

The sun spike was a weird plant. Not quite a succulent and not quite a tree, it rose from the desert sand on its spindly trunk, an improbable support for the pod-like leaves and bright orange fruit that puffed out from its upper arms. The sun spikes weren't native to Seed; they were an introduced species, just as the Humans who tended them were.

Tessa watched the sun spikes go by in neat rows as she flew the low-hovering skiff down the orchard road and back toward the village. 'What'd I tell you?' she said to her passenger. She threw a glance over her shoulder to the bed of the skiff, full to the brim with bushels of fat fruit.

Ammar raised his calloused palms. 'You win,' he said. 'I'll never question your pollinator maps again.'

Tessa nodded, satisfied. Drawing up a new rotation for the pollinator bots hadn't been hard. Geometry and logic, that was all. Move this shape here, fill that gap there, and hey presto, you've got more efficient field coverage. That part had been a cinch. The hard part was convincing the settlers who'd been there far longer than her – people who didn't trip over their own feet when looking up at the sky, who didn't freak out over bugs that weren't food, who no longer stared at the unending horizon until they felt dizzy – that her suggestion had a good chance of boosting the next harvest. That part had been hard, too – waiting. Seasons on their world moved fast, but still, she couldn't just grab a few spare aeroponics parts and put her plan into action. She'd drawn up the map in winter, waited until spring to actually do anything, and crossed her fingers until late summer in the hopes that she'd be right.

And she had been. She couldn't help but feel a bit smug about it. It was a good way to feel.

Ammar reached back, plucked a choice sunfruit from their haul, and took a huge bite. '*Mmm*. Stars, I love these.'

'Hey,' Tessa said, slapping his knee. 'What is that, your fourth?'

'If I pick 'em, I eat 'em,' Ammar said. He took another bite, his lips already stained from the previous three. '*Mmm mmm mmm*.' He looked down at Tessa's arm. 'Did you forget your jacket again?'

A bit of the smugness faded. 'I'm fine,' she said tersely.

Ammar laughed. 'You are goosebumps from shoulder to wrist. Tess, you gotta remember that weather exists.'

Tessa stuck her tongue out at him as she flew around the construction site for the new water reclamation building. Days on Seed were hot, and it was easy to remember to dress cool when you woke up with blankets kicked to the floor. The bit she kept forgetting was that the sun going down meant the warmth went with it. A lifetime of disconnect between *light* and *air temperature* was a tough thing to shake.

The sky was a hazy pink by the time they got home, and Tessa was starting to shiver. She warmed up quick, though, as she and Ammar and the villagers who saw them approach worked to get the fruit into the storehouse before dark. The liftbots – which had lain unused and in disrepair before Tessa's arrival – accepted their new inventory, emptying the heavy bushels into stasis crates, carrying their burdens silently. In contrast, the busy Humans unleashed a loud chorus of chatter. Tessa heard people talking about the size of the fruit, the colour, how it compared to the year before, and the year before that, and the year before that. They talked about who was going to make jam, and who was going to make kick, and how the suddet root should be coming up soon. Simple talk. Harvest talk. She'd never had interest in the farms back home – back on the *Asteria*, that is. This was different, somehow. Something about the dirt, maybe, or the added chaos of wild bugs and desert chickens (which weren't actual *chickens*, of course – they weren't much like Earthen birds at all – but you made do with the words you had). She wasn't entirely sure what the reason was, but she liked being part of the farm crew here. To her unending surprise, she liked it.

A herd of kids ran over, the eldest and fastest at the front, the little ones trailing dutifully. They were followed by two elderly folks – the childminders. Their careful eyes were belied by their unfussed stroll and minimal interference. The kids waited the barest of seconds to get an approving nod from an adult, then swarmed upon the fruit. They took them into their hands, gnawed in starting points, then scraped out the sweet pulp with whatever stage of teeth they had. Tessa saw Ky, shadowing Alerio as usual. His idol was an impressive *six and a half*, and everything five-year-old Ky wanted to be. But though Alerio always generously put up with his devotee, he failed to notice that Ky couldn't reach the top of the bushels.

Tessa made her way over and crouched down behind Ky. She put her hands over her son's eyes. 'Guess who,' she said.

Ky ducked down out of her hands and spun around. 'Mom, don't *do* that,' he giggled.

'Oh, I'm very sorry.' She raised her eyes to the out-of-reach sunfruit. 'Do you want one?'

'Yes!'

'Yes, what?'

Ky bounced up and down. 'Yes, *please.*'

She stood, picked him up around his midsection, and lifted him within reach. Stars, he was heavy. Ky made a move for a fruit that was about half the size of his head. 'You're never gonna finish that one, bud,' Tessa said. 'I think you should get one you can pick up with one hand.'

Ky grabbed a more moderately sized one with both hands. 'I can finish this one.'

'All right,' Tessa said. Compromise had been found, in a way, and besides, her back couldn't take much more of him deciding. She set Ky down, and he wasted no time in running back toward the pack. Tessa called after him. 'What do you say?'

'Thank you!' Ky shouted in motion.

'You're welcome,' she said, even though she was sure he'd stopped listening. She scanned her eyes over the kids, looking for a tall head of choppy black hair.

Where was Aya?

Ammar was leading the charge with harvest storage, and there were more than enough hands, so Tessa had no qualms about walking home in search of her errant kid. It was properly dark by then, and she hurried along with hands in her pockets and bare arms pressed to her sides. She passed the school, the fuel depot, the med clinic. She passed the gathering hall, still decked with bunting from Remembrance Day. She passed the sculpture of a homesteader standing in the middle of a growing wreath of desert plants, the plaque below inscribed with heat-etched words:

In honour of all who carried us this far.

She arrived, at last, at a mud-and-metal home, not particularly different from the others. This one, though, had a painted sign beside the door. *Santoso*, it read, underlined by four handprints – two big, two small. She relaxed as she saw a familiar red scoot-bike tossed unceremoniously onto the front porch. Aya was home. She'd be receiving yet another talking-to about putting her things away properly, but still – she was home.

The warm air inside made Tessa melt with relief, and a wonderful smell met her nose. George stuck his head out of the kitchen doorway. His beard and belly were streaked with flour, and he wore a pair of oven mitts. 'You are about fifteen minutes away from a kickass desert chicken soup and what is, I believe, my best bread yet,' he said. He looked her up and down. 'Did you forget your jacket again?'

Tessa rolled her eyes. 'What's so special about this bread?' she asked as she pulled off her boots.

'Nuh uh,' he said, ducking back into the kitchen. 'A chef never reveals his secrets.'

Tessa shook her head with a smile. The previous winter – their first on Seed – when there'd been little to do but stay warm and go bonkers, George had discovered a previously unknown love for baking. He was honestly talking about quitting the construction crew to open up a shop. George. Her husband, George. Tessa privately thought he could do with a few more loaves that weren't gooey on the inside before he made the leap, but she wasn't about to squash his enthusiasm, and besides, she was happy to eat her way through as many experiments as it took.

Stars, but it was nice having him around.

'Where's Aya?' she asked.

'Talking to your dad,' he said.

Tessa raised her eyebrows and made her way to the living room. There indeed was her daughter, covered in dirt from head to toe, having an animated discussion with Pop on the sib.

'And *then*,' Aya said, 'Jasmin was like, I bet you can't jump that ditch, and I said, yeah, I can, and I *did*. I crashed when I landed, though. Look, see.' She raised up her elbows toward the screen. 'I've already got crazy bruises.'

'Yikes,' Pop said. Light glinted off his ocular implant as he nodded approvingly. 'Those are impressive.'

'Yeah, tomorrow we're gonna go off the dock into the lake. Tommy built a ramp, and it's fine, the water's real deep.'

Pop laughed from way deep in his chest. 'You'll have to show me when I come visit.'

'When are you coming?'

'Early next standard. Takes a long time to get there. Think you can find a scoot-bike for me?'

Aya giggled. 'I dunno.' She turned her head. 'Mom's here, do you want to talk to her?'

'Nah,' he said. 'Don't have time.'

Tessa raised her voice. 'Thanks, Pop.'

Pop leaned toward his screen confidentially. 'Tell your mom I can't talk because I've got a hot date.'

Aya craned her head back. 'Grandpa says he can't talk, he's got a hot date.'

'Oh, stars,' Tessa said. She pinched the bridge of her nose, then walked into frame. 'Lupe?'

'Psh,' Pop said. 'Old news. I'm meeting Marjo at Top to Bottom.'

'And I'm sorry I asked,' Tessa said. She gave a sarcastic wave. 'Have fun.'

'Bye, Grandpa,' Aya said.

Pop was still waving and smiling as the screen went dark.

Tessa put her hands on her hips. 'So speaking of scoot-bikes . . .'

'Oops.' Aya gave her a charming smile.

Tessa was not swayed. She plucked at her daughter's shirt. 'Have you been strolling around this house in this nasty shirt?' She moved her hand to Aya's scalp. 'Stars, *your hair*.' Crusty bundles of dirt clung to her daughter's locks.

Aya looked down as if seeing her clothing for the first time. 'Oops,' she said again.

Tessa brushed the transferred crud off her palm, wondering just how much of Seed was now coating the inside of her home. 'Kiddo, you have got to remember that dirt exists.'

'And *you* have to remember to bring a jacket.'

Tessa ignored the poorly smothered laugh from the kitchen. She narrowed her eyelids. 'Shower. Clean clothes. Now.' Aya made a face, but she obeyed, and received a gentle swat on the shoulder from Tessa as she went.

Tessa sighed and surveyed her wreck of a living room. Toys, tools, visible footprints. She bent over and started tidying up, knowing her efforts would be made futile by tomorrow. Her limbs were sore from the day spent in the field, and she knew that while the next day would be less strenuous, it'd be just as busy.

They had to start covering the roots before the first fall frost hit, and the pollinators needed to be cleaned before they got packed away. Plus, there was laundry that needed doing, and globulbs that needed replacing, and a draughty wall that needing patching, and . . . stars, it never ended, did it?

'Hey,' George called. 'You're not cleaning, are you?'

'I'm just tidying up.'

'Tessa. It's not hurting anybody, and I can do it in the morning. Sit down, have some kick, warm up.'

She opened her mouth to protest, but then . . . why not? The mess *wasn't* hurting anybody, it wasn't going anywhere, and there'd just be another one tomorrow. She picked up the bottle of Whitedune and an accompanying glass from the top of one of the shelves. She sat on the couch, pretending she didn't see the puff of dust that rose up when she sat down. She poured herself a splash. She didn't need more than that. Just five minutes of a warm throat and stillness. That would do nicely.

She thought, as she closed her eyes, about home. Seed was a good place, better than she'd expected. But it wasn't *home* yet, and she worried, sometimes, about whether it ever would be. There were nights when she lay awake, missing the hex so much she could hardly breathe, or when she was so unaccustomed to the luxury of having George home all the time that she went and slept on the couch for the familiarity of sleeping alone. Sometimes she snapped at the kids when they didn't deserve it. Sometimes she got sad over silly things – the oxygen garden, her old mek brewer, even the stupid cargo bay. It was hard, life on the ground. Yes, homesteaders had to worry about water and crops, too, but if one of those systems failed, if your ship fell apart, there were others you could go live on. It wasn't like that out here. Leaving Seed meant leaving the system, travelling for tendays, figuring life out again. Part of her still couldn't believe that she'd done this. Part of her was still unsure. Maybe part of her always would be.

She opened her eyes. Something was off. With a sigh, she

realised – she hadn't heard any sounds of showering. She hadn't even heard the water turn on yet. She got up, walked to the bathroom, pushed the door open, and – the scolding died on her lips. Aya was in there all right, still clothed, still filthy. But she had the window propped open, and she was halfway out of it, twisting her torso to look up at the sky. Her dirty hair swayed in the evening breeze. Her face was turned toward the biggest moon, shining bright and beautiful overhead. She hadn't noticed her mother come in, and was talking to herself. Whatever the words were, Tessa could not hear. Some story, perhaps. Some idea she didn't want to forget. But while her words were lost, the expression on her face was unmistakable. She was curious. She was unafraid.

Tessa stepped back out, taking care to lean the door shut silently. She made her way to the kitchen. George was facing away from her, transferring his precious bread from oven to cooling rack. She walked up behind him, wrapped her arms around his middle, and rested her cheek between his shoulder blades.

'Hey, you,' he said.

'Hey,' she said.

'I think I fucked up this bread,' he sighed.

She laughed and shut her eyes, soaking up the warmth of him. The bread, fucked up or not, smelled great. So did he. He always did. 'That's okay,' she said. She held him tight. 'You'll make another one.'

ISABEL, THREE
STANDARDS LATER

The assembly hall was decorated as it always was – cloth flags, metal stars, shining ribbons. There were differences, of course. Some of the other archivists had been fed up with the worn flags they'd dragged out standard after standard and took it upon themselves to make a batch of new ones (Isabel had to admit, they were much better). The seedlings on the favour table weren't sky vine anymore, but four-toes, which had come back into fashion (she'd found their fussy flowers so old hat when she'd been in her youth). But details didn't matter. It was still a Naming Day, and she never tired of those. They were the best kinds of days.

She felt someone looking at her, and she glanced over from her out-of-the-way corner to Tamsin, who'd tagged along for this one. The Mitchell family from hex 625 was the one getting an extra name record that day, and their cooking was legendary throughout the neighbourhood. Tamsin had taken a chair off to the side of the room, and very much looked the part of an innocent old woman who needed to rest her legs. Isabel knew her too well for that. Her wife had chosen a strategic spot that would put her right at the front of the buffet line once the formalities were over. Tamsin locked eyes with her, and gave a purposeful tilt of her head toward a man setting down a giant bowl of noodles mixed with crispy fish, a rainbow of vegetables, and all sorts of tasty bits Isabel couldn't make out at a distance. Tamsin held her hands close to her stomach and gave Isabel two secretive thumbs up.

Isabel smothered a laugh and looked elsewhere. She had to be respectable today. Tamsin didn't always make that easy, but then, that was part of the fun.

The young family arrived, hanging back in the hallway. Isabel made eye contact with the musicians, and they began to play. The crowd parted. The couple approached, baby in tow. They stopped at the podium, as they knew to do. But Isabel did not move. Instead, she looked to another, and nodded.

Isabel watched her new apprentice as he took his place. He'd filled out well in the years that he'd been away. He'd grown into himself. He had a full beard, and his voice had settled steady and low. He'd completed an academic track in Post-Unification History, which he'd passed by the skin of his teeth. He spoke spaceport Reskitkish, and his arm sported a swirling bot tattoo he'd picked up from some market stop, like you do. He'd gained a soft spot for snapfruit tarts. He liked letting ocean waves run over his toes. But he drank his mek hot and his kick ice cold, and found no meal as comforting as a hopper topped with twice-round pickle. He peppered his Klip with Ensk, his Ensk with Klip, and thought Martian accents were the funniest thing there was. He knew that the sky was best viewed below his feet. And he'd told her, when she'd demanded to know why he was back, that seeing so many singular things had made him realise he came from somewhere singular, too, and even if it was ass-backwards and busted – his words – it was *theirs*, and there was nothing else like it. The Fleet was priceless. The only one. If it was gone, there wouldn't just be nothing for other Humans to learn from. There'd be nothing for *him* to learn from.

She'd put in an order for his robes right then, the same robes he wore handsomely now – bright yellow with a white apprentice's stripe on the shoulders. He was nervous, she could tell, more than his face gave away. Of course he was. She'd been nervous her first time, too.

She looked out at the crowd waiting for him to begin. They

smiled warmly at him. They understood. They had his back. He was one of theirs.

Kip cleared his throat and gave a brave smile. 'We destroyed our world,' he said, 'and left it for the skies. Our numbers were few. Our species had scattered. We were the last to leave. We left the ground behind. We left the oceans. We left the air. We watched these things grow small. We watched them shrink into a point of light. As we watched, we understood. We understood what we were. We understood what we had lost. We understood what we would need to do to survive. We abandoned more than our ancestors' world. We abandoned our short sight. We abandoned our bloody ways. We made ourselves anew.' He spread his hands, encompassing the gathered. 'We are the Exodus Fleet. We are those that wandered, that wander still. We are the homesteaders that shelter our families. We are the miners and foragers in the open. We are the ships that ferry between. We are the explorers who carry our names. We are the parents who lead the way. We are the children who continue on.' He picked up his scrib from the podium. 'What is his name?'

'Amias,' the man said.

'And what name does your home carry?'

'Mitchell,' said the woman.

'Amias Mitchell,' Kip spoke to the scrib. A blue square appeared on screen. He took the baby's foot and attempted to press it to the square. The baby kicked mightily, and for a moment, Kip looked intimidated by the person a fraction of his size. A quiet laugh rippled through the crowd. Kip laughed, too, and with the help of the child's father, got the foot in order. The scrib chirped. Record had been made.

'Amias Mitchell,' Kip said. 'Born aboard the *Asteria*. Forty Solar days of age as of GC standard day 211/310. He is now, and always, a member of our Fleet. By our laws, he is assured shelter and passage here. If we have food, he will eat. If we have air, he will breathe. If we have fuel, he will fly. He is son to all grown, brother to all still growing. We will care for him, protect him, guide him. We welcome you, Amias, to the decks of the *Asteria*, and to the journey we take together.' He spoke the final words now, and the room joined him. 'From the ground, we stand. From our ships, we live. By the stars, we hope.'

ACKNOWLEDGEMENTS

This book had the unusual experience of starting with one editor and ending with a different one. This is the sort of thing that would make a writer panic (and there may have been a bit of that), but my luck on both sides of this equation has been amazing. Thanks forever to Anne Perry, who pulled me out of the weeds and gave me a place to lay down roots, and to Oliver Johnson, who helped me find the rhythm of the whole thing. Thanks, too, to Sam Bradbury, Jason Bartholomew, Fleur Clarke, Becca Mundy, and the entire team at Hodder.

On the science side, the Exodan caretaking tradition was inspired by real-world efforts to establish human composting as a funerary practice. Big thanks to Katrina Spade of the Urban Death Project and Recompose for taking the time to chat with me and answer my questions. Additional thanks to Mom and Dad for letting me bug them about gravity.

As always, I'd be nowhere without my posse: my family, my friends, and Berglaug the incredible. Much love to all of you.

ABOUT THE AUTHOR

Becky Chambers was raised in California as the progeny of an astrobiology educator, an aerospace engineer, and an Apollo-era rocket scientist. An inevitable space enthusiast, she made the obvious choice of studying performing arts. After a few years in theatre administration, she shifted her focus toward writing. Her creative work has appeared at The Mary Sue, Tor.com, Five Out Of Ten, The Toast, and Pornokitsch. *The Long Way to a Small, Angry Planet* is her first novel, and was funded in 2012 thanks to a successful Kickstarter campaign. After living in Scotland and Iceland, Becky is now back in her home state, where she lives with her partner. She is an ardent proponent of video- and tabletop games, and enjoys spending time in nature. She hopes to see Earth from orbit one day.

www.otherscribbles.com
@beckysaysrawr